Deathlehem
Revisited

Deathlehem
Revisited

Edited by
Michael J. Evans
and
Harrison Graves

A
Grinning Skull Press
Publication

DEDICATION

To all those who enjoy a little darkness
during the holiday season.

TABLE OF CONTENTS

ACKNOWLEDGMENTS

First off, we would like to thank Barry Lee Dejasu for creating an awesome interior graphic for this year's volume and Jeffrey Kosh for another great cover. Also to Hal Bodner and all the authors who made this year's volume possible. And to the readers who embrace all things Christmas, light and dark.

HAPPY KRAMPUSNACHT

There's been a lot of talk on the News lately regarding a war on Christmas. Maybe you've heard about it. Starbucks has recently come under fire for removing the snowflakes and other seasonal images from its coffee cups, opting, instead, to go with a simple red cup. In this day and age where somebody is always finding offense in the simplest of things, maybe they (the Powers That Be at Starbucks) thought that going simple would be the least offensive path to take (or maybe it was a financial decision in that a plain red cup was less expensive than a printed red cup). Little did they know there would be those who take offense at not having anything to be offended by. Never mind the fact that red is the color typically associated with the holiday season. After all, what color suit does Santa wear? And God forbid you wish somebody a Happy Holiday instead of a Merry Christmas. You might be accused of being Satan himself trying to take the "Christ" out of Christmas. Suddenly, trying to be politically correct and as inoffensive as possible has become offensive.

Many years ago, when I was a kid, my mother always

told to wish somebody a Happy Holiday instead of a Merry Christmas. It wasn't meant to be offensive; quite the opposite, actually. As it was explained to me, what if the person you are bestowing a holiday greeting upon was Jewish? What if the person was an atheist? What if they celebrated Kwanza (not really, as this was before we were even made aware of that particular holiday, but you get my drift)? They might take offense being wished a Merry Christmas, so instead wish them an all-inclusive Happy Holiday.

Is it any wonder why I've turned my back on all things festive and bright and embraced the darker spirit of the holiday? Some folks say I've taken it to an extreme, and maybe they're right, which is part of the reason why Deathlehem was created (for the full story behind the creation of Deathlehem, check out the first in this anthology series, *O Little Town of Deathlehem*); it combines the darkness of the holiday that I've come to love [Krampus, Grýla, the Yule lads, Jólakötturinn (the Yule Cat, and if you don't know about him, just be thankful for the underwear Aunt Patty gave you this year, and so what if it looks like the Underoos you wore as a kid)] with the spirit of giving, as proceeds are donated to charity.

If this is your first visit to Deathlehem, I should warn you: there are no happy endings here. In Deathlehem, Krampus is King, and even old Saint Nick shows colors some folks would rather not see. In fact, Hal Bodner opens this anthology with "Scarlet Sacrifice," a tale that takes us back in time to when Christianity is just beginning to impose itself on a pagan population. In it, we get a glimpse of ol' Saint Nick before he becomes the popular holiday icon we know today. In Stephen Roy's "Checking It Twice," we do get to see the benevolent Santa, but the jolly old elf's niceness is overshadowed by a threat that follows the main character into adulthood. And if you think Santa and Krampus are bad, wait until you meet the elves that visit here. Nasty, repulsive creatures that thrive on torment and fear. Can't wait to meet them? Then check out Patrick Freivald's "The Red Man" and Max Vile's "Leo."

What else can you expect in Deathlehem? Murder and mayhem are commonplace, and nowhere is that more obvious than at family gatherings. Need proof? Just check out DJ Tyrer's "Christmas Vacation" or RJ Faherty's "Holly, Jolly Christmas." And what about that neighbor who goes overboard with the outdoor decorations every year? You know the one I mean. The one with enough lights so it's like midday when you venture outside at night. We've all wanted to commit murder—or worse—where that one is concerned, and Flo Stanton has a field day in "Happy Christmas." And even though he's supposed to be immortal, not even Santa is spared the attempts on his life, as Mark Allan Gunnells so gleefully depicts in "The Boy Who Killed Santa Claus."

In Deathlehem, there's no comfort in holiday traditions either. After reading Chantal Boudreau's "Breaking Tradition," you'll never look at the fruitcake the neighbor gave you the same way again. And if the annual gathering at the town center is anything like the one in A.P. Sessler's "The Night I Stopped Believing In Santa Claus," you might choose to forego it and spend the holiday at home with your family. Oh … Wait … That might not be such a great idea.

In Deathlehem, expect visits from the Ghosts of Christmases Past and Present. The future is questionable as the odds of you surviving your visit to our quaint little town are slim to none. In Deathlehem, serial killers lurk around practically every corner and the malls and stores hold unexpected, unpleasant surprises. Even our popular tourist attractions often prove fatal, especially if you managed to land a spot on Santa's Naughty List.

Scared yet? No?
Well, c'mon, then, and don't say I didn't warn you.

Welcome to Deathlehem…
Again.
And whatever you do, don't buy any Christmas trees!

Michal J. Evans
and the staff at
Grinning Skull Press,
Best Wishes for a Happy Krampusnacht,
and a frightful New Year!

S*CARLET S*ACRIFICE

Hal Bodner

The chill air teased goose bumps from Aelwyn's bare skin. He closed his eyes and concentrated on what little warmth he could glean from the hearth fire. If anyone saw him shiver, he was afraid that they would think it was from fear and not merely because he was freezing.

"Steady, lad," Berthe murmured.

The old woman ran her wizened fingers up the inside of his naked thighs, her touch as light as the lilting tread of a spider upon its web. Her roughened palms brushed his buttocks and, involuntarily, he clenched the muscles.

"Have you found anything yet?" The imperiousness of the question barely covered the unease beneath it. Pedr, the blacksmith, realized that his tone had betrayed his fear and scowled, silently daring anyone to comment.

"These things take time," Berthe told him as her hands continued to stroke and probe Aelwyn's flesh.

"If she finds a blemish …" someone from the back of the crowd whispered, too loudly. Someone else quickly hushed them while several of the onlookers made gestures intended to ward off bad luck.

Aelwyn's muscles tensed anew when the ancient hands moved to examine his manly parts.

"It's a good thing we're not doing this in spring. If that was the kind of harvest we've to look forward to …"

Pedr shook his head ruefully and pointed to Aelwyn's groin.

In spite of the young man's resolve to stand fast and unflinching, his privates seemed to have a mind of their own. His testicles retreated as far into his body as they could, seeking respite from the cold; his staff shriveled and looked not much bigger than an overly fat worm.

Berthe chuckled, though her hands never ceased moving. "Appearances can deceive, isn't that right, lad?'

She slapped his bare stomach just below the navel to make her point and the unexpected contact made Aelwyn flinch.

"It's a proud staff, it is, when there's warmth to be had. You needn't worry about that."

"I hope so," the blacksmith grinned back at her. "We've pampered the lad for a twelvemonth now. I'd hate to think all that effort's been wasted."

"There's still the bogs," someone pointed out.

Aelwyn felt the muscles in his neck tighten involuntarily against the thought. Strangulation was not one of the ways he would choose to leave the world.

"True," the Pedr conceded. "But it won't do much good. Not this time of year." He glanced at the sky through the open window of the hut. "Hurry up. It'll be full dark soon. Time for that papist bastard to make his appearance."

"Mind your tongue." Berthe's tone was sharp, though from the expression of deep concentration on her face as she searched every last inch of Aelwyn's body, one would not have known she was annoyed. "We should be thankful that holy men are the only things Rome still bothers to send this far north."

"Holy men!"

Pedr spat onto the ground, but the hard-packed earth was too frozen to absorb the extra moisture. Berthe glanced at the gobbet and frowned before fixing the blacksmith with an expression that made it clear she did not appreciate the addition to her floor.

"At least he respects the old ways," someone said.

"He *is* the old ways," said another, and a susurration of unease rippled through the small crowd of onlookers.

Aelwyn wished Berthe would hurry things along. Standing completely bare-assed in front of half of the most important people in the village was not only cold, but embarrassing as well. He focused on his shame to keep his mind from dwelling on the fate that his duty commanded him to suffer. In the meantime, he resolved to stoically endure the temperature even though he had hoped when everyone crowded into Berthe's small home that their combined body heat would ease the chill. As his poor, freezing privates could attest, that hadn't happened.

"That'll do." Berthe clutched his arm for support and painfully rose from her knees. "You'll want to cover up now."

Aelwyn didn't need to be told twice. He snatched his trousers and shirt from where he'd hung them close to the fire and gratefully pulled them on, relishing the feel of the warm, rough fabric against his skin.

"Clean limbed," the old woman announced. "Without a mark."

As one, the crowd breathed a collective sigh of relief.

"That's the first good news we've had yet," Pedr said, grudgingly. He glared at the younger man who, fully dressed now, rubbed his arms to warm them. "Maybe the choice meats weren't wasted after all."

"Or the good ale," someone quipped. There were some uneasy chuckles at the joke.

Pedr stepped forward.

"An unblemished youth, never having known a woman …?"

He paused and the question hung in the air. Aelwyn nodded and hoped his cheeks hadn't turned scarlet.

"You are prepared to do what you must do?"

Aelwyn nodded. "Aye."

"We should have fed the bogs," the voice repeated.

The speaker, a portly man of middle age, stepped forward and Aelwyn saw that it was Gwilym, the merchant. His clothing was colorful and noticeably finer that the drab homespun cloth most of the others wore, and a thin ring of real gold glittered on the middle finger of one hand.

Pedr scowled. "The decision's been made, Gwilym. No more of your harping on it." His expression softened slightly when he faced Aelwyn once again. "It's a brave lad who'll do what must be done without flinching. I don't see either of your fine sons standing here for Berthe to paw over, do I?"

"You'll not take that tone with me, Pedr. Both my sons wives are with child, as you well know …"

"That doesn't mean your sons are responsible," called a wit from the back of the crowd.

Aelwyn stifled a grin; levity wasn't appropriate for someone in his position.

Gwilym spun with a glare, daring anyone else to comment at his expense while he could see who was speaking.

"The Italian won't like it," Gwilym insisted.

"Who is he to object? They eat the flesh of their gods, and drink their blood," Pedr pointed out. "Besides ..." He rested one hand on Aelwyn's shoulder in a way that was meant to offer comfort. "If there were any other way ..."

"For seven hundred years, we've kept our traditions," the old woman added. "And we've never had cause to regret it. Have you forgotten that it was my own two granddaughters taken last solstice?"

"And my baby, Sior," someone called out. "Barely nine years old."

"My sister's twins the year before," another added.

Other voices joined in and it was clear that almost everyone in the room had been touched with tragedy.

"You've not lost a child, though. Have you, Gwilym?"

"I had the good sense to build my home of stout timber and strong stone ..."

"And you had the gold, too," taunted the same jokester.

Gwilym spun to face the crowd. "I'll not apologize for that. You'd all do the same to protect your families if you could. Besides, who provides the animals for summer sacrifice? You, Gildas? Your husband, Morwen? No, it's me who you come to, isn't it?" His tone became mocking. "'Oh please, Gwilym. Surely you can spare a plump goat for sacrifice? You have so many when I've only the few. And perhaps some fruit as well? Your orchards must be blessed to be so bountiful. Look at my trees, all warped and withered.'"

He captured several of their gazes with his own, but none could meet his eyes for long.

"I respect the old ways," he continued. "They've been

9

good to me. This Christ is a Roman god and I'd very much like the Romans to keep him!"

"I don't disagree," said the blacksmith.

Aelwyn was glad to see Pedr making an effort to calm the merchant's temper. Gwilym had a reputation for nastiness when he was angry. Aelwyn didn't want the evening to become any more difficult than it already was.

"I have no use for this Christ myself ..." Pedr began.

A high, cheerful tenor interrupted him from the back of the crowd.

"Your use for the Christ is not the point, my child."

A tall, slender man wearing a simple robe of undyed cloth over thick trousers made his way to the front of the crowd. Most people would have had to push to get through, but Aelwyn noticed that the villagers hastily moved aside to let the man pass, almost as if they were reluctant to brush against him.

This was the closest Aelwyn had come to the Christian priest since the man's arrival several weeks before, although he had sometimes seen him from a distance. Up close, the man's hair was impossibly black where it was not tinted by wide streaks of grey. His bare forearms were taut and well veined with the muscles of someone who was no stranger to physical labor. Yet the priest's visage, though showing the lines and wrinkles of incipient old age, was somehow strangely youthful and not nearly as weathered as the faces of some of the villagers who were a decade or more younger. Despite the snow outside, and the bitter chill, he wore no cloak.

"The point," he said in a lilting accent that bordered on musical, "is that the Christ has a use for you."

With his elegantly long index finger, he lightly tapped the blacksmith in the center of the chest for emphasis.

"Forgive me, Father Caravella, I meant no disrespect."

Caravella's expression was gentle, but his eyes sparkled as if he was trying to refrain from laughing at a joke that no one else had heard.

"Of course you are forgiven, Pedr. That is another point of the Christ. Forgiveness."

His attention shifted to Aelwyn, and the young man's breath caught in his throat for an instant. Perhaps it was the dimness of Berthe's home that caused the illusion, but from where Aelwyn stood, Father Caravella's eyes looked as black and as deep as the village well.

"Is this strapping lad...? No!" He clapped his hands to his cheeks, pretending dismay. "To condemn one so handsome is surely a sin."

Aelwyn reluctantly took a step forward. Though he had the courage to face death to protect his friends and neighbors, there was something about this Italian holy man that prickled his skin. At Berthe's prodding, he took another step and lowered his eyes respectfully.

"I am Aelwyn, my lord."

"No, no, no," the priest exclaimed, playfully shaking his finger in Aelwyn's face. "I am no one's lord, my child. Merely the humble servant of God."

"Not my god," Pedr mumbled under his breath.

Somehow, the Italian heard him anyway.

"Perhaps not," he agreed, outwardly cordial but with a hint of mockery. "Perhaps your old ways are indeed best. You would strip the boy naked, bind him to the altar, and plunge the knife into his belly like ... so!"

He pantomimed stabbing Aelwyn in the stomach, ending the motion with a vicious twist of an imaginary blade. In spite of himself, the young man flinched. Father Caravella saw the slight movement and raised one eyebrow, amused.

"We shall gut him then, no? Like one of the little hens

running about in Senore Gwilym's yard. *Squawk*! *Squawk*!"

Comically, the priest flapped his arms and turned around in tiny circles in a surprisingly accurate imitation of the chickens that the merchant kept in a little enclosure behind his house.

"Should we reach inside ..."

Someone gagged as Caravella formed his hand into a claw and thrust it at Aelwyn's middle to demonstrate.

"... and pull out his ... what is your word? Ah! His guts! Shall we pull out his guts, all glistening and moist, so that you may wrap them around your sacred oak? Or shall we, as Senore Gwilym would have it, wrap the boy's neck with rope, twisting and pulling ..."

The description was accompanied by another, even more graphic, performance in mime. Aelwyn felt his gorge rise as he watched it, and for the first time in a year, he felt uncertain of the path he had chosen.

"... until the balls of the eyes go ... *Pop!* ... and this oh-so-handsome young man's features are twisted and blue, like so?"

Caravella made an outlandishly grotesque face, rolling his eyes and allowing his tongue to hang out.

"But no!"

He held up a single finger to command silence, even though no one had spoken.

"We will *not*! For you have already done such horrible things, have you not? And what is your result? I, Father Lucenzio Caravella, will tell you your result." He lowered his voice to a whisper and made a gesture as if he was releasing a small insect upon the air. "Pffft. Niente."

"But Father ..."

"Shh ... shh ... shh." He held the finger to his lips. "Caravella speaks. You have tried these things and still this ... this ... *pezzo de merde* ..." He paused almost infinitesimally to cross himself and mutter "*mea culpa*" before continuing as if he had not interrupted himself. "This … this … *brutto figlio di puttana bastardo…*"

Though not a single soul in the room other than Caravella spoke Italian, there was a collective gasp at such language coming from the mouth of a holy man.

"My apologies … *mea culpa ancora* … in my anger, Caravella forgets himself." He made the sign of the cross several more times and hung his head in exaggerated shame. When he felt he'd presented the appearance of atonement for long enough, perhaps a second and a half, he continued. "This unholy *thing* that preys on your children, that steals them away never to be seen again … I, Lucenzio Caravella, with the grace of Our Lord and the help of this brave youth, will see that it bothers you … *no more!*"

With a flattened palm, he sliced the air to make his point.

Aelwyn was not alone in being transfixed by the priest's performance. Like everyone else, he held his breath, waiting to see what histrionic thing he would do, or say, next. Instead, Caravella merely gave a casual shrug before flinging his arm across the boy's shoulders.

"If it doesn't work and the lad survives his arms and legs being torn from his quivering body by the godless creature …," he grinned, "… we have always the knotted cord and the knife for the slicing of the belly in reserve, do we not?"

Aelwyn swallowed several times. He'd never before heard his possible fates discussed with such gruesome cheer.

"This, *il miei amici*, is the unblemished youth that your ancestors commanded you to sacrifice to the false gods of your woods and rivers. For a year, you have feasted him and pampered him, readying him for this day when he will happily lay down his life to protect yours. It is an old tradition, and an honorable one, dating from the time of the Greeks … ah, the Greeks!" He chuckled with affection. "But, no more about the Greeks! I am now a man of the cloth, no? And I say to you that this honorable custom of yours will be as chaff in the wind before this thing that torments you. I, Lucenzio Caravella—if God wills, of course!—will remove the pestilence from your village. Now, we go!"

Aelwyn found himself seized by the collar of his tunic and hauled through the crowd and out of the cabin, where he found the sky busily crafting fresh snowflakes into a mantle for the frozen ground.

❄ ❄ ❄

They wasted no time leaving the village behind and heading up the mountain. Aelwyn was surprised to see how extraordinarily quickly the priest scampered over the rocks, especially for a man of his age. As they climbed higher, the youth found he had to push his body even harder to keep abreast. Caravella, on the other hand, seemed able to maintain the pace without much visible effort.

Ordinarily, Aelwyn would not have minded the exercise. But he was sweating like a dray horse, and after leaving Berthe's house, the priest had not allowed him time to return home and fetch a cloak. His clothing was damp with it, and rather than trapping the warmth of his body, the cold clammy cloth meant that his teeth were in danger of chattering.

"When we arrive," Caravella told him not unkindly, "I will see you are warm. That is a promise."

He lent Aelwyn a hand over a particularly rough patch of ground. To the boy's consternation, the older man showed not a trace of perspiration on his brow, nor did his breath frost in the air except when he spoke. It was as if the priest was casually strolling across a level pasture rather than in the midst of clambering up the face of a sacred mountain where the only approach to the shrine had been made deliberately difficult.

On and on they climbed. To Aelwyn, it seemed they had been laboring for many hours, though, in truth, it had not taken them much longer than two. He was fast approaching exhaustion, but he refused to succumb to fatigue and ask Caravella to slow down. The indefatigable gusto with which the Italian attacked each new outcropping made the boy ashamed of his inability to match the man's efforts. His legs were cramped and sore, and he filled his lungs with great gulps of air. Just when he was about to give up and beg for a brief rest, the old priest spoke.

"We arrive!" he announced, as if it was an event worthy of celebration.

Aelwyn hauled himself past the final boulder and onto the ridge where the path to the place of sacrifice was located. He collapsed onto all fours, gasping and sweating. When Caravella approached, his arm outstretched to help Aelwyn to his feet, the boy noticed something astonishing. The Italian priest had made the entire journey wearing only a pair of open-toed sandals, practically barefoot.

Awed and a little frightened by someone who could accomplish such a feat without complaint, Aelwyn ignored the proffered help and struggled to stand on his own. He was beginning to understand why so many of the villagers seemed loathe to get too close to the man.

Caravella was oblivious to the mild rebuff. Instead of expressing offense, he busied himself gathering twigs and dried grass to pile onto the iron brazier at one end of the long, carved expanse of the sacrificial stone. As soon as he regained his breath, Aelwyn scurried to help, all the while unsuccessfully trying to ignore the thick metal rings set deeply into the four corners of the altar. He could not stop himself from wondering, since Caravella had brought along neither a pack nor a bundle, what the priest planned to use to secure him to the altar.

Either the older man observed his uneasy surreptitious glances at the altar, or he was able to sense what Aelwyn was thinking. He dropped a final arm full of bark and leaves onto the brazier, brushed his hands clean of dirt, and addressed the boy's fears.

"Bah!" he said, with a twinkle in his eye. "You believe you will be bound to the stone? That I will cut your throat ... *Szzzst!*" Once again, the demonstration was uncomfortably graphic. "Or open your belly so that your lovely red blood will be spilled upon the ground. This is what you think?"

Aelwyn nodded.

Caravella burst into hearty laughter. "Fear not, my handsome young friend." He winked as if the two of them shared a secret. "What a terrible waste that would be! No, there will be no binding of the limbs, no sharpening of the knives nor twisting of garrottes. And the flames are only for warmth. You need not worry that you shall be cast into their midst. Go now and light it. And mind your steps."

The priest made one of his expansive gestures to indicate a crooked line of feeble-looking saplings and twiggy bushes on the opposite side of the plateau from where they had mounted to the summit. Aelwyn saw the meager foliage hid a steep, sheer drop overlooking the river below. Anyone who toppled from it, in the unlikely event they survived the fall and were not battered to pieces on the rocky slope, would plummet through the ice and be whisked downstream by the frigid water to be lost in the glacial depths of the sea beyond.

Confused, Aelwyn did as he was told and gathered up

whatever he thought might burn. Though the wind had cleared the mountain top of the worst of the snow, some of the leaves and twigs were still damp. It took Aelwyn some time before he could get a spark to catch and, even then, the flames paled in comparison to the amount of smoke that was produced. Still, a little fire was better than none and he gratefully rubbed his hands together as close to the burning wood as he dared.

Throughout, Caravella continued talking. At first Aelwyn got the impression he was speaking his thoughts aloud and did not expect any contributions from his traveling companion.

"There will be changes this night," the priest said. "I, Caravella, will make it so. Does he think he can continue threatening the safety of the rest of us? It is a new age, this age of the Christ. Julian! Ah, now *he* was an Emperor! A true pity his time was so short. I fear the pagan days are gone forever."

He sighed so heavily that Aelwyn looked up to see what was the matter.

"This new Christianity, this new empire of East and West, it means trouble for all of us. I, Caravella, have seen this. Precautions must be taken."

Abruptly, he ceased his odd, one-sided chatter and his eyes seemed to focus on Aelwyn once more, as if he'd only just remembered that he was not alone.

"Why, *caro mio*, you are freezing! This must not be allowed."

He sprang to the altar and knelt beside Aelwyn by the fire, briskly rubbing the boy's shoulders and arms to stimulate the circulation.

"This night may bring many outcomes. And none of them, I think, will be quite what you expected."

Once again, he found something amusing to smile at,

something only he was privy to. Then, he grew more somber than Aelwyn had yet seen him.

"Your purpose here in not an enviable one. You are to serve as … what is your word again? As a trap … No! As bait. Yes, you are to be the tiny worm that wriggles in the stream to entice the fish to snap him up and catch himself upon the hook. Yes, my handsome little worm, this is your task."

"I will not be sacrificed to the old gods?" Somehow, Aelwyn found the courage to ask the question.

Caravella seemed to consider the question seriously for long moments. "There will be sacrifices made, this is true. We do not, sadly, have time to do things as I would wish. You may suffer …"

Aelwyn winced at the word, but Caravella met his gaze squarely and the younger man realized the priest did not mean what he'd thought at first.

"You may suffer some small … inconvenience in the future. But Caravella will be with you to guide you. Hopefully, you will not find things to be so terrible." He winked as if sharing another joke. "Not so terrible as the bloody knife and the tightening cord, eh?"

"Your god …," Aelwyn began. "The Christ …"

"What have you heard of Him?" the priest asked with only mild curiosity.

"That it is as Pedr said. That your god wishes his followers to eat his flesh and drink his blood."

"Posh!" Caravella said. "Those falsely pious men with their ridiculous symbolism! No one is eating the flesh of anyone."

"Does that mean you do not drink his blood either?"

An uncomfortable silence descended for several moments. They seemed to Aelwyn to last far longer than they should have.

"That," Caravella finally admitted, "is not exactly correct. There will be time for that discussion later. For now, you must lay upon the altar and act as the little worm. We have a very large fish to catch, you and I. A large and dangerous fish."

Uncertain at first, Aelwyn stretched himself out atop the altar stone. But when the priest failed to whip out hitherto unconcealed means of restraining him, his wariness eased. He lay there for some time while Caravella read from a small parchment scroll, bound with gold and scarlet thread, that he'd taken from inside his robe.

At first, the harsh inflexibility of the stone pressing his sweat-dampened clothing against his body was merely uncomfortable. He fidgeted and shifted his body's position on the altar, seeking respite, but it did no good. The moisture soaked clear through the cloth and he feared the shirt would eventually freeze to his skin. Now, without the body heat generated by climbing, the cold thrust vicious fingers at Aelwyn's shivering flesh as if seeking to tear an opening so it could take up residence within his innards. The temperature was extreme enough to be painful, but Aelwyn stiffened his resolve to bravely endure whatever trials this night might hold, and he refused to complain.

The priest droned on in the background. The chanting was strangely relaxing, and without intending to do so, Aelwyn closed his eyes. When he flexed his fingers, they had gone numb, and he could no longer feel the sting of the wind on his face. Soon, drowsiness threatened, and Aelwyn found to his surprise that his chest was inexplicably flushed with warmth.

"He arrives."

The sharpness of the priest's tone snapped Aelwyn wide

awake. Too quickly, he sat up and winced at the agony that engulfed his arms from fingers to elbow. Instinctively, he thrust his hands into his armpits, but it did little to abate the torture of a thousand tiny, invisible knives.

"Stay there," Caravella warned. "We must make him believe you are a sacrifice. And whatever you witness, you will invite great danger should you interfere. *Capisce*?"

Aelwyn nodded. His thigh muscles were racked with painful cramps. In vain, he tried to feel his feet, but from the ankle down there was no sensation other than a faint tingle. He foresaw no problem following the priest's instructions; he doubted his legs would hold him upright for more than a second or two should he be foolish enough to disobey.

The air grew heavy and thick and took on an ominous quality. Though the snow had ceased falling while he was asleep, the wind had increased. Aelwyn watched as it seemed to seize the surface powder from a small snowdrift and whirl it into a column of sparkling ice crystals. Father Caravella's chanting increased its intensity. Now, his voice colored with a note of command. As if in response, the column darkened and solidified. With not a small amount of fear, Aelwyn began to suspect that the disturbance was caused by something far more unnatural than the mere wind.

The center of the maelstrom became translucent and seemed to gather in upon itself. A few seconds later, a large mass formed within it, as scarlet as blood. Ice and snow exploded outward, and where there had been a whirlpool of sleet only seconds ago, an enormously fat man appeared.

He was slightly shorter in height than the priest, but he more than made up for it with his girth. He was quite simply the largest man Aelwyn had ever seen. Had he not witnessed it with his own eyes, Aelwyn would have refused to believe that any human body could support such massive rolls of fat. In his entire village, he doubted there existed a chair that would not collapse into kindling under the man's bulk.

The stranger was clad in a robe made from more scarlet-dyed cloth than even someone as wealthy as Gwilym could ever hope to afford. The cuffs, collar, and hem were trimmed with white fur—ermine, unless Aelwyn was mistaken—and the robe was held closed by a belt of shiny black leather unlike any leather Aelwyn had ever before seen. His cheeks were reddened from the stinging wind, and his eyes were little buttons of blackest night, almost lost within the fleshy folds of his face. A luxurious beard, as white as snow, cascaded from his cheeks and chin down to his massive belly.

"Who summons me?" the new arrival demanded.

His voice was deep and resonant, commanding. Yet, the sound of it grated on Aelwyn's ears and increased his shivering. The man cast about and, seeing only the two of them, his eyes narrowed to slits. He focused on the priest.

"Was it *you*, blood drinker?" he asked, astonished. His belly started to jiggle, then his chest and shoulders rocked with mirth as he gave in to deep, bellowing laughter. "What could one of *your* kind possibly want with *me*?" he finally choked out.

"There have been rumors, Nikolai," Caravella said sternly.

"Rumors," the man repeated. The laughter ceased abruptly and his tone was flat and wary.

The priest nodded. "All the way from Brittany to Rome, we heard them."

"How do these … rumors concern me?"

"They don't. Not yet. But a new church rises in the south. And unlike the old religions, it is not very tolerant of our kind. We must exercise care. I have been sent to ask you to be more … discreet in your undertakings."

"*Our* kind?" The man called Nicolai started chortling again though Aelwyn could not see that Caravella had said anything amusing. "We have nothing in common, you and I."

"Not true. I, Lucenzio Caravella, tell you this. We are few. The humans are many. There is danger in that."

"I've never known a blood drinker who wasn't a simpering parcel of fear when it comes to humans. You're no different, *Signore* Caravella." He bestowed the honorific with a sneer.

Suddenly, his nose wrinkled as he caught the scent of something upon the air. His eyes snapped toward where Aelwyn was still seated atop the altar.

"Chaste?" he asked, as if impressed. "*You* brought me a virgin?"

"I am the Unblemished Youth," Aelwyn said without thinking.

Caravella shot him a look of warning, but Aelwyn knew his duty and ignored the priest.

"I am the sacrifice so that you, my lord, if you are pleased with me, might be willing to spare the children of our village."

"How old are you, boy?" Nicolai demanded.

"Seventeen summers."

"Seventeen summers and not yet pushing out urchins with some buxom wench? I find that hard to believe."

Aelwyn lowered his eyes modestly. "From birth," he said formally, "I was destined to be the Unblemished Youth until such a day as this, when my life would willingly serve as a sacrifice for …"

"It used to be," Nikolai abruptly interrupted with mild disgust, "they would give us kings. Stand up, boy," he ordered.

Aelwyn complied. He steeled his features against wincing when his full weight came down on his feet and sharp spears of pain shot up his legs. He had to grasp the edge of the altar to keep from falling, but almost immediately he let go. He was supposed to be unblemished; it would not do for him to show frailty at this late stage.

Nikolai walked slowly around the altar, his eyes never leaving the youth.

"Clean limbed," he said in a tone very much like that of a man discussing the attributes of a horse he might wish to buy. "Some decent meat on his bones, thank goodness. Children are all well and good, as I assume you know ..." He shot Caravella a meaningful glance. The priest's upper lip curled with distaste. "But they're not very satisfying. A virgin, though, of his age and size? Now, *that* is a treat!"

The fat man smacked his meaty lips. When he grinned, Aelwyn saw that his teeth were extraordinarily long and jagged things, half rotted with bits of gristle still stuck between them. Aelwyn's stomach contracted into a tight knot of horror when the nature of his fate became clear.

He was to be devoured alive!

It was a far more terrible prospect than anything he'd dared imagine. He quailed at the thought. For a moment, he struggled with the urge to bolt back down the mountainside, but he knew that if he did he would be shunned by everyone he knew. He wondered if, perhaps, his cold-crippled legs would bear him far enough so that he could throw himself off the cliff. Even being drowned or frozen in the river, or broken on the rocks below, would be preferable to the agony he'd feel as the fat man's horrid teeth sank into his body and ripped away chunks of his still living, quivering flesh.

Panic blossomed and, in spite of his resolve to meet his fate bravely, he took a single stumbling step toward the cliff edge. But before he could take a second step, he caught the priest's eye and saw the slight warning shake of his head. Even that would not have been enough to quell his burgeoning terror, except that Caravella also favored him with a reassuring wink and a half smile. In the face of the priest's amused confidence, Aelwyn's fear, though it did not vanish, was banked and he was able to master himself and stay where he was.

"There will be no virgin on your plate tonight, my friend," Caravella said. "Nor will there be any children in your future. I must ask you to refrain. In fact, I'm afraid I must insist upon it."

"Or else?" Nikolai's attitude toward the priest was one of disdain.

To Aelwyn, it seemed he had no more respect, nor fear, of Caravella then Pedr the blacksmith would have had for a fly. Caravella, however, did not grace him with an answer. He merely held up the scroll he'd been reading from earlier and shook it gently from side to side as if showing it off.

Nikolai shrugged, as if the roll of sheepskin was of no concern. In response, the priest reached inside his robe and withdrew a small bit of greenery, several leaves and red berries tied together with a length of string.

"Mistletoe and holly. So?"

The man in red shrugged again except, unless Aelwyn was mistaken, there was now the slightest suggestion of caution in the gesture. Caravella sighed, as if with exasperation, and dipped back into the folds of his garment. This time, his hand emerged holding what looked like a simple lump of coal.

"You're showing signs of senility, old man," Nikolai sneered. "You're mixed up. That may scare your friend the Krampus. Not me."

"Not even if it is soaked in oil of peppermint?" the priest asked with feigned innocence.

The fat man stiffened and hastily backed away a few steps.

"Maybe you do know what you're doing after all," Aelwyn heard him mutter. Then, in normal tones, he addressed Caravella once again. "I suppose," he began with studied casualness that rang entirely false to Aelwyn, "I might be convinced to perhaps skip this year's ... er ... harvest." He patted his massive belly. "It's not as if I'll starve if I miss a meal," he chuckled with self-deprecation. "This is merely because I have no wish to be inconvenienced by your trinkets and talismans, you understand."

Now it was Caravella's turn to smile. Aelwyn wondered why he'd never before noticed how white the priest's teeth were.

"Hardly mere trinkets, my jolly friend," Caravella told Nikolai. "You!" He pointed at Aelwyn. "Back onto the altar. Hop, hop!"

Uneasy in spite of the priest's promise that he was not to be offered as a sacrifice, the youth resumed his perch atop the frigid stone.

"I take the bouquet ... like so! And I place it around the neck of this youth, this young man who has not yet brought forth the urchins, as you have said ..."

Aelwyn reached up to examine the little bundle of foliage laying against his chest, but Caravella lightly slapped his hands away with a brisk, "Tssk!"

"In his left hand, he holds the coal ..."

The smell emanating from the rock was pungent enough to make Aelwyn's eyes water. Though the tears froze on his cheeks, he was glad that the peppermint scent wasn't entirely distasteful, merely strong.

"And in his right ...?"

Caravella paused, as if thinking deeply. Nikolai watched him through narrowed eyes, suspicious. But as the moments passed and the priest did nothing more, the huge man in red seemed to regain his previous arrogance.

"In his right?" he prompted.

"*Silenzio*," he said. "The brain, it continues to think."

"In that case," Nikolai responded with a truly gruesome smile, "I revoke my earlier offer."

He took an ominous step toward where Aelwyn sat shivering. Again, Aelwyn felt his eyelids wanting to close. He fought desperately to remain awake, but slumber tempted him with imagined warmth he found hard to resist.

"I'll have this stalwart young virgin first, and if I'm still peckish ..." His expression was more of a leer than a grin. "... there are children in the village below. In fact, I may visit the little tykes anyway. For spite. And to teach *you* a lesson."

"Just as I thought." Caravella made a business of sadly shaking his head. "These demons, they are not to be trusted," he told Aelwyn.

The boy slumped on the altar stone. His chin was sunken down upon his chest, and had the priest not wrapped his fingers around the lump of coal, he probably would have dropped it.

"You will, I trust, remember that in the future, *caro mio*."

But Aelwyn was afraid that any future of his was likely to be short. Even now, he was finding it difficult to focus his eyes and his body's demand that he succumb to sleep was increasing.

"Just a few moments more," the priest told him, kindly.

"Ah, look what I have here!" Caravella exclaimed. "*Stupido*, I had forgotten."

"What is that?" Nikolai demanded.

"It is the hoof of a reindeer, wrapped with a strand of little silver bells and blessed by ..." Caravella paused, "... elves."

"You don't dare!"

"I put it in the boy's right hand ... *ecco!*"

The instant Caravella closed his hand around the precious artifact, Aelwyn felt a surge of energy course through his body, erasing the bitter cold's effects from his limbs and keeping it at bay. His eyes snapped open and he felt more aware, more alive, than ever before. An intense warmth flowed through him, originating from the little bundle of greens against his chest; the fragrant coal matched it with an iciness that was invigorating. And from the tiny silver bells attached to the animal foot, sparks flew in all directions.

Effortlessly, Aelwyn rose to his feet. Holding the talismans at arm's length in front of him, he took his first slow and deliberate step towards Nikolai.

"No!" screamed the fat man.

He flung up his arms as if to ward off a blow, but it did no good. For every step the boy took forward, Nikolai was forced to back away to maintain an equal distance. The fat man's early steps were halting and tentative, but as Aelwyn continued his slow and inexorable approach, Nikolai was soon stumbling and tripping over himself in his haste to get away. He bellowed furiously and gestured with his ermine-trimmed arms. The powdery snow stirred and rose into the air, once again taking the rough shape of the column by which he'd arrived. But with the first words Caravella read aloud from the scroll, it collapsed into an innocent snow drift once again.

Alternately spitting threats of dire revenge and gibbering with terror, the fat man continued to retreat. The saplings at the far side of the plateau were no match for his bulk; he forced them to bend out of his way. Then, he tripped over one of the leafless bushes and stumbled, barely stopping himself on the lip of the cliff's edge.

"Touch him, boy," Caravella murmured, far too quietly

to register on human ears.

But Aelwyn somehow heard him anyway. He reached out with both hands and, oh so lightly and almost infinitesimally, the peppermint-soaked coal and the silver-wrapped hoof made contact with the hem of Nikolai's robe. A sharp crack like lightning striking split the air and the tiny bells jangled, miraculously filling the mountaintop with the chimes of a thousand cathedrals.

The man in red's reaction was both immediate and extreme.

Instantly, his entire body stiffened; his knees locked and his arms straightened and slammed against the sides of his body. A look of horrified rage appeared on his face just before his eyes rolled back in their sockets. Then, like a tree cut by a woodsman's axe, Nikolai slowly toppled backward. His feet left solid ground and, without uttering a sound, his body vanished over the edge of the cliff.

Aelwyn watched. From this distance, Nikolai's body resembled a huge red ball bouncing down the side of the mountain. Normally, Aelwyn might have winced every time the fat man slammed into a rocky outcrop, or when he careered past trees and boulders with renewed speed, but the flush of energy was fading and he didn't have the strength. He barely remained on his feet long enough to see Nikolai roll up a slight incline to be launched into the air and out across the river. The fat man's body smashed into the ice and vanished, leaving behind a large hole filled with bleak, black water that, even as Aelwyn watched, began to freeze up and close in upon itself as if by magic.

Fatigue overcame him and Aelwyn sank to his knees. The frozen ground would shortly leach the last bits of warmth from his body, but he had done what he was born to do. The current below the ice was strong. Aelwyn took solace in knowing that, in the next few moments before he succumbed to the cold, the river would have carried the body halfway to the sea. And long before the spring thaw, when the villagers would climb the mountain to collect whatever parts of him had not been food for winter scavengers, the fat man in red would be sinking to the bottom of the deep, black ocean, never to trouble anyone again.

Aelwyn felt the priest lift him and carry him back to the altar. Once there, he sat with the younger man's head cradled against his breast. Dimly, he heard Caravella muttering about not having enough time to do things properly, something he seemed to recall the priest speaking about earlier. Now, as then, he had no idea what it meant.

"Am I dying?" Aelwyn managed to whisper. With the moment upon him, he was afraid.

"Only for a little while, *caro mio*," Caravella told him while he gently stroked the boy's hair.

Aelwyn found the older man's voice soothing and relaxing. If he could only concentrate upon it, perhaps it would help to banish his fear.

"Your Christ god teaches of a resurrection," he said, hoping he would prompt the priest to continue talking. "Do you think he will resurrect me, even though I do not believe in him?"

"Not exactly," Caravella said.

The priest leaned forward and Aelwyn saw that his teeth were not only impossibly white, but impossibly sharp as well. An instant later, Aelwyn felt a searing pain in his throat that vanished as quickly as it had come, replaced by a languorous feeling of sensual pleasure unlike anything he had ever known.

With his fangs buried deeply in the boy's flesh, Father Lucenzio Caravella lost himself in the rich, red flow of Aelwyn's blood.

T̲HE N̲IGHT I̲ S̲TOPPED B̲ELIEVING

A.P. Sessler

y nose was buried in the Sears Wishbook as I searched for the next entry on my Christmas List, my head swimming with visions of plastic robots and starships—but that could have been the fumes from the paper and ink. I already had twelve items, enough for each day of Christmas if we were rewriting that lengthy carol.

Mom's big belly bumped into my elbow. My hand jumped across the page, leaving a long line across the ruled sheet of paper.

"Hey!" I complained.

"I'm sorry. And so is your little brother or sister," Mom said, and let her belly rest a moment on the kitchen table.

I smirked. "It's all right."

I twirled my pencil upside-down and rubbed the paper

vigorously until the line disappeared in a pile of pink rubber particles. Now all I could smell was eraser dust.

"That sure is a big list. You think Santa can bring all that?" said Mom, leaning over my shoulder.

"Sure. He has all the toys," I said.

She giggled. I looked at her jiggling belly. It looked like she took a basketball and stuffed it up her dress. Not the deflated one we had in the garage, but a good one that you could play with.

"You think he'll be a boy?" I asked.

She laughed.

"Well, if it's a he, of course he'll be a boy. But if it's a she, she'll be a girl," she said, and laughed again.

I didn't understand. "Will he be born by Christmas?"

She laughed. "I sure hope not."

"Why not?"

"That would mean he'd be born early."

"You always say getting up and going somewhere early was good."

She stooped over and kissed my head. "Not with babies."

I didn't understand that either.

"It's like cooking a turkey," she said. "I can't let you eat the turkey until it's fully cooked or you'll get sick."

The comparison of cooking and babies was not one I wanted to dwell on, but I think I understood.

Nicky stepped into the kitchen. She placed her bulky backpack on the counter and walked to the fridge.

"How was school?" Mom asked.

Nicky groaned.

"That good?" Mom teased.

"Hey, Nick. You wanna see my Christmas List?" I asked.

"No," she said, her head buried behind the opened refrigerator door.

I heard her shifting bottles around in search of something.

"You sure?" I asked.

"I'm sure," she said, closing the door and placing a jar of grape jelly on the table.

She stood on her toes, opened a cabinet door, retrieved a box of graham crackers, and put it beside the jar. She opened the box and the jar, and before she could turn around to reach for a butter knife from the dish drain, Mom placed one in her hand.

"Thanks," said Nicky, reaching for a cracker from the package.

Mom smiled.

"Aren't you going to make your list?" I asked.

"For what?" Nicky asked as she smeared jelly on a cracker.

"For Christmas."

"Duh. I know Christmas, but why?"

"So Santa will know what to bring you."

"Doesn't *Santa* already know?" she asked, staring without blinking.

"He knows if you're good or bad because he watches you, but he can't read your mind," I said, unsure how I even came up with such an answer.

She smirked. "I'm not going to make a list because it doesn't matter. *Santa* only brings you what Mom and Dad can afford anyway. Isn't that right, Mom?"

I looked at Mom. She opened her mouth but didn't speak. After a moment, the words came.

"Santa reads your list, and Mommy and Daddy pay him to make your toys," she said.

"Then why are all the toys at the toy store?" Nicky asked, her mouth full.

"That's enough, young lady," said Mom.

"Well, if you need help, I'll help," I offered and placed

my sheet of paper in the catalog and closed it. I slid the thick book toward her. "And if you want to look at my list, I'll leave it right here."

Nicky huffed and pushed the catalog aside.

"Where's Dad?" I asked.

"He's straightening out the Christmas lights," said Mom.

I went to the living room window and pulled back the curtain. Dad was having a time with those lights. I went outside and walked past him to the open garage. Inside I found my basketball sitting atop a pile of junk like a cherry on a sundae.

I reached for it, standing on my tiptoes until my fingertips pushed it off balance and brought it tumbling down. It lay on the garage floor, not even enough air to make it roll properly.

I carried the limp ball outside and tried to bounce it on the concrete driveway. When it failed to return to my hands, I retrieved it and made a shot. It flew through the air and into the hoop, then plopped onto the driveway like a pile of orange bird crap.

I expected some sympathy from Dad, but he was too busy untangling the spaghetti of Christmas lights at the end of the driveway. I cleared my throat.

"Dad, can I ask Santa for a new basketball?" I asked.

"The one you have is fine," he said without looking. "It just needs to be pumped up is all."

"You always say that. Maybe we need to ask Santa for a pump."

"We have one. We just need to find it is all."

"You always say that, too," I said, throwing my hands up.

"Don't worry, Son. I'll look for it."

He always said that, too, but I felt reminding him would result in little difference. I kicked the ball, intending to send it through the air, across the street, and into the neighbor's yard. It landed a mere few feet away from me. I made my way to the front porch when he stopped me.

"Hey? You gonna put that up?" he said, suddenly interested in my activity.

"Why?" I asked.

"Because you're done playing with it, aren't you?"

"No. I didn't play with it."

"Are you lying to me?"

"No. I didn't play with it because it's broke."

"Don't be smart with me. Now put it up. You know Santa won't bring you any toys if you don't take care of the ones you have. He doesn't like when children lie, either."

I couldn't argue with that. I picked up the lifeless ball and laid it down to rest inside the garage graveyard with all the other ghosts of Christmas toys past.

❄ ❄ ❄

Nicky and I stepped off the small porch and made our way to the sidewalk. She eyed the yellow piece of paper with disdain.

"Eggnog," she said. "Who drinks eggnog?"

"I do," I said with more enthusiasm than she approved.

She rolled her eyes. "You're the only one Mom and Dad buy it for. They don't like it, and I don't like it. How can you drink it? It tastes like soap."

"Not the carton kind. The can kind is the bad kind."

She re-read the item aloud. "Oh, that's too bad. Mom specifically said to get the canned kind."

"No!" I yelled and snatched the list from her.

"Hey!" she objected, trying to take it back.

I hurried ahead of her and read the small list, pinched

tightly in both hands, and found the item. "It says to get the carton kind!"

"I was just kidding, nerd," she said, and mussed my hair. "Now give me the list back or I *will* buy the canned kind."

I gladly handed her the list. We were nearing the corner of our street when she stopped in her tracks. I had walked a few steps before I noticed she wasn't with me. I looked back and saw her staring at the sidewalk.

"Did you step on a crack?" I asked.

She didn't answer. I approached her and looked carefully at the position of her feet. They were well within the acceptable safety zone. Mom's back had been spared.

"Nope. You're okay," I said, but she wasn't comforted by my assessment. "What's wrong, Nicky?"

She stood still. I pulled at her shirt tail. She faced me, her mouth open, no words coming out at first.

"Remember these berries, Rudy," she said, and pointed.

I looked at them. They were small and red. I looked up and down the street. There were no berries in any of the trees.

"What are they?" I asked.

"Holly berries."

I looked at the trees again. "Where did they come from?"

She glanced over each shoulder, then up in the air.

I bent down and picked them up. "What's so special—"

"No, Rudy!" she said, and slapped them out of my hand.

My eyes turned red and my lip began to quiver.

"Geez, Rudy. Don't go crying," she said.

"But you—"

"I said *remember*, not *touch*."

"But you hit me."

"I didn't hit you. I swatted them out of your hand because they're bad."

I looked at them. They didn't look bad to me. "You didn't

have to hit me," I whined.

"You better stop it, Rudy, or I *will* hit you."

I fought back my tears and confusion and accepted the ultimatum. "What's wrong with them?"

"Holly berries are a sign," she said. "And whenever you see them, you need to know that something bad will happen real soon."

Even half in tears, I was intrigued. The way children are when learning of a new superstition. Enough to stop crying—mostly.

"What will happen?" I asked, still sniffling.

"Rudy, I know you think I don't like you, but I do. And even though I can't tell you why, I'll never lie to you."

"What are you talking about?"

"That's just it. I can't tell you. It's just the way it is."

"What way?" I asked.

"Our way."

"You mean me and you?"

"No, Rudy. I mean *our* way. Mom and Dad's way. Our family's way. The way of Danny Boston's family. The way of our whole town."

"That doesn't make any sense."

"I know it doesn't, but that's our way. Even if it's not right, it's the way we all do it. Danny's sister had to do it. I have to, and so do you.

"Danny doesn't have a sister."

"Not anymore, but he had one. That's what I mean. Everyone will pretend it's not the way it is, but it is the way it is. Don't let anyone fool you."

"That's stupid. I don't have to do anything. And you're stupid, too," I said, and took off running.

I heard her call my name, but I didn't look back. I just kept running. There was only one place I could think to go.

As I ran to my best friend's house, I heard hammering half a block away. It echoed through the whole neighborhood.

When I finally got to Danny Boston's house, I was half out of breath. The hammering was really loud. I saw him playing catch with a baseball in the fenced-in backyard. I walked across the small front lawn to the chain-link gate.

"Hey, Danny!" I yelled.

"Come in, Rudy," he said.

I went inside. Mr. Boston was working on Danny's treehouse, high atop a giant ladder, hammering nails into wooden planks.

"Hey, Rudy. What you up to today?" Mr. Boston asked.

"Nothing," I said.

"Same thing Danny's up to," he said.

"Nuh uh," said Danny, looking at his dad with a squinted eye.

Mr. Boston laughed. "I'm just kidding. Danny's been playing catch. I'd offer you my mitt but it'll be too big for you," he said, glancing at me.

I looked over at the picnic table he had made. The leather mitt sat on top, and he was right—it was way too big for my tiny hand.

"That's okay. I don't need one," I said.

Danny walked past the tree house to the far side of the yard. I went to the other side—not too close to the fence in case he threw it too hard. He threw me the ball. It stung a little when I caught it, but I didn't let on.

"Are you going to the wreath ceremony Friday?" he asked.

"Of course, we have to," I said and threw it back.

He had a mitt on so it didn't sting at all. "I hope we win."

"Me, too. I mean, I hope my family wins," I said.

Ow! He threw the ball a little too hard that time. I returned it with equal strength, not that he felt it.

"Really I just want me and Mom to win. I don't like my dad or sister, but mostly my sister. I hate her," I said.

"You shouldn't say that. It's not right," he said.

"I only hate Nicky 'cause she hates me."

"It's 'cause you're the youngest. Older brothers and sisters always hate younger brothers and sisters."

"Why?"

"Mom says it's because they're jealous."

"Of what?"

"You get all the attention."

I knew that wasn't the truth. "No, I don't."

"That's what my mom says. She also says that's why they make up imaginary friends."

"Your brother Brian has an imaginary friend?"

"Nicky doesn't?"

"No. But she said you had a sister."

"I don't have a sister."

"That's what *I* said, but *she* said—"

"She's wrong," he insisted. "But maybe she knows about Brian's imaginary friend. Her name is Shelly."

I noticed Mr. Boston's hammering had slowed down. When I looked at him, he returned to his normal pace, but one eye stayed focused on us.

"I bet Shelly doesn't yell at Brian like Nicky yells at me," I said.

"Why did she yell at you?" Danny asked.

"'Cause I picked up some stupid holly berries."

"Holly berries?"

"Ow!" I heard Mr. Boston yell just before his hammer came crashing into the scrap pile of planks.

We looked at his dad. He shook his hand and sucked his thumb.

"Are you okay, Dad?" Danny asked.

"Yeah. Just hit my thumb is all. How 'bout you get inside. I'm sure Rudy has to be getting home now," said Mr. Boston as he descended the ladder.

I was about to throw the ball to Danny, but his back was still turned. "No, I don't—" I started.

"I'm sure your parents are wondering where you are right about now. Go ahead and get on your way," he said and picked up the hammer.

He gripped it and pointed at Danny with the claw end. "Inside. Now."

Danny glanced at me and took off ahead of his dad. Mr. Boston glanced back at me over his right shoulder as he followed Danny inside the back door. It slammed shut behind them.

I was all alone in the small backyard. Dead leaves gathered at my feet in the afternoon breeze. I placed the baseball in the hollow of Mr. Boston's mitt on top of the picnic table and went to the cold chain-link gate and left.

❊ ❊ ❊

It was Friday night. We finished our light dinner of tuna fish sandwiches and were busy getting ready for the big ceremony. Well, Mom, Dad, and Nicky were.

Mom and Dad ran back and forth in their dizzying attempt to get dressed. Between the "How do I looks" and the "Where's this" and "Where's thats" I stayed out of the way on the couch in front of the TV playing video games.

"Son, are you ready?" Dad asked.

"Yep," I answered as I mashed buttons on my game controller.

He walked into the living room and stood between me and the TV.

"Dad!" I yelled. "You're in the way."

"I thought I told you to get ready," he said, straightening the tie over his button-up collar.

"You asked if I was ready," I corrected him.

"And are you?"

"Yeah."

"No, you're not," he said and called to my mom. "Honey, where are Rudy's clothes?"

"I laid them out on the bed for him," I heard her yell from somewhere.

"Son, go get dressed," he said.

"But I'm still playing my game," I argued.

He spun around and pushed a button on the TV, sending my video game world hurtling off into oblivion. "Now you're not."

"Dad!" I whined and reached for the TV remote.

"I don't think so, young man. You get upstairs and dressed right now."

I slammed the remote on the couch (not a very impressive act of rebellion) and stomped off to get dressed.

❆ ❆ ❆

Nicky and I sat in the backseat, both disapproving of our current station in life. I stared at the back of Dad's smoothly shaven neck. Mom sat in the passenger seat, occasionally looking at something out her window. I don't know what; Christmas lights weren't even up, yet.

To my right, Nicky nervously picked at her dress. It made me more conscious of my own itchy sweater—a red thing with snowflakes and reindeer knitted into its threads. I could barely hear Dad humming some tune over the car heater.

"Mom, what does it mean if you find holly berries?" I

asked.

Her head spun aside and Dad stopped humming; it was like I just said a four-letter word.

"What did you just say?" she asked.

I was about to answer when I noticed Nicky's stare burning into me. I glanced over and found her face puckered into an angry expression. She shook her head at me.

"I was wondering what it meant if you found berries," I said softly, with occasional pauses between words.

"You said holly berries," she corrected me. "Why would you ask that?"

I glanced at Nicky again before answering. She looked even angrier. "I found some berries today on the sidewalk."

Mom faced the road. I thought I heard her sniffle, but it was hard to tell with the heater blowing in my ears. Dad glanced at her, reached over with his right hand and placed it on Mom's. She raised a fist to her mouth and looked out the window.

Dad looked back at me and exhaled before facing the road. Nicky swatted my leg and crossed her arms. I gazed out the window to my left. Nobody's lights were on at home, except an occasional porch light. Only the street lights on the telephone poles looming overhead were consistently lit.

Dad didn't hum the rest of the ride. We arrived at the town civic center at 8:08. That's what the light-up clock on the radio read.

✳ ✳ ✳

"We want to thank everyone for coming out tonight," said the bald man dressed in a suit and tie. He stood behind a podium, his hands planted on its frame, as he spoke into the microphone. "As is our tradition since the founding of our town, we bestow the Berryville Christmas Wreath upon one special family.

"This family will carry both the joy and the burden of the Berryville Blessing, which will see to the continued prosperity and safety of our little paradise here in the greatest country on earth."

The audience applauded. I looked to my left, past Dad and Mom to Nicky, who sat with her arms crossed. I wondered if she had once uncrossed her arms since we got out of the car. I felt kinda guilty for bringing up the whole berry business. Then again, maybe Nicky wanted me to feel guilty.

But despite her sour mood, she was pretty—for a sister. Her white dress was a few shades lighter than her skin and barely reached her knees as she sat. It had a red fur collar that swallowed her neck. It matched her lipstick, which Mom didn't let her wear often. I always thought her lips were kinda funny. They were like little rectangles. Whenever I got real mad at her, I called her Lego Lips. She hated that.

Around her waist was a black belt with a gold buckle like Santa would wear. It matched her gold hair clips and bobbed black hair that fell just below her ears.

I noticed everyone had stopped clapping, so I stopped. She glanced at me and rolled her eyes.

"And now for the moment we've all been waiting for," the man at the podium said with a smile and reached his fat hand into a big glass fishbowl full of paper that looked like it went through Dad's document shredder.

I saw Dad put his hand over Mom's, like he had in the car. It looked like he squeezed her hand real hard, but she didn't seem to mind.

The man's face turned red as his hand squirmed through the bowl. After a moment, he pulled out his hand with a shredded piece of paper. He unfolded the small piece with both hands and tilted his head back to look at it through the bottom of his glasses.

"And, the lucky family is—," he said and glanced at the drummer behind him, who proceeded to patter the snare drum with his sticks.

"Nick and Donna Wilson!" the man shouted into the microphone, which answered with ear-piercing feedback.

The brass band broke into *For He's A Jolly Good Fellow*. The whole audience looked at Mom and Dad as if a spotlight had appeared, but it hadn't. My parents stood up and smiled with red, teary eyes. Nicky's eyes were red, too, but she wasn't smiling.

Dad took my hand, and Mom, Nicky's, and we all made our way past pairs of legs, tucking and turning aside until we exited the row of chairs. We walked up the red carpeted aisle to the stairs and up to the stage, where we turned to face the audience. The music was so loud my ears hurt.

A pretty blond woman in a short, sparkling red dress and white fur collar came from the opposite end of the stage with a big, jingling wreath and handed it to Mom and Dad like they had just won a brand new car on a game show. She kissed Mom and Dad on the cheek, then Nicky, and lastly me.

It was wet. I rubbed my cheek and got lipstick all over my hand. Mom and Dad each held the wreath in one hand, like they were going to walk it across the street.

The fat man motioned with his hand and the band stopped playing and the applause ended. Finally. My ears continued to ring. He stepped aside and motioned again, so Dad handed the wreath to Mom and stepped up to the podium.

Dad leaned over the microphone. "I just want to thank everyone," he said, and wiped a tear from his eye. "Berryville is a truly special place. We are blessed with so much. We have the lowest cancer, car crash, crime, and divorce rate in the country. You might not know that, but I do, because I, along with my darling wife, Donna, handle most of Berryville's legal and insurance needs."

The audience laughed.

"And on a serious note, I just want to say thank you to my children, who are the best children a man could have," he said as he turned to face us. "I couldn't be prouder than I am of Nicole and Rudy. You two mean the world to your mother and me. We love you very much."

The audience stood in applause.

I had never heard Dad say such kind words. I don't know if he actually meant them, but at that moment, I couldn't have been happier. But Nicky, I don't think she could have been any more miserable.

❄ ❄ ❄

The next morning, Mom and Dad went about their routine in silence. She prepared our breakfast, drank coffee, did dishes. Dad didn't finish half his bacon and scrambled eggs. I eyed his plate like a begging dog, but Dad didn't get the hint.

"Are you going to finish that?" I asked.

He smiled and slid the plate over to me. "Here you go, Sport. Have at it. After breakfast, me and you will go find that air pump in the garage."

"Really?" I asked, my mouth already filled with his scrambled eggs.

"Yes, really," he said.

I stared at Nicky's plate. "What about Nicky?" I asked.

"Easy, Sport. She needs to eat, too," he said, and immediately went silent again.

I saw Mom turn back to the dishes. Even though the rack

was full of clean dishes, she turned on the water and began to fidget with something in the sink.

When I finished breakfast, Dad and I, but mostly Dad, sifted through the treasure trove in our little garage. A lot of the items were too heavy or wrapped around something else and triggered small avalanches, but he didn't yell at me or scold me a single time.

"Eureka!" he said, and held up the air pump like it was Excalibur.

"Yay!" I shouted and carried the deflated basketball onto the driveway.

Dad followed me with the pump and set it down. Each time he pushed the plunger down, I heard imaginary sticks of dynamite go off. The ball slowly came to life. After a minute, my mind wandered away from exploding mine shafts to Nicky's bedroom window. She stood there, looking out, at what I don't know. Mom stood behind her, her lips moving.

When Nicky noticed my stare, she pulled the curtains closed. My gaze lowered to the naked front door. I glanced back at Dad and the ball. It was almost full.

"After this, can I help put up the wreath?" I asked.

Dad stopped pumping. "Do you want to play with your basketball or not?" he asked, his voice sharp and cutting like it always was before.

"Yes, sir. But after I play can—"

"Your mother and I will put it up," he said and continued pumping the ball.

"But I want to help."

"That's not how we do it."

"But—"

"It's tradition!" he shouted and removed the air line from the ball. "Take your ball and go play."

He stood up with the pump in his grip and threw it into the garage, triggering another avalanche. He stomped up the porch steps and into the house, slamming the door behind him.

Sometimes I wish he were dead.

❄ ❄ ❄

Nicky and I stood in the driveway, facing the door and the green wreath speckled with red and gold hanging on it. It was made entirely of holly leaves and berries, with small golden bells tied to it. Nicky put her hand on my shoulder and pulled me close.

I leaned my head on her waist. "Merry Christmas," I said.

"It's not Christmas yet," she said.

"Then early Merry Christmas."

"It won't be merry, Rudy. Not now or ever. Remember what I said. Those berries. The next time you see those berries, you run, Rudy. Run and don't look back. Leave this little town and never return."

I didn't know what to say, so I didn't.

❄ ❄ ❄

"Rudy, could you go pick up these things for me?" Mom asked as she handed me a small grocery list and a twenty-dollar bill. "You can buy yourself a Dr. Pepper, too."

I looked at the few items written on the list. "But Nicky usually gets groceries," I said.

"I know, but Nicky will be busy today. She and her father are going to have a little father–daughter time."

"He never has father time with me."

"It's different, Rudy. Your sister is growing up. She needs this."

I half-crumbled the list and the bill in my hand. "I need it, too," I grumbled, and went out the front door.

❋ ❋ ❋

I stood at the grocery store counter with the bottle of Dr. Pepper, can of evaporated milk, and bag of marshmallows on the counter, waiting for the cashier to ring them up.

"There's the Wilson boy," I heard a woman say.

I looked out the corner of my eye and saw two old ladies.

"Were they the ones chosen this year?" the other asked.

"Yes."

"It's about time. They've gotten off lucky all these years."

Gotten off lucky?

"Will that be all, Rudy?" the cashier asked.

The women caught me staring at them. Not that I cared—they were staring at me first.

"Rudy?" the cashier asked again.

I faced him. He was a nice old fellow. Bald, with little patches of hair on either side of his head.

"Yes, sir," I said, and handed him the twenty-dollar bill.

He gave me the change.

"You want me to pop that top for you?" he asked.

"Yes, please," I said.

He took the glass bottle of Dr. Pepper and removed the top with the counter-mounted bottle cap remover. He handed me the steaming, cold bottle and my bag of groceries.

"Take care of yourself, Rudy. And give your sister Nicky a big hug for me," he said, his eyes all red.

I never saw him so emotional. But everyone was acting all emotional.

"Yes, sir," I said, sort of uneasy, and carried my groceries out of the store.

* * *

With a burning candle atop every table, each downstairs room smelled like a different spice. The living room smelled like pine to help the artificial tree put on a more convincing act; the dining room smelled like cinnamon; the kitchen, vanilla.

Whatever bad mood that had plagued everyone but me was miraculously dispersed and healed by the aromatic craft of these waxen apothecaries. Not to be denied, our remaining senses were tantalized by Christmas music playing on the stereo and a burning yule log that crackled in the fireplace.

Our near-empty plates rested on the dinner table. Scraps of ham, sweet potato souffle, buttered biscuits, and cranberry sauce sat uneaten.

"Who wants eggnog?" Mom asked, removing the beautiful white-and-green carton from the fridge.

"Me!" I said, raising my hand.

Mom took two small glasses from the cupboard and placed them on the kitchen table. She opened the cardboard carton and filled my glass to the top; hers, only half-way.

"I'll take a glass," said Nicky to my surprise.

I laughed as I took a sip, making bubbles rise and pop atop the thick, yellow confection.

Mom placed a third glass on the table. "Nick?" she asked, one hand on the cupboard door.

He shook his head behind a lowered newspaper. "None for me, thank you."

I laughed another mouthful of bubbles into my glass.

"Hmm. This doesn't taste like soap after all," said Nicky in surprise; a thin, yellow mustache adorned her pink Lego lips.

"Told you so," I said.

Mom drank her glass quickly and placed it in the sink. I guess Nicky was right—Mom didn't really like it.

"Maybe I should have given this a chance before," said Nicky, placing her empty glass on the table.

She reached over and hugged me. "Sorry I didn't believe you."

"It's okay," I said.

With that she released me. Even with the sound of sleigh-bell music filling our house, it seemed suddenly quiet.

Dad cleared his throat and placed his paper flat on the table. "Alright, kids. It's time to get to bed," he said, tapping the face of his wristwatch.

"Aww," I moaned and motioned for my sister to follow me. "Come on, Nicky."

"You go ahead," she said, but I waited.

"What are you waiting for?" said Mom. "You heard your sister."

"But if I have to go, she has to go."

"Go to your room, Son. She'll be right behind you," said Dad.

"What about the cookies and carrots for Santa and his reindeer?" I reminded them.

Mom opened the fridge and removed two plates filled with their respective items.

"Don't worry, I didn't forget. I have them right here," she said and placed them on the kitchen table. "Now up you go."

With drooped shoulders and crouched back, I made my way up the stairs to my room. I lay in bed, waiting to hear Nicky's footsteps. It wasn't fair. She got to stay up late while I had to lay in bed unable to get to sleep. It was some time before she came upstairs.

My door creaked open. "You awake, Rudy?" I heard her whisper, but I didn't answer. I was mad at her.

"Rudy? You awake?" she tried again, but again I ignored her. "Merry Christmas," she said and pulled the door shut.

I wish I hadn't been so mad at her, but I couldn't help it. It took me a good while to fall asleep, but eventually I did.

※ ※ ※

I was startled awake by a noise. I was about to fall back asleep when I heard it again.

"Nicky?" I whispered. "Is that you?"

I waited a minute. I heard something again, like shuffling or dragging feet—that, and the jingle of a bell. I sat up.

"Nicky?"

I threw my blanket aside and got out of bed. The Berber carpet was warm beneath my feet. I cracked open my door and peeked through to see if Mom and Dad were up. If they caught me wandering around on Christmas Eve, they would go nuts.

I pushed the door open and stepped into the railed hallway overlooking the first floor. The hardwood was cold, as was the dark fireplace, but Santa can't come down the chimney with a roaring fire going. I gazed at the silver star crowning our Christmas tree. In the light of the blue bulbs, it, too, looked so cold.

I stepped towards the stair when my foot landed on something colder than the hardwood floor. It stuck in the bridge of my foot like a stone. When I raised my leg to see what I had stepped on, I saw a crushed red berry on the floor.

It was a holly berry. As my eyes cleared from sleep, I saw more—not a whole pile of them, just the occasional one here and there. I turned back towards Nicky's room. They were scattered along in that direction as well.

I thought of waking her, but I knew she would yell at me, complaining she needed her beauty sleep or just calling me dummy, so I decided to venture on my own. Besides, the way I had ignored her earlier surely wouldn't win any points with her.

I walked as softly as I could, still the stairs offered their creak of alarm. Each time they sounded, my shoulders tensed up, as I expected Mom and Dad to come storming and screaming from their bedroom.

I found another holly berry with my opposite foot. Who knew something so small could hurt so bad? I made it to the bottom without any further incident.

I saw a berry between the landing and the dining room to the left. I entered, expecting any moment to find Santa Claus nibbling the cookies we left on the adjacent kitchen's table. Both the cookies and carrot we left for his reindeer were untouched.

I could never figure out how Mom was so messy when baking cookies for Santa. She always left a pile of flour on the floor that she never seemed to leave when baking any other time. In fact, I never saw her make cookies she hadn't bought from the store in a plastic bag or cardboard tube.

But when I wandered into the kitchen, there it was—the floor generously floured. In it, I saw a reindeer's hoof prints. I carefully avoided the space so not to betray my presence.

I heard the jingling of bells once more.

I ran into the living room. There was something in the fireplace. It was a sack! Santa's sack!

It went right up the chimney, followed by a cloud of soot that came raining down. Santa had just left! I hurried to the fireplace and looked up. I saw black, then as a shape exited through the top, the starry sky appeared.

I felt something beneath my hand. I raised it to find a

crushed holly berry in my palm. I gazed down in the freshly fallen soot, where the print of my hand rested between that of hooves.

I ran back upstairs to my bedroom and opened the window. I twisted to get a peek at the roof. The snow had already settled on top the chimney and on every shingle edge. I put on my shoes and climbed out onto the roof.

I looked up, and there it was—the reindeer—visible between every red and green flash of the MERRY and CHRISTMAS lights above the plastic Santa Claus figure. Its antlers peeked out from just behind the rooftop. I wasn't sure if I could scale the snowy shingles, but if I didn't try, I would never have this chance again.

I climbed the low incline, my foot slipping only once. I stood on the top of the roof, prepared to say "Hello" or "I see you" or "I gotchya!" but my brain forgot any such greetings along with the ability to speak at all.

It was no reindeer. No Santa Claus. No animal or man I had ever seen. I don't think it was either. More like both. It stood upright like a man, but had the body of an animal. Its calves bent back, and right above its hooves there were great tufts of dangling hair, I supposed to keep its "feet" warm— just like those horses on the beer commercials.

It didn't know I was standing just behind, staring at its humped back, I'm sure because it fought to keep the squirming sack it carried from leaping out of its clawed hands. That is, until the quarry it captured emerged from the sack. A lone hand squeezed through its grip and out into the winter air. I never saw her face, but I know she saw mine.

It's like when you hide beneath a blanket. If you hold it real close to your eyes, you can just barely see through the spaces between the threads.

"Rudy, help!" I heard my sister cry out.

The thing turned its head. Around its neck was a collar of holly, much like the wreath that hung on our front door. Suspended from the coarse sticks that formed the collar's frame were the jingling bells I had heard from my bed.

I knew from the look in its eyes I had turned white, paralyzed in its gaze. It didn't have to make any threatening gesture or command, I was helpless.

"Please, Rudy! Help me!" she cried from inside the sack.

It shoved Nicky's hand back into the sack and turned away.

"Hey!" I yelled when my courage only briefly returned, but it ignored me.

It leaped into the air, off the roof, and disappeared into the dark, snowy night. I scurried toward the edge of the roof, where resting in the snowy blanket were two red berries. I listened to Nicky's voice as it faded, like dim light in darkness.

I returned to my room, trembling from cold and fear. I didn't sleep well the rest of the night. The only time I got to sleep, I had a horrible dream. It was like watching a movie.

Everything that happened that night replayed in my mind. The only difference was that just before the thing jumped off the roof with Nicky, she poked her head out of the sack. Her black hair was a tangled mess, full of holly berries and leaves.

Her skin was ghostly pale and her cheeks and eyes lined in thick black, like a stage ghost in a theater play.

"Next year, Rudy! It'll be you, next year!" she shouted without blinking.

I woke up. It was dawn, Christmas morning—the time I usually jumped out of bed and ran down the hall to wake up Nicky. I didn't bother going to her room, but I did gaze down the hall. All the berries that lined the hall and stairs the night before were gone.

I looked in the living room. There were colorful boxes with bows waist deep at the foot of the Christmas tree. I didn't care.

"Merry Christmas, Son!" greeted Mom and Dad as they came out of the kitchen, their voices jubilant.

My frown spoke volumes while my words were few. "It's not a Merry Christmas."

"Aw, Son. Why would you say that?" said Dad.

"Nicky's gone," I answered.

They looked at one another.

"Nicky?" said Dad.

I nodded.

"Nicky?" repeated Mom.

I sniffed as the snot trickled down the back of my throat and tears crept down my cheeks.

"What's wrong, Son?" Dad asked.

"The monster took Nicky," I cried.

"What monster?"

"I thought it was Santa's reindeer, but it wasn't. It was a monster. He took Nicky and stuffed her into a sack and carried her away."

He smiled, sort of. He glanced at Mom and back at me, then laughed. "What are you talking about, Son? Did you have a nightmare?"

I did have a nightmare, so I nodded, but I didn't mean to.

"Aww, I'm sorry," he said.

"It was just a dream. It can't hurt you," said Mom. "But don't think about it. That was last night and now it's Christmas morning and you have a whole bunch of presents to open. Isn't that exciting?"

I glanced at the living room full of presents, but only out of habit. I wiped the tears from my eyes with my palm.

"But I want Nicky back," I whined.

"And Santa took Nicky away?" Mom asked.

"Not Santa. The monster," I tried to clarify.

"Santa has many helpers," said Dad. "Sometimes his helpers look like him, sometimes they look like you or me, and sometimes they look like elves or reindeer because he knows all kinds of magical creatures. Isn't that what you mean?"

"No! I mean the monster. I saw him put Nicky in a sack and jump off the roof."

"Son, you must have been dreaming. You couldn't go out on the roof. You'd fall off. And with all that snow? You'd get frostbite or freeze to death."

"But—"

"And who's this Nicky? Do you mean, Saint Nick, as in Saint Nicholas? Santa Claus?"

"I mean my sister!" I yelled.

"Calm down, Son, there's no need to raise your voice."

"But you keep saying Nicky's not real."

"Come here, Son," said Dad as he put an iron grip on my shoulder and led me to the kitchen, where the plates set out for Santa and his deer sat empty. "Saint Nicholas is very real. There are his bootprints right there. See?"

Beside the hoof prints in the flour sat a fresh pair of heeled boot prints that I instantly realized were not there the night before when I had wandered through the house.

Santa had never visited our kitchen, not on any Christmas past nor would he on any Christmas future. Those weren't Santa's boots.

"I don't mean Santa Claus," I said. "I mean Nicky. Nicole. You know who I mean."

"Son, it's alright to have an imaginary friend. Your mother had one, and so did I. It's often what we do when we grow jealous of our younger siblings."

"I don't have a younger sib—" I couldn't pronounce the word.

"No, but you soon will. And even though you might feel like your mother and father aren't paying as much attention to you, we are. It will only seem that way because your younger sibling will require a lot of attention until he or she is old enough to look out for his or herself. Does that make sense?"

How could I argue with the logic of a grown up? I simply nodded. "Yes, Sir. Yes, Ma'am."

✳ ✳ ✳

Years went by without our family "winning" the Berryville Blessing. My little brother was born and grew up to be quite the pain. I hassled Donny any time he tagged along or was left in my care. The rest of my time would be spent with my imaginary friend, Nicky.

What adventures we would have together, just the two of us. She knew me better than anyone; someone I could trust with all my secrets and darkest fears. She never left my side until the chilly Autumn day we stumbled upon the holly berries on the sidewalk running up our street.

"Sorry, Rudy," she said. "I have to go now, but I'll see you soon."

And like that, she disappeared. Now it would be just me and my little brother. And soon he would be alone, talking to his imaginary friend Rudy, unless I took the advice my sister gave me years ago and left town right that moment.

In all its years, Berryville had never filed a Missing Persons report. There was no need to. Everyone was in on the dirty, little secret. That was part of our deceptive charm. Lowest cancer, car crash, crime, and divorce rate in the country. My parents would know. Now the world outside our town would know *why*, and our town would no longer be so safe, nor home to the "blessing" that plagued the innocent children of Berryville.

B̊reaking T̊radition

Chantal Boudreau

itch!"

The phone cracked in three places as it hit the wall.

Serena had planned on spending the night doing traditional Christmas things—stringing popcorn, baking gingerbread men, and making gifts for her friends. She also had all the fixings for old-fashioned fruitcake. What said traditional Christmas more than that?

She had assembled everything for her baking, including the all-important rum, when she had answered a call from her cousin, Jessica.

"Did you invite Claire to your party?" Jessica had asked.

"Of course, I did. She's my best friend."

"Well, she won't be bringing a date."

"Why not? I thought she was hot and heavy with someone?

She suggested they might be getting married soon."

"That's true, but she won't take him to your party because she won't want to ruin your Christmas. She's dating Tyler."

Serena's hands had been shaking after Jessica had hung up. This was before she had launched the phone at the wall and screamed profanity. Serena and Tyler had once dated, for four long years, beginning with their last year in high school. When she had made it clear she thought it was time for something more, he had chosen instead to end things rather than offer her a real commitment. The break-up had broken her heart.

That had been two and a half years ago. Serena had liked to think she was over him, but in truth, she wasn't. She hadn't even considered dating anyone else, was reluctant to move on. Serena suspected Claire knew it, and she also knew Serena would see her relationship with Tyler as the most heinous of betrayals. That was no doubt why Claire had been hiding her current love from her best friend, but she had made the mistake of not keeping the truth from Jessica. Serena's cousin lived for gossip, the nastier, the better.

Crushed, Serena set upon the rum—after all, she only needed a small portion of it for the actual fruitcake. She drowned her hurt feelings more than she did the batter, stewing in negativity as she mixed. She had been hoping Tyler might come back some day, realizing the mistake he had made when he had left her. That likely wouldn't happen if he married someone else. It also suggested Tyler's problem wasn't with marriage, but with her. That hurt even more.

Serena couldn't help but wonder if Claire's betrayal had gone farther than just picking up the boyfriend who had dropped her. Had the two been seeing one another while Serena and Tyler were still involved? Did Claire's betrayal run even deeper?

The drunker she got, the more she blamed Claire.

"How could you do this to me? A best friend doesn't do something like this. You're just awful—a heartless harlot. I never took anything from you."

Fierce anger fermented into hatred, and by the time Serena was soused, she was plotting inebriated revenge. She wanted to kill the one she blamed for her heartache. She decided the best way to do that would be to poison the gift she had been planning to make for her.

Barely able to stand, she teetered her way over to the sink. In the cabinet below it, she kept an industrial-sized bottle of ant poison. She poured it liberally into the bowl before adding the last of the rum.

"Chew on that, you slutty s-s-snake," she slurred, barely able to keep the mixture from spilling. Her alcohol-sodden brain wasn't making sense of much, but she did decide she needed a way to mark the cake as Claire's. "Claire, Claire, Gummi Bear." Serena recalled the fact that she had had bought a bag of the candy that served as Claire's nickname, purchased to decorate a gingerbread house. She could spare a couple for Claire's homemade gift.

The rest of the night was a blur. Serena wasn't sure how she managed to get the cake in the pan, the pan in the oven, and then the cooked results onto the cooling rack without scorching herself or burning down the house. Aside from a small sear mark on the inside of her wrist and a horrible hangover, including some minor memory loss from the night before, she was unscathed by the entire debacle.

The fruitcake—topped with two semi-melted gummi bears: one red and one green—was slightly lop-sided. When looking at it, something about it made Serena feel uneasy and nauseous, but she couldn't remember her additional murderous extra ingredient. If she had, now sober, she would never have wrapped it and sent it. Wanting to poison Claire was something her drunken mind had concocted and was keeping to itself. She despised her once best friend, but Serena thought she would be the better person.

"Don't stoop to her level."

Serena packed up the fruit cake and dropped it off at the post office with the necessary postage.

✳ ✳ ✳

On Christmas Day, Claire stared down at the lumpy-looking fruitcake in the tin before her, the twin gummi bears staring back up at her like a pair of bulbous, mismatched eyes.

"I'm sure she was trying to be sweet," she said to Tyler with a shrug. "She handmade all her gifts this year—she warned us about that. And look, she put gummi bears on top, just for me. I'm surprised she's still willing to send me anything for Christmas."

Tyler rolled his eyes and ran his hand through his dark hair. "If she were still that good a friend, she'd remember you're off gluten. We wouldn't have to hide that we're together either. She'd already know by now, and she wouldn't care."

"Of course she's going to care. She's still stinging over you. And I'm sure someone has blabbed about us to her by now, but I'm going to tell her everything after Christmas when the timing's better. Until then, it may seem like just a nasty rumor. Maybe she thought this was the most I deserved … a lumpy Christmas cliché."

Claire was going to just throw out the fruitcake when she recalled a tradition her mother and an old friend had going when she and Serena were kids. As a friendly joke, and a Christmas tradition, the two women would send the same fruitcake back and forth to one another every year, along with whatever other gift they sent. Claire laughed.

"Wait a minute! I know why she sent this. This is a Liz-and-Margaret cake. She really is reaching out to me as an old friend this year." Claire grinned, rewrapping the cake. She would stow it away in the freezer until the following year.

"A Liz-and-Margaret cake?"

"A playful tradition. Serena never meant for me to eat this. She'll be getting it back next year."

Tyler gave her a cold hard stare. "You plan on playing games with her. I don't think that's a good idea. If she decides she can't forgive you for hooking up with me, she'll hold a grudge. I've told you before, you'd be better off severing ties. You can make new friends. She gave you a crap gift, hoping you'd resent her for it. I bet she's jealous. Toss it and get rid of her at the same time."

The look he was giving her made Claire uneasy. His expression could go from charming to menacing in a single breath, shifting as quickly as his moods. At times it was easier to give in to his fouler moods than to fight. While she usually would concede, giving up her long-time friendship with Serena—if her bestie was willing to forgive her indiscretions—was not up for concession. She would defy Tyler even at his growliest for Serena's sake.

Claire didn't openly argue, however. She set the fruitcake aside with the intention of hiding it at the back of the freezer once Tyler had been distracted by other things. He would forget about it, and as long as she didn't mention it again, she could return it to Serena next year as planned.

Claire knew engaging with Serena that way would never make up for the hurt she had caused her—would cause her as long as she stayed with Tyler—but at least it would keep them connected. She had never meant to damage their friendship.

She hadn't been all that interested in Tyler at first, but then she had had one too many at a party they were both attending and woke up in his bed the next morning with a terrible headache and the realization she had just betrayed her best friend in one of the worst ways possible. Tyler had used her guilt against her, threatening to tell all to Serena if she didn't come back for seconds. Then thirds. Then Claire was hooked.

She wasn't typically drawn to forceful men; he was somewhat of a bully, but he did manage to grow on her after a bit. She didn't like that he often played off her insecurities when they argued, and perhaps he was manipulating her in the process. On the other hand, he was an exciting lover and took care of a lot of things she preferred not to bother with. Plus he had a good job with a promising future. Claire didn't want to see herself as a gold-digger, but the idea of not having to worry about money was a pleasant one. Her family had struggled to pay the bills while she was growing up and avoiding that as an adult was a top priority.

And while she hadn't let Tyler know it yet, she had another reason keeping her from leaving now.

After he had left the room to go watch football outtakes on his desktop computer, she reached for the rewrapped fruitcake with one hand and stroked her still-flat belly with the other. She would have to disguise the fruitcake with foil, but Tyler hardly ever went into the freezer, and then it was only for something microwavable. He considered cooking woman's work.

"Until next Christmas," Claire sighed as she wedged the cake between a bag of frozen peas and some pork chops. "Here's to tradition."

❋ ❋ ❋

Serena gazed at the open package in her lap.

"I don't get it. I gave this to her last year. She regifted it. What the hell??"

Her new boyfriend, Andy, tilted his head thoughtfully. Then he shrugged his shoulders and laughed. "It's the old revolving fruitcake gag. The only reason people can do it is because these things never go bad."

He reached towards it as if to pluck off a morsel, and unexplained panic made Serena start. She batted his hand away violently, almost dropping the cake in the process. Andy cradled his stinging fingers in his other hand, grimacing.

"What was that for?"

Serena wasn't sure why, but she couldn't let Andy touch it. Just looking at the cake, with its warped little gummi bears, filled her with an inexplicable sense of dread. This, even though she couldn't remember baking the damn thing. That might explain why it looked so awful. It would probably taste awful, too.

"I can't send it back nibbled. Besides, you don't know for sure it's not bad," she warned him.

She hadn't realized Tyler was bad either until she had stopped pining for him. It turned out Claire had done her a favor rather than a disservice. Now that Serena was in a relationship with someone like Andy, far more relaxed and content, she could see how controlling Tyler had been, bordering on abusive. She was sure things would have escalated if they had gotten married—the way they had for Tyler and Claire.

Instead of being angry at Claire, now she was worried for her. First, there had been a sudden engagement followed in quick succession by a hasty wedding and then, only a month later, poor Claire had suffered a miscarriage. Serena had tried to be there for her, but Tyler had made it difficult.

Nobody had been able to see Claire while she was recuperating without her husband allowing it, and he had made it very clear that Serena was not welcome.

After such a chilly rejection, Serena hadn't been surprised when Claire had refused the invitation to Serena's annual Christmas party. That was why Serena hadn't been expecting to see her when her old best friend suddenly showed up at her door that day. Claire had looked exhausted, her face drawn and her eyes shadowed and puffy. She had seemed cowed as well, not even meeting Serena's gaze as she had handed her the gift.

"I'm sorry, I can't stay," Claire had mumbled, passing her the brightly colored package. "But I brought you this. Merry Christmas."

Serena had begged Claire to stay, if only for a few minutes, to have a coffee or some eggnog, but Claire had shaken her head and slipped away despite Serena's objections. She suspected Claire had made an undeclared escape from Tyler and couldn't afford to be gone long enough to have her absence noted. That notion struck Serena as disturbing, but what could she do about it? She had volunteered her help in the past, but the offer was only good if Claire was willing to act on it, and so far she hadn't been.

Serena glanced up at Andy, eyes sad. He gave her a sheepish grin.

"Fine. I won't touch it then. I was only going to nab a mangled gummi bear, but I suppose you're right. I won't spoil your fun. Stick it in the freezer until next year. Then you can send it back to her."

Serena nodded and bit at her lip. Considering the prison-like existence Claire now found herself in, Serena wondered if hiding a file in the cake next year might be a worthwhile idea. Not that the restraints confining Claire could be done away with with something as simple as a file. They were partially self-imposed at this point, and almost entirely psychological, unless Tyler had begun to actually rough her up.

At least the returning of the cake next year would remind Claire that their friendship still endured, despite all their trials and tribulations. It might only be a small gesture, but it was one way Serena could let her know that she still thought of her and that none of those thoughts were negative ones anymore.

* * *

Tyler clenched his fists in frustration. Claire apparently hadn't realized he was home when she had answered the door to the postal worker. She had taken the package and cached it away behind the sofa so he wouldn't notice it, rather than placing it with the other gifts. He hated the fact that she was hiding something from him. He had to know why.

She angered him easily nowadays. He had been upset with her when she had tricked him into marrying her based on a pregnancy that went nowhere. He was still convinced that she had done something to cause the miscarriage, just to spite him once he had given in and said "I do."

Then, to make matters worse, Claire had changed. She had grown moody and sullen, a ghost of the woman she used to be, skulking around the house with no flair. She made only a half-assed attempt to listen to him when he told her to smile, and it had taken several months and just as many arguments to convince her that it was in her best interest not to spend any time with her rotten friends. None of them liked him, and they all kept trying to sabotage their relationship. It was about time they minded their own business.

And none of this had stopped her from occasionally giving him lip, usually after one of her so-called friends had telephoned. This meant him having to put her in her place all over again. After all, he was the man of the house. She barely contributed anything to the household. He even had to coax her to have sex with him. He couldn't understand why she wasn't more receptive. She owed him.

When the second pregnancy had come along, followed by another miscarriage, Tyler had been absolutely sure it was Claire's fault. She used it as an excuse to deny him what he needed, playing the sympathy card. So he had gone out and gotten what he needed from someone else. She wasn't some sorry excuse for a woman like Claire. She had gotten pregnant, too, and was already six months along. There had been no miscarriage there—proof it wasn't his fault. Claire just didn't have what it takes to be a mom. She was damaged goods.

After Claire had headed up to bed, Tyler retrieved the stashed gift from behind the sofa. He recognized the handwriting right away. It was something from Serena. A wave of hatred ran through him. He hated that cow, still interfering in his life long after they had called it quits. With a muffled growl, he gritted his teeth and punched at the package. The paper had torn where he had struck it. Considering this a good enough excuse, he ripped more of it aside.

Grabbing his whiskey—he often drank straight from the bottle when in a foul mood—he placed the box on the kitchen table and slumped into a chair next to it. After taking a couple of swigs, he shredded the rest of the gift wrap and pulled the box open to look inside. A couple of misshapen gummi bears atop a familiar, ugly, lumpy Christmas fruitcake looked back at him. Tyler rolled his eyes and took another swig, preparing to launch it in the trash. First, though, he plucked one of the gummi bears, the red one, off the top and flicked it across the room. That was when he noticed a pastel-colored card peeking out from underneath cake, like something you'd expect to find in a board game. Serena had added some writing to it.

"If you need any help, give me a call. You are always welcome here, and I'll always be here for you. You are not alone."

This enraged Tyler. *"You are not alone."* Of course Claire was not all alone. She had Tyler, and he was all she needed. If he had to push her around a little or give her a good shake from time to time to remind her of that, he was prepared to do so. He wasn't about to let her leave him either. If she did, she would try to take some of his money with her. She didn't deserve that. He'd kill her before he'd let that happen.

Tyler was so angry that instead of just throwing out the cake, because Claire might manage to rescue it from the trash, he decided he would make sure to ruin the two women's Christmas tradition for good. If he ate the cake, there would be no getting it back. The last thread tying Claire to Serena would be severed.

Taking several more swigs of whiskey to steel his nerves and dull his taste buds, Tyler dug his fingers into its stale, crumbly center and began shoveling handfuls into his mouth.

❄ ❄ ❄

Claire stole downstairs early on Christmas morning. Tyler liked to get drunk on Christmas Eve and never got up before ten on holidays or weekends, so she figured she could safely retrieve her gift from Serena, open it, then hide it in the freezer before he began to stir. She was only partially right.

She discovered right away that her attempt to hide Serena's gift had failed. Claire reached behind the couch where she had stashed it the day before and came up empty handed.

A nervous knot formed in her stomach immediately. If Tyler had found it, that meant he would be angry with her, and even though it was Christmas Day, there was no telling just how badly he'd react. If he decided to "teach her a lesson" for ignoring his request that she end her friendship with Serena, she could end up with a few new bruises for Christmas rather than a box of chocolates and a pair of gloves. That's what he usually gave her.

She chewed at her fingernails as she approached the kitchen with trepidation. She caught sight of Tyler within, from behind. He was slumped in his chair, torn wrapping paper to one side of him and a near-empty whiskey bottle to the other. He made no sound, much to Claire's surprise. Whenever he passed out at the kitchen table, he tended to snore like a chainsaw. He also smelt like vomit. That didn't surprise her at all, a common side-effect of his drinking to excess.

She said his name quietly, but he didn't respond. She said it a little louder with still no answer. He didn't even stir. That was when she made up her mind that she would try to clean up everything around him, with the exception of the near-empty bottle, and maybe he would not remember finding the fruitcake at all. She might even be able to rescue Serena's gift from the table and preserve their tradition in the process.

As Claire reached for the shredded gift wrap, she accidently nudged Tyler ever so slightly. It was enough to shift him off balance and he started to toppled. Reflexively, she made a grab for him, but he was too heavy for her—

dead weight—and all she succeeded in doing was twisting him face up towards the ceiling as he landed on the floor.

Finally getting a good look at his face, Claire let out an ear-piercing scream. Tyler stared lifelessly up at her, stiff and glassy eyed. He wasn't just covered in his usual boozy vomit, but in a slimy mixture of whiskey, sodden chunks of cake, blood, and a single green gummi bear. His stubble was also dotted with pinkish, frothy flecks of spittle.

Sobbing, she pushed him away from her and scrabbled as far away across the kitchen as she could manage. It took a few minutes for her to regain her senses, the initial shock of the moment finally passing. She was ashamed by how much relief she felt along with being horrified. She had heard about drunk people asphyxiating on their vomit, but she had never expected things with Tyler would end like this. She had no idea what to do.

That was when she spotted the card that had come with the gift. She approached long enough to snatch it off the table before skittering away again.

With shaky fingers, Claire reached for the phone. She decided she had to call Serena. She was, after all, the only friend Claire had been able to keep despite her history with Tyler, even if his last living gesture had been to break their Christmas tradition.

She thought to herself, still a little dazed how ironic it was that in breaking their tradition, he had also broken himself—and there would be no fixing either, both the cake and Tyler were beyond repair.

Staring at the lone gummi bear resting on his chin, she giggled plaintively as she clutched at the phone, waiting for Serena to answer.

HOLLY, JOLLY CHRISTMAS
JG Faherty

ate Marino looked at the dead bodies on the dining room floor and smiled. Music drifted in from the den, the soft strains of Nat King Cole's "The Christmas Song" matching nicely with the flickering candles and the mouthwatering aromas of baked ham, lasagna, steamed broccoli rabe with garlic, and sweet potatoes drenched in butter and brown sugar.

Aunt Janice had been a perfect kick off to the party. Glutton that she was, she'd had two glasses of poisoned wine and half her equally tainted soup before anyone else finished more than a couple of mouthfuls. Only her grotesquely massive size had kept her from collapsing too soon and warning the others. Nate's smile grew wider as he remembered the increasingly amusing events of the past ten minutes.

Without warning, Janice had suddenly gone rigid in her chair, the sacks of fat on her neck and arms quivering like the cheap cherry Jell-O mold she'd brought as a gift. A single sound, the cry of a toad crushed under a boot, squeezed from her throat, forcing its way past a hunk of heavily buttered bread. Then she'd slowly tipped to the side, hitting the floor so hard the glasses in the breakfront created tinkling accompaniment to the holiday songs.

Nate—Nate Junior to the family, although he refused to acknowledge it as his real name—feigned surprise while he watched the rest of the family react to Janice's collapse. Several people jumped to their feet, banging their knees against the table. A few gasped in shock. Uncle Fred shouted for someone to "Call 9-1-1!" while Nate's father, Big Nate, just stared with an open mouth at his unconscious sister.

Cousin Joe ran for the kitchen phone, giving Nate Junior a momentary scare. But the habitual ass-kissing suck-up only made it three steps before keeling over. Nate Junior barely contained a gleeful shout as Joe's face lost the battle between ceramic tile and human flesh. _Smash._ No contest at all, really. Blood from Joe's split lips and crushed nose splattered the white tiles in delightful patterns, and the crunch of shattering bone was audible across the room.

"Jesus Christ!" Big Nate had finally found his voice. "What the hell's going on?"

Abby, Big Nate's wife of six months, reached out a hand heavy with diamond rings. "Oh my God, Nate! Do someth--"

Nate Junior had to slap a hand over his mouth to cover his smile as his third—and least favorite—stepmother grabbed her cosmetically enhanced chest and slid down in her seat, her anorexically thin body easily slipping through the small space between chair and table. As she disappeared from view, one of her rings snagged the table cloth and pulled it just far enough to bring a bowl of steaming lentil soup down on top of her.

"Abby!" Big Nate stood up, his porcine face flushed and sweaty. "Somebody call the goddamn ambulance!"

"I'll do it," Nate Junior said, grateful for the opportunity to get away from the table and hide his glee. At the same time, he wanted to make sure no one managed to dial for help. Ducking around the table, he grabbed the phone and punched in 9-9-9.

"Hello? We need help," he said into dead air. "People are unconscious. Send an ambulance. In fact, you better send a couple." After reciting the address, he added, "Please hurry!"

He hit the disconnect button. "They're coming."

"Thank God." Big Nate was frantically patting Abby's cheek, which had already grown pale. Then he gasped as Cousin Larry, Cousin Jill, and ancient Uncle Fred collapsed in rapid succession, like victims of an invisible sniper.

That left Nate Junior and his father staring at each other across the wide, food-laden table. Neither of them spoke. Nate Junior had time to count to twenty, while the festive music played on in the background.

"Have a holly, jolly Christmas, it's the best time of the year. Don't know, if there will be snow, but have a cup of cheer ..."

Understanding slowly dawned in Big Nate's eyes. Nate Junior watched it blossom, wondering how the hell such an idiot had ever managed to rise to a position of power.

"You!" Big Nate let go of Abby's hand, which fell onto the hardwood floor with a soft *thump*. "You did this. Why?"

Careful to stay on the opposite side of the table from the still-dangerous man who'd sired him, and then essentially ignored him all his life, Nate Junior shrugged. There were plenty of reasons he could give. Emotional abandonment. Physical abuse. A mother he was pretty sure his father had either killed or had killed. All legitimate enough reasons taken singly, let alone as a group. But time was running out, and Nate Junior didn't feel like spending their last moments together explaining something his father would never understand anyhow. Instead, he allowed himself a soft laugh.

"Like the commercial says, why ask why? Does it really matter?"

Big Nate's face went even darker, and his eyes narrowed to slits. "You little bastard. I should've gotten rid of you—"

"What? When you killed Mom? Maybe you should've. Too late now, though."

His face all violent lines and angles against a purple background, Big Nate slapped his hand on the table and stood up. "Just like you. Never thinking things through. Big deal. You killed everyone. Now what? Go to jail for murder? Or maybe you think you can steal some money and start a new life?"

"Actually, I had something better in mind." Nate Junior took a step to the left, countering his father's movements and keeping the table between them. "When I actually call the police, they'll find the bottle of poison in your pocket, with your fingerprints on it."

"And what about you?"

"That's for me to know and you to never find out, unless you can watch from the afterlife." Nate Junior smiled, knowing how much it would piss his father off.

And it worked.

Rivers of sweat ran down Big Nate's forehead, whether from fear or anger or poison Nate Junior couldn't tell. But the heavy man's hand was as fast as ever and rock-steady as he drew the two-shot derringer he always kept in his pants pocket and aimed it at his son.

"Then I guess there's nothing to stop me from blowing

your sorry ass to hell." A smug grin twisting his thick, wormlike lips upwards, Big Nate pulled the trigger twice.

A bray of laughter burst from Nate Junior as he watched his father's eyes widen in surprise when the gun did nothing but click.

"It works better with these in it." Nate Junior took two bullets from his own pocket and held them out, then had to duck to the side as his father threw the gun at him.

"You son of a—"

Big Nate stopped in mid-sentence, his lips a pink donut framing a black cave filled with grayish-yellow tombstones.

"Hurts, doesn't it?" Nate Junior pocketed the bullets again. "Kinda like a knife twisting inside your chest. That's what it said online, anyhow."

Big Nate made a choking, wet sound and extended his hands in an inarticulate plea for help. He fell to his knees, one elbow smashing Abby's delicate nose sideways. Big Nate never noticed, too occupied with his own agony. Tendons bulged on his neck and forearms, protruding up through the layers of fat laid down from decades of excessive living. Nate Junior had often wondered, if they cut his father open, would the fat be in rings, each one representing another year of overindulgence?

For a few moments, Big Nate managed to hold himself up. Then his muscles gave out and he toppled over.

"That's it. Die, you son of a bitch," Nate Junior whispered.

Big Nate looked up with eyes that dripped bloody tears. "Go to Hell," he gasped. A violent cough shook his body, and he spat up a fist-sized glob of blood and mucous.

His eyes closed, and a final breath wheezed out.

Nate Junior stared at the body. "Always had to have the last word, didn't you? Hope you enjoyed it."

The holiday carol came to an end, rousing Nate Junior

from his reverie. He glanced at the clock. Time to get moving. If the bodies sat for too long, the coroner would be able to tell the time of death didn't match Nate's story.

"That's right. *Nate.* Hear that, Dad? I'm not Nate Junior anymore. Fuck you."

Using a napkin, Nate wiped down the bottle of poison, the bullets, and the gun. After pressing his father's fingers against everything, he loaded the derringer and slipped all the evidence into his father's pants pockets. Then he stood and looked around the room.

This may be the happiest moment of my life. Too bad I can't take a photograph to remember it by.

He picked up the phone and dialed 9-1-1. "Hello? Please send an ambulance. Everyone's sick. I think … I think they might be dead. I don't feel … It hurts! Help!"

Nate let the phone drop to the floor. He figured he had ten, maybe twelve minutes before help arrived. He sat back in his chair and pulled his untouched soup close.

Three spoonfuls should do it.

Enough to make him sick, maybe even pass out. Not enough to kill, although it might be close.

A dangerous plan. But well worth it, and not just for the money he'd inherit.

For the freedom.

He lifted the spoon and sipped warm salvation.

Merry Christmas, Nate. After fifteen years, you finally have a reason to celebrate.

T*HE* O*THER* S*IDE* OF THE W*ALL*
Tracy L. Carbone

Ronnie was agoraphobic, so said his doctor and his daughter. *Bullshit.* He wasn't afraid to go out and leave his property, the small ranch house on a fifth of an acre. There was just no sense interacting with people if he didn't have to. Everyone was mixed races now and mixed genders and he couldn't stomach what the world had turned into. He ordered his food and essentials online. They even delivered Sophie's dog food. On the rare occasion he or his dog had to see a doctor, his daughter stopped by and brought them. He and Sophie didn't like leaving the house, but they did when it mattered. So it was a bullshit diagnosis.

He had no front yard to speak of, which was fine with him. His property faced the wash, bone dry about three hundred and sixty days a year and a raging torrent the other five when it collected the town's rainwater. No neighbors across. No one to the right either. There was a house on his left, but it had been empty for, oh … four years now. He bought his house when he landed the part of Elwood in *Scream on a Summer Night*. Little Ginger was a toddler then, and Elma, God rest her soul, was alive and smoking hot.

Elma was in the movie with him. His first film. Her's, too. Elma screamed her lungs out and was killed in the first scene. He had the lead role as a disgruntled mailman who'd been badly burned and hated the world and all the young pretty people in it. It was a cliché plot, but it had made Ronnie a star. Well, star was a funny word in Hollywood. He was a star of B movies no one remembered a year later. But he did a bunch of them and bought this house in the early 80s. Had owned it free and clear for the last twenty years. His dog, Sophie, was old like him, and the two of them were content to just be, safe and sound in their cozy little house in their safe yard.

He didn't do much now except battle the gophers over the lawn, watch old movies, and update his blog. He had twenty thousand some followers, but half of them were gays or homos or whatever he was supposed to call them now. They only followed him so they could complain. It pissed him off that he couldn't write about his wholesome views without all of *them* filling his page with negative comments. *You're not fair! You're a jerk! We have rights!!!* And those were the tame ones. He'd had four death threats, broken windows, and hundreds of letters sent to his house saying *he* had no right to judge. A group of them got together and stated, in writing, they'd boycott his movies. Hollywood listened. He hadn't had an acting job in ten years.

But a good amount of his followers actually agreed with him, and it was for those folks he wrote the blog, to remind the world how things were supposed to be. No one was gonna tell him what to think or what to accept. He was retired from acting, but it was worth it. He circulated his own petitions and had done his share of damage right back. Ronnie wouldn't stop writing that blog until the day he died.

Ronnie was just finishing his newest post about the damage being done to children raised in same-sex homes when the doorbell rang. *Who the hell can that be?* He looked to Sophie, a messy gray Schnauzer badly in need of a proper haircut.

He walked to the solid wooden door and slid the black panel to view the visitor. A young Mexican stood before him.

"I ain't buying," Ronnie said.

"Not selling. I'm your new neighbor. Thought I'd stop by and say hello."

Ronnie studied the man who carried a basket of food. He didn't like company but didn't want to risk making an enemy of someone in the next yard. He disengaged the lock and opened the door.

"Name's Beto," the man said.

"Ronnie," he said.

"Wow, some place you got here. Mind if I come in?"

Ronnie did mind, but the man walked in before he could say so. "Place looks a lot smaller on the outside." He whistled. "You got some great touches in here. Looks like a 1930s Hollywood bungalow with all the original fixtures."

Ronnie crossed his arms. He knew damn well the guy was casing the joint, assessing his valuables. *Well, good luck. I don't have any.* Sophie stood at his feet, staring at the stranger. "Some original, some we bought to make the place look authentic. My wife did the decorating."

"Hey, I love the movie posters." Beto looked at several of the large framed posters lining the entranceway and hall.

"Hey, you were in these, weren't you? You're Ronnie O'Shea! Wow, that's awesome. I gotta say, you scared the hell out of me when I was a kid."

"Sorry," Ronnie said.

"No, hey, it's cool, man. You inspired me. And my partner. He lives next door, too."

"Your partner?" *Shit.*

"Yeah, you know, my, uh, husband kind of, but we're not married yet."

Ronnie searched the room for something he could use as a weapon. He didn't believe for a second that Beto just happened to move in next door. He was up to something. Probably wanted to drive him out of the house, or kill him right here on the spot.

The guy smiled at him, looked friendly as hell. Maybe he was the one gay guy out there who didn't know about Ronnie's blog or views. "Huh. Well, um, welcome to the neighborhood. Pretty quiet here. Just me, and now you and your, um, *partner*."

"Eric."

"Got it. Eric. Listen, hate to be rude but my show is on and Sophie and I like to settle in and watch it live. I don't go for that DVR crap."

Beto's face fell, and truth be told, Ronnie felt a little bad about it. But not so bad he'd lose sleep over it. He'd hated the old neighbors, too. Bunch of Mexicans with revolving houseguests. He'd called INS on them and the whole lot of them got deported. *The good old days. Now everyone had rights. Rights, rights, rights coming out their asses.*

"Okay, sure. Just wanted to say hello. Brought you some fruit and crackers and stuff. I can set it over here if you want."

Gay and Mexican, goddamn double whammy.

He placed the basket on the empty side table in the living room.

Good a place as any.

"Thanks." Ronnie gestured to the television. "It's starting in a minute. I really have to—"

"Yeah, no problem," Beto said. "I'll let myself out."

The man left and Ronnie followed him, bolting the door behind him. He wished he'd opted for more locks.

Sophie stood on her hind legs, both of them shaking. She sniffed the basket. "Nothing in there for you," he said. "You get down. I'll dump that in the trash when it gets dark out. It's probably got poison in it."

The dog complied and the two sat on the couch. Ronnie flicked the television on and frowned when the lights from the Christmas tree reflected smack in the middle of Lauren Bacall's face. He rose and turned off the tree lights. "There, now we can watch TV in peace."

❄ ❄ ❄

What in blazing hell is that?

It was six o'clock but already dark because of daylight savings. Ronnie walked into his backyard. He had eight-foot cinderblock walls on all sides of his house, but there at the top, on the left-hand side, he saw the top of Beto's slick and shiny black hair.

"What are you doing up there?" Ronnie yelled.

Beto climbed a little higher and Ronnie was able to see the top half of his face like the guy on that sitcom in the 80s. "We heard there are crow problems here so I'm hanging these plastic owls. It's supposed to help."

Ronnie couldn't argue with that. Damn crows were everywhere, cawing so loud he couldn't hear his programs. And always taking all the food from the feeders meant for the little birds.

"You think that'll keep them away?" Ronnie called up.

"According to the Internet, yeah. It should. Gonna put one here and in the other corner so they'll stay away. I'm putting some on the other side of our yard, too, by the street."

"All right then. Just don't make a habit of going up on that ladder. I like my privacy. You wouldn't want me looking over your walls would you?"

Ronnie didn't wait for a response. He was damn sick of apologizing for wanting to be left alone in his own damn yard. He called to Sophie and the two of them went back inside and drew the curtains. Damn house next door had been empty so long he'd forgotten how it was to have neighbors. He didn't like it. Not one bit.

The first thing that got to him was the chanting. Ronnie sat up with a start. *What the hell?* He threw his robe on and padded down the hall. Sophie growled but stayed in the bed. She was too old to jump off anymore, and he saw no reason to involve her.

The sound grew louder as he neared the French doors off the living room, the ones that led to the backyard and his new neighbors. He carefully opened the back door and stuck his head out. It wasn't happy, quiet, monk chanting, like on TV. This was the eerie devil-movie type. There were more than two voices, too. More than Beto and his *buddy*, Eric. He strained to count. *Must be five or six people over there. What the hell are they doing?*

Ronnie didn't like being scared. He acted in those movies but couldn't watch them. Hated horror movies and books and hadn't been to a fun house since he was seven and pissed his pants. A soft yellow glow rose from the other side of the wall. He sniffed and smelled … incense? Maybe the marijuana these kids all got with their pot cards. The yellow light made him think of fire, but he didn't smell fire.

He walked in bare feet through his grass until he was right up against the wall. His feet were cold and the damn grass was wet. It was watering night and the sprinklers would've gone off an hour or two ago. *Hope I don't step in dog shit.* As he listened, ear pressed against the stone as if that would help, the chanting grew louder. Excited and frantic. He heard the sound of a chicken squawk and scream. *Jesus Christ, what are they doing over there?* He ran back into the house, ignoring the slimy, stinky mound his foot stepped into along the way. He rushed inside and locked the door.

Sophie was barking from the bedroom. His right foot was covered in dog shit. He limped to the sink, flicking on lights as he went. He used half a roll of paper towels to wipe down his foot and then the floor.

Bark bark!

"Sophie shut up. I'll be there in a minute!"

He turned on the hall light and the bedroom light. Sophie was whimpering in the bed. She stood over a small wet circle. "Great." He picked up the dog and set her on the floor. She ran down the hall and to the dog door in the living room. He pulled the blanket from the bed and checked the sheets below. Still dry.

Walking to the hall closet to get a new blanket, it hit him that Sophie was outdoors. With those devil worshippers, or Santeria or whatever hell religion they were practicing over there.

He ran to the back door and did his best loud whisper. "Sophie, get in here!" The chanting continued and he heard the ungodly howl of a cat. It sounded like it was being tortured.

What the fuck? "Sophie, get in here!" The little dog toddled back inside and he shut and locked the door. He locked her small door, too.

Ronnie opened the bathroom cabinet and found his bottle of Xanax. One left. He fumbled as he tried to open it. Damn hands were trembling. He'd have to call his doctor if the neighbors kept this shit up. He was safe in his house and rationally he knew it, but his anxiety and fear didn't believe him.

Sleep was out of the question now. He turned the TV on loud—louder than the chanting—and sat with his dog watching whatever black and white movie had just begun on Turner Classic Movies. Soon the pill kicked in and he fell asleep.

❄ ❄ ❄

The sun woke him up. He was groggy from the Xanax but relaxed. The lights were on throughout the house. *There goes the electric bill.* He set Sophie on the floor and let her out back. Everything looked okay out there from what he could see. He sniffed, but nothing was out of the ordinary.

By afternoon, the terror from last night was all but forgotten. He'd received a delivery from the grocery store and another from Amazon. He knew the Amazon package contained the DVD of *The Bishop's Wife* and couldn't wait to open it.

He settled in with Sophie and watched the movie, enjoying the simplicity of the old days when men and women got married and lived happily ever after.

❄ ❄ ❄

Sophie stood on his chest, scratching at his face with her

paw. "What is it?" She whimpered. He didn't want to have to wash blankets again so he carried her off the bed and together they walked to the back. He'd locked her dog door at sunset so he opened the big door.

He saw dust flying up from over the wall and heard the sounds of someone or something running. He hadn't seen the yard next door in years, but since no one was there to tend the grass or run sprinklers or battle the gophers, he assumed it was a dirt pit. *What the hell is it?*

Something was running around back there at three in the damn morning. Sophie barked. "Quiet!" he whispered. Again he walked to the wall to get a better listen. He was afraid but curious. Like those high school bimbos in the movies he'd starred in. The ones that made ridiculously stupid decisions. Still, though, he was safe on his side of the wall; he just wanted to know.

He went to a racetrack back in his acting days. On location for *The Jockey Murders*. That's what the noise sounded like. Horses running in circles, stirring up the dirt and dust. Hooves pounding the ground. But it was softer. *Dogs?*

Maybe they'd had their vocal chords cut. He'd heard of that. There were all kinds of nuts in the world today.

He heard a thud. Some of the running stopped. Another thud. *The sound of a head being smashed with a bat*, he thought with panic. Now only one animal or whatever it was running. A final crack. A bat hitting a skull and cracking it open. Or a crowbar. Three dead creatures.

Then silence.

Shit.

He heard the creak of a door behind the wall. His neighbor's house. *Someone going in or more people coming out?*

Ronnie scooped up his dog and ran into his house, locking the back door. He turned on all the lights again. "What the hell is going on over there?" Sophie looked at him. He ran into his bathroom and found the empty bottle of pills. *Damn.*

He picked up his phone to call the police but what would he say? He had no proof of anything. The police wouldn't come running to investigate silence. Best case, they would humor him and come over and maybe go to the neighbor's. But if there was nothing to find, Ginger would start talking about assisted living facilities again.

He set his phone down. From behind his drapes he saw a glow. He rose and ever so carefully drew back his blinds. Yellow light from behind the wall again. And then the chanting started.

"No. Shit. No!" He wrapped himself in an afghan and put the TV on. He raised the volume as loud as it would go, until it hurt his ears, and poor little Sophie's. He turned on the lights of the Christmas tree and the lights in the garland he'd layered on the fireplace. Several times he glanced toward the back door, expecting something to come in, or bang against it. A knock, or the sound of an intruder turning the knob. But there was nothing.

When the sun came up, he fell asleep. *Safe for one more night.* Sophie tried to get out, but he didn't let her. She peed on the floor and then pooped, but he didn't care. He was not going out there again in the dark.

A loud knock and Sophie's resultant shrill bark ripped Ronnie from his sleep. It took him a minute to focus. The Christmas tree lights were what he first saw. Flashing blue, green, yellow, and red. And the voice of Humphrey Bogart.

The knock and Sophie rattled him again, roused him fully. He got up, limping on his left foot that had fallen asleep. "Coming!"

He slid the panel on the front door and saw a tall, thin man with rimless eyeglasses. "I'm Eric. I live next door. We heard your TV all night and were worried something might have happened to you."

Something might have happened. Right. You sick bastards.

"I'm fine. Just fell asleep *late*. Had a hard time resting." He stopped short of complaining or asking what the hell kind of activity they were up to over there.

"Okay. Well, if you need anything, we're right next door. Just over the wall." The guy sort of snarled when he said it. No doubt his partner forced him to come over to feign being neighborly. These two knew who he was and what he stood for and no doubt loved that they could come right over, proud as you please.

"Good fences make good neighbors." Ronnie slammed the panel shut and walked away from the door.

He dug into the cabinet next to his TV and rifled through his CDs. He lowered the TV's volume and popped a Christmas CD in the player. He opened a window by the back door and played it. Loud. He smiled as music about Christ played in his yard and subsequently into theirs. "Take that, you heathens."

Truth be told, Ronnie was more of a commercial Christian. He hadn't been to church since Ginger got married. And before that, it was only a handful of times for his sacraments, and Ginger's. At times like this, though, boy, did he pray that Jesus and all His miracles were real. It was Mumbo Jumbo most likely, but if there was any chance it was real he'd take it.

Tomorrow was Christmas Eve. Ginger would be coming over with her husband and kids. She had her annual tantrum trying to get him to come to her house, but he refused. He had his own annual tantrum. She'd bring the main course and he'd be cooking side dishes all day.

When they came, he'd tell them about the neighbors.

Ginger would know what to do. Her husband wasn't the sharpest tool in the shed, but he was a good guy. He was a card-carrying Republican and member of the NRA. Ronnie reflected that at times like these a gun might come in handy.

One more night to get through and then Ginger would give him advice about the neighbors. Jim would go over there and scare the shit out of them. See how *they* liked it.

The evening was quiet. Ronnie drank two servings of Nyquil. He gave Sophie a Benadryl. He fell asleep by eight o'clock.

At nine o'clock he heard a crash. He sat up. *Is that an earthquake?* It wasn't. It happened again. A loud crash. He flung his front door open. No one there. His car was fine. The moon lit the driveway and the wash. Nothing out there. *Smash.*

The backyard. The neighbors.

He ran back inside and through the house to the back door. Pulling back the curtains, he saw yellow light again, interrupted by shadows. He couldn't see what the hell was going on, but it was something. Ronnie heard grunting, and chains rattling. He pictured people, women, chained outside, their mouths taped shut. Duct tape. Chained to the outside of the house. His adrenaline surged as fear gripped him. *If you need anything, we're right next door. Just over the wall.*

"What the hell kind of monsters are you?" he whispered.

The moaning and chain rattling persisted. He slid his shoes on and crept toward the wall again. If the sound kept up, he'd call the police. He'd say the neighbors were having a party or playing loud music; whatever he had to accuse them of so the cops would check out the neighbors. He'd posted a blog last year about the proud gay police chief, and since then they didn't so much as lift a finger. He'd called three different times about threats he'd received and they wrote reports but didn't help him. This time, though, this time they'd take him seriously. They'd find last night's dead dogs smacked on the head, and tonight's women shackled to the wall. They might even find an altar. *Shit, maybe those are children tied to the wall.* He got a sick feeling, a sudden bad stomachache.

The yellow light grew brighter, the moaning louder. And then the chanting began again. Above the chanting he heard, "Help me!" in a child's voice.

I need to do something. He looked back at his house, knowing his cell phone was way back in his bedroom. *I need to do something. Now.*

"Stop it! Whatever you're doing over there, stop it right now! Do you hear me? I'm calling the police. I'm going to call the police and I'm going to come over there. I've got a gun!"

His whole body was shaking now. He could barely stand, much less crash a satanic ritual and save anyone. But he had to act. His living room called to him. He could just go inside. Lock the doors and call the police. There was no way he would come out alive if he went to the neighbors. No way if he crossed his property line that he'd survive. Fine, maybe he was agoraphobic but this was actual danger.

"Help me!" another child cried out. A different voice for sure.

In the movies, he'd always been the villain. The writers would cast a fool to fight him and the fool won time and again. *I am that fool. I can do this.* He looked to the shed against the wall. He opened the door and spotted his rickety wooden ladder. It was old and hadn't been used in years. He moved the lawnmower out of the way and dragged the ladder out. It took all his strength to move it to the wall, but he managed.

A familiar plotline. He'd read the scripts, knew how it worked. Weren't movies based on life anyway? *The underdog wins all the time in movies.*

He heaved the ladder against the wall. His legs were like jelly as he climbed one rung at a time. He felt dizzy and his chest hurt.

"I should go back to the house." He began to retreat, one rung at a time. "I'm a stupid old man. I can't save anyone."

He heard a howl then. *Sophie. Are you on their side of the wall? How is that possible? I left you in bed.* He knew her bark, knew it like his own voice. Fifteen years was a long time to spend alone with a dog and he knew it was her. "Sophie!"

Again she yelped.

He rushed up the ladder. He got closer to the top, his chest tightening as the seconds passed. He reached his hands to the top of the wall. The yellow light grew brighter, the moaning louder, the chains closer. Sophie's crying intensified.

Finally, he crawled to the top of the ladder. He could barely breathe and his chest ... So much pressure and pain. But he moved ahead and managed to look down into the neighbor's yard.

And then his heart stopped and he tumbled down from the ladder and slammed onto his lawn, breaking a hip and two ribs. But by then he was already dead.

❉ ❉ ❉

"Go, go, go!" Beto said from below, to Eric, who was swiftly climbing their industrial red metal ladder. "Get the owl cams from the front and the back." Eric pulled down one of the plastic owls and tossed it down to Beto. He ran across the wall until he got to the other side, where he took down the second plastic owl casing with the camera inside. He tossed that down to Beto as well.

"This wasn't supposed to happen. We were just supposed to scare him. Give him some payback for treating us all like shit."

"I know. Jesus, I know, Eric. Can you see him? Is he moving?"

"I don't know. Shit. We're not going to be able to use any of this footage now. So much for our Internet Indie movie about the old creep."

"Forget that. Is he okay? Is he breathing?" Beto called up.

"I'm gonna use his ladder to get down." Eric climbed down the ladder and saw Ronnie's broken and still body. "I think he's dead."

"Shit!" Beto called over the wall.

"I need to go in his house and get the camera out of the fruit basket."

"Okay, but hurry. Don't leave any prints."

Eric bolted into the house and followed barking to Ronnie's bedroom. Sophie stood on the bed, growling. A wet circle spread under her. "It's okay, sweetie. You'll be okay." He gently lifted her from the bed and set her down. She ran and hid under the bed. "Good girl. Ginger will come get you tomorrow. You can live with her now."

He walked back through the living room and grabbed the snack basket, popping out the camera from it and slipping into his pocket. He left the basket to explain away any residual prints in case it came up.

Eric scaled the ladder, then knocked it over onto Ronnie's lawn beside his body. When he got back on their property, Beto glared at him. "Is he really dead?"

"Yes. We need to get the hell out of here."

"What about his dog?"

Eric smiled at his partner. "His dog is fine. She'll be

better off with his daughter. I read Ginger has a couple of dogs already, so she'll take her."

"I feel really bad. He was an asshole and all, but Jesus. We were just trying to scare him, show the horror master homophobe getting the shit scared out of him. Show everyone he wasn't so tough after all."

"Yeah, well, it happened, so let's pack up." Beto was the emotional one in the relationship and Eric knew now was not the time to lament.

Eric surveyed their yard with the mannequin body parts sprawled on the ground. A length of heavy chain rested in the middle of the property, as well as a few speakers and lights, all part of the set designed to scare a mean old man to tears.

"What do you think was the last thing he saw?" Beto asked. "You think he knew it was all fake?"

Eric shook his head. "I bet his last image was in his imagination, a horrific torture scene replete with devils and dead animals. Just on the other side of the wall. Way scarier than the reality."

"Probably so. You're right. Let's grab this all up and get out of here," Beto said.

The young filmmakers packed their gear into their van. They left the film permit tacked to the house, in case the police questioned why there was activity in a seemingly abandoned house. They had permission, had done everything by the book, and researched their subject extensively to make the perfect found footage film.

The fact an old man got nosey about their filming and snooped and fell off a ladder? Well, the story would go that it was a heartbreaking coincidence. A Christmas tragedy.

CHRISTMAS VACATION

DJ Tyrer

"Surely, this can't be the place?" Abbie asked her dad.

"Sure is!" he replied, looking back with a grin.

"Keep your eyes on the road," Mom snapped. Winter was coming in hard and fast and conditions were getting poor.

"Don't worry, honey, we're almost there." He glanced back at Abbie. "Wonderful, ain't it? The perfect place for a Christmas getaway."

"But how could you afford it, Dad?" Abbie asked.

"Probably been dealing drugs. Eh, Dad?" smirked Joe.

"Less of that lip, please!" his Mom responded.

"It wasn't all that expensive," he told them as they pulled up in front of the house. House? It was a veritable mansion, not the backwoods cabin they'd been led to expect. Out here, in the woods with the mountains behind it, the place did have a bit of a Transylvanian vibe, as if it ought to be the palatial holiday home of Dracula, or, perhaps, the Addams Family. Not that they'd let a little thing like that put them off; it was lovely.

"Really?" Mom asked, her tone sceptical.

"Really," he replied, then changed the subject. "We'll have to make a dash for it; the weather's atrocious! Grab what you can from out the back and head for the door!"

They did as they were told, carrying as many bags as they could, and headed for the front door, their heads down against the wind and snow. Dad unlocked it and they all tumbled inside.

"It's cold," whined Abbie.

"It's better than out there," her brother retorted.

"I'll go fire up the boiler and the generator," said Dad, "and pretty soon this place will be lovely and warm. In the meantime, there are logs for the fireplace if you want to get a fire started."

He headed down to the basement as they began to explore. Mom started a fire in the living room grate.

A little while later, when Dad rejoined them, the place was beginning to feel a bit more like a home and a little less like a chilly tomb.

"I've made hot chocolate," Mom told him as he entered the living room; with the fire going, it was quite inviting.

"With marshmallows?" he asked.

"With marshmallows," she smiled back.

"Now, perhaps you can tell us how you got this place so cheap," said Abbie.

"Yeah, all the gory details," added Joe.

"Oh, there are gory details," Dad replied, relishing the look of surprise on his son's face. "You see, this place was the site of a grisly murder, sort of like out of *The Shining*. A guy brought his wife and kids up here for Christmas, back in 2000, and completely flipped out, killing them all: Mansion Fever, I suppose you could say!" He laughed and Mom gave him a stern look. "Nobody has wanted to stay here since. But don't worry; they replaced the chiller cabinets."

"Chiller cabinets?" asked Mom.

"Yup! He chopped 'em all up and stashed them away. Some say he ate bits ..."

"You're making it up," said Mom.

"Nope, it's the honest truth. That's why it's cheap."

"Gross!" exclaimed Joe with a tone that implied anything but.

"So you drove us up here thirteen years later, on Friday the thirteenth, in 2013?" asked Abbie, rolling her eyes. "Are you trying to make some kind of point?"

"Probably planning to celebrate the anniversary by gutting us all in our sleep," joked Joe.

"Don't say that!" exclaimed Dad.

"Joke!"

"Yeah, Mom's more likely to butcher us than him!" laughed Abbie.

"Hey!"

"Joke!" she replied, mimicking her brother.

"Anyway," commented Dad, "I couldn't stuff you in the chiller cabinets, even if I wanted to."

"Sorry?" said Mom.

"They're full to overflowing with food, as are the freezer cabinets and the pantry. We're well stocked. We have all the food and fuel we need to last weeks. So, don't worry about getting snowed in. We can take anything Mother Nature throws at us!"

"Good," Abbie nodded. "The old dear can be a bitch!"

"Language!" snapped Mom.

The news was reassuring, though, as the snow was falling steadily and the odds were that they'd shortly be snowed in. They'd probably made it just in time. Knowing that they didn't have to worry about supplies allowed them to appreciate the Dickensian nature of the scene as snow piled up against the windows.

"I'm not much of a fan of the cold," Joe said over his second hot chocolate, "but this is… pretty cozy." He said the words with an embarrassed tone, as if coziness wasn't something respectable.

"Romantic," commented Abbie, before proceeding to elucidate the relevance of the term Dickensian to the scene in a somewhat tedious monologue that was offset by the pleasure of chocolatey marshmallows.

"I'm going to explore," she told them a little later. They'd only had a quick look around when they arrived. "This place looks absolutely fascinating."

The building was just as large and interesting as it had looked from the outside. It dated from the early part of the 20th century and was ornately gothic, with enough room to serve as a hotel, and there was even a not-too-secret passage in the library, where a bookcase full of fake books swung out like a door, leading up to the largely empty attic.

"This place would be awesome for a murder-mystery weekend," she told her brother when their paths crossed in an upstairs corridor.

"Served well enough for murder," he replied.

"Spotted any bloodstains yet?"

"Nah! And believe me, I've been looking …"

They all met up later for dinner.

"This place really is well stocked," Mom said, showing them the meal she'd prepared for them.

The next week went swimmingly, even with the cable

out due to the blizzard. There was plenty to do: decorating the house had kept them busy, the library was full of books— some of which Joe was certain his parents wouldn't approve of, but he found extremely educational. They had a Blu-ray player and plenty of discs, and Joe had brought along his Wii, and there were board games for when they felt more nostalgic.

"Okay, *Clue*'s beginning to get boring, now," said Joe when his sister won it for the thirteenth straight time in a row. "This is probably what caused the murders!"

"Well, the board is reminiscent of the house," Dad joked.

It was at that moment that a tree came crashing down, its branches smashing through the window and allowing a swirl of snow mixed with glass into the room, sending them into a panic as they sought to seal the breach. Dad sent Joe to find an axe for him to chop off the branches. Once the window was clear, he taped a tarpaulin across the vacant space before shoving a bookcase up against it.

"Well, that rather ruined the evening," sagged Mom.

"I don't know," Abbie replied. "It helped pass the time …"

"That's the frontier spirit!" said Dad, leaning the axe in the corner. "Right, now let's get this room tidied up." There was melting snow, broken glass, and the hacked-off branches all over the floor.

Abbie found herself barely sweeping as she replayed the scene in her mind: the branches smashing through the window like the reaching fingers of some hideous clawed hand attempting to seize them; her father hacking at the branches in a frenzy she'd never imagined him capable of. She dreamt the scene again that night, waking in a cold sweat.

"Hey, Joe," she called to her brother as they left the kitchen after the breakfast. "What did you think of Dad yesterday?"

"What do you mean?"

"When he was waving that axe around. I mean, did he seem a bit psycho to you?"

"Not really. A bit down on the tree, but no wonder!" he laughed.

"I suppose ..." In her dream, he'd been terrifying.

Joe laughed. "You don't mean you think he's going to go axe crazy on us like that guy did thirteen years ago? Oh, priceless! And, everyone thinks *you're* the sensible one!"

"No need to be a jerk!"

"Whatever ..." He flipped her the bird and headed for his Wii.

She spent the rest of the day scrutinizing her father, watching for any sign that he was going to flip out.

"Stop looking at me like that," Dad snapped, annoyed.

She flinched, wondering what he'd do next; he flipped the page of the book he was reading and continued with it.

Behind him, the edges of the tarpaulin that extended past the bookcase barricading the window sucked slowly in and out as if the house were breathing. As she watched, it was as if his breaths were synchronized with the movement of that membrane.

"I said," he snapped again, "stop staring at me!"

"Sorry!" she snapped back, storming out the room, scared of what he might do. He hadn't been himself since the tree smashed through the window. As much as she'd hoped to blame it on annoyance at that incident, his mood hadn't improved; in fact, if anything, it had grown worse.

She dreamed the dream again that night: the branches reaching in to seize them, only, instead of hacking them, Dad was hacking at her and Joe and Mom as the fingers of that awful hand held them firm, while the walls of the room sucked in and out as the house breathed in the smell of slaughter.

She awoke sobbing and sweating, grateful that she hadn't screamed and woken her family.

She cornered Joe the next morning and told him what she'd been dreaming.

"Dad killed us all!" she finished.

"But it was only a dream, Abbie. It wasn't real."

"Yeah, but he's been acting strange. Ever since that tree came in through the window, he's been … odd. Angry."

"Well, can you blame him? He's probably still upset about the tree. Makes sense."

"No, it isn't that …"

"Then what? All I'm hearing is a load of paranoid nonsense. It's worse than when you were obsessed with those Birther websites."

She sniffed. "Better than the websites *you're* interested in."

"Ouch! Someone's in a foul mood!"

"Shut up!"

"You started it! If Dad goes axe-happy with anyone, it'll be you. You're in a right mood."

"Fine, whatever! Just don't blame me when it all goes to hell, Joe! Don't blame me!"

"It's not going to go to hell, Abbie," he laughed, jogging off in search of something to do.

"It will …" she muttered. "It will …"

The rest of the day passed by with a frostiness that almost matched the chill outside. The only difference was that there was a calm inside, unlike the storm raging outside. That would soon change.

She had the dream again that night: the branches smashing their way in, seizing them; Dad going mad with the axe, killing them all; and the house breathing in the smell of slaughter.

Waking drenched with sweat and sobbing with the echo of fear from her dream, Abbie rose and dressed before stumbling downstairs to the living room. She went straight to the smashed window and watched the sides of the tarpaulin sucking in and out.

With a shriek of frustration, she seized the bookcase and pulled it away, throwing it to the floor with a crash. Freed of the obstruction, the tarpaulin billowed in and out, breaking free to flap loose as snow blew in.

Her dad burst in, demanding to know what was happening. She quailed from his rage.

Mom entered a moment later, followed by Joe.

"What's happening?" shrieked Mom.

Dad rounded angrily on her. Abbie could see he was looking towards the axe that was still leaning in the corner of the room where he'd left it. She knew he was planning to kill them all.

Without thinking, she lunged across the room and seized the axe before rounding on her father and shouting at him to stay back, to leave them alone.

Dad bellowed with rage, the shout merging with the howl of the snow-laden wind raging in through the window past the fluttering tarp.

He took a step towards her and she didn't pause to think, just raised the axe and swung it at him, bringing it down with a wet *thwack!* on his head. He staggered and fell to his knees.

"Quick! Run! Get away!"

Before her father could do anything, she raised the axe for a second time and brought it down on his shoulder in a crimson spurt of blood that splashed her face like an obscene baptism. Slowly, bloodily, he slumped to the floor.

Just to be certain, absolutely certain, she hit him again. And again. Then, just so there was no chance of him harming any of them, she dismembered what was left.

Breathing heavily, she looked around. Mom and Joe were gone, fled before Dad could harm them. They were safe now. She was thankful for that. She'd saved them.

Trailing the axe behind her, Abbie headed for the door, keen to make sure they were okay.

Before she'd taken more than a step, something smashed into her face and she was bowled over backwards.

Her Mom loomed over her, a kitchen stool in her hands. "I'll kill you!" she shouted down at her.

"Mom …?" she gasped. Her Mom had gone insane!

Mom raised the stool, ready to bring it down on her head. She was going to kill her!

Not knowing what else to do, Abbie groped behind her for the axe and, managing to grasp the haft, swung it at her Mom's leg, the blade embedding deep into her ankle with a bloody spurt.

With a shriek of pain, her Mom fell sideways.

Pulling herself to her feet, Abbie looked down at her Mom, who gazed up at her with rage-filled eyes. Her mother was infected with the same madness that had afflicted her dad. If she let her live, she'd only come after her again; after Joe.

With a heavy heart, Abbie raised the axe. She didn't want to do it, but she had to …

Before she could bring it down on her, Joe burst from the kitchen, screaming at her, a large knife in his hand.

She turned and jumped back from the stabs.

He was confused; he had to be.

"Joe, not me! It's her! She's gone mad, like Dad! She wants to kill us, just like Dad did!"

But Joe wasn't listening. From his incoherent cries of

rage and the contorted look of hate upon his face, she knew he'd been infected with the same evil that had got their parents. They were all infected. She was the only one who was still sane. She had to kill them, kill both of them, before they killed her.

"Put that knife down!" Abbie cried one last time, hoping to get through to him.

"No damn way!"

With a sigh, she hefted the axe and swatted him with it; the blade smashed into Joe's hand and tore off half his fingers. The knife fell to the floor in a bloody mess and he staggered away, howling and clutching the wound. She felt guilty as hell, but what else could she do?

Turning her back on her brother, Abbie went after her mom, who was crawling away across the floor, doubtless seeking another weapon to use against her.

A few whacks were all it took to still her twitching and chop her up into pieces so that she was no longer a threat.

That just left Joe.

He'd conveniently left her a trail of bright-red splashes to follow and she did so, heading into the kitchen. The knife holder and knives were scattered across the floor next to a pool of blood; she guessed he'd gone for another weapon. Joe obviously wanted her dead as much as Mom and Dad had. Reluctantly, she knew she'd have to kill him. Kill or be killed, that was Mother Nature's way, and Abbie was a dutiful daughter.

She followed the blood trail to the half-open back door and out into the snow. In the pale morning sunlight, the red droplets were easy to see, even where the falling snow was already filling and obscuring footprints.

Joe was headed for the trees, obviously hoping to lose himself in the shadows, then return to kill her when her guard was down. Not that she'd let him …

There he was; she could see him now through the snow and shadows. Blood loss and the chill air were making him slow.

She came up behind him and swung the axe, burying it deep in her brother's back. Joe let out a soft sigh and fell face down in the snow. She paused only to chop him up, then left his remains to be concealed by the falling snow.

Slowly, Abbie stumbled back towards the house. The pain in her head from her mother's blow was growing worse and she could feel the chill spreading through her body, penetrating deep into her bones. She needed to rest; she was so tired. Now that the adrenaline of fear had dissipated, the exhaustion only grew worse. She just wanted to sleep.

Staggering back to the kitchen, she dropped the gore-smeared axe and headed for the hallway. There she saw her mother, hacked into bloody bits and pieces, and the realization of what she'd done struck her and she fell to the bloodied floor, sobbing, hammering her fists against the wood. And as she pounded her fists and sobbed and screamed, she began to wonder: had Mom and Joe truly intended to kill her or had they merely mistaken her pre-emptive attack on Dad for a homicidal rage? And as she wondered that, she had to ask herself if Dad really had been murderously angry and about to go for the axe, or had she been mistaken? Had she stopped a killer, or was she the one infected with the evil of this place? Had she re-enacted the evil of thirteen years before?

She'd slaughtered her entire family. She was the murderer. She was nature red in tooth and claw, gone insane. She was infected.

She knew what she had to do.

She had to die.

THE BOY WHO KILLED SANTA CLAUS
Mark Allan Gunnells

Seven year old Henry Childers crawled reluctantly under the covers of his bed. "But, Mom," he whined, "I'm not sleepy. Can't I stay up a few more hours?"

"It's almost ten already," his mother Tonya said with an indulgent smile. "If you don't get to sleep, Santa won't stop here tonight."

"Do you think Santa got my letter this year?" Henry asked, sitting up against the headboard.

"I'm sure he did, honey."

"'Cause I don't want it to be like last year."

Tonya sighed heavily and rubbed at her temples. She'd been hearing this same tirade from her son for an entire year now. "Henry, there was nothing wrong with what you got from Santa last year."

"I asked for an XBox, and he gave me a Playstation. It's not the same."

"As I've told you a hundred times, maybe Santa was all out of XBoxes," Tonya said, pulling the covers up to just under Henry's chin. She and her husband had gone to every store in the city looking for an XBox last year, but they'd all been sold out. It had been a Playstation or nothing, but still it hadn't satisfied Henry.

"I mailed my letter in *October* last year," Henry said. "That gave him plenty of time to have his elves whip me up an XBox."

"Henry," Tonya said, a little more sharply than she'd intended, "you're being awfully ungrateful. There are children in the world who have nothing. If you don't start being more appreciative, Santa may decide to just skip our house altogether."

"Okay," Henry said, his lower lip poked out like a shelf. "I'm sorry."

"Just get to sleep," Tonya said, leaning over and kissing her son on the forehead. "When you wake up in the morning, you just might find that bike you've been wanting waiting under the tree."

"You think Santa will like the cookies and milk we left for him?" Henry asked.

"I'm sure he'll think they're delicious. I'll see you in the morning, sweetie."

Tonya turned off the light, the small nightlight plugged into the electrical socket by the closet throwing a muted yellow glow throughout the room. She eased the door closed, leaving Henry to dream of Christmas morning.

✳ ✳ ✳

"Do you think it's safe to start?" Jonas Childers asked his wife. They were sitting in the living room, watching a SciFi channel marathon of the *Silent Night, Deadly Night* films.

Tonya glanced at the clock, saw that it was just past one o'clock in the morning. "He should be sound asleep by now," she said. "I think we can get started."

"Good," Jonas said. "It'll probably take me 'til dawn to get that bike put together."

They went up to the attic, careful to avoid all the squeakiest boards, and brought down all of Henry's presents. Tonya began arranging all the smaller gifts around the tree while Jonas unfolded the instructions for the bike and began assembling it.

"Shit," Jonas cursed under his breath, trying to fit together two pieces that simply refused to fit together. "As much trouble as this is, Henry better like this damn bike."

Tonya knelt next to her husband, took the uncooperative pieces and easily snapped them together. "Are you kidding? He'll absolutely *love* it."

"He better. I don't want to have to go through another year hearing him bitch and moan like he did about that damn Playstation."

"It did get a bit tiresome," Tonya said with a giggle. "But Henry just wants what he wants, and he won't settle for anything else."

"Like mother, like son."

Tonya swatted her husband on the arm. "That's not true. I settled for you, after all."

"Very funny," Jonas said. "How about you settle for passing me those cookies."

Tonya had baked a batch of oatmeal raisin cookies, half of which her family had eaten, the other half of which had been placed on a plate for Santa. She took the plate and handed it to her husband, who immediately scarfed down two of the cookies.

"Careful," Tonya said, reading over the instructions. "You keep that up, you'll soon be fat as Santa."

"This isn't for me," Jonas said around a mouthful of cookie, spewing crumbs like a fine mist. "It's for Henry. Think how disappointed he'd be if he woke up and saw that Santa hadn't eaten the cookies he left for him."

"Don't talk with your mouth full," Tonya said with a smile.

"Hand me the milk, please."

They did not leave out a glass of milk for Santa since that would curdle, but they placed it in a thermos to keep it cold. Tonya passed the thermos to her husband.

Jonas popped the top of the thermos and gulped down several swallows of the milk. Suddenly he retched, spitting milk into the air like a geyser, the thermos dropping from his hand and leaking its contents onto the carpet. Jonas clutched at his throat, making strangled gagging noises as milk and blood dribbled down his chin.

Tonya screamed and grabbed her husband as he collapsed onto her lap. His body was jerking with violent spasms, his eyes rolled up to the whites. He coughed violently, and more frothy blood sprayed Tonya's arms, and she thought there were chunks of tissue mixed with it.

"Oh God, Jonas," she screamed, crying. "What's wrong? What should I do?"

"What's going on?" Henry said, stepping into the room wearing his pajamas, rubbing the sleep dust from his eyes. "I heard screaming."

"Henry, get the phone and call 9-1-1," Tonya yelled frantically. "Something is wrong with your father; he needs an ambulance right away."

"What is it?" Henry asked, wide-eyed, stepping further into the room.

"Henry, call 9-1-1 NOW!"

Henry started to turn toward the phone, but then he spotted the spilled thermos of milk and froze. "Did Dad drink the milk?" he asked, snatching up the thermos and waving it at his mother.

"What?" Tonya said, feeling her husband's spasms tapering off, afraid to contemplate what that might mean. "Your father needs help."

"Did Dad drink the milk?" Henry said again, his old stubborn self. "This milk was for Santa Claus, not for Dad."

"Henry!" Tonya screamed, desperate tears of frustration and helplessness streaking her face. "This isn't the time—"

"THIS MILK WAS FOR SANTA CLAUS, NOT FOR DAD!" Henry roared, throwing the thermos across the room.

A numbness began to spread throughout Tonya's body, starting in her chest and reaching out through her limbs. Comprehension came slowly, and it made her feel cold inside. Cold and empty.

"What did you do?" she croaked, her voice raw and raspy. "Henry, what did you do to the milk?"

"I poured Drain-O in it," he said matter-of-factly, as if stating that he'd brushed his teeth.

Tonya was on her feet in an instant, the still form of her husband stretched out on the floor. She grabbed Henry by the shoulders and shook him, shook him hard. "Why would you do such a thing?" she shouted into his face. "Why in the name of God would you do such a thing?"

"I wanted an XBox!" Henry shouted back, wrenching out of his mother's grasp. "Not a Playstation, an XBox, and Santa knew that. He knew that, and he gave me the wrong thing anyway. I wanted to teach him a lesson, make him pay for giving me the wrong gift last year."

Tonya stumbled back, hands to her mouth, and watched as her son turned and ran back to his room, slamming the door behind him. She snatched up the phone and quickly dialed 9-1-1 while Santa chopped up a topless teenager on the television behind her.

W✳HOSOEVER D✳IGS A P✳IT

D.H. Lewis

errance Whatley wasn't always the weird kid.
Brandon and Terrance lived in the small community of Gabriel Hill. They had attended the same school, and for a while the same church, and they went out trick-or-treating together on Halloween. But things changed.

Brandon learned about the word "divorce" one Christmas when Terrance's mother went away. During the summer months, Terrance would spend time with his mother in northern California and then return for the school year to be with his father, one Gus Whatley, known locally as Ol' Cussin' Gus. Such circumstances made maintaining a friendship difficult.

Brandon's family witnessed strange incidents when riding by the Whatley house. Once, during a storm, Terrance was seen squatting in a dug-out hole while holding a cinder block over his head. Ol' Gus sat in a folding chair under a beat-up umbrella, reading scripture out of a worn Bible. Brandon once saw Gus pacing around Terrance, shouting something about losing his wife because of his son's bad behavior.

"Wicked ways bring wicked days!" shouted Gus.

Brandon tried to hear what else Mr. Whatley was saying as his father drove by, but only caught words that had given the man the title of "Cussin'" Gus. Brandon's father would speed past the house when both Whatleys were outside. Sometimes his mother would quietly say, "That poor boy."

Others witnessed strange events. The neighborhood was full of whispers.

"That poor child."

"That awful man."

"Know what I heard?"

"Know what I saw?"

"Know what I think?"

Life in Gabriel Hill rolled on.

❄ ❄ ❄

Brandon woke on Christmas morning, having survived his first semester at college. He considered this his first Christmas as a true adult. No matter what his status, the family traditions remained the same; the Eve was spent talking while watching cheesy holiday specials, then the Day spent exchanging gifts.

Santa as the bearer of gifts had ended when Brandon had puzzled out that the Jolly Old Elf was really Mom and Dad, having woken one Christmas morning before his parents had put the presents under the tree. He had been ordered back to bed. Once back between the covers, Brandon had heard his parents frantically rushing about the house, plucking presents out of hiding. His mother had shouted out that he could come out, and lo and behold … a Christmas miracle: there were the presents. Santa must have been in a mischievous mood last night, they had said sheepishly.

Brandon had been curious about why Santa had left the price tags on the gifts. His parents had realized then that the magic particular to the holidays was extinguished. The memory of his parents' sadness, his mother even stifling a tear, remained, but they had been happy after he had thanked them for the presents.

It all seemed so long ago.

Brandon put on his leopard print bathrobe, a gag gift from his girlfriend, before heading downstairs. He thought it strange that the familiar aroma of nutmeg coffee and Christmas waffles, a holiday tradition, wasn't filling the house, and there was a numbing cold draft.

The downstairs was quiet. The tree was missing. Brightly colored packages were scattered about the room, although some were missing. The front door was wide open. Brandon called out.

His parents didn't answer.

* * *

"What you think you're gonna get this Christmas?" asked Brandon as he added another layer to the snow fort.

"I saw my mom buy Blobbiemorphers, so I'm probably getting that," Terrance said sullenly.

Brandon shook his head. "No, what did you ask Santa to bring you?"

Terrance looked straight to the ground. "Mom didn't take

me to see Santa 'cause Dad said not to. He says that Santa is Satan spelled a different way."

Brandon puzzled over this bit of information. "That's stupid."

Terrance sniffed, rubbing his nose with the back of his hand. "Yeah. That's what I thought."

* * *

Brandon looked around. The land line phone was missing, along with his parent's smartphones. His own, which he had plugged in downstairs to recharge, was also missing. Shattered ornaments covered the floor. along with a broken plastic Santa and his reindeer. Dasher looked as if she had been crushed under a five-ton press. The stockings hung by the chimney with care had been ripped apart and the contents thrown about the house.

Brandon searched the rest of the house and found Christmas cards stuffed in the toilet, Christmas cookies ground into the hallway carpet, and waffle batter covered the kitchen counters and floor. He saw red mixed in with the thick, sticky residue and immediately thought the worst, but saw that it was only raspberry jam from a broken jar. Everywhere there were signs of violence. He found the rest of his mother's Santa Claus figurines outside in yellowed snow. He noticed that all the tires of the family cars had been slashed, including his well-abused twenty-year-old Corolla. There was evidence on the white ground (for it had been a White Christmas) that there had been much travel back and forth from the house.

The trail was unmistakable. Brandon went to the garage to collect a tire iron. He put on his boots but still wore his bathrobe, sweat pants, and t-shirt. Brandon followed the trail, knowing it would lead to the Whatley house, knowing that he would be seeing his old friend again.

✳ ✳ ✳

Terrance shook as the class sang. Brandon leaned over to ask what was the matter. The strange look in his friend's eyes almost caused Brandon to call the teacher, assuming that his friend was ill.

"The other reindeer names, they're the names of old demon gods. My dad said so. What am I supposed to do? This is a bad song. I need to be good, or Santa won't come."

Terrance grabbed his friend's shoulder. "I'm not bad. Really. I'm a good boy."

Brandon pulled away from his friend's grip. "Of course you are. It's just a stupid song." At this point in the song, the other reindeer had accepted their red-nosed brother. Brandon always thought it weird that the other reindeer only acknowledged the red-nosed wonder because he had helped them out. Seemed that in the Spirit of Christmas they should have welcomed him as-is.

Terrance stood up. "I'm a good boy."

By coincidence, he spoke at the silence right after song's end. The children all turned to stare, then laughed at Terrance's comment. The boy's eyes went glassy. Brandon shivered looking into those blank eyes. He was scared to even touch Terrance lest the boy say something more embarrassing. His friend sat motionless as the red and green cake was passed out, along with a sugary punch in plastic cups. Children talked and laughed. The principal walked in dressed as Santa, decorated with the cheapest fake beard that could be found at the local drug store, bellowing out a hearty "Ho, ho, ho!"

Terrance came out of his stupor. Brandon thought he heard Terrance say, "I don't understand" before he ran out of the room. No one else noticed. Brandon was about to follow, but a small green-wrapped box was placed in his hands. "Ho, ho, ho, little boy, Merry Christmas!" He ripped off the thin paper to discover a box of crayons. Santa, aka the principal, asked about Terrance. Brandon said he didn't know. Santa gave Brandon a red-wrapped box. "Then I'll trust you to give him his gift. You'll do that for me, right? Ho, ho, ho!"

Brandon forgot. Pretty little Christy gave him a quick kiss on the cheek under a picture of mistletoe. The red box was left on the teacher's desk.

It was the last year that Brandon shared a holiday with his friend.

❆ ❆ ❆

The sun reflected off the snow with a vengeance. Blinded and sweating in the cold, Brandon followed the trail, noticing bits of tinsel and other holiday debris marking the way. He regretted not grabbing a coat.

Rudolph, the Red-Nosed Reindeer, sat partially submerged in the white. Brandon remembered coloring the balsa wood ornament with markers when he was six. Mom had said it was the best reindeer ever. It had survived twelve Christmases only to be abandoned. The red nose had started to run from contact with the snow, making it look like poor Rudolph had been punched in the face by a rowdy drunk. The icon still smiled, despite the recent hardship. Brandon reflected back on the raspberry jam mixed in with the waffle batter and how it looked like blood.

He started to run.

❆ ❆ ❆

Brandon edged his friend toward the red and white dais.

The department store intercom announced another spectacular sale in housewares. Shoppers caught in the holiday frenzy heard it and dashed to housewares to see what was going on. "C'mon, just tell him what you want. He makes a list. As long as you're good, you get at least … I'll say 80% … of what you ask for. He'll know if you've been naughty or nice."

Terrance shuffled closer to the red-shrouded bearded figure. Brandon thought that one of the elves looked an awful lot like a derelict that his parents had gifted a few dollars to one evening. He remembered his mother whispering, "But there for the grace of God go I," after raising the car window. The man had stuffed the dollars into his left sock. Brandon remembered thinking that it was a silly place to put money.

He also remembered the man saying, "God bless you" as the car pulled away. The sincerity was overwhelming. Brandon had found himself praying about the man later that night.

"Just tell him what you want," he said. Santa sat dispassionately upon his red and gold throne.

"I'm scared," said Terrance.

"Just tell him. It works out."

Brandon watched his friend shuffle toward Saint Nick like a man on his way to the gallows. Terrance looked back, his face pale. Brandon gave him a thumbs up. A sprightly elf in candy stripe leggings and green tunic hoisted Terrance onto the big man's lap. Brandon couldn't understand his friend's fear or the strange ideas from the boy's father, and then noticed the look of panic on the faces of the younger children, some of whom he was sure were about to wet themselves, approaching the big man. Suddenly Brandon felt it was all a bit silly.

Pretty Christy suddenly went by in tow with her parents, giving him a shy smile and a small wave as they headed toward housewares. All other thoughts left Brandon's brain as he clumsily followed after them while trying to figure out a good way to approach Christy without seeming like a complete spaz.

Christy's father was irritated by the interruption in a family affair while the mother was delighted and went on about "how cute" Brandon was. Christy giggled at Brandon's discomfort. Christy's family bid Brandon a goodbye. He went back to Santa's Workshop to find Terrance sitting near a particleboard gingerbread house. Terrance's face held a tight smile. Brandon didn't know why the grin disturbed him so. The helpful elf near Santa stared at Terrance as if he were some sort of mutant. Even Santa nervously glanced at the boy.

"I-I told him, Brandon. I gave him my list and said I had been a good boy. I told him everything I've done; I've listened to Paw-Paw, said my prayers at night asking Jesus to burn all corrupters in Hellfire, and for Mom to die of AIDS."

❄ ❄ ❄

Icicles hung off the edge of the Whatley house roof like rotting alligator teeth. Peeling paint gave the house the appearance of having a terrible rash. The front lawn stood in an uneven jumble. The front door was open. No suggestion of the holiday season was apparent except for the few strands of silver tinsel along the path to the door. The windows were blocked by yellowed newspapers. Brandon scanned the old headlines, some from when he was a boy. Gripping the tire iron, he took a deep breath before entering.

The scent of mildew and staleness hit Brandon's senses before the underlying odor of rot. The house seemed to not to have been cleaned in years; however, a large section of the living room had been cleared away for Brandon's family

Christmas tree. A few surviving gifts were placed underneath the tree's green branches. Brandon thought it looked like Holidays in Hell.

Other smells became evident. Bugs. Old food wrappers. His mother's perfume. His dad's deodorant. Burnt toast. Gingerbread cookies. Rotting wood. Grease. Oranges. Old paper. Sour milk. Turpentine. Candle wax. Old meat. Glue. Plastic. Nutmeg. Mold.

A *thud* from where he remembered the kitchen to be. He tried to say "Hello," but found his mouth too dry to make a sound. He licked his lips, then tried again. "Terrance? You here? Hello?"

The house was quiet for several seconds until heavy footfalls came from the kitchen. Terrance came into the living room, complete with a red hat with a fuzzy white ball at the end. He was bigger than Brandon remembered, monstrously so. Long, matted hair concealed most of Terrance's face. His old friend stood upright, looming over Brandon like an ogre from myth.

"H-hey Brandon. W-what … What you … What have you been up to?"

❄ ❄ ❄

Brandon studied the back of Christy's head during Social Studies, not noticing Terrance doodling pictures of candy canes and wrapped presents in his notebook. Terrance reached over to Brandon's notebook and wrote: *What did you get for Christmas?*

Brandon hastily wrote down what he got, ignoring the unwanted sweater and socks sent by his Aunt Joann.

Terrance stared at the list. Brandon returned to his vigilance of Christy's gold hair until he heard a stifled sniffle and noticed his friend was fighting back tears. He scribbled down, *What did you get?* in Terrance's notebook. Suddenly, Christy noticed Brandon and gave him a mischievous smile. Brandon blushed. Terrance's reply went unread.

Wasn't good enough—had to drink coal ash—was naughty—naughty don't get presents.

Brandon and Christy exchanged a few more shy glances before the teacher noticed and directed the pair to turn their attention back to the front of the class. The other students giggled except for Terrance. His thoughts were elsewhere.

Brandon turned red and waited for the attention to die down. He glanced at Terrance's drawings. Among the candy canes and presents was one of a round Santa, the beard spiky, almost like a projection of needles, and the eyes circular with giant pupils. The mouth was wide open, containing a row of shark teeth.

Brandon reached over and wrote under the drawing. *Really Cool.*

Terrance looked horrified. Brandon's attention returned to Christy.

Terrance spent the rest of the class writing in his notebook. *Naughty or Nice. Naughty or Nice. Naughty or Nice.*

Brandon stood motionless. The tire iron slid from his hand, landing softly on a pile of old newspapers. He reached down to pick it up. Terrance watched unconcerned.

"Where're my parents?" Brandon asked quietly.

Terrance stomped his feet while grabbing his greasy head. "W-why you gotta say it that way? I wouldn't hurt them! You're just like the people in town. I like your parents. I liked your mom's peanut butter and jelly. Remember when she used to make that for us? I don't want to hurt them!" Terrance's fist swung out, hitting the nearby wall. Brandon thought that the entire house shook from the blow. Terrance clutched his head like he was containing an explosion.

"I'm not bad," said Terrance.

Brandon studied the room. He looked for anything that would be a better weapon than the tire iron. There was nothing. All danger from the room came from simple filth and neglect. He then noticed that the majority of the newspapers contained Christmas advertisements from years long past. Crushed between layers of newsprint were cheap plastic elves, reindeer, and snowmen, with other holiday paraphernalia.

"I'm not bad," repeated Terrance. "Am I?"

Brandon looked directly into Terrance's eyes and saw a lost soul.

"No. You're not bad," he said.

Terrance tensed. "Then why hasn't Santa ever visited me?"

❄ ❄ ❄

"Do you think that Santa is in with God?"

Brandon laughed. Terrance shrunk from the sound. Teams were being chosen for dodge ball. Christy was on Ben's team, and Brandon wanted to be on that team. "What do you mean?"

"Does he work for God, or is he God? Because he seems like both, you know? So is he like another son of God? Or an angel? Maybe a prophet?"

"What are you talking about? Christmas was two months ago." Brandon jumped up and waved frantically when it was Ben's turn to choose. "Grow up."

Ben picked Brandon and he ran off to stand beside Christy.

They smiled at each other before blushing and looking away. Terrance wandered off. It was only after the game that Brandon noticed his friend sitting alone nearby. A worn Christmas card was in his hand. Brandon wondered if it was from Terrance's mother, but then Christy walked by and stuffed a small note in his hand. It was a blue ink picture of a heart with an arrow through it.

Terrance was forgotten.

Brandon never saw his friend in school again and later heard rumors that he was being home schooled by Ol' Gus.

❋ ❋ ❋

Terrance kicked at a stack of odds and ends. "I don't know what I'm supposed to do to be a good boy! I don't know what's right and wrong anymore. If Daddy was lying, then what's truth? Why hasn't Santa Claus ever given me any presents? Santa gave you presents. Tons of them. What do you do that makes you so good?"

"Where's your dad?" Brandon wondered if it was for good or ill if Terrance's father was around.

Terrance stomped the floor again. "He's in the pit! That's where liars go to. He was buried upside-down and lit on fire. Liar, liar, pants on fire! His legs danced in the air like he was trying to run on the vault of the sky." Terrance stooped forward. Brandon thought Terrance was about to fall over. "He's in the pit."

"What pit?"

"The Pit of Hell. I dug it in the backyard a long time ago. But I filled it in, with him in it. Come on, I'll show you."

Terrance gestured for Brandon to follow as he walked into the kitchen. Brandon obeyed and took the opportunity to look around for any sign of his parents. He saw one of his father's slippers on the kitchen floor but nothing else. There were three doors in the kitchen and from childhood memory he recalled one was for a pantry, one went to the basement, and the other lead outside. Terrance directed him to the one leading outside. The door gave a shrill shriek as Terrance opened it. Brandon almost cried out, thinking it was one of his parents screaming from somewhere outside.

The backyard landscape was a collection of holes, big and small, spread out around the yard. Piles of earth in different states of weathering accompanied the holes. One was filled in, a rusty shovel staked into the ground nearby. Two blue-and-yellow canisters of lighter fluid with an empty box of wooden matches lay nearby. A pair of skinny blackened legs crookedly stood out atop the earth mound as if attempting to mount an invisible upside-down horse. The shoes were still on the feet. The pants had been burned away. The exposed flesh showed a spectrum of red and black and pink. Brandon thought the legs appeared almost artificial, but the closer he got to the protruding limbs the stronger the stench of charred flesh became. Brandon could only think of a badly burnt order of barbecue.

"I d-don't think I did wrong, Brandon." Terrance slowly crouched on the ground. "He lied. When I saw him get shot, I knew he wasn't telling the truth. I saw him as he really was, a liar, a sinner, ah-ah-fabricator of deceit. Liars burn in the Pit. 'His wickedness will be exposed in the assembly.' That's in Proverbs." Terrance started quietly chanting, "*Liar, liar, pants on fire.*"

Brandon felt lost in a sea of insanity. He took a stab in the dark. "Do you want to know the truth about Santa Claus?"

Terrance ran up to him. Brandon gasped, unprepared for Terrance's imposing mass towering over him. Possibilities bombarded his mind of Terrance bashing his head in with a shovel, or being dragged to a pit for an inverted fiery burial, or merely stuffed into an oven for an ecclesiastical baking. He was not prepared for Terrance's tear-filled eyes.

"C-can you make things right with Santa?"

✻ ✻ ✻

One event concerning the weird Whatleys briefly became a Holiday tradition in Gabriel Hill, and that was the Christmas Eve tirade of Gus in the town square. He would arrive downtown around midday, apparently drunk, screeching that the Christmas celebration was a pagan observance and that it should be banned. People mostly ignored him. Terrance was always there, marching behind his father while holding a wooden sign covered with hand-painted biblical verses. By late afternoon, there would be enough complaints from merchants for a sheriff's deputy to come out to escort the Whatleys back home. Gus would be shouting toward the Heavens, beseeching God not to hold back His divine wrath. Terrance would be staring at the ground, embarrassed or just confused. Every year, Brandon would notice that his old trick-or-treat pal grew to look more like a hunched-over juggernaut potato than a human. If he had played football for the local school, Terrance's mere presence would have intimidated the opposing team into forfeiting.

It wasn't just Terrance's size that made people feel uncomfortable, but the feeling one got from looking at the boy that caused a level of fear. As the deputy dealt with Gus, the youth would stare at the window display Santas and other Christmas decorations about the town. The townsfolk watched the show as the police escorted the pair away; they'd make comments on how weird the father and son were, chuckle at tactless jokes. There were some who were waiting for the boy (who obviously had to be messed up) to explode in an episode of craziness. Terrance didn't erupt, but merely obeyed the officer's orders and sat in the patrol car when the unlucky deputy drove them home.

Brandon would watch the Whatley's being carted off as his father did the last-minute shopping. Afterward, the town Christmas pageant would play out with a local newborn playing the part of Baby Jesus. Later, Brandon's family would drive home for the traditional cheesy TV holiday fare. They would drive past the Whatley house: all lights off, no decorations, all quiet.

The family would have their Christmas morning ritual of waffles and nutmeg coffee, hot chocolate for young Brandon, and after all the presents were unwrapped, Brandon would spend the afternoon playing with his new toys. When he went to bed that night, Brandon would look out the window and sometimes imagine Ol' Gus standing outside with Terrance, pointing at his house while putting on a B-movie performance worthy of the Academy. At the center of the show would be Terrance, staring at the holiday decorations with a strange longing.

Brandon actually once heard Gus cussing at Terrance one Christmas Eve night, his shrieking voice carried by the chill December breeze to his window, the tone full of insane anger. In school, Brandon had learned that cold air allowed sound to carry further due to an effect called refraction. He opened his window to listen.

"They get all the presents you don't get. You're such a wicked boy, breakin' apart the family, chasin' away your mother. Santy Claus would like nothin' better than to give you presents, but you just keep being so wicked! What could be worse sin than driving away your mother? Maybe in your case suicide wouldn't be a sin but a blessing."

Brandon had felt sorry for his old friend. But as familiarity bred contempt, distance bred apathy. Brandon developed his own life.

But Brandon often thought of that cold Eve night, of Gus's shrill tirade echoing against the rural landscape, and no one listening, or if anyone heard, a way was found to ignore it.

Life in Gabriel Hill went on.

❄ ❄ ❄

"Wait a second!" Terrance ran back into the house. Brandon stared at Gus's red, black, and pink legs. Terrance burst through the back door carrying a string of lights attached to an extension cord. Brandon recognized the lights being those that had decorated the bushes at home. Terrance quickly wrapped the string around the burnt legs, then clicked the lights on. In the bright morning, the electric lights took on a pastel hue.

Brandon and Terrance stood and stared.

"Merry Christmas," said Terrance. "A merry, merry Christmas to all."

Brandon almost threw up when one of the legs twitched.

After Brandon composed himself, he found Terrance looking at him. "W-what am I doing wrong? Why hasn't Santa stopped by? I just don't understand."

Brandon often wondered about the illusion, the absurdity, of Santa Claus, wondering why bratty kids got magnificent presents while those of lesser means received so little. He remembered reading an article online about children in the 1920s sending requests to the North Pole asking for a job for their father, that their mother would get better, for new shoes and clothes for themselves. Such requests seemed so much more worthy than a new toy or game. How could Santa deny such a humble request? But year after year he did, and from that grew the idea that maybe the man didn't exist. Brandon realized that he knew Santa didn't even exist before his parents' morning mistake.

"Let's go back inside," whispered Brandon. "I'll tell you everything about Santa."

Terrance grabbed a notebook and pencil before settling into a well-used armchair. He opened the notebook to a blank page before gnawing the pencil end to a point. Once satisfied, he looked to Brandon with the eagerness of a man awaiting the Rapture.

Brandon weighed truth against the myth. There was tremendous power in the myth; mischievous children would be on their best behavior, donations to charities would increase, the media would be filled with feel-good stories of mysterious benefactors and examples of holiday cheer. There was the opposite; people injuring others to get the best box store deals, human parasites tricking others to give to a phony charity, or angry individuals screaming about a War on Christmas. In the middle of it all was this chubby man in a red and white suit passing out rewards to the children determined worthy by a randomly concocted set of regulations.

Terrance sat in the worn chair. Eyes wide, awaiting revelation. Brandon made his choice.

"Santa Claus ... doesn't exist. He's fake. A lie told to children to make them behave. No one watches you to see if you're naughty or nice. It's just a story, a fairy tale. No elves. No North Pole workshop. The guys at the stores are just men paid so parents can get a picture of their kids with Santa." Brandon felt like he was on a roller-coaster right at that moment before the slow crossing of the crest to the rapid rushing decline. "Your dad was messed up. He lied to you.

There just isn't any Santa Claus. Never was. The parents buy the presents."

Terrance stared down at the blank pages. Meaty hands closed around the notebook, crushing the pages and spiral wire into an unusable mess. Slowly, Terrance began to tear off sections of the crumbled notebook. The pieces fell to the floor. Brandon watched the pieces fall, afraid to interrupt Terrance's mental process. *Surely*, he thought, *Terrance would come to realize that Santa was simply a myth.*

"Why do you lie to me? What reason? I'm due. For so long … the truth, just want the truth. Everyone wants to deny me what is mine. Two guys in white shirts and black slacks riding bicycles came to my door and asked me if I knew God. And I told them yes, God was Santa Claus. They said that Santa wasn't real, and I knew that wasn't right, that it was a test, so I … I … Liar, liar pants on fire, nose as long as a telephone wire …" Terrance's voice diminished to a mumble.

Brandon's mouth went dry. Words struggled to come out. "Terrance, where are my parents?"

Terrance looked at Brandon, the right dark pupil three times larger than the left. "Santa is God in a red suit. He judges, and those in the Right are rewarded. The Right get presents and toys and candy and cake and … love and warmth … and hugs goodnight. I wasn't good and you know what Santa did? He took my mother away. And when I didn't improve, Santa made my mom sick. She died because I wasn't a good boy. That's what my dad said—"

"Your dad lied."

Terrance dropped the mangled notebook. Ends of broken wire had scratched Terrance's fingers, but he did not react. "Liar, liar, pants on fire, britches … hanging on a telephone wire …"

"Where are my parents?"

"I need the truth, Brandon," said Terrance. "I'm c-confused. So just tell me, truthfully, what can I do to make Santa judge me worthy?" The right pupil grew bigger. Terrance's grasped his head. "I'll do whatever he wants. I just have to know what that is! Tell me. I've suffered enough. I really don't see how this is fair."

Brandon slowly withdrew toward the front door. "I'll go get Santa, the man himself. I know how to do that. Let Santa tell you what you need to do."

Terrance violently rubbed his temple. Dirty fingernails left red lines on his skin. "You can do that?"

"Yes," said Brandon. "Just give me a little while to contact him."

Brandon felt the bitter cold through the holes torn in his sweat pants from the numerous times he had stumbled running home, his hands numb from countless plunges into the snow.

He had come up with a crazy plan to deal with a crazy situation. It would only work if his old friend were truly mad.

Brandon raced straight to the attic and threw open all the boxes marked XMAS. He breathed a sigh of relief when he found the old Santa Claus suit his father had worn long ago for an office party. He wasn't his father's height or weight, but if Terrance was too far gone from reality, Brandon hoped that the imperfections wouldn't matter. He disrobed in the chilled attic, not knowing if he were shaking from the temperature or fear. An old throw pillow provided the bowl full of jelly, a discarded tube of red lipstick made the rosy cheeks. Brandon placed the foam-covered wire hooks around his ears that supported the curly white beard. Clumsily making his way down the stairs, he stopped at the closest bathroom to check his disguise in the mirror.

"Only a crazy man would believe I'm Santa," he said. In tears, he ran back to the Whatley house.

✳ ✳ ✳

The tradition of Cussin' Gus's Christmas Eve Town Tirade ended due to the actions of a new deputy, one young Clarence Campbell by name. Nervous, inexperienced, given a gun, and sent out on what was supposed to be a mere handling of the local eccentric, the situation dissolved into Gus crying in the streets from a bullet to his right knee. Clarence, sweating as large snowflakes fell around him, called for an ambulance while apologizing to Gus. Terrance stared at his father, the titan, face covered in tears, wiggling on the asphalt while clutching his knee. The wound was not life threatening and some of the locals laughed at the scene. Brandon remembered the look in his old friend's face. Discovering his father's frailty had ignited something sinister behind Terrance's eyes, giving life to a new perspective of the world. This time, Terrance looked at the Santas and holiday decorations with a look of violent defiance. Brandon believed he was the only one in the crowd who had witnessed the change.

Gus was carted off to Gabriel Hill Community Hospital. Terrance, forgotten, walked the seven miles back home. Later, the deputy was nicknamed Barney Fife and was frequently asked about the "one bullet" that the sheriff allowed him to carry.

Life in Gabriel Hill carried on, with one new story to tell.

✳ ✳ ✳

The Christmas before heading off to college wasn't as magic-filled as those experienced in youth. The cookies and milk by the fireplace, along with threats of the dreaded

Naughty and Nice list, were gone. All gifts were now under the tree. No more surprises from Saint Nick.

Cussin' Gus did make an appearance downtown that Christmas Eve, but without his usual fire and damnation. Fear dominated his eyes as he meekly held onto his handmade sign proclaiming condemnation. Terrance followed, but only stared at his father like a cat ready to pounce on a toy mouse. A humbled Gus that wasn't cussing was not entertaining, so the man was ignored. Brandon was there with his family, drinking eggnog at the town diner after shopping, watching flakes of white descend outside.

Terrance watched the man who had commanded his life for the past several years sink further into decrepitude. Brandon felt that he was the only one who had noticed his old friend no longer stood hunched over, but straight and tall and now loomed over the cursing prophet. Ol' Gus seemed afraid of the towering figure that shadowed him. He openly drank from a bottle stashed in his coat pocket. Terrance quietly smiled at a secret revelation.

Life in Gabriel Hill went on, without much of a story to tell.

❉ ❉ ❉

The blinding white glare of the morning was now replaced by a sky of gray. Brandon knew from having grown up in the Midwest that a snow storm was coming. By the time he reached the Whatley house, a mixture of sleet and snow had started to fall.

Brandon remembered his appearance in the bathroom mirror; a scrawny college kid in a bad costume. He was playing the part of a Jesus, Buddha, or a Muhammad to the singular audience of a crazed seeker. Terrance had to believe.

"Ho, ho, ho, my boy!" Brandon slammed open the front door, hoping the action would unsettle Terrance, hoping it would give him an advantage. There was no reply. The living room was empty. Brandon started to choke, then realized that he was inhaling strands of the fake beard into his mouth. His heart pounded in his ears.

I'm panicking, he thought, *I'm panicking and my parents need me. They'll die unless—*

"Santa, hmmph, is that really you?"

Terrance stepped through the doorway leading in from the kitchen; he was crunching on a gingerbread man cookie. Brandon saw the head of the cookie sticking out from Terrance's mouth, its expression condemning.

You're next, college boy.

"Oh Santa, I've waited so long." Terrance didn't look Brandon in the eye. "And I have so many questions."

Terrance's shaking hands covered his face. Brandon thought that the boy/man was about to cry before realizing he hadn't thought of what to do beyond tricking Terrance. "A good boy would tell me where Brandon's parents are at. You do that, and you can have Brandon's pres—"

"Follow me, Santa." Terrance gestured for Brandon to follow, his large hands still shaking. "They're all just cozy and fine." Brandon followed Terrance into the kitchen. Terrance opened the door to the basement. The smell of mold and damp earth overwhelmed Brandon's senses. Terrance flicked on a light switch then descended. Cobwebs lined the space above the stairwell like a mist. The wooden stairs creaked under Terrance's thudding weight. Brandon felt his mouth go dry. He couldn't move.

Terrance stopped halfway down and turned, angry tear-streaked eyes boring into Brandon.

"Get down here."

Brandon obeyed.

The basement stench hit Brandon like a physical force. Terrance didn't seem bothered. A single yellow bulb provided a dim vision of a muddy indoor swamp. Small bits of ice floated in the brown water.

"Dad never could fix the leak in the kitchen sink, and he didn't want anyone messing around in the house to work on it. Plus, after every heavy rain the basement got wet." Terrance pointed to a far corner. Brandon's parents sat partially submerged in the mire, bound by scraps of clothing to wooden chairs, their heads covered with reflective red and green wrapping paper secured by coils of clear tape. "See, just fine and dandy."

Before Brandon could calculate his next move, Terrance spoke.

"You're a false Santa," said Terrance. "I recognize a bogus Claus when I see one. Don't know why you lied to me, Brandon. I explained my problem."

Brandon gathered up courage born of outrage. "You kidnapped my parents, wrecked my house, and want to meet Santa. You're sick, Terrance. You need help." Terrance responded with humorless laughter.

"What I need is to know why I've been skipped over. I'm challenging Santa so I can figure out what exactly is naughty and nice. I don't feel that you've been so nice, especially since you lied, so I'll give you a chance to redeem yourself in His eyes. Go save your parents. Give me your boots and the suit. Trust me, those will only bog you down." Terrance gestured to Brandon's parents. "See, I can be nice. Ho, ho, ho!"

Brandon passed the boots and costume into Terrance's beefy hands while dropping the pillow into the surrounding muck. The cold air already starting to numb his skin, Brandon placed one foot into the freezing brown water and sank to his calf into the thick mud underneath. Holding onto the stairway banister, Brandon stepped forward with his other foot, now sinking into the water waist deep. The mud unwillingly released his leg for the next step. As his foot went down, it met resistance.

"I should warn you that we threw a lot of garbage down here: broken glass, anything plastic, metal stuff," said Terrance as he took off his stained pants to put on the Santa suit. "Dad stopped paying for garbage pick-up years ago. Who knows what's slicing into your feet. That's what I worried about whenever Dad sent me down here to do penance. Feet would get so numb I just couldn't feel them anymore." Terrance placed the hooks of the wispy beard around his ears. "I think ... Santa is imperfect. That He doesn't see everybody, but makes us believe that He can. You see, every Christmas Eve I would go to people's houses and watch them, even yours. I'd return the next night to see what Santa brought them. Such awesome things. Even such people that I know—I KNOW!— were naughty got presents. They would spend the year lying, cheating, stealing, doing anything and everything bad, yet every Christmas I had to drink coal ash. Everyone believes in Santa. People dress like him, act like him, make movies of him, have images of him ... why waste so much time in an illusion? Santa is a god, the true god of the season. More powerful than any other god." Terrance stood up, the Santa costume stretched to its limit over his behemoth frame. "I will go find the true Santa and demand answers."

Terrance thumped up the stairs. "I'll be like Paul, and maybe have a vision on the way to Damascus." Terrance sighed before closing the basement door. "I hope you succeed, really. I'm sorry for all this, but Santa has a lot to answer for."

The door slammed shut.

Brandon stepped closer to his parents. The cold of the water numbed his physical sensations. He knew that something had punctured the heel of his left foot. He realized that tears were flowing from his eyes. His parents were just feet away.

"Mom? Dad? I'm coming." Brandon stumbled, the mud unwilling to give up his right foot. Cold, fetid water entered his mouth. He regained his balance.

"Mom? Dad?"

No response.

Brandon pushed forward, his parents now just inches from his reach. There was no movement from either one. "Could one of you say something?" He found himself praying for a Christmas miracle.

When Brandon reached his parents, he hugged them before tearing off the wrapping paper. He had been granted part of his wish; one parent was alive, the other was not.

❄ ❄ ❄

It had been six years since Brandon rescued his mother from the basement. She had developed post traumatic symptoms from the encounter. Christmas time had become subdued after the "incident." Brandon caught himself staring at images of Santa during the season. Every depiction was so horribly artificial.

He wondered what it all meant, what purpose did it all serve? People dashed madly to buy presents. A bald man on TV squawked that there was a war on the holidays and chastised those that did not say "Merry Christmas." Charities vied for attention because this was the one time of the year that people seemed willing to give. Above it all loomed the figure of a fat, rosy-cheeked man in red and white. Brandon had to admit that his old friend was right about Kris Kringle: He was the God of December, no other stood before Him, and woe to those who said anything against Him.

Every season Brandon found Internet news concerning the disappearance of one or two mall Santas in the Midwest, their fates unknown. There were also the stories of a large man traveling around in a tattered Santa suit who had a devoted following of homeless lost souls who were searching for the true Santa Claus. The large crazy man was quoted saying, "Death to false images of Santa." The bizarre man was now soliciting money for a trip to the North Pole to meet the Big Man himself.

The fake beard had been replaced by a real one, although bleached white by peroxide, but the craziness burning behind the eyes was unmistakable.

Brandon found himself wishing the man success in his mission.

Life in Gabriel Hill rolled on, with no more stories to tell.

The Ringer

G.G. Silverman

A man ringing a bell stood alone in the middle of nowhere, a frozen, stark white landscape under an ice-gray sky. He didn't know why he was there; he had forgotten the purpose of ringing his bell, or how he arrived there in the first place, where the cold frost stung the exposed skin on his face, rendering his lips numb. Beside him, a red kettle of coins hung from a chain on a tripod stand. He kept ringing his bell, unable to stop, his arm and hand controlled by an unseen force that he fought against, to no avail. Nor could he move his feet, or any other part of his body except his bell-ringing hand. He screamed until his throat grew raw, and he gave up, hoping the sound of his bell would carry far into the distance and spur his rescue, though the small voice of his conscience told him that no one could hear him.

He stole a sideways glance at the kettle of coins, searching for clues about his past, or what brought him here. The words on it had been partially rubbed off, the only remaining letters reading *Sal Arm*. The bell ringer decided this was his name, Sal Arm, and that his bell-ringing arm was a relentless perpetual motion machine.

He attempted to pass the time, trying to think of songs he could hum. Fragments of winter songs came, but not enough to comfort him. *God rest* … God rest what? *Ye merry* … hmmm. There was another song he remembered, something about a little boy who liked to drum, or was it something else?

The perpetual motion machine of his arm kept swinging, swinging.

The hours passed, and the sky grew darker, and a sense of despair crept over him.

He closed his eyes. Shards of more memories came. Something about a former life.

There had been an alley. He had dragged a kettle of coins into an alley. Was it his kettle? He wasn't sure. There had to be have been something more. There had been noise, shouting. Maybe a scuffle.

Think. *Think.*

There had been a dark parking lot.

And, there had been a beating. Someone. A man.

A man was beaten. There was blood. A head wound.

The man cowering as someone brandished a tire iron, swinging, swinging.

The man screaming, *Don't. Don't.*

He remembered now.

It was he who held the tire iron.

Laughing, taunting, *No one can hear you scream.*

The man limp on the pavement, his blood pooling on dirty, cracked ice.

He had beaten the man and left him to die, and dragged off the kettle into the night.

The man had been a bell-ringer, as he was now, in this frozen karmic wasteland. And now his bell-ringing arm kept swinging, swinging; a perpetual motion machine.

He scanned the horizon for someone, anyone. The white sclera of his eyes burned, unable to produce tears. He opened his mouth wide, and raged against the vast expanse of snow and sky. It was a cold day in hell. And no one could hear him scream.

Leo

Max Vile

December 22, 7:30 pm

Jessica pulled the key from her front door and waved her new friend inside. Christopher smiled a nervous thank you and entered. She locked the door behind him.

"I don't usually do this," he half stuttered.

"Do what?" she asked.

He turned away, embarrassed or not able to explain. She didn't force him. Instead, she pulled him closer and gave him a light kiss on his lips.

Over his shoulder, she searched for Leo. He wasn't on the couch or under the table or snuggled in the fireplace where sometimes he slept. She glanced into the dining room. He wasn't there either.

You're nothing but a slut, a voice whispered in her ear.

She shook her head until the voice vanished.

"Are you okay?" Chris asked.

"Fine. Too much to drink."

She took Chris's hand and led him toward the stairs.

"You have a nice house, Jessica," he said. "No Christmas decorations?"

"I don't celebrate the holidays," she said, "and call me Jay."

They walked up the stairs to the second-floor master bedroom. She paused at the closed door.

How long had it been since you stepped foot through this door?

Her body tensed when she felt Chris's fingers slide around her waist to her stomach. He pressed himself against her. He was tall, maybe two hundred pounds, but nothing about him was intimidating—like a grown child trying to play as if he was a man. Yet the bulge that grew harder against the back of her thigh as he hungrily kissed her shoulder said he knew enough.

Before his hands moved farther down or up, she stepped out of his embrace and pushed the bedroom door open. She didn't invite him through this door. Through this one, he came willingly.

While he removed his suit coat, she again searched for Leo. Her eyes combed the space beneath the bed frame, behind the television, atop the dresser, past the curtain into the connected bathroom. No sign of him.

"You know, I don't even drink." Chris laughed. "I'd never been to that bar, *The Cornerstone.* I stopped for the hell of it after work … No Christmas plans, not traveling … Maybe depressed. You ever feel that way?"

"Yeah." She slipped off her jacket and let it fall to the floor.

He kept rambling, still nervous. "I was celebrating the one year anniversary of my divorce ... Sorry, you probably don't want to hear about it ... She wasn't a good person—"

"Who is," a deep nasally voice spoke from the shadows in the corner.

Jay flipped on the lamp on the nightstand. The dark retreated. No one stood in the corner.

Chris continued, unfazed, unaware. "—you never know, I guess. I'm happy. I wasn't drinking because I was sad about her ... I mean, look where I'm at ... I mean, I like you—"

"Good God," the voice said again, not from the corner but across the room. This time, its owner revealed himself.

Leo sat atop the vanity. His skinny green legs wagged over the lip of the first drawer but were too short to reach its center. He slid the red knit pointed cap off his head and rubbed his wrinkled cheeks. "It's a good thing I don't want his tongue."

Jay crinkled a face at the elf for him to shut up. Leo shrugged.

Chris continued, "—it's a long way out here to your house, in the country ... I live the opposite way, apartment in the city ... Is that a lake behind the house—?"

Leo tossed his hat onto the vanity. "Kiss him so he'll shut up, please."

Jay didn't hesitate and pushed herself higher on the balls of her feet to put her lips on his. It worked. Again his hands groped at her waist, beneath her blouse, against her skin. His fingers were cold from outside. They didn't feel like a man's, not because they were smooth, not the hands of a working man, but a lawyer, not like Leo's calloused palms. Despite their hunger, they felt dead, as if they were her own hands that had fallen asleep, foreign and lifeless.

She pushed him away.

"What?" he asked.

Behind her, she heard Leo giggle.

"Take off your clothes," she said.

Instinct took over. He slid off his tie and was through the buttons of his dress shirt in seconds. She pushed him onto the bed. He kicked off his shoes, then slid further up to rest his head on the throw pillows. She retrieved his shirt and tie, took his right hand, and raised it to the bedpost. Slowly, she wrapped the tie around his wrist to bind him. He didn't protest. Instead, he grinned like a madman, so eager.

She walked around the bed with his dress shirt and tied his left arm the same.

"Wait," he whispered as she finished, "aren't you going to undress—?"

She put a finger to his lips. "No more talking."

She leaned over the bed and undid his belt and zipper. Her fingers hooked through both his pants and boxers. With one pull she yanked them to his ankles. His manhood stood already fully erect, too eager.

"You can take your pleasure first, if you desire," Leo said.

"Let's just be done with it," she answered.

Chris cleared his throat. "Whatever you want … You have protection? I didn't, I don't carry—"

"I have my husband's condoms," she said.

"You're married?" Chris asked.

"Divorced. Two years. They're his old ones."

She returned to the nightstand and slid open the top drawer.

"Two years ago? They might not be good anymore—"

"I wouldn't worry about it," she said.

Jay withdrew her ex-husband's old Ruger from the drawer and aimed it at Chris's chest. He stared at it blankly for a moment, his eyes only growing larger upon realization when she pulled the trigger.

She'd never fired the gun before. The room instantly went silent, replaced by a sickening single high-pitched tone that threatened to make her vomit.

Chris's mouth strained open so wide she thought his cheeks would rip. She knew he must be screaming, yet she heard nothing except the wail in her ears. A red hole in his chest pooled blood over his diaphragm onto his stomach, then drained in rivers between his flexed ribs as he kicked and strained his arms against the clothes that bound him. Already his right hand had frayed the fabric of his tie.

Her fingers trembled around the gun, but she tightened them and fired two more times into his chest. The impacts splattered the blood covering his torso onto her face. Her arms lost the strength to hold the pistol. She let it fall onto the soaked red comforter.

Chris no longer fought. His mouth spat up more blood, twitched twice more, then froze open, like his eyes, toward the ceiling.

Jay doubled over the trashcan beside the nightstand, unable to control the nausea, and vomited.

You killed another innocent person, Jay. Another fucking innocent—

"Look at the hog on this one!" Leo spoke, closer. "Powerful hips. Big boned, any way you mean it."

Jay wiped her face and lifted herself from the trashcan. Leo crawled over the lawyer's body. His spindly clawed fingers dug new holes into the corpse as he climbed. His tiny black boots left ripples in the blood. He plopped himself to a sit onto Chris plump stomach and smiled at Jay.

"I don't want to do this anymore," she said. Her voice echoed in her skull though she knew what came off her tongue was far weaker.

"Yes, you do, Cupid," replied Leo. Despite the ringing, his voice spoke as clear as day between her ears.

"Yes, I do," replied Jay. She felt tears in her eyes. Or maybe it was only the man's blood.

Leo nodded. "Good girl. I love you, Jay."

"Go to Hell."

The elf slid off the corpse onto the stained red comforter. Jay's hearing began to return. She heard the tarnished silver bells attached to the heels of Leo's boots chime while he squished his feet over the bed to Chris's blood-soaked suit coat. His minuscule body vanished into the folds for a moment, then he slid himself free and shook like a wet dog to rid himself of the blood on his long, withered mutton chops and beard. In his hands he held a pack of Marlboros and a lighter rummaged from the inner coat's pocket.

Leo popped a cigarette into his mouth, lit it, and sucked in a deep drag before resting on a throw pillow beside the corpse's head. He ashed into Chris's open mouth, then nodded his head toward Jay. "Now, get to work."

December 23, 12:03 am

Jay ran the towel through her wet hair. She'd showered off the man's blood, then tucked her ruined clothes and his into a bag that she'd brought downstairs into the den after she'd finished her work. He was too big to drag to the basement; she'd had to do the cutting upstairs, which only worsened the mess. The comforter and sheets and all the pillows went with the corpse, with no love lost.

"You haven't stepped foot in this room since you kicked out that bastard of a cheating, beating fool two years ago," Leo had said. "What fucking difference does it make that we ruined your sheets?"

Over the months, she'd sprayed air freshener in the room to keep it from smelling stale but never crossed the threshold until last night. The mattress was ruined and thoroughly soaked, sure to smell in the next few days. Then again, in the next couple days, when Leo's work should be completed, who knew how the world would concern her anymore.

What Leo hadn't needed from the man, she'd disposed of in weighted garbage bags in the lake. What remained of the lawyer, Christopher Whittaker, rested at the bottom in the sludge near the other bagged body parts and a plumber's truck she'd let roll underwater less than a month past.

She opened the wood furnace. The fire was lit but low. She tossed in a log and followed it with the bag of clothes, then shut the metal gate. In moments, she felt the heat flare inside, the fire as hungry as her dead suitor's smile.

How many has it been? Three? No, with the lawyer, four—?

Her phone rang.

Jay stared at it for several rings, unsure if what she heard was real. She'd barely, if at all, slept in the last week. She couldn't be sure. She heard too many things that weren't real and the elf's presence never helped. It was so hard to focus between the work that had to be finished—so little time left ... Leo said it had to be done before the holiday—and the nightmares that she couldn't remember if she had while she dreamed or was awake ...

Before it went to voicemail, she grabbed the phone and checked the screen.

Melissa. Her sister.

It was late and she'd never call at this time unless it was an emergency. Both their parents were dead. They had no other immediate family that might've died and warrant such a call. Only one reason, Jay knew, could be so pressing.

Jay answered, "Hello?"

"Uh … Jessica?" Melissa asked over the phone. "Didn't think you'd be up. I was going to leave a message for you to get in the morning."

"It's fine. I couldn't sleep."

"The dreams again? About mom?"

"I don't want to talk about it."

"I know it's a hard time for you, this time of year."

"I'm really tired."

"I'm here, if you need, Jessica—"

"Why won't you ever call me, Jay?"

"Because that's not your name."

"Okay, *Mel*."

Jay couldn't help but smile at their bickering, sisters until the end. Even though Melissa had left their family home as soon as she turned eighteen, they'd never lost touch, despite her never speaking to their parents ever again. She was always watching out for her little sis.

The smile quickly soured.

"Why'd you call so late?" Jay said. *Please don't say you're coming here. Please don't have changed your plans.*

"Well," Melissa said, "I'm no longer going to be stuck in New York for this damn last-minute consultation the firm dropped on me. My boss is a lowlife, but on the holidays? He went to Maui. That makes him a new kind of scum."

Jay silently begged her to stop, to tell her anything except what she expected.

She stepped to the doorway and looked out of the den into the hall. Leo wasn't visible. That didn't mean much. He could be hiding under nearly anything, or invisible, or …

She glanced up at the ceiling. Sometimes he'd surprise her from above, crawling along the plaster like a spider.

"Are you coming here?" Jay blurted.

"Don't act happy or anything," Melissa said. "You wanted me to call you ASAP if my plans changed, right?"

"Yeah."

"And they did. I'm going to Maui!"

Jay coughed, almost choking. "What?"

"Maui. Scummy boss turned out to not be so scummy. I'm getting on a plane in about an hour. Better, right?"

"Yeah." Jay kept her throat tight. Her eyes watered. She wiped them with her wrist. "That's why you called me at midnight?"

"I was going to leave a message. I know you turn your ringer on silent at night. Next time, don't make me swear to call you if my plans change. I'm the big sister. I'm the one who's supposed to be looking out for you."

"I have to get back to bed."

"Go. And don't dream anymore. I'll call you tomorrow when I'm beachside. Love you, sis."

"Melissa?"

"Something else?"

"Is it snowing in New York?"

Melissa sighed. "Yes. I'll talk to you tomorrow."

Jay hung up the phone. She tossed it onto the counter beside the old antenna TV, then flicked on the TV to Channel 3 and let herself collapse onto the couch. Under her breath, she thanked God, though not aloud, in case Leo was closer than he appeared.

She doubted she'd sleep, though the static on the TV helped, like white noise. Back when they were kids and shared a room, when Melissa passed out, Jay would flip on the TV and watch whatever played until the station went off the air for the night. The static always sounded so soothing. She'd drift into sleep minutes after it started.

It worked less in the last weeks, or at all in the past few days, but it was habit, and in habit came her only peace. It was hard to tell if she really woke in the mornings or if she'd simply been staring at the blank screen so long her mind drifted off, her body still going like an automaton. Perhaps Leo crawled inside her during those times, wheeled her around, like a test run.

The thought made her stomach turn. She shifted her focus back to the screen

The static looked like snow. She couldn't recall when the real thing had fallen. The fizz and haze from the speakers swelled like the cold winter wind to blow the flakes every which way until they became a web over her eyes. The black speckles between were the trees around her house, barely seen in the background through all that white—everything washed away in a blanket of light.

She lied to herself. She'd become good at it. She did remember when last it had snowed.

The world was white on Christmas day, twenty-two years ago, when she was seventeen, the day her mother killed herself.

In two days, Jay would be the same age as her mother when she died.

December 23, 1:00 pm

Upstairs she listened to the shouting. It was her voice, but not hers, not anymore, the past. Louder than her pleas, her ex-husband's voice commanded her silent. When she refused, she heard her pleas became screams.

"*Stop it!*" she yelled at the basement ceiling. Jay swallowed the memory deep until the sounds faded.

They weren't there. Only a memory.

Her finger bled. She'd pricked it on the needle. Cursing,

she snatched the plastic bottle of alcohol by her feet and doused it over the break in her skin. She hated touching the dead skin of the bodies, but gloves were too clumsy for her to sew. Even so, Leo wouldn't allow her to wear anything when she worked on his gift. "Naked flesh for naked flesh," he said.

Leo sat on her shoulder. He nudged a heel into her clavicle and waved for her finger. She presented it to him. He took it in his tiny hands. Gently, he placed the tip against his lips and kissed the wound. His tongue grazed past the twin rows of razor teeth that slid in and out of his gums when he smiled. It licked a droplet of blood on her skin that he'd sucked out.

She took back her hand and rethreaded the needle. The doll thread was tough but slippery, the bodies' skin leaking fluids she couldn't name. The plugs in her nose kept the smell out but forced her to breathe through her mouth. She swore the missing stench formed a film on her tongue, their taste like a rotten tooth.

The bodies—the *golem*, as Leo called it—was nearly complete. It had to be, in two days' time, by the elf's instructions or else—

"We still need another arm, the right one," Leo said. He combed his hand through her red shoulder-length hair. The catlike claws slid against the lobe of her ear but didn't break the skin. "And a head."

The naked golem lay in a seated position against the basement wall and was covered in potpourri at Leo's insistence, as if in ritual. It only worsened the smell, adding the rot of dead flowers to the decaying mess.

Finally, the random parts resembled something close to the human form. She'd managed to pull the golem upright after stitching the lawyer's hips to the torso and legs, the latter donated from her female personal trainer during her final home visit. Even without life beneath the skin, her muscles remained taught, both in her abdomen and chest with her small firm breasts, and her thick thighs down to her calves. Her black skin had turned partially purple from rot, the woman being her earliest collected victim. The shift in hue made the matching of the parts with the lawyer's hips and another older white man's feet more grotesque.

She'd gotten the feet, hard strong feet, from a self-employed plumber, her third. She'd grown smarter by his turn. With the trainer, if she had anyone who cared about her, they might've checked her books, come knocking to ask if she'd been there, though no one had. Jay found the plumber's number on a flyer from the community board at the post office. She'd asked for his latest appointment so no one would be calling for him that he'd missed prior and so it'd be dark when she'd need to dispose of whatever vehicle he had. The van had sunk easier than she would've guessed.

The last part, its left arm, came from a homeless man she'd found trekking along the highway. She'd have had both of them, but he was lame in his right. He barely spoke when she picked him up or when she offered him food, shelter. He barely spoke or looked surprised either when she raised a hammer above his head and he turned too soon, as if somehow he expected it.

"When will you let me go?" Jay asked.

"That's a silly question," said Leo. "You can go whenever you want. I'm not controlling you."

"You're not controlling me," she said, "but you won't let me go."

"Is that what you want? Like your husband let you go and into the arms of another slut? Like your father wanted to send you away because of that pretty face. Just like your mother's. To beat the flesh away until he could forget her name."

Jay dropped the needle and started to stand when she felt Leo's claw lay itself onto her inner thigh. Her skin dimpled along each of his nails' curved points. She didn't dare move or else they'd sink into her to the muscle, into the nerves. He'd punished her before.

"I'm the only one who loves you, Cupid." He sneered, knowing it wasn't the truth. "Don't you love me, too?"

He slid his palm further up her thigh. The skin of his palm felt like sandpaper. It hurt. He didn't care, perhaps enjoying the fact since he touched her there so often. In her squat, his head only reached her calf, his newly dyed red hat bobbing in line with his grip. He didn't meet her eyes. Instead, his slitted yellow eyes followed the path of his fingers.

"Why do you think everyone leaves you, hates you, Jay? If they hadn't taken you away from him, how far would your father have taken his beatings of pleasure? Did he touch you like I do?"

"Yes," she answered.

"Then you replaced him with a man who couldn't stand the sight of you either. Is that why he beat you, too?"

"I don't know."

Leo's hand stopped only an inch from her vulva. He lightly stroked the sensitive skin along the cleft between her pelvis and thigh, his eyes turning from his hand to her hips.

"And your mother ... How did that pan out?" he said. "So I know you don't want me to leave you. Because if I do, there's only one other person I can go to ... And your sister's not as pretty as you, Cupid."

"You stay away from her."

Leo shrugged. "Then finish the work—"

A knock came from upstairs, at the front door.

"Goddamn it," Leo cursed. "Ain't it just the damnedest

shame, every time you want to get some touch? Go see who it is!"

His hand left her thigh. She immediately stood and rushed up the stairs.

She left the basement, grabbed her pajama pants and the old black band shirt she used whenever she left her work below, and threw them on as fast as she could. She blew her nose hard to dislodge the plugs and tossed them in the kitchen trash. She knew she must stink. Dark-colored stains blotted her arms and legs.

Again, the knock came, louder, from the front door. She crept to the peephole but stopped short when she saw Leo balanced on the windowsill. He peeked through the blinds onto the porch.

He chuckled. "Let him in."

"Look at me. I can't let someone see me—"

Leo laughed louder. "I don't think he'll notice."

Jay used her shirt to make a cursory wipe of her face, then unbolted the door and opened it.

On the porch stood a young man dressed in a teal polo shirt, slacks, and once-white tennis shoes worn tan from what must be a long route to get from house to house out in the country. A backpack's straps hung over his shoulders and he carried a stack of pamphlets Jay recognized instantly as Jehovah's Witness.

"Hello, do you have a minute for me to speak to you about our Lord and Savior, Jesus Christ?" he said, oblivious to her appearance. She wondered if he could see anything behind his black-rimmed Coke bottle glasses.

"As a matter of fact, I believe we do," said Leo. She felt him standing between her ankles. "Nice arm."

Jay nodded and moved aside for him to enter.

"Don't feel bad, Cupid," Leo said. "They don't celebrate

Christmas either."

December 23, 5:05 pm

Jay stood at the edge of the lake and stared into the mirrored surface. The breeze was calm, the water still. She saw her face clearly.

Her mother's face.

They looked so much alike, their photographs often mistaken for each other.

In the reflection, she saw her father step beside her.

"So beautiful," he said. His finger caressed the line of her neck.

Jay closed her eyes until the memory passed, then opened them once more. The water was so shiny above, murky below. She couldn't see more than a foot past its veil. She wondered if those she'd wronged below gazed up at her from the sludge, their faces frozen in silent screams.

Again she closed her eyes. She saw another person screaming in silence, her mother, through the glass window in the double doors of the hospital hallway as the orderlies dragged her away. Her father returned. She could never escape his memory.

"She's sick," he said, not looking at her.

Suddenly, her mother's screams found her ear. Jay glanced up to see her bursting through the doors before the orderlies that had held her caught her again and wrapped their arms around hers to bind her.

"Don't listen to him, Jessica!" her mother screamed. "Don't listen to him!"

Her father clamped his hand onto Jay's shoulder so hard she whimpered. The orderlies dragged her mother back to the doors. Before they closed again, her mother screamed,

"I'm sorry, baby. I'm so sorry."

She opened her eyes. Her father stood again in the reflection, his arm wrapped around her. Suddenly, he grabbed her shoulder and twisted her around.

Jay's ex-husband stood in front of her in her father's place.

"You worthless bitch!" he shouted and he slapped her across the face.

Jay shook her head.

It's not real. Just a memory.

She stepped away from the lake's edge and sat on the muddy shore.

The day in the hospital had been a few weeks before today. On Christmas Eve, they'd locked her mother in a padded room because she'd become violent with the staff. The next day they'd found her somehow freed from her straightjacket, her hospital gown torn into shreds, and the pieces stuffed down her throat until she'd choked to death.

It had been Leo. Her mother wouldn't listen to him. She'd saved those same people, different faces that Jay had murdered. She'd been brave enough to die. Did she know he'd come for her instead? Did she know if Jay didn't obey, that'd Melissa would be next?

Melissa had found out about her father's abuse and called the police. Jay knew she would've never said anything. Her sister had found out the same thing about her husband and helped her use it against him to divorce him and make sure he never returned under threat of imprisonment. Jay knew she would've never said anything about him either. Maybe she wouldn't have said anything even when he killed her. Sometimes she wished he had.

Had she seen Leo then? She couldn't remember when he'd first appeared. A year ago? At first, she'd thought him her nerves, then later her mother's disease. He'd remained even after she took the medicine her doctor had given her. He remained until finally she began to believe. He'd remain until she gave him what he wanted or she failed and he was inherited by another.

There was no one else in the world worth saving except for Melissa. Even if everyone else in the world had to die.

Jay bit her lip, but she couldn't stop the tears.

"You're worthless," she heard her ex-husband whisper in her ear. *He was right.*

But she wouldn't let anyone harm the only person who loved her. Not even if it meant her own life.

She tucked her head between her knees and drew her arms around them until she could no longer hear herself cry.

"It ends tonight," she said.

Everything.

❋ ❋ ❋

Jay pushed herself to her elbows. Somehow she'd laid prostrate into the mud. She must've fallen asleep. The sky was much darker, the sun long gone.

A loud thud from the house made her shuffle around. She rubbed her temples and listened, wondering if she'd imagined it.

Through the basement window, she could see the light was on. It shouldn't be. She always turned it off whenever she left. Something moved behind the glass, then vanished.

Jay stood.

"Hello?" she said. "Leo?"

There was no answer. She brushed the mud from her pants and face and hurried onto the porch and inside.

❋ ❋ ❋

Jay halted on the second to last of the basement stairs and stared at the blinking lights strung over a bright green Christmas tree she'd never put up.

Red and blue bulbs hung along the branches. Silver ornaments of Santa Claus, snowmen, reindeer, and angels draped the gold tinsel that looped it in circles. At its base spread a crocheted green-and-white tree skirt.

Black railroad tracks circled the edge of the skirt. Jay watched a toy train glide along the rails with two cars and a shiny red caboose in tow. It honked as it passed by the feet of the headless golem who sat where she'd left it, leaning against the wall, at the base of the tree, like an expectant child waiting for a few more hours to flee.

The tree shook. Jay jumped on reflex. In its center, the branches trembled, then convulsed. Some of the ornaments fell off their wires. A blue glass bulb shattered on the concrete floor.

At the noise, Leo's head poked through the branches to see the damage, then he noticed Jay and spread open his arms, almost losing his balance. He grabbed a branch to keep from falling, then slid down through them, scraping off fake pine needles under his claws, until the tree spat him onto his feet atop the toy train tracks.

"Tada!" he cheered. "Familiar?"

She shook her head, then stopped.

She did recognize the tree, the train, the colors. She remembered them from a picture, a photo taken when she'd been an infant.

"You might not remember, but I see everything," Leo said. "It's your first Christmas, Cupid."

"*No!*" she screamed. Leo stepped back. "No more games. It ends now, tonight."

He cocked his head. "Tonight?"

"I only want one thing."

Leo jumped up and down, clapping. "A present!"

"What are you?" she whispered.

"Nothing."

"No, Leo, I deserve to know."

"Then ask the right question."

"*I said no more games!*" She rushed toward him and snatched the elf off the ground. "*Why?*"

The elf wasn't in her hands. Instead, she held a curly red-haired rag doll.

Her mother had sewn the doll to resemble her. Her first gift.

She threw it against the basement wall. Leo sat on the golem's lap and twirled the whiskers of his beard.

She repeated, "Why?"

The elf shrugged, his answer for everything. "Christmas magic? Winter solstice? Humanity's collective belief in dreams and candy-cane wishes? Perhaps I'm the Devil and on the day the most glorious birth is celebrated, ol' hellfire wants to take the biggest shit he can muster, and *voila*, here I am. Of course, I don't believe in the Devil, but who believes in me either … Except you? Could be there's no meaning, coincidence and happenstance, nonsense and shadows. Or maybe you're just fucking crazy—and crazy's the birthplace of miracles."

"I'm not crazy," Jay answered.

She knelt and picked up the saw she used to sever the bodies for the golem. She placed its serrated edge by her throat. "I'm the final piece."

"You can't—" The elf shook his head and chuckled. "I'm the *only* one who loves you, Cupid."

His sneer vanished. He crawled beneath the tree. Slowly, he used his weight to push a cardboard box twice his size from under the tree. A bow adorned its top. Dark stains crept down its edges.

Leo peeked around the box. "You've already given me my final gift."

He pointed toward the basement window. Jay looked.

It was light outside. That shouldn't be right. When she'd left the lake, the sun had set.

Her mouth trembled. "What day is it?"

Leo smiled. "Christmas Eve, silly."

Jay reached into her pants pocket and took out her phone. She swiped it on.

The date read the 24th. There was a notification, too, a missed call. The contact name read *Melissa*.

Leo undid his belt and let it clank to the floor. With both his clawed hands, he ripped off his green tunic.

Jay had never seen him without it. His body wasn't there.

Where his torso should be, his flesh looked like a nest of worms. Uncovered, the tendrils snaked in the air as if tasting it, others reached to the floor. One of their featureless heads dove against a puddle of dried blood by the elf's feet and pounded on it until its nub crushed itself. Another picked up a stray bit of bloodied skin and shook it before it tossed it as if unsatisfactory. Several more fell free from Leo and slithered across the floor toward the golem.

Jay watched them slide up the stringed-together corpse, then burrow into its skin. More dropped off the mass in Leo and rushed to do the same.

Leo picked up the needle and thread from the floor. His body shriveled as more and more escaped toward the corpse, until the skin beneath his face sunk in on itself, like an emaciated child.

He smiled. His gums had receded so that his teeth gleamed like a mouthful of razors. He wheezed, his voice like the static from the TV. "I can finish the last stitches … No more pupa, true flesh ... Cupid ..."

Jay pressed on her voicemail. Melissa had left a message.

Her sister's voice played through the speaker. "Don't be mad at me. I lied about Maui. I wanted to surprise you, and I know you would've said no if I asked. Can't say no now, I'm at the Nashville airport! I already rented a car, so don't worry about picking me up. You know you live in the middle of nowhere. Just be home okay! I'll be there late on the twenty-third—"

Jay saw the stairs. Blood stained the steps, as if something had been dragged down them.

She dropped the phone and ran up the stairs. Her shoulder slammed against the basement door and she sprinted into the living room.

The house was freezing. She felt wind, the cold outside.

She stopped in the hall. The front door lay open, the breeze unhindered. And lying inside, over the threshold, was a body.

Jay screamed.

December 24, 8:49 pm

Jay held her sister's hand. The fingers had long went cold, but she couldn't let go. The tears had come for hours. Now, nothing. *Nothing.*

"*Why didn't you listen!*" Jay shrieked. There was no anger in the words, only meaningless sound, like the answer she already knew.

There is no Leo, is there, Jay? You are your mother's daughter.

If the thing existed or not, neither answer mattered anymore.

"I wanted to see you." Her eyes stared out the still-open front door into the dark. The wind had picked up. It threw the trees' limbs in her yard into a frenzy and flowed into the house. Her skin prickled with goosebumps, but she couldn't feel the chill.

Only her sister's fingers.

No sound came from the basement.

Why should it? Leo wasn't there, if he'd dissolved or if he ever existed at all. Nothing was there except the dead... Except those her psychosis had caused her to murder for a reason that no longer held any meaning.

Don't lie to yourself, Jay. You didn't kill them to save Melissa, did you?

She squeezed her sister's fingers.

You killed them to try and save yourself.

"He wasn't real. I did this."

And Melissa won't be the last. Will she?

"I'm so ..."

Jay let go of her sister's hand. She pushed herself to her feet, her legs long ago fallen asleep. Despite the rush of needles, she forced herself to the stairs and heaved herself against the railing.

Halfway to the second floor, she heard shouting. It wasn't real, another memory. She didn't stop. Behind her she heard her own whimpers and pleas, then the sounds of knuckles striking her face.

"You want me to kill you, you stupid bitch. Is that what you want?" her ex-husband threatened.

You should've killed me. I never deserved to live.

She reached the upstairs when she saw her father's back near the closed spare bedroom door. Gently, he knocked.

"Open the door, Jessica," he said. The door crept open. Jay saw herself, fifteen, watch him unblinking from the crack. He pushed the door wider, then reached for her face to caress it with the back of his fingers. "It's just us now."

He stepped inside, past her. Jay's younger self met her

own eyes with nothing but hatred.

No more pain, for anyone.

Behind the girl, her father said, "Close the door, Cupid."

Jay turned away and knocked open the master bedroom door.

The room was silent. No Leo waiting to surprise her. No more ghosts from the past. Only a bare mattress where she'd killed the lawyer. Atop its surface, a curved red stain stretched where the man's blood had outlined his body. It seemed to smile at her. Jay smiled back.

She opened the nightstand drawer. Inside she found the Ruger. With the smile still on her face, she brought the gun to her temple and fired.

December 25, 7:06 am

Jay awoke.

She was on the floor. Her cheeks felt the rough carpet, hard with the dust that had caked in it over the past two years.

She tried to lift her head. What little strength she had left refused. Blood matted her hair, holding her firm. Pain seeped through her skull and ran like a river down the sides of her neck to empty in her throat. She gagged on her breath until she could spit up the tacky blood that had clumped against her windpipe. The coppery taste stung her tongue.

Her eyes opened but barely focused. The world washed into hues, melting, diluted in a wave of grays. Light crept around the end of the bed where she must've fallen when she shot herself. It came from the blinds against the glass doors that lead to the bedroom's balcony.

It was morning. The sunlight reached almost to her face through the blinds. It only came that far inside when the sun rose in the east where the window faced.

She crawled her hand up her chest, then her neck until it found her tattered hair. Her fingers crept over her skull. They seeped into a deep gash above her temple that ran the length of her fingers up her skull. She felt the torn flesh, the bone beneath, perhaps exposed. Her fingertips sunk deep in the wound, yet no pain, the nerves still in shock or dead where she'd failed to do what she should've done from the beginning.

Jay ground her teeth and pushed her head to turn toward the open bedroom door. The gun lay against the door stopper. There had to be at least one more bullet. This time, she'd stick the barrel into her mouth. No missing this time.

A noise came from downstairs.

No, not below. On the stairs.

Her vision blurred worse. She clenched her eyes shut and tried to focus on the sound. It grew louder. They were footsteps, coming up.

She opened her eyes. The colors worsened. They burned. She squinted as someone stepped into the door frame. Whoever came up the stairs flipped on the overhead hall light. The bulb cast them in silhouette, though she couldn't see well enough to discern their face regardless.

"Jay?" spoke the shadow.

Melissa? It resembled Melissa's voice, but her ears had begun to ring and made it difficult to tell. The sound of her name echoed in her skull, deeper and muffled, as if the word had traveled through the speaker's nose instead of her mouth.

Her sister wasn't dead. Had she only imagined it?

Jay struggled to say her sister's name. Blood must still be in her throat or else her lungs hurt too much to obey. Clots had formed in her nose to stuff out any help of breath from there, the smell of the world washed clean.

You are your mother.

Her sister came into the room. Jay felt her kneel beside her, felt her hands on her tacky hair, but couldn't move her head to see her.

"What did you do to yourself?" Melissa asked, the voice still distorted.

Had she made up everything? Were there bodies in the lake, the basement?

You are your mother's daughter, aren't you, Jay?

Melissa! Jay wanted to scream. Her voice didn't rise above a whimper, spit bubbling out of her lips. *Please ... Call no one. Let me die, Melissa. Just let me die.*

Jay tried to lift her head higher, squint her eyes clear. Both refused. Her sister stood and walked past her, further into the bedroom.

She pressed her lungs, anything to get out one word in case this moment's awakening had only been a small reprieve before her life finally fled.

I'm sorry, Melissa. I'm so sorry—

Her nose cleared, the clots pushed out enough for air to rush into her nostrils. Jay sucked in deep to get enough to speak. The room smelled of the sanitizer she'd sprayed on the mattress days ago after the lawyer, but the stench of decay overpowered it, though she'd cleaned nearly all of his corpse from the bed.

No, you're imagining the smell. There was no lawyer. You didn't kill anyone.

There was also another odor, like rotting potpourri.

The world bled white. Light poured through the window.

Jay tilted her head around the bed with all her strength. She saw Melissa standing in silhouette against the pulled-back blinds.

Jay squinted her eyes to force them to focus. Her sister's

silhouette smeared against the sunlight, its parts all wrong, misshapen.

"Merry Christmas," said the shadow. "It's snowing, Cupid."

S⁂anta's ❄Village

Evan Purcell

Nate felt a blast of cold air on his face. It wasn't winter yet, but they were already high enough on the mountain to feel a change of temperature. Unless it was just his imagination. "Almost there?" he asked his older brother.

Jeff ignored him.

Nate tried again. "Hey, Jeff!"

Still nothing.

When Jeff was with his girlfriend, he tended to block out the rest of the world. Well, he tended to block out Nate.

"I think your brother's talking to you," Maxine whispered loud enough for Nate to hear.

"What?" Jeff said. "I thought that was just the wind." He wrapped his arm around her narrow shoulders.

"You're so mean," she said, pulling away and slapped

him on the shoulder. Nate could tell she didn't really care about his feelings because she was laughing as she said it.

"I am not," Jeff said, and he was laughing, too.

Nate knew he was the tagalong. As soon as Maxine agreed to come along with them, Nate knew he would be the unwanted extra person. He knew that he'd be struggling to keep up with them and their long, teenager legs.

They'd been walking up the side of the mountain for the longest time, but they finally reached the top. Jeff and Maxine saw Santa's Village first because they were faster, but Nate wasn't too far behind.

"Dang," Jeff said. "This place is …"

"Creepy?" Maxine asked.

"Awesome!" he said.

Nate wasn't impressed. He knew the place had been closed for decades. He knew the rides wouldn't work and the decorations would be half-broken, but he wasn't expecting … this.

Santa's Village.

The workshop was water-damaged and boarded up. The little stone elves were all missing body parts. A human-sized gingerbread man with half a face was stuck in the dirt at their feet. Everything—every single thing in this awful place— was crumbling into nothing.

It didn't look safe.

Without realizing what he was doing, Nate grabbed onto Jeff's shirt. "I don't like it here."

Jeff shook him off. "Just give it a chance," he said. "This place is crazy."

The three of them walked through the candy cane entrance. They explored the little yellow pathway for a few minutes, but Jeff and Maxine sped up once they got to the dark cave tunnel behind the workshop.

"Jeff!" Maxine squealed. "It's the tunnel of love!"

None of the swan-shaped cars were functional anymore, but that wouldn't stop them from at least walking through it.

"Okay," Jeff agreed, his eyes lighting up. "Let's do it."

"Okay!" Nate said, trying to sound excited.

Jeff turned around, acknowledging his little brother for the first time since they got there. "This is a two-person ride," he said.

"What?"

Maxine tapped Nate on the shoulder. "It means you should probably explore another area of the park," she said.

"But …"

Jeff sighed. "Just go."

"But …" Nate said again. He knew his voice sounded whiny, but he couldn't help himself. He'd been looking forward to this stupid trip for weeks. It was bad enough that none of the rides were working. Now he had to walk around the park by himself? That wasn't what he'd planned.

"This is our alone time," Jeff said. He squeezed Maxine's hand and she kissed him on the cheek. "Alone time." That was what Mom and Dad said when they locked the bedroom door and wouldn't let Nate into their room.

"Fine, then!" Nate said. "I'm gonna have so much fun by myself."

Jeff didn't say anything.

"So much fucking fun!" He wasn't supposed to say the f-word. That was for grown-ups. He knew that would get a rise out of Jeff.

But Jeff still didn't say anything. Instead, he half-waved at his little brother and then led Maxine in the other direction.

And Nate was alone. Totally alone.

Whatever.

He stood there for a bit, just in case Jeff changed his

mind or felt guilty or something. When Jeff didn't come back, Nate mumbled the f-word one more time—just because he could—and walked toward the big Christmas tree in the center of the park.

The tree didn't move or light up or do anything special. It just sat there. Like a tree. It was behind a tall glass cage and had presents all around its bottom. Most of the glass panels were broken and dust had gotten inside. Stupid thing.

He picked up one of the presents—a little purple one— only to find it wasn't real present at all, but a painted wooden block. It wasn't even purple all the way around, just on the side that would've been seen by the public. The rest was unpainted.

Nate suddenly got the urge—the uncontrollable urge—to smash the present into a million purple pieces. He wasn't quite strong enough for a million pieces, but he stepped on it and the rotted wood crumpled like a cardboard box. Which was okay.

He left the ruined present on the ground outside the tree's enclosure and then walked toward the snowman area. On the way, he saw a half-faced gingerbread man lying on the ground. It looked so sad—what with half a face and all—and the mushy ruined half reminded him of the present he'd just smashed. He stared into the man's fake gumdrop eye for the longest time. "Sorry," he muttered. He was apologizing for the present, and for the two times he said the f-word, and for everything, really. He was sorry that the gingerbread man had to sit there with half a face for all eternity.

But mostly, he was just sorry for himself. Maybe Jeff would find him and take him home soon.

❊ ❊ ❊

The tunnel of love smelled like animal urine, but Jeff didn't seem to notice. He was too busy exploring the rough surfaces of Maxine's tongue with his own. She tried to say something, but he kissed her harder.

He wanted this to be a magical moment, dammit, and he knew that if he let her talk, she'd tell him that they needed to check on Nate.

Maxine's mouth was so warm. He wanted this moment to last forever, or at least the next few minutes, but she pushed him away. "We need to check on Nate," she said.

He knew it! He saw that coming, and damn the little brat for acting so defenseless all the time. Even when he's not around, he still ruined things.

"Five more minutes," Jeff said, and kissed her again.

"No more minutes."

"Two more minutes."

She pushed him away a second time. "Jeff," she said, "how old is your brother?"

"I don't know," he said. "Six? Ten?"

"Come on," she said. "This place has a lot of holes and rusted metal and stuff."

"Fine," he said. Together, they walked out of the tunnel of love. Once they left the darkness, Jeff realized how weirdly quiet the whole place was. No wind. No animal noises. Nothing at all, really. "Nate!" he shouted.

No answer.

"Nate!"

Still nothing.

Jeff felt a pinprick of fear in his bellybutton area, and it started to grow. He was getting a little nervous. Christ. Why did Maxine have to talk about rusted metal and all that stuff? His little brother was a royal pain, but anything happened to the kid ...

"NATE!"

It wasn't like Nate to run off like this. He was a boring little kid, scared of everything except video games and Star Wars. He couldn't have gone too far.

Jeff walked around the snowman area and the peppermint sticks, but he didn't see anyone. Maxine followed him every step of the way, but she didn't seem too nervous. "Where'd he go?" Jeff asked.

Maxine shrugged. She was useless, too. This whole trip was not turning out like he'd hoped. And *BAM!*, Jeff accidentally slammed his foot into one of the stone elves lining the path.

"Christ!" he shouted.

"Are you okay?"

"No, I'm not okay! Look at this stupid thing!" The elf was looking up at him with a giant smile and two squinty black eyes. Its suit used to be green, but most of its paint had chipped off over the years. "What are you looking at?" he asked the statue.

It didn't respond, of course.

"I said … what the hell are you looking at?"

"Come on, Jeff," Maxine said. "I think he's cute."

"Well, I think he could use a face lift." With that, Jeff picked up a rock and bashed it against the elf with all his strength. Its nose crumbled off. So did half its jaw. "See? Doesn't he look better now?"

Maxine didn't even look at the elf. "Let's go find your brother," she said.

Jeff was done listening to everybody else. He'd taken them up here to have a little fun, and he was going to have some fun, Goddammit, even if he had to do it alone. "Jeeze, Max," he said, "stop being such a downer."

Maxine's face went blank, but only for a second. "I'm

bringing you down? This is my fault?" she said.

As soon as the words left his mouth, he realized he'd made a mistake. His girlfriend was not the best at taking criticism.

Maxine puffed out air through her nostrils. She walked over to the elf and pushed it as hard as she could. It teetered at first, then went crashing to the ground. On impact, its head popped off.

"Are you happy?" she said, annoyance flashing across her face like a traffic light changing from yellow to red.

Before Jeff could say anything else, he saw a small figure dart behind the cottage. Apparently it didn't want to be seen, but Jeff had seen it nonetheless.

That has to be Nate, he thought. Nate was the only other person here, and the figure was about his size.

Christ, if he's playing a game, so help me God ...

They followed the shadow without talking. Maxine looked a bit confused. It was clear she hadn't seen or heard anything

"Hello?" he called. "Hello?"

Nothing.

"Hello?"

And then the silence—that throbbing, powerful silence— gave way to something else. A skittering noise. It seemed to come from every direction at once, alternating between loud and quiet, loud and quiet, until Jeff felt dizzy from the noise.

He wanted Maxine to clutch at his side, to cling to him for support, but she didn't, and he kind of hated her for it.

The skittering noise crescendo, each tiny rustle converging into loud, single pair of footsteps. Footsteps that were approaching them from the darkness. At first, Jeff couldn't see the figure approaching, but he knew it was there. He knew it was small and dark—and walking directly toward them, but he didn't know what it was.

Until he saw the pointy hat. And the pointy shoes. And

the black eyes that grew larger—impossibly large—as the figure approached. It looked angry. No, it looked furious.

"Uh, Jeff," Maxine whispered. She clung to his side now, but by this point he didn't even notice. He was staring at the approaching elf statue. Its movements were awkward, like a child taking its first steps. Something that was not accustomed to moving about.

Something … that shouldn't exist—but did.

"Go," Jeff whispered. "Go now."

When Maxine didn't start running, Jeff did. Sure enough, she followed. They barrelled through the park, over rocks and other broken things, until they made it to the workshop.

The footsteps behind them didn't stop. They didn't run, either. Just slow, even *thuds* against the ground.

"Is it safe in there?" Maxine asked.

Jeff didn't answer. He gripped the rusted handle and twisted and pulled as hard as he could. He felt pieces of it— cold slivers of the metal—jab into his palm. "Open, please open," he whispered.

But it didn't. They were trapped.

❄ ❄ ❄

After sulking around for fifteen minutes, Nate had had enough. He'd seen everything he needed to see, and it sure wasn't a lot: some concrete snowmen with missing carrot noses … a carousel that had been half-dismantled before people realized it wasn't worth anything … even a bathroom shaped like a gingerbread house. He was done.

Besides, fifteen minutes was a long enough time for Jeff to start feeling guilty about how he had treated his little brother. Head held high and hands jammed into his pockets, Nate began walking back toward the main courtyard.

He wasn't scared. He was alone, but he wasn't scared. He only thought about his brother, about what he could say to make him feel guilty for abandoning him.

When Nate passed by a maintenance shed shaped like an igloo, he heard low breathing coming from within the building through a partially open window. "Hello?" he whispered. He put his face against the glass, squinting his eyes to make out any shapes inside. It was too dusty, though. He couldn't see anything.

Well, he saw movements. Something was inside, something low to the ground. It swayed back and forth. What was it?

Nate tapped three times on the glass. "Jeff," he whispered. Then he raised his voice a little. "Jeff?"

No answer.

But the figure inside heard him because it turned around and started walking toward the dusty window.

"Jeff, are you okay?" Nate asked.

The figure shook his head no. He gestured for Nate to lean closer. He wiggled his impossibly long fingers through the air. Jeff didn't have such long fingers but maybe had found something in the park, a costume or something, which he put on in the hopes of scaring Nate.

This doesn't feel right, Nate thought. His whole body was tense and his neck hairs were standing up. He felt, deep down in his bones, that something was very, very wrong.

Still … he should always listen to his big brother. He leaned closer.

The figure on the other side of the glass leaned closer, too. It raised one hand and wiped away at some of the dust.

What was it? Nate still couldn't see it clearly because there was so much dust.

The figure cocked its head.

BAM!

In a burst of sudden movement and loud shattering noises, the window broke open and the wall collapsed. Glass flew everywhere. Dust did, too. Something large and white dove at Nate. It had a spherical head and two black lumps for eyes. There was a perfect hole in the exact center of its face, where some small bird had made a nest.

Snowman!

The thing clawed through the air. Three twig fingers on each tree branch arm, all reaching toward Nate, digging at his shirt.

Nate felt jagged fingertips tear at his shirt. He twisted to the side, just managing to wiggle out of the snowman's grasp. It grunted like an animal.

"Jeff!" Nate shouted. "Jeff! Help me!"

There was no response. Not even an echo. Then, rising out of the silence ... his brother's voice! "Nate! Nate!" It sounded far away.

The voice had come from the workshop!

Nate looked around but the snowman had disappeared. He couldn't see it anywhere. The area around that igloo was silent and still. He circled around and headed toward the workshop.

The sky grew darker. The clouds were thick and full of rain and blotted out the sun.

Nate struggled to catch his breath. "I'm ... here," he whispered. But where was his brother? He looked around the corner of the workshop. Two figures—Jeff and Maxine—were standing at the door, trying to yank it open.

"We're here," Jeff said, but Nate had already seen them.

With a groan, the workshop door shifted but didn't open. There was a padlock in the way, something they hadn't noticed in their panic, and from the look of it, the damn thing had rusted shut a long time ago.

Nate ran to his brother. "Did you … Did you see that snowman?"

"Give me room," Jeff ordered. "It's gonna break soon. It'll open."

Nate trusted him. Besides, Jeff was big and strong. He played lacrosse.

Creeeaaaaak.

The weathered wood splintered and the hasp fell away. Jackpot! But before the door could open completely, it stopped. A foot of open space. Light spilled from the inside of the building. And slowly, an elf hobbled out. He was smaller than any of the statues they'd seen. Part of its leg had crumbled away, and it looked like a pirate with a peg leg. "Tis the season," the elf said.

Maxine backed away.

The elf took them all in with a sweeping glance. "You know, children always get what they deserve at Christmas time."

"What does that mean?" Jeff said.

Another elf stepped out of this shadows. This one was headless. "It means payback," the creature said. God knows where the voice came from. Perhaps from the hole in his open neck.

Nate wanted to throw up.

The headless elf pointed straight at Maxine. "Get them," he ordered.

Jeff jumped. Nate had never seen his brother this scared before. It didn't seem right.

More elves surrounded them, their movements jerky, like broken toys. Paint chips flecked off them and left trails on the ground.

There was nowhere to run. They were in the middle of an abandoned theme park on the top of a mountain. People were forbidden to come here. Hell, people were afraid to come here. And now Nate knew why.

Nate noticed Maxine nudge Jeff. It was some sort of secret boyfriend–girlfriend code. She expected him to do something, although Nate didn't know what his brother could do against so many.

He had faith in his brother, though. Whatever plan Jeff had, it would totally work. His plans always worked. Nate trusted that his big brother would take care of them. He just wished it would happen faster.

"Hey." Jeff motioned for the first elf to come forward.

It did. Its peg leg made crunching noises. In slow, deliberate movements, it tried to attack Jeff. Its fists pummelled the air. Jeff dodged it easily. He smiled, the little victory clearly going to his head.

"Be careful," Maxine warned.

"Yeah, yeah," Jeff said. He steadied himself, pulled back his own fist, and punched the elf right in its face. There was no damage done to the elf, but Jeff let out with a loud, painful scream.

Jeff's knees buckled and he collapsed onto the grassy ground. Maxine grabbed him under his armpits and tried to pull him back to his feet.

"You're okay," she said. "They're tiny."

Jeff shook his head. "They're stone!" he said. He held up his hand for her to see. It was twisted unnaturally, and there was a sharp bump under his ring finger. "I think ... it's broken."

The elf pushed Maxine away. He got closer to Jeff. "You get what you deserve," he said. In a single motion, he balled up his stone fist and punched Jeff right in the face. Nate couldn't describe the sound it made, not in words, but it was a sound that echoed through his brain and wouldn't leave.

Jeff's nose and jaw shattered in a cloud of gore.

Nate's big brother, the kid who was supposed to protect them all, fell backward and didn't move. Blood pooled under him.

"Please," Maxine whimpered. "Don't. Please."

They didn't listen.

"Let me go," she begged. "Take the boy, but let me go. I wasn't even supposed to be here."

The elves were upon her now and rode her to the ground. Grabbing at her. Tearing at her. Their little fingers with their sharp, irregular edges ... They tore at her clothes, her flesh, her eyes.

"Please," Maxine howled. "I don't deserve this. I didn't do anything."

The headless elf walked to her and placed his head into her hands.

"Oh," Maxine moaned from a place deep inside her. She lowered the elf head to the ground.

The next elf—this one wearing red—limped forward. One of its legs was twisted. He held a long, metallic stick painted like a candy cane. He set the curved end to the ground and positioned himself next to the sobbing girl.

"I'm sorry," Maxine said. "I didn't mean ..."

The red elf giggled. He tapped the candy cane against Maxine's temple. She was moving too much, so he put one pointy shoe on top of her head to keep her still. He raised the candy cane high over his shoulder, like a golfer.

"Please."

Three.

Two.

One.

The red elf brought the cane down. Maxine's head made a juicy noise and was separated from her body. It flew through the air. As it hit the ground and rolled, all the elves did a little victory dance.

Nate didn't realize he'd been screaming the whole time.

❋ ❋ ❋

Pain. Searing, unimaginable pain.

When Jeff came to, his brother and girlfriend were gone. He wiped the blood from his eyes, careful not to touch the torn, ragged gash where his nose had been.

"Nate," he croaked. "Maxine. Nate."

With a grunt, he bit back the pain and managed to sit up.

There was a red trail that started in his own crimson pool and led toward the workshop. Someone, perhaps two someones, had been dragged there.

With two fingers, Jeff reached up and touched his face. Slickness—that was the blood—and lumps—those were the twisted bone. He was mangled, probably beyond recognition.

He'd always seen himself as a goodlooking guy. His jaw was strong, and his aunt always told him that his great-grandfather was a Native America, which meant he had some killer cheekbones. He rarely got zits, and the freckles along the bridge of his nose weren't particularly obtrusive.

Yeah, Jeff had been handsome.

But nNow he had mush for a face.

How was he possibly going to live the rest of his life like this? How could he find a girlfriend? How could he show himself in public?

Jeff coughed a little. Blood and small amounts of bile dripped out of his mouth. He didn't throw up, but he probably would've felt better if he had.

He didn't have time to think about his own blood. His girlfriend and his brother were still out there, and there was a blood trail leading back to the workshop.

He crawled toward the building. He didn't call out anyone's name, though. He kept quiet.

There was a rosy glow coming from inside the workshop. That hadn't been there before.

Using the doorframe, he was able to stand, and once on his feet, he gave the door a push. It creaked open. He was in too much pain to think of a plan, so he was just going to have to see how things played out.

On the inside, the workshop was cozy, warm, and inviting. Rows of elves happily banged away at toys on an assembly line. A Christmas tree rotated in the center of the workshop, shining its multicolored lights in all directions. And at the far end, a massive Santa Claus sat on a throne, and in his lap was Nate.

It.

Not his.

This Santa wasn't quite human.

Just beyond them, a few of the elves were decorating Maxine's headless body as if it were a tree. They sang nonsense words. Some of them laughed. Otherwise, there was no other sound in the workshop. Even the machinery didn't make any noises.

Nate looked at Jeff, his eyes blank. He didn't seem afraid of the Santa. He seemed almost … comfortable.

Jeff motioned his younger brother to come to him.

Santa ignored him. The elves ignored him, except for one who threw a handful of glitter in his direction. The only person to acknowledge Jeff was his brother. Nate looked over and said, "I don't know."

"What do you mean you don't know? What don't you know?" He didn't even know if Nate could hear him.

"You should've protected us," Nate answered. "You should've protected Maxine."

"Yes, but I'll ... I'll protect you now." His voice caught in his throat.

Nate leaned his small body against Santa's giant gut. "I don't need protecting. You guys were naughty, but I wasn't. I'm safe here."

Jeff watched the Santa as its black eyes blinked and its head swayed left and right. It looked wrong, simple as that. It looked like what a toy factory's cheap copy of a human would look like.

"Nate," Jeff begged. "Come on. Come with me. Slowly."

Santa laughed, its whole belly trembling. Nate shook in its lap.

"Don't listen to bad children," Santa told Nate. It stroked his hair with one gloved hand. Jeff noticed with horror that there were little red spots on its white gloves. Blood.

"Yes, sir," Nate said.

"And you," Santa continued, "have been a good boy. You didn't hurt anyone. Not like those other two." He was talking about Jeff and Maxine, the naughty ones.

Jeff touched his face, smearing some of the blood down his cheek. "But we can leave, then," he protested. "I already paid my price." Like the elf he had destroyed, he'd suffered a shattered nose and a mangled chin. An eye for an eye. It should've been over.

Santa shook its head. Its shark eyes never left Nate, though.

An elf walked into the workshop. He held a smashed present in both hands. It was purple and crumpled.

Santa continued to stroke Nate's hair. "It looks like someone crushed one of my darlings," it said. "There's one more price to pay."

Jeff didn't understand. He didn't remember smashing any presents. He hadn't seen any presents like that anywhere.

Then he saw Nate, saw the widening sense of horror spread across the younger boy's face, and he realized what his brother had done.

Oh God!

"We can't accept that," Santa said. He scratched the tip of his red nose. "We believe in giving what you deserve. Now, if you come clean, I will be nice. I will only crush your bottom half, not the rest. But you need to admit what you did."

Nate looked at his big brother, panic across his face.

Crush?

Santa gestured toward a toy-making machine in the corner of the room. It looked like a trash compactor decorated in alternating stripes of white and red. It had a hole in the top where could be lowered into the machine. It was big enough for a person to fit.

"Please," Jeff said. Blood was dripping into his mouth again. "I … Please."

"If you lower yourself inside voluntarily," Santa continued, "I will only crush you halfway." His deep, booming voice laughed. "Your little brother can leave … and come back with help if he so chooses. However, that deal is only if you admit to crushing the present."

Jeff looked at his little brother. Then the machine.

He would lower himself into the machine. He knew he would. If he survived that thing, if he could crawl out of it with his upper body still functional … what sort of life would he be able to live? He couldn't imagine. No legs. Half a face. He'd be nothing.

But he was the big brother. He had to protect Nate, even when life wasn't fair.

Wordlessly, Jeff stumbled toward the machine and climbed a small ladder until he was able to pull himself onto the top of the machine. Then he lowered his legs inside.

Santa clapped. He laughed and clapped.

"Now," Santa said to Nate.

Now?

Next to Nate was a large peppermint stick lever protruding from the wall.

Jeff saw the look on his little brother's face. At first, it was confusion, but that quickly morphed into a mixture of horror and queasiness. Nate was going to have to pull the lever himself. He wasn't just allowing his brother's legs to be crushed; he was actively making it happen.

Nate—eyes wide—looked straight at Jeff. Christ, he looked at Jeff for permission. He was asking Jeff to willingly sacrifice his legs so that Nate could go free. After everything …

Jeff looked away. He couldn't. He couldn't bear to look at his brother anymore.

"I, um …" Nate said.

Jeff tried not to move his lower half. Metal pieces were cutting into his legs.

Nate walked over and grabbed the candy cane lever.

"Wait," Jeff said. He couldn't do it. He couldn't go through with this. There had to be another way.

Nate looked at his big brother. He had a blank look on his face. No expression at all. "I'm so sorry," he whispered.

Then he pulled the lever.

At first, nothing happened. Then the floor beneath Nate opened up and the younger boy disappeared into darkness. The machine never started. Jeff was safe, and Nate was gone.

Jeff didn't understand. He looked at Santa for some explanation.

The elves started cackling. Like their voices, their laughter was shrill and loud. Even the broken elf head laughed.

Santa joined in, and his laughter was loud enough and

deep enough to rock the entire building. When it finally stopped, he turned to look straight at Jeff. "Santa hates liars most of all," he said.

HERE HE COMES A-WANDERING

Matt Cowan

Kevin had been lying awake in bed, lamenting his grandmother's insistence on confiscating the kids' phones during their visit, when he heard a knock at the front door of her house. Excitement for upcoming days filled with snowball fights, family games, and delicious feasts around a packed table, topped off by the opening of gifts on Christmas morning, kept sleep at bay. Getting up, he wiped a layer of frost from the window that overlooked the front porch.

At first, he thought it might be late-arriving relatives, but reconsidered upon seeing the huddled figure wearing a long black overcoat and tall top hat in the dim glow of the porch light. The figure withdrew a thin, pale hand from the door while holding a package tucked under one arm. When the door opened, Kevin strained to listen through the floor. Grandmother was saying something about him having to make deliveries so late on the night before Christmas Eve. The other's reply was too muffled to understand. A moment later the door closed and he watched the man slink back toward the street. Kevin wondered where his car was; none were visible that didn't belong to people in the house. The man turned to look up at him from the driveway; his face was pallid and gaunt and pools of darkness shrouded his eyes. He wore an old-fashioned suit with a vest and necktie, the style of which reminded Kevin of the men illustrated in *A Christmas Carol*. Originally, he'd seemed short, but this was because he walked so hunched over, like one stiff from a long slumber. The hint of a smile played across his gray lips as he gave Kevin a tip of his hat before continuing on to disappear into the darkness of the winter night.

✻ ✻ ✻

Kevin was still in his pajamas the next morning when his favorite cousins, Greg and Tanya, arrived. They gathered around Grandmother's long dining table heaped with an assortment of breakfast foods.

"Who was at the door last night, Grandma?" Kevin asked between bites of bacon.

Grandmother put her hands on her hips. "You mean the man who arrived while you were supposed to be sleeping?"

Kevin gave her a sheepish grin. "I tried. I just couldn't."

"Well, if you must know, it was just a man delivering a package."

"What was it?"

"You'll see in a bit. Finish your breakfast," she ordered.

✻ ✻ ✻

After breakfast, the kids moved into the cinnamon-scented front room. It was a wonder to behold. The wall paintings were adorned with garland. Red and green candles stood beside wooden nutcrackers on end tables and window sills. "God Rest Ye Merry Gentlemen" chimed softly from the stereo. At the core of the festive room was a massive pine tree with multicolored blinking lights flowing toward a giant star that nearly touched the ceiling. Bulbous glass and ceramic ornaments of all shapes and sizes were visible behind a rope of silver garland. The kids ignored all these adornments, their eyes drawn to the mountain of colorful packages surrounding the tree's base. Soon they were circling it, examining the offerings, each seeking out ones bearing their name.

Kevin had uncovered five belonging to him when he spied one apart from the others. Its wrapping paper seemed out of place. Swirls of dark gold, rich crimson, and fluid silver flowed across its surface. To Kevin, it looked like something that belonged under the tree of a royal family in ancient England. Its tag was a piece of red silk with stilted ink handwriting that read "To: Kevin." It did not say from whom it came.

"That was what was delivered last night," Grandmother said. "Do you have any idea who would have sent it?"

Kevin ran his fingers across the slick paper. "I can't even imagine." He lifted it and was surprised by its weight. "Can I open it?"

"Later," his father answered. "Everyone can open one present after lunch, like always. For now, you should get dressed and find something to keep you occupied while the adults get everything ready for tonight."

"Can I have my phone back?" Tanya implored.

"No," Grandmother answered quickly. "Today and tomorrow are family time. You can have your phones back on

Christmas morning."

"Can we go outside and play in the snow?" Greg asked with a broad smile.

Grandmother nodded. "So long as you stay on our property. We don't want to go searching for you kids like last year."

They agreed, vanishing to their rooms to get ready while Kevin's aunts and uncles split off to either help with the cooking or watch football in the living room.

❊ ❊ ❊

Kevin and nine of his cousins traded the smells of indoor baking for the crisp scent of snow that was mounded in the backyard. A large-scale snowball fight was waged before some decided to go back inside and others moved to the front yard to make a snowman. Kevin, Tanya, and Greg slipped beyond the tree line that skirted the edge of the yard.

"Let's go back to the same place as last year," Tanya suggested.

"I don't know about that," Kevin said with a frown.

"Why not?" Greg asked. "You scared because of what happened?"

"No," Kevin answered sharply. "It's just that we said we wouldn't."

"We won't stay long," Tanya pleaded. "I just want to see if it's still the same."

Just then a call rang out from the house. "Who's ready to open presents?" Grandmother yelled.

That ended the discussion as everyone raced to the back door as fast as the ankle-deep snow would allow.

❊ ❊ ❊

When it was Kevin's turn to choose a present, he picked the heavy one. The kids all sat Indian-style on the floor near the tree as the adults settled into the couches and chairs. Kevin shredded the unique wrapping paper that adorned the present, eliciting a few regrets from his aunts. A plain cardboard box, held together by knotted twine, lay underneath. Using his father's pocket knife to cut it open, Kevin wasted little time pulling the box apart to look inside. The smile faded from his face.

"Kevin?" his father said, moving forward to see what was wrong.

"He's gone white as a ghost," Grandmother added.

Inside the box was a craggy, nine-inch-tall angel statue made of marble, broken into two pieces.

Kevin's father removed it with both hands. "What an odd gift," he said, examining it. "Don't worry, son. I should be able to glue it back together for you."

❉ ❉ ❉

Kevin sat next to his grandmother on the couch, his mind tangling with unanswerable questions.

"You're looking rather peakish," Grandmother said. "Are you feeling alright?"

Forcing a weak smile, Kevin met her gaze. "Have you ever heard of someone named Edward Corbin?"

She frowned and looked up at the ceiling, as though searching out memories trapped there since seeping from her mind years ago.

"Corbin? There was something … from way back. Yes, I remember my grandfather telling me a story about a man named Corbin. I was just a girl, but I still recall it … most of it anyway, but it isn't a pleasant tale; not one appropriate for such a festive time as this."

Tanya's eyes seemed to read Kevin's from across the room. "I want to hear it," she said, jumping up and setting aside the book she'd just unwrapped to kneel at Grandmother's knee.

"Me, too," Greg said eagerly, following his sister's lead.

"Sakes alive," Grandmother sighed. "I can see I won't have a moment's peace if I don't tell it to you, but I'd best not hear a lick about anyone being too scared to sleep tonight."

"We won't," they answered in unison.

"I was around your age when my grandfather told me of Edward Corbin. He was a local school teacher here in Cedarville with an unabiding love for Christmas. One year, he was inspired to demonstrate this love by traveling into the Talbot Forest to obtain the greatest pine tree the town had ever seen. A group of young men agreed to assist him, so they grabbed a large cart and trod off into the snowy woodlands.

"The intensity of Corbin's drive to find a suitably impressive tree drove him ever deeper into the ancient woods to the point where his companions became uneasy, imploring him to turn back. Even today, there are vast sections of that forest where no man ever goes," Grandmother said, looking out the window toward the trees. "Just then, he came upon the perfect specimen. Tall, stout, and full, it was exactly as he'd envisioned, but it grew dangerously close to the edge of a deep ravine. Neither that nor the worsening snowfall or plummeting temperatures would deter him, however, which proved to be a terrible mistake. Lines snapped, causing the tree to break free and tumble toward the crevasse. Corbin leapt forward in a foolish attempt to halt the tree's progress but ended up being carried over the side along with it. The villagers helplessly watched the resulting impact below. Survival from so great a fall was impossible, and they had no way to retrieve him, so they headed back in great sadness."

"How terrible," Tanya said.

"Indeed," Grandmother replied with a glint in her eye. "But that wasn't the end of his tale. Against all possibility, he walked back into Cedarville unharmed two nights later, single-handedly pulling the majestic tree behind him. Everyone gathered around in shocked awe asking how he survived such certain death. He didn't answer, merely smiling at them instead, his mouth filled with too many, inhumanly long, curved teeth. Realizing they were looking upon not a man but an abomination, everyone fled to their houses, bolting their doors and praying for deliverance from whatever it was that had emerged from the forest wearing Corbin's face. Only the sheriff stayed behind to try and deal with the demonic beast, unloading a full clip into him. But the bullets failed to keep Corbin from lunging forth to bite his head clean off with one snap of his massive jaws."

"Did Corbin kill them all?" Greg asked, awe evident in his voice.

"Heavens, no! Do you think Cedarville would be here today had that happened?" Grandmother said, pinching his cheek. "Things were dire, though. After feasting on the sheriff's headless body, Corbin began dancing around the pine tree he'd erected in the center of town, casting discarded entrails across its branches all the while."

"How did they stop him?" Kevin asked, unable to hide the desperation in his voice.

"Legend has it that the clanging of church bells from nearby Dawn Haven chiming the arrival of Christmas morning caused him to collapse. Noticing this, the townspeople came out and promptly chopped his body into pieces, which they gathered up and buried beneath a special tombstone from which they believed he could never escape."

Hope rose in Kevin's chest. "Do the bells still ring on Christmas morning?"

"No, the church in Dawn Haven had their bell removed after it was damaged in a storm. Cedarville had one for a while, but that church was recently torn down and replaced by a strip mall. Don't worry, though, the whole thing is nothing but a foolish legend. Such things don't really exist."

Kevin wished he could share in his grandmother's assurance.

✳ ✳ ✳

Later, Kevin sat on his bed with Tanya and Greg. They stared at the marble statuette atop the chest-of-drawers, whole once again due to his father's diligence.

"It can't be the same one," Tanya said.

Greg picked it up and held it out to Kevin. "You got the best look at it. Is this it?"

With the exception of a thin, hooked nose, the statue's once-delicate facial features were worn away. The wings on its back looked tattered and pockmarked with holes. Grandmother said it must be some antique that had sat outside for years.

Kevin looked away with a shiver. "That's it. That's what was on top of the tombstone I knocked over last year."

Tanya shook her head. "But no one besides us knew about that. Who would send it to you?"

"I don't know," Kevin said, closing his eyes to recall the man who had delivered it the previous night. "Let's pray I don't find out."

✳ ✳ ✳

The rest of the night Kevin tried to join in with the games the kids played downstairs, excusing himself from hide-and-seek when the thought of being alone in some dark corner of the house got to be too much for him. At 11:00, the adults herded the kids into their beds. Kevin tried to talk his Father into letting him sleep in the same room as Greg but was refused. Once again he lie awake listening to the quiet murmurs of the adults through the floorboards until they, too, retired for the night, leaving the house still and silent.

Kevin got up to look out the window several times during the next few hours, expecting to see the man with the top hat walking up the snow-blanketed front lawn, but by 2:00 am, with no sign of him, Kevin relaxed enough to drift off to sleep.

His dreams returned him to the secluded graveyard he and his cousins snuck off to last year. They were throwing snowballs at one another, weaving in and out amongst tombstones in the forest. He was at the far edge of the graveyard when Greg caught him square in the face with a damp projectile. Kevin fell backward, hitting something solid that toppled beneath him. It was a tombstone. Its topper, a weathered marble angel, separated from the stone and lay broken in two pieces. The marker's epitaph read,

Edward Corbin
May the guardian forever watch over this spot,
And keep him bound,
So to rise again he may not
1813 – 1849

Kevin snapped awake. He wasn't sure what had roused him, but as he lay listening, he heard the crunch of snow outside. Cold fear clawed down his body, but he forced himself to rise and return to the window. The man with the top hat and hollow eyes strode across the white lawn, stopping to look up at Kevin, smiling and tipping his hat once again. Kevin flung himself back into his bed, burying himself under the covers. He waited, holding his breath as the clock ticked off endless seconds. He'd be safe inside the house, he thought. His father and uncles wouldn't let anyone in this late, and he doubted the man could reach him on the second floor.

A scraping sound came from overhead as the shadow of a large top hat filled the wall across the room. Kevin looked up to see long, pale fingers grasping the bottom of the window, letting in more than just the frigid outdoor air. He tried to cry out for help, but his body refused him. The oddly dressed man stepped past the bed into the room. He turned toward Kevin, his lips stretching to allow his absurdly long teeth to push forward. Approaching the bed, the thing leaned in close to Kevin, his breath smelling of tree sap and rotting meat. "Thank you for freeing me, Kevin. My sleep was long and my reassembly slow, but now I can finish what I started so long ago," the raspy-voiced thing said.

"Why?" Kevin blubbered.

Corbin's smile widened. "Because your people trespassed someplace they shouldn't have, a place where primordial beasts have waited, trapped for centuries behind barriers meant to protect you from us. Mortals are so easily manipulated; make one of those mystical barriers resemble something they desire, and they immediately start cutting it down, punching a hole to be crawled through."

"There are more like you?" Kevin asked, licking his dry lips.

"Millions, some like me, many far worse. More will discover my little breach and escape as well, but I'll be finished here by then and will have moved on to another town. But all this talk of food is reminding me just how hungry I am. It's time I had a light snack."

Kevin wanted to scream for help but only managed a whimper as the twisted man above him unhinged its huge, jagged, toothy maw and opened it wide above his head.

A deafening clang exploded into the room.

The man's face contorted, his mouth snapping shut as he whipped his head around.

Another clang rang out from behind them.

A small figure stood silhouetted in the open doorway.

Edward Corbin leapt off the bed, looking confused as his body wavered with each new clamorous bong. His bloodless skin, stretched across his face, opening up garish sores. His nose broke off, falling to the hardwood floor with a moist plop. Tiny white worms erupted from crimson festering wounds. They wriggled and squirmed as they feasted on his rapidly disintegrating face. There was little more than a skull left when his immense teeth began to loosen and fall out.

A second later, reduced to nothing but a skeleton in baggy clothes, it collapsed into a heap on the floor.

Standing in the doorway, Tanya lowered the phone she'd been holding above her head and silenced its booming chime.

Kevin could see the terror in her eyes, despite the darkness. "What was that?" he gasped.

"I found where Grandma hid my phone and searched out a live broadcast of Christmas morning church bells," she mumbled, still staring in disbelief at the pile of dusty bones beneath a tattered old top hat.

* * *

Kevin's father and uncles spent the early morning hours that Christmas reburying Edward Corbin's remains. Reattaching the broken grave topper proved challenging, but a temporary fix was achieved.

Afterward, Kevin snuck back out to Corbin's grave to assure himself the nightmare was truly over. A fresh layer of snow had fallen, blanketing everything in white. Nothing more to be done, Kevin started back toward the house.

An icy breeze swept out from the forest, carrying an exhilarated giggle to Kevin's ear; it caused him to stiffen and hold his breath as he regarded the swell of trees. He tried to convince himself it was drunken holiday revelers, until the cackling returned, louder and more ecstatic, the laugh of one stumbling upon an extraordinary surprise—something they couldn't wait to sink their teeth into.

W✷HITE ✷HRISTMAS

Jeremy Simons

Have you ever heard that song, *I'm Dreaming of a White Christmas*? Of course, you have. Everyone has. I used to despise that song, mostly because I was jealous of the lyrics; jealous of the fact that I'd never had a white Christmas.

I'm almost twenty-eight years old now, and I've only had one. That one came a little over two months ago. It was a memorable experience for everyone across northern Louisiana. I know I will most certainly not ever forget it. That was, after all, the day the bodies started piling up around me.

You probably think I'm exaggerating, but I assure you I am not. Just continue reading and you'll see.

I awoke that dreary Christmas morning with an odd sense of urgency although I had nothing in particular to do. No Christmas dinners. No family. No gifts. No friends.

No loved ones. I was forever alone and still am ... in some sense.

I was on my way to the grocery store for a can of Joe (thank God for greedy corporations that care more about making a dollar than the importance of family values). It's funny to me now how a man can be so forgetful over something he deems a necessity. With that in mind, I'm still unsure of whether to blame my forgetfulness or my nasty coffee habit or a combination of the two for the events that transpired. I suppose it doesn't matter either way. What's done is done.

I was traveling north on Highway 165 when things went awry. The snow was coming down heavy. Thick powder littered the road, lessened only where previous drivers had left their tire tracks behind. I hit a patch of ice—black or regular, I don't know—and lost control. I began sliding quickly to the right, towards the ditch and the trailer houses beyond it. Logical thinking escaped me then, but I knew one thing for certain: if there was going to be an accident (which seemed evident even then), it was not going to involve me running through someone's house. I refused to run through a sleeping family's home.

I broke the Number One Rule of Thumb right then and there by slamming on the brakes while skidding. I jerked the steering wheel in the opposite direction of the skid. The nose of the truck snapped around away from the trailers and towards the other two lanes of traffic. The rear end fishtailed towards the same ditch in front of the trailers. I was completely sideways in the turning lane and headed for the two lanes of oncoming traffic before I finally started getting control. Little by little, I was bringing my big old Ford back to stability.

Things went really bad from there.

A car—a little red Dodge Neon (I'll never forget that

car)—came zipping along. A man and a woman (married, I knew then even before I met them) were the occupants. They may very well have been the last two people my sanity encountered.

The man was driving. He could have stopped it. He could have prevented it all. He could have stopped the car easily but didn't. Now I don't know if this man simply did not see me until it was too late, or if he thought I was going to correct my slide before things turned fatal, or if he simply had a death wish, but he did nothing in the beginning. He was driving in the outside lane, the fast lane, the lane nearest me, and he did nothing.

Finally, when it was seemingly too late, he made his move. It was the wrong one, though. I could see his wife bickering with him even through the falling snow and despite the situation. It is amazing what the mind can focus in on during dangerous situations. Rather than stopping (he still had time to do that, I'm almost certain) or getting over to the inside lane to give me more room, he swerved right at me. I know what you're probably thinking: *what an idiot;* right? I thought so, too … then. Now that I've had ample time to think, I see it differently. He must have thought I couldn't get hold of my truck, that I was going to continue drifting over and cream him. It was a rational afterthought.

The turning lane was a treacherous go with thick patches of ice masked by fallen snow. The Neon caught a patch, but rather than sending him on over into the other lanes like the patch I'd hit had done, it slid him right towards me. We hit head on.

I recall the initial crash. The impact was far worse than anything I had ever experienced. Whiplash from the seatbelt catching still affects me today. I have imprints across my chest and waist from where it caught. My head smashed into something. I'm assuming the steering wheel … or maybe the driver's side window. The semantics don't matter much now. I have an improperly healed scar the length of my forehead that I allowed to heal on its own. I couldn't allow myself to be seen in public after what I did. I most certainly could not risk going to a doctor and leaving an easily traceable paper trail behind me, but I'm getting ahead of myself.

The blow knocked me unconscious. When I woke, the snow was still falling. My windshield was caved. A fire was burning briskly from beneath the Neon's hood. I did not know that then. I thought it was coming from beneath my own hood, which was why I got out as quickly as possible, ignoring the blinding pains throughout my entire body. But the most shocking revelation I discovered just before getting out was I now had a passenger. I didn't have one before.

I could tell by the way he was crumpled up and bleeding there was no hope for him. His chest wasn't moving. His face was splintered with gleaming shards of glass. Blood covered his face like someone had poured a bucket of red paint over his head. There was no way for me to be sure it was the driver of the Neon, but I had my assumptions. And even before I noticed the absence of both occupants of the Neon and the matching holes in the other car's windshield (directly in front of the driver's seat) and in my own windshield (directly in front of where my new passenger was hunched over), I knew my assumptions were right. I'll take the blame for everything that happened that day, and everything that has happened in the months since, but I will not take the blame for his carelessness. Honestly, who doesn't wear their seatbelt in a snowstorm? You can make your arguments that seatbelts destroy just as many lives as they save, but not on this day. I'm still alive, and the woman lived—not living now, though—but she survived the crash.

I couldn't waste my time with the man. He was a lost cause. But the woman might not have been. I was already guilty of vehicle manslaughter, but one count was better than two.

I got out and went over to the Neon. The flames were dancing out from beneath its hood. Time was of the essence. The passenger's seat was indeed empty, but there was no proof of impact on the windshield from her. That was when I first realized she must have been wearing her seatbelt. It saved her life. I wish now it wouldn't have, though. I wish the crash would have killed her just as it had her husband. That might have changed things drastically.

I found her leaning against the fender well on the passenger's side. The flames were almost touching her hair. I knew then she must have been in shock … or maybe concussed. Her face and head looked like mine felt. She was conscious, so that was good. At least I thought so then. She told me her name was Jillian. I told her my name was Bobby Thomas. It wasn't the entire truth, but it was not necessarily a lie either. Robert is my first name. Bobby was a nickname I never acquired a taste for. Thomas is my middle name. I didn't disclose my last name to her then, and I will not disclose it now … at least not yet anyways. It is not important just yet.

Jillian was hysterical. I couldn't blame her. But at least she was coherent. I don't know if I ever got through to her that the Neon was on fire and could explode at any minute, but she finally allowed me to drag her away. I led her around the backside of the car towards the ditch I had initially drifted towards. I didn't want to. Lord knew I didn't, but I had to. She was safer over there. And one of us had to call the cops. She was better suited to do that. I was more composed, but hysterics have a way of working miracles for emergency calls.

I had her convinced to go knock on the nearest trailer and ask to use the phone ... or at the very least, to tell the owner to call 9-1-1 and the fire department. It took some convincing. She kept babbling about Mark: *Where's Mark? Is Mark okay?* I told her I would find him and take care of him. I told her I was certified in CPR and first aid; I wasn't lying. I had been certified once upon a time. My cards for both, of course, had expired many years ago, but she hadn't needed to know that.

Finally, she was ready to go. She took the first few steps down the shallow embankment before turning to take one final look at the wreckage. That was when she saw him crumpled over in the passenger's seat of my truck.

Jillian let out a blood-curdling scream that still haunts my dreams today. She ran right past me toward the truck. She was quick. She was back at the truck and jerking at the door handle before I caught up with her.

I tried talking some sense into her. It didn't work. I tried pulling her away, but she wasn't having any part of it. The door was jammed. There would be no getting it open for the two of us. There was only one thing I could do.

The driver's side door was still open. My only chance was to pull him out through there. There was no hope for him, but it was the only way to get her away from the truck.

I ran over to the driver's side, leaving Jillian on her own. The fire from beneath the Neon's hood was dancing even more wildly now. It wouldn't be long now before it exploded. I grabbed hold of his left arm and pulled. Everything that happened next happened so quickly it took quite some time for me to register the validity of it.

I pulled mightily. His head lolled over, pivoting like a victim in a horror movie that has had his throat slit. Mark's throat had been slit, either by my windshield or his own. He fell over into the seat. His head was thrown back. His neck opened up like Pacman gobbling cherries. I felt my stomach rising in my throat and told myself throwing up would only make the situation worse (as if that was even possible).

Well, it was possible.

Jillian let out another one of those blood-curdling screams. The fire continued dancing, jigging its way to beneath the hood of my old pick-up. She was coming for me now, around the bed. I met her halfway. She was mumbling something; it wasn't audible over the howling winds. She needed some comforting. I was the only one who could give it to her.

Need and want are two entirely different things. What I thought she needed was not what she wanted. She slapped me across the face before I could get a word out. I saw red immediately but maintained control. I pinned her arms and held her while she cursed me and accused me and told me it was all my fault. I held her until the explosion happened.

Apparently, my old pick-up was a little more prone to igniting. It blew both of us nearly twenty feet (rough estimate) from the wreckage. We landed awkwardly. Her coming down on top of me hurt almost as much the wreck. It knocked Jillian unconscious, which was a lucky break. But she didn't stay out for long. When she came to, she was more persistent than ever. She went through the same old song and dance of cursing and screaming and blaming me once more. I had a pounding headache that had only gotten worse after the blow threw us. There was a puddle of blood rapidly disappearing beneath freshly fallen snow where my head had landed. That couldn't be good. I felt fine, but I had lost a lot of blood, and the puddle was evidence I wasn't through losing just yet.

My mind raced over whether I could survive the blood loss or not, slowly drowning out the sound of her dreadful voice, when it hit me. It literally hit me. Jillian had slapped me once more. The side of my face stung like a cold hand plunged into hot water. I tried to protest, but she hit me again. She hit me again and again. I lost count of how many times she hit me before I finally hit her back. I slapped her. I was no animal (at least not then). The shock spread across her face was more troublesome than it had been when she first discovered Mark.

"You *bastard!*" she screamed.

Those were the last words she ever spoke. She came at me again ... slapping, kicking, and—I believe—biting. I hit her again, with my fist this time. Blood flew from her nose in a fine spray.

I didn't stop there. I couldn't. I swung again. I felt the bone in her cheek collapse beneath my fist. She fell to the ground.

I still couldn't stop. My head was pounding. Hitting was acting as my Aleve. Hitting her was the only thing making me feel better. I pummeled her. Her head bounced off the asphalt like a dribbled basketball with each lick. I could hear bones shattering over the howl of the wind. I think I even heard her skull fracture.

The only thing that stopped me was the scream of an approaching engine. Normally, I would have freaked out. Normally, my paranoid mind would have envisioned a police cruiser skidding up beside us while I straddled Jillian and pummeled her face with a vengeance like an MMA fighter. But these were not normal times. I was not normal ... not anymore. I won't say I was in a haze or a blackout because that would be a lie. I do not want to lie to anyone. I was fully conscious. I was fully aware of what I was doing, but yet, I could not stop. It felt so good.

The engine screamed louder as it drew closer. It was a diesel of some sort, big, but not a rig.

It went dancing past me just as I rose to my feet. They saw me. Maybe not Jillian, but they had definitely seen me. My blood-drenched body and the vehicles blazing behind me would have been enough to make anyone stop. The only thing I couldn't figure out then—and still cannot figure out now—is of all the times throughout the entire ordeal another vehicle could have come by, it came then. That has haunted me since. If the truck had come five minutes earlier, I would have gotten off with a ticket for reckless operation and maybe an accusation of vehicular manslaughter. If it had come by five minutes later, I would have been long gone before the cops showed.

But it hadn't come earlier and it did not come later. It came then. It stopped. And the man pried. Why did he have to pry? The driver was a big black man, much bigger than me, but he was nice. Nice guys finish last. He introduced himself as Shane. No last name was given. He offered to call the police, to which I lied and said I already had. He offered to sit with me until help arrived, to which I gratefully declined. But he was persistent.

Shane went over to where Jillian lay. I'm not sure if he was checking for a pulse or just checking her injuries, but he was hunched over her lifeless body when I decided he had to be taken care of also.

"This woman took one hell of a beating," Shane said with his back still turned to me. "If I didn't know any better, I'd say this happened after the wreck." He began rising and turning slowly. "Hey, pal!"

My fist slammed into his nose. There was a loud *POP!* just before the blood sprayed.

Shane continued rising, now more shocked than anything else.

I hit him again. He fell to one knee. My right knee shot

up, an involuntary reflex. Fresh blood exploded from his mouth onto my jeans. I would find three of his teeth clinging to my jeans later and the teeth marks on my leg beneath the heavy material.

The second his big ol' head crashed to the softened asphalt, I was on top of him like a ravenous predator. He was gurgling and gagging, choking on his own blood and teeth, but that didn't stop me. I started working him over. I continued to do so until my knuckles were bleeding and I couldn't open my hands. And the son of a bitch was still breathing. He was a tough one; I'll give him that much.

But in the back of my mind, I kept thinking, *What if another vehicle comes by right now?*

I'll have to kill them, too, I said, answering my own question.

You have to finish killing him first. That voice wasn't mine. It wasn't in my head either. It was behind me.

A hand reached out and grasped my shoulder. I've always heard Death's touch is cold, but I don't believe even it could be that cold. The hand seized me; my heart skipped a beat. It was much cooler than the falling snow or the ice caked around my knees. That coldness was inexplicable and still is.

I turned slowly, half-expecting to see Death himself in his black-hooded cloak, scythe in hand, ready to drag me down into the depths of Hell. After all, I had sustained some rather severe injuries. The other half of me expected to see nothing but the falling snow, and coming to the realization that the voice had been inside my head all along.

I got neither.

What I actually saw when I turned was more frightening than either of the above. What I saw was Mark; Captain of the S.S. Neon Mark; Mark with his Colombian necktie; Mark speaking out of his neck like Pacman had he been able to talk.

I couldn't believe it. Mark was alive. Well, I wasn't sure if he was alive then, but he was most certainly standing there.

I won't say I was entirely crazy … at least not right then. The odds of him surviving going headlong through two windshields during a head-on collision at more than forty miles per hour was next to nothing. The odds of him surviving the Colombian necktie he'd received as a parting gift in the wreckage was even less. And the odds of him surviving the explosion when he had been sprawled across the front of my pick-up were impossible. The odds of him surviving these three events simultaneously were astronomically impossible.

But yet here he was, standing behind me, grasping my shoulder in a discerning manner like he was the coach of a little league baseball team giving a pep talk after the player lost the big game. He was mumbling continuously, "You must kill him first. You must kill Shane. Finish him now."

The mantra chilled my bones in a way his touch couldn't, in a way the falling snow couldn't, in a way the ice caked around my knees couldn't. The words thudded in rhythm with my headache. It was like a shotgun exploding inside my head each time the words sounded off. The craziness came then. I felt it wash over me in a wave. I can only imagine it a feeling similar to someone catching the Holy Ghost.

The words floated into my ears again as I—the new me— looked down at Shane once more. It wasn't Shane … not anymore. What was beneath me was a monster. I had to kill it.

But how?

I had beaten this man senseless. I had pummeled him until my knuckles bled and were busted. He wouldn't let go. This son of a bitch would not die.

"You must kill him. Kill Shane. Finish him now."

The words had gotten stronger. It was becoming

unbearable. I put my hands up to my ears to block it out. I realized the words were just as much in my head as they were coming out of Mark's purple lips. I also realized that somewhere throughout it all, Jillian had arisen as well. I didn't question whether she was alive or not. I knew the answer. I had killed her myself.

She was hunched over in a sitting position a few feet to the right of where Shane and I were. Her head was lowered. The falling snow mixed in with the freezing blood in her hair to make an unorthodox polka-dot pattern I would lose sleep over in the nights to come; a pattern I hoped I would never have the misfortune of seeing again, although I would eventually see it every night in my dreams for the next week or so, and even longer still in waking moments. I could hear her voice clearly even over Mark's; it, too, spoke inside my head every bit as much as it did outside my melon. I could hear her so clearly; in fact, I could vividly depict the noticeable lisp in her voice. There hadn't been a lisp before … well, before I beat her to death. I was sure of this much even before she raised her head to look at me. Teeth were missing; her nose broken and laid over to one side; her tongue had been split open straight up the middle (I don't know if she had bitten it or cut it on one of her fragmented teeth). She was smiling. It made me shiver. Dried blood cascaded down her chin.

"You must kill him," she said. Her eyes were locked on mine. "Kill Shane." I couldn't look away. Holding my hands to my ears seemed to be amplifying the voices rather than silencing them. "Finish him now."

My hands shot down towards Shane's face. I want to say it was involuntary because that was what if felt like. But I think I'd be lying if I said that. I don't want to lie to you.

My fingers found Shane's eye sockets and began

pushing. Jillian's grin grew wider. Mark's grip on my shoulder grew tighter. My fingers sunk in deeper. Two loud, audible pops rang out as Shane's eyeballs exploded beneath the pressure. I continued pushing until Shane finally quit squirming.

That involuntary feeling left me then. I was myself again … Well, almost. Mark and Jillian were still with me—as they still are today.

I rose to my feet warily. The snow was still falling. No more vehicles had passed. No police had been by. No sirens were wailing in the distance. All was quiet except for the howling wind, which had become calming to me.

"We should go." It was Jillian speaking. She didn't seem as benevolent or excited then.

"I agree," Mark said, completely compliant.

I agreed as well—wholeheartedly—but I didn't voice my enthusiasm. I didn't need to. They were in my head. They were a part of me now. I don't know if I knew it then, but it made itself apparent on numerous occasions over the next several weeks.

My mind may have been cluttered, but I knew what I needed to do. I had only two perceivable options: I could wait for the police, or I could run, become a fugitive from justice. I chose the first. Mark and Jillian opted for the latter and voiced their opinions strongly.

As I stood in the turn lane on what would have normally been a busy area on Highway 165 in the falling snow next to a man I had killed, one of three bodies that had yet to reanimate itself, arguing with the other two that had come back alive, my perspective changed drastically. It was Shane who changed my mind.

The last thing I remember saying was I wasn't going to run away and hide, and that was final. That was merely seconds before Shane sat bolt-upright. His arm shot up; his finger pointed directly at the trailer nearest the ditch I had almost slid into.

I looked. I had to. I followed his finger and noticed the curtains in one of the windows falling closed the second my eyes past over it. Someone was watching me ... watching us. I didn't know at the time my new acquaintances could not be seen by others. I would find that out later.

The thing that was most frightening to me wasn't the realization I was being watched, but the fact Shane could see without eyes. I would come to realize over the next few weeks my friends could do a lot of spectacular and useful tricks, but it caught me by surprise then. I was preoccupied with Shane. His eye sockets were black holes like a doll on an assembly line. Thin lines of blood trickled down his cheeks. It was a sight I knew I would never get used to, and I haven't been able to do so even now.

Mark and Jillian were arguing somewhere behind me. I imagined the lady inside the trailer was dialing up the sheriff's department right then. And I was mesmerized by an eyeless corpse that wouldn't stay dead.

The point is everything would have fallen apart right then and there had it not been for Shane. His voice was strong when he finally spoke. It drowned out Mark and Jillian entirely. I'm not sure why. I think it must have had something to do with the manner I disposed of him. It was more personal than Jillian.

"You must go, Robert," Shane said. His voice was as serene as the second he introduced himself.

I understood then that he really was in my head ... all three of them were in my head. How else would he have known my name? My real name?

"Kill her, Robert. You must continue. We have more work

to do."

I was crossing the two northbound lanes toward the ditch and trailers before I even realized it. Mark and Jillian's voices had joined Shane's, but I barely noticed. I was on a mission.

I saw the curtains open once more and then close again more quickly than the first time when she saw me coming. I knocked softly on the door. There was no answer. I hadn't expected one. I knocked harder. Nothing. Finally, I started beating. I heard footsteps scurrying through the trailer. Something fell over inside.

"Who is it?" a woman's voice said softly. She was caught. She tried to disguise her voice, make it sound groggy as if she had been sleeping, but I knew better.

"My name is Bobby Thomas." Lying was starting to come easy to me. "I need to use your telephone, please. I had an accident. I need an ambulance. And I'm pretty sure the two people in the other vehicle may be dead."

The footsteps fell quiet just on the other side of the door. It took a moment for the dead bolt to click open. I couldn't believe she was actually going to open the door, which led me to think that maybe whoever was on the other side of that door hadn't seen anything at all. Maybe this woman had only been watching the falling snow. After all, it never snowed in Louisiana. The idea was not so far-fetched.

The door had opened only inches before the chain latch caught. "I already called 9-1-1, sir," she said shyly. "I heard the screeching tires and the crash. I called immediately. I don't know what is taking so long. Maybe there are some more accidents between here and there, or maybe they just have to take their time on the roads."

I smiled politely. It hurt to do so, but I was convinced it was a must. I had to gain her trust. She had seen too much. She had lied to me already. There had been no screeching tires. I was sure of that. And the cops should have been there by then had she called in the beginning. No. She had been spying. She saw me with Shane. She had to die.

"I'm grateful, ma'am," I said as cordially as possible. "I know you don't know me, ma'am, but I'm gonna catch my death out here in this cold if they take much longer. If I could just step inside the door, I'd be greatly indebted to you. That heat hitting my face feels like Heaven, ma'am. I promise I won't hurt you." I said the last with a reassuring smile I am sure could never be duplicated no matter the situation.

I saw the fear in her eyes. She wasn't going to open it. She knew better than to believe a complete stranger, and I had to give her credit for her intelligence.

"Kick the door in, Robert," Shane said as plain as day. The woman's eyes widened as if she had heard him. I wouldn't find out until later that no one but me could actually hear or see my new tagalongs.

Jillian: "What in the hell are you waiting for, Robert?"

The door eased shut in my face. I didn't lose my cool … not then anyways. There was still a small possibility she hadn't seen what I had done and that she was just shutting the door to remove the chain link.

Mark: "You have to get in there, Robert. She saw too much."

I couldn't hear the chain sliding across the lock. The door did not open. I was beginning to lose hope when I heard it. I heard the monotonous drone of numbers being pressed on a telephone. She was calling out. But who? I already knew that answer.

I kicked the door, hard. The chain ripped away and the bottom of the door splintered. The knob turned easily in my hand. The foolish woman had forgotten to lock the other two locks.

She was standing a few feet inside the door, the phone in hand and pressed against her ear. Her mouth dropped open in shock. I lunged without thinking. My fingers engulfed her throat. We fell to the floor.

Sirens wailed in the distance. I didn't have time for this. My eyes caught a glimpse of the knife holder on the counter that was within arm's reach. I grabbed the handle of what I thought would be the largest one and pulled. The entire holder fell to the floor beside us. I grabbed the largest one I saw in my hurry. She grabbed the one nearest her hand.

I stabbed her in the throat but not before she got me in the shoulder. I don't know what was coursing through my veins at that moment, but I never felt the knife. I wouldn't feel it until later on while safely hidden at my home when I finally pulled it free. She died quickly, much quicker than Shane or Jillian. I'd like to say, *Thank God for small favors*, but I'm positive He played no part in the events of that day or in the months following until now.

I left in a hurry, but not before wiping my prints away from the knife handle. It was a small afterthought, but I had become a killer. Killers can never be too careful. Also, I had heard in a movie once, *never cut forensics a break*. It seemed fitting. I wouldn't think until later of how the knife I had originally grabbed may have not been the one I stabbed her with; or how my muddy, bloody footprint was plastered on the front door; or whether my truck was still visible enough to pull a positive ID from; or if I had actually witnessed Shane and Jillian rising from the dead or if it had been just their spirits; my DNA would have been all over them. There were so many things I had not thought of, but I was merely an amateur.

I ran through the woods and eventually ended up

somewhere familiar. I made it to the house and went into hiding.

As you know, I have referenced a few months passing, which means my story is far from over. Not a lot of memorable things have happened since. I'll tell you about those and try to keep the details to a minimum in the process.

I've never put much faith in police in general; my faith in the Caldwell Parish Sheriff's Department was even less than that. If you want reasons, I'll give you the greatest one: it was eleven days following Christmas before the first cop finally showed up at my home. Eleven days. That was pitiful.

In those eleven days, I had time to do a lot of things; mostly, I used that time to recollect and get to know my new friends. Yes, they became friends in every sense of the word. If you think going crazy is bad, try going crazy alone. In some deranged way, those four spirits have kept me sane (ha ha).

Anyways, the cop showed eleven days following Christmas with a warrant in his hand. He ended up letting himself in by kicking in my door. I was smart enough to know to keep my presence unknown until the right time.

The gold-plated ID badge pinned to his uniform shirt read Deputy Green. He was persistent. He checked thoroughly … a little too thoroughly. I was willing to let him walk away with his life (we all were, except for Suzanne; Suzanne was the lady from the trailer; she was quiet and reserved and didn't want to be here with the rest of us; I cannot say I blamed her), but he couldn't walk away without something. Deputy Green kept digging and searching until he found my hiding spot. That is not the entire truth. He was about to find me, but I surprised him.

I rushed him from beyond my closet door and stabbed him repeatedly with my old buck knife. He died slowly (I regretted not slitting his throat first off, but after being with him for a while, I'm glad I made it painful; he is one nagging, annoying son of a bitch). It was messy, but by then, I didn't care. Deputy Green not only had a warrant to search my home and the premises, but he also had a warrant for my arrest for three separate counts of murder and a possible fourth. It had taken them eleven days, but they had discovered my secrets. And where there was one, there were bound to be others.

I went on the run then. I have never stayed in one place more than a day, and I have never dropped more than one body in a day. I have been in or around Caldwell this entire time, and no one has found me. You have to love the police around here.

After Deputy Green, I was lost. Victims were meaningless unless I had something against them. I had no enemies. Even the people I had killed up until then, I had held no grudge against; they were simply wrong time, wrong place deals. I wandered around aimlessly for what must have been a week or more. I considered suicide. I considered turning myself in. I considered going to another country and starting all over. I considered every option I could fathom, but none of them seemed right.

It wasn't until I was wandering through a bar's parking lot, breaking into trucks and cars (not my proudest moment) when an idea hit me. It was a little blue car—a Dodge Neon, oddly enough—that brought me to this realization. It's funny how the same type of car that put everything in motion would be the same type that kept it going when it was on the verge of ending abruptly. It was the car in general that caught my attention although the silver-plated NEON emblem on the trunk made me stop. It was merely a bumper sticker that put things into perspective.

The bright-red background of the sticker standing against the sky-blue bumper grabbed my attention. The yellow smiley face with devil horns and its tongue sticking out compelled me to get a closer look. *The voices inside my head tell me what to do.* That wasn't the exact quote, but it's close enough. The point is, it got me to thinking. I wondered briefly if the driver of this particular Neon did hear voices before deciding no. But I did. I heard voices; voices that had kept me out of prison; voices that had stood beside me throughout my indiscretions.

I decided right then and there that it was time for me to literally allow the voices inside my head to tell me what to do. And boy did they have some wonderful ideas.

My voices had a lot of enemies, people who wronged them over the years. I settled the scores. They gave me the names; I tracked them down and disposed of them in whatever manner the voices wished. I must say, nagging son of a bitch or not, it has been a blessing in disguise to have Deputy Green with me. He turned out to be a lot smarter than he looked and a lot smarter than what I gave him credit for the day he first showed up at my house. Deputy Green has kept me safe.

More voices have joined me now. Some strong, some weak, all with their own names. Everyone has contributed except my dear Suzanne, the beauty from the trailer.

But alas, Suzanne spoke to me this very morning. She spoke clearly and adamantly. Her voice temporarily outweighed the others. I didn't think that possible. Suzanne said only two words: a name. Randy Reed. That name may not mean anything to you, but it did to me. It did to Suzanne.

I am going to stop right here and tie everything in because you are most certainly wondering by now what exactly I want from you. I assure anyone reading this, I want nothing from you. This is not a confession. This is not a suicide note.

This is merely a story ... my story.

I have two copies of this story. One I left out in the open at my house with Deputy Green's body. I assume since I haven't heard anything about it on the news that either that letter has not been found (which would also mean Deputy Green has not been found) or the cops are merely keeping the story out of the news. Either option is plausible, but either way, it just goes to show why my faith in the local sheriff's department is what it is.

The other copy—this copy—stays in my pocket at all times, which means one of two things: either I've been killed or captured. Either way, I do believe my final attempt was thwarted, or maybe it wasn't; maybe it was a success, and I was gunned down escaping. Either way, it doesn't matter. What's done is done. I cannot change the past.

I merely wrote this to show everyone the things I have been dealing with. The voices in my head may have told me what to do, but they are not responsible. I am still a human being at the end of the day. I possess free will, the freedom to pick and choose. The voices may have chosen the victims on numerous occasions, but I—I, alone—chose to go through with it. I could easily have said no, but didn't. I rather enjoyed it. You may think I'm crazy, and I guess I am, but at the end all of this, I believe those voices had been with me all along, hiding in the shadows of my mind, waiting for the most opportune time to strike, waiting for my breakdown. When they finally showed themselves, they were relentless to say the least.

Now to get back on topic, the name Randy Reed (the name Suzanne said in my head) may sound familiar to you. In fact, if you're from around these parts, I'm positive you know the name. Deputy Randy Reed, as he was called ten years ago, arrested a man named Simon Singer, Suzanne's younger brother, for a felony drug-possession charge because he supposedly wouldn't cut in Deputy Reed on the profits. Simon had a parole hearing come due a few years back that never came about due to unforeseen circumstances (the unforeseen circumstances was a dead inmate said to have been murdered by Simon Singer). I have heard—a little blonde birdie told me so (ha ha)—that Deputy Reed (now Sheriff Reed) had the inmate murdered and pinned it all on my little blonde birdie's baby brother.

Is it true? Who knows? I sure as hell don't. But that doesn't matter. With this being Suzanne's first victim, I am unsure if it is genuine or a setup to end my charades. It doesn't matter either way, though. I will pay Sheriff Randy Reed a visit today. I will kill him just like I have the rest. And I will be wearing a smile when I do it. But just before I do him in, I will ask him the truth about Simon Singer. You can tell a lot by a man's body language. You may not ever know if he was lying or not, but I will. Suzanne will. Sheriff Reed may die an innocent man, but that is not for me to judge. Only God can judge.

In closing, I have nothing left to say, but my friends do. I believe they have just as much say in this story as I do; so here goes:

Mark Jones would like to tell everyone on God's green Earth to kiss his white ass. (I wish I would have gotten a chance to meet him before all of this; I think we would have gotten along fantastically; ha ha).

Jillian Jones is not as vulgar. She wishes everyone the best and would like to say she has buried numerous coffee cans around her property containing money. (Between you and me, I think she's full of shit, but hey, feel free to look. You never know what you might find).

Shane Butler would like to send his best to all of his family (a classy man, as always).

Deputy Green would like to apologize to his family for his misdeeds over the past couple of months. (For what it's worth, I believe him; you should, too.)

And finally, Suzanne Singer would like to apologize to her brother. She would also like to tell him that redemption may be just, but revenge is so much sweeter.

There are many others here now, but you do not know them (at least you do not know they are with me). If I survive, they'll get their word out.

I would like to say I bid you all *adieu* until we meet again, but I would advise you all to pray to whatever God it is you call your own that you will never have to meet me. If your name finds its way inside my head, I will find you, I will track you down, I will kill you, and I will wear a smile while I'm doing it.

Sincerely,
Robert Thomas Livingston a.k.a. *Bobby Thomas*

✴ CHRISTMAS TREE

Philip Thorogood

O Christmas tree, O Christmas tree!
Thou tree most fair and lovely!
O Christmas tree, O Christmas tree!
How doth this empty house wish for thee!

The sight of thee at Christmastide
Would uplift us, before our fireside
O Christmas tree, O Christmas tree
How do we all now yearn to see!

Tradition would have it, in the Archibold family, that while the great and wonderful decorating of the Christmas tree would commence on—and never before—Christmas Eve, the specimen itself would be gathered and retrieved to their front lawn in the week preceding the event. This year, however, by the time the sun began to drop in the sky on the eve of Christmas Eve, no such plant was to be seen. Sampson Archibold—head of the family, father to David and wife to Georgina—was massaging his temples from his favorite armchair, which was situated before the roaring fire. A shadow fell over him; his wife stood between him and the soothing heat of the flames, hands pointedly placed on her curved hips.

"That was uncalled for, Sam," she enunciated clearly. She was referring to his sending their eight-year-old son up to his room not five minutes ago. He hadn't done it quietly. "He was only asking." Sam looked at his wife. She looked beautiful in a green-spotted dress that hugged her buxom figure.

He sighed and lowered his head. "Gina—" he started, but she interrupted him.

"Don't you 'Gina' me!"

"I really don't want to fight. Not again. It's almost Christmas."

"Exactly!" she seized on his statement. "Tomorrow is Christmas Eve, Sam. Christmas Eve! The night before the celebration of Jesus' birth. You do remember what this family does *every* Christmas Eve, right?" He nodded despondently, but she was adamant. "Hmm?"

"Decorate the tree," he mumbled.

"Decorate the tree! And do you know what the *one* problem is with us decorating the tree tomorrow, Sam?" She was really on a tear now, and he sighed again. She tossed her head, flinging her platinum-streaked brown hair over her shoulder, and rolled her eyes.

It was enough for Sam. He shot out of the chair and began pacing. "We don't have a tree. And you know *why* we don't have a tree, Gina? Because I've been so busy at work that if I'd have stepped out for even a few minutes, I probably wouldn't be receiving that Christmas bonus! And there remains the fact that you could've just as easily taken a few minutes out of your busy schedule to—"

"I would have happily popped out to get one from the store if you didn't *insist* on getting a *natural* tree *every single year*."

"Oh no. Hell no, I'm not paying for some fake plastic thing that'll smell like chemicals and an industry sweatshop!"

"Then you can't expect me to be able to take time out of *my* work to go gallivanting about in forests looking for the right tree. You know Christmas is the busiest time of the year for the church."

"So your work is more important than mine, just because I don't work with people?" his voice was low.

She shook her head and visibly took a breath. "That's not what I meant, Sam. I just thought that with both of us so busy it would be easier ..." Her voice trailed off, and he knew what she meant. Yet again with the fake tree push. Every year.

"You say the same every year, and every year I tell you—it's tradition!"

"A-ha! Tradition! *Just* like our tradition of decorating it on Christmas Eve!"

"Goddammit, woman!" he shouted and lunged out of his chair, heading for the hall.

"Don't you dare use the Lord's name in vain, Sampson!" she called after him.

He hesitated just for long enough to grab his keys and stuff himself into a puffy overcoat before slamming the door with a final, resounding "Jesus Christ!" as his parting shot.

❊ ❊ ❊

Gina walked through the drawing room, away from the deep warmth of the fire into the sitting room and watched her husband trudge through the gathering snow to get to the car. Taking another steadying breath, she turned and headed upstairs to their bedroom. Once there, she changed into her nightie and proceeded with her nightly ablutions, before kneeling beside the bed. She clasped the tiny golden cross that hung from the chain around her neck and closed her eyes. Out of instinct, she turned her head towards the church that she was vicar of—three streets down the road—even though she could not have seen it. She recited the Lord's prayer, and her normal nightly offering of words, and a final addendum.

"Lord, please give us strength. Bring us closer as a family, and enlighten us to our true, immaterial value."

She sighed and got into bed, already missing the warmth of her husband beneath the cold, heavy sheets.

❋ ❋ ❋

Sam was driving slowly through the drifting precipitation, the car's full-beam headlights not helping visibility in the slightest. After his initial aggressive jolt out of the parking space at the end of the drive—he wouldn't chance parking on the icy slope that was their driveway during the coldest part of winter—he had slowed right down. Even though he was angry, he wouldn't let that change his normal careful driving habits. The only difference in his manner was his gritted teeth and the creaking of his leather driving gloves as they squeezed the steering wheel.

"The Lord's name my arse," he muttered. Despite his strong love for his wife and his pride in her advanced career and clear devotion to her cause, Sam had never been a believer. A bunch of superstitious mumbo-jumbo and silly mutterings was his secretly kept opinion, though he never said it, of course. He had so wanted to avoid a fight; he'd been planning on getting up at dawn to go collect a tree for their traditional decorating anyway, so this argument was pointless. He ground his teeth harder and flicked the lights down to normal, then back up to high beam. The falling snow was annoying; with the high beams on, the flakes reflected the majority of the light, stopping you from seeing, and on normal intensity, you couldn't see far enough ahead.

He forced himself to take a deep breath in, held it for as long as he could, then let it out slowly. He did this a few times until he was calmer. The one thing he was glad for was the axe and lengths of rope that were already in the boot of the car, placed there earlier so he would be ready for the morning's expedition. An hour passed of the snow driving into the windshield before he arrived at his destination; it was a journey that should have taken ten minutes but was lengthened by the weather and his limited speed. With a resigned sigh, he braced himself and opened the door of the car. The heat that the engine had built up was gone in a moment and, shivering, Sam pulled the axe and rope out behind him.

Four hours after Gina had gone to bed, the front door slammed open, shaking the house. Unable to sleep properly while her husband was away, she had been reading, and at the sudden noise, she threw the book quickly onto the bedside table. Slipping on her husband's dressing gown—it was warmer and softer than hers, and swaddled her comfortingly— she went downstairs, meeting James on the upstairs landing. Taking his hand and keeping him safely behind her, they went down the stairs.

Immediately before them, on the landing, were heaps of trampled snow. More of the frigid white flakes were flurrying in through the wide-open door, which Gina hurried to close. A muffled curse came from the drawing room, and together they followed the trail of fallen snow to the culprit.

Sam stood in one corner of the room, straightening the branches of a magnificent green-needled pine tree. They stood together, mother and son, mouths agape at the brilliant specimen before them, until little James broke the spell, running and jumping for joy around the room. Gina recovered, the ice around her heart from their earlier argument melting instantly at this grand gesture. She went straight to him and threw her arms around him, ignoring the sludgy snow and dirt on his clothes.

"Oh Sam, it's fantastic," she gushed. He nodded, his face flushed with the sudden heat of the house and the exertion of fighting to get the tree inside by himself. When he had pulled into the driveway, he had been ready to be smug and snarky with her, but Gina's outpouring of love and affection banished that in an instant. He grinned.

"It is something, isn't it? Hey, James!" He collared the exulting boy and, getting down to one knee, dragged him playfully into a one-armed hug, his other arm around his wife. "Do you know what we're going to do tomorrow, my boy?"

"Decorate the tree!" James crowed. Sam laughed.

"Yes, we are, and the entire house, too! So you best get on up to bed and get rested, hadn't you?"

The boy needed no more encouragement, and after giving his parents a quick peck on the cheek each goodnight— pulling his mother down to his level to do so—he scampered off upstairs. They heard his bedroom door slam shut and the audible click of the switch-string of his light being pulled.

They smiled at each other knowingly with shared love—he'd never been so quick to get off to bed. Gina sighed happily and turned to look once more at the tree—it almost radiated green.

"How did you manage such a splendid find on the night before Christmas Eve?"

Sam bit back the truth—she wouldn't have approved, and he didn't want another argument—and winked at her instead. "A man has his ways and means, my dear lady."

O Christmas tree, O Christmas tree!
You stand in verdant beauty!
O Christmas tree, O Christmas tree!
Now this house is complete with thee!

Your boughs are green 'gainst twinkling light
And do not fade in winter's blight
O Christmas tree, O Christmas tree
How tall and strong and mighty!

Sam was up early as planned the next day—almost at the crack of dawn, in fact—and was out to town and back home before even Gina had got up to start the pre-Christmas cooking. She was just coming down the stairs, her hair balled up in a towel turban, and narrowed her eyes at him in mock suspicion.

"And where have you been out to so early?"

Sam's answer was to grin and hold up the many large bags he carried, the hundreds of pounds worth of decorations almost spilling out over the tops of the overloaded carriers.

"Don't let the door..." she began, but it was too late. The wind caught it and slammed it shut, the impact echoing throughout the house. Moments later James was running down the stairs, his eager feet pounding onto each step. Gina struck her hands-on-hips serious-mothering pose. "Don't run down the stairs. You'll—"

Their son tripped on the last step and face-planted the carpeted hallway floor. In a second, before either of them could react, he was back up on his feet, grinning widely at them both.

"I'm fine! No harm. What's in those?" It was like he was high on sugar, and they hadn't begun to open their traditional Christmas sweets tin yet.

After a mild scolding from Gina—who Sam could see was struggling not to laugh at their son's over-eager spill—the three of them entered the drawing room.

"Does it seem … bigger to you?" Gina ventured slowly as James tucked into the bags that Sam had just put down on the floor.

Sam stood back a little and took in the tree's girth. Had it brushed the ceiling last night when he'd brought it in? He couldn't remember. Eventually, he shrugged. "We were tired last night, and over-excited after I brought it home. I can't remember how high exactly it was, but clearly it's four meters! Good job we chose a place with high ceilings, eh?" Sam frowned slightly as he noticed how close the branches were to the three-piece suite in the room, and wondered briefly how he had managed to haul it in without knocking any of those down, but quickly dismissed the notion. As Gina moved off into the kitchen to breakfast ready, he got down on his knees next to James and began to help him sort the decorations into piles.

After the first load of dishes were prepared and bubbling or roasting away, Gina joined the guys in decorating the tree and house. The only disruption to their day was when their cat, Fridge—James had named him when he was younger and had insisted that they call her Fridge through many a tantrum and strop until it stuck—entered the room. Sam held out his hand to their pet, taking a pause from their ministrations, and recoiled with a sharp intake of breath as her claws raked his fingers.

"Ow, Fridge! What was that for?"

Her fur was raised all over, every claw on her paws extended and visible, her teeth bared in an aggressive hiss.

Concerned more than angry or hurt, Sam shuffled forward on his knees to scoop her up, but she turned tail and bolted from the room. Even as Gina fussed over his fingers and retrieved a plaster from the first aid kit under the kitchen sink, he frowned his worry until James' remonstrations and demands brought his attention away from her and back to the decorating.

❄ ❄ ❄

Later that night, with an exhausted James tucked away sound asleep in bed, Sam and Gina crept about the ground floor. From the hidden cupboard behind a false back wall in the tiny pantry, they ferried each load of brightly colored presents, taking four trips until every gift was safely pushed underneath the lowest branches of the Christmas tree. James wasn't the only one who was tired; Sam had been run off his feet chasing after his son, keeping him out of Gina's way whenever she took to the kitchen and helping him decorate the entire house. Gina had split her time between cooking all their meals for both that day and the next and helping the boys decorate. Sam yawned and stretched, laughing in reflex as Gina poked his side mid-stretch. She waved him to follow her tiredly, heading for the stairs and their bed. Sam reached the hallway and leaned back into the drawing room to flick off the main light. Instinctively, he glanced around the room and paused, remembering what he had to do.

The room was brightly lit by the thousands of twinkling lights wrapped around the tree, the dulled-neon colors reflecting off the tinsel, ceiling streamers, and window-ledge ornaments. By the dying fire, three stockings hung, all stuffed with goodies—Sam had done Gina's, and vice versa—and atop the mantel piece a saucer held a glass of milk, three cookies, and a carrot, ready for Santa and his reindeer. He had forgotten those. Walking back into the room, he took as big a bite as he could manage out of the carrot's side, spitting it out into his hand to take to the bin in the kitchen, and followed it up by cramming two cookies into his mouth in four large, crunching bites. Washing them down with the milk—making sure to leave a fair scattering of cookies on the plate—he turned to go to the kitchen bin and froze.

His favorite chair—the one he always sat in to feel the soothing warmth of the fire—was closer to the tree. A frown creased his forehead, and he scratched his chin, feeling another yawn building.

"Must have knocked into it when we did the presents," he said to himself. With a mental shrug, he walked over to it and pulled it out, his frown deepening as he saw the worn indents in the carpet where it had sat in the years since Gina had bought it for him. He remained confused as the chair bumped into the sofa, which apparently hadn't moved. He shook his head, dismissing his concerns; whatever had happened, he could sort it all out once the decorations were done. Sam popped out to the kitchen and dropped the carrot piece in the bin, then headed up to bed, sticking his head in to switch off the drawing room light.

O Christmas tree, O Christmas tree!

How laden are your branches!
O Christmas tree, O Christmas tree!
Over night you still enhance!

The sight of thee fills up the room
Hidden mysteries in gloom
O Christmas tree, O Christmas tree
How strange and unearthly!

Sam woke up to his senses jarring horribly. A heart-breaking wailing was echoing up the stairs from the drawing room, and he was out of bed and to the top of the stairs before Gina had even properly thrown back her side of the covers.

"What's going on?" she mumbled, but her husband had no reply for her—he was already halfway down the stairs.

He skidded into the drawing room, incredulity rooting him to the spot. James stood in the middle of the room, bawling his eyes out like he hadn't for several years now, his head raised to the ceiling in what could only be described as despair. Gina bumped into Sam as she came into the room, a lack of understanding enabling her to speak where he could not.

"Where are the presents?"

What Sam couldn't force past his tightening throat was that that was the least of their problems. What Gina apparently couldn't get her eyes or mind to process was that the tree had grown to swallow the presents, and the entire fireplace could no longer be seen. His favorite chair was somehow gone, as was the sofa and the other armchair, the myriad giant branches of the tree stretching almost entirely around the outskirts of the room. Sam's paralysis finally broke as he noticed the branches were still moving, stretching now that they were all in the room in an attempt to close in and trap them all.

"Move!" he bellowed, and such was the sudden force of his voice that Gina obeyed instantly, Sam following a moment later after he had thrown James over his shoulder. The boy's crying fluctuated oddly as he bounced on his father's shoulder, the top of his head just scraping the grabbing branches as they slipped out of the room. Without thinking, Sam followed Gina as she ran into the kitchen, almost hitting her with their son's body as she pulled up short just inside the doorway.

"Back! Back!" she shouted, her voice trembling. It was in here, too, gnarled and twisted roots had pushed through the floor, turning it into a squirming carpet; bulbous knots had tipped over and broken open all of Gina's hard-worked food. They stumbled backwards as the living carpet writhed forwards in response to their presence, and Gina screamed, "Demon!"

As one, they turned to surge up the stairs. Branches were now extending from the drawing room, too, and before they began to climb, Sam caught a glimpse into the living and dining rooms—both were crawling with green and brown activity. Turning, he herded Gina up the stairs.

Back in their own bedroom, the door shut firmly behind them in the vain hope of keeping out the tree, Gina cradled and soothed James. Sam moved back and forth around the room, pushing things against the door. From their position on the bed, Gina watched her husband move, still not quite able to believe what was going on.

"This is a nightmare … the work of the devil. This is a nightmare … I'm going to wake up in a minute."

Scratching sounds came through the bedroom door, and Sam was suddenly at her side, looking deep into her eyes and stroking her hair.

"This isn't a nightmare, it's real. If only we could get to the fire ..."

She saw something there, in the depths of his gaze. A hint of something. Was it guilt? Suddenly, something clicked in her mind, and a current of anger managed to thread its way through her fear. "Where did you get that tree, Sam?"

He looked away from her piercing gaze and moved to push their chest of drawers against the pile of furniture in the doorway.

"Sampson Archibold, answer me! Where did you get that tree!?"

Sam paused mid-stride, his whole body seeming to deflate. With his head hanging and his arms limp at his sides in defeat, he said, "The army base ... on the grounds."

"What?" Her question was steel.

"A tree had brought down the fence. I noticed on the way home from work on Friday afternoon, so when I went out to get our tree ... that tree ... I went there."

"You *stole* a tree? From the *armed forces* of all people!?"

He nodded at her shrill words, but she continued none-the-less.

"You lied to me *and* committed a crime by axing down and bringing home that thing down there and—"

She was cut off as he danced forward and kissed her on the forehead.

"The axe! That's it!"

Without another word he was at the front window, hauling it open as fast as he could fumble the lock free. He glanced back at her and winked. "I'll sort this out, love. Sit tight."

Before she could say anything, he dropped from the window, her shriek following him out.

Sam's impact was muffled by the snow drifted up

against the side of the house, but he had forgotten that he was only wearing pajamas. Shivering, he brushed off the worst of the clinging flakes as he waded through shin-deep snow to the car. Glancing quickly at the house—and noticing the crazed map of branches and roots entangling the majority of the structure in the morning light—he elbowed the car window. Pain shot up his arm —he'd cut himself or stuck a piece of it in his arm—but he ignored it. The axe was right there on the passenger-side seat where he'd left it. So armed, he returned his attention to the house and, aiming himself at where the front door should have been, attacked in a frenzy.

Wood splintered and cracked, boughs fell and the fingering vines writhed away from his assault. He was a man with a weapon, and his family was in danger. With surprising ease, he made his way into the hallway, dismantling the front door with a few well-placed strikes of his heavy tool, and continued his savage chopping on into the drawing room. The demented Christmas lights continued to sparkle in amongst the main mass of the tree where he and James had set them, and the thought of his poor son and wife upstairs huddled on the bed in fright urged him on faster. The axe swung and fell and blurred as he cleared his way to the fireplace, yelling in triumph as he broke through into the little space, heat spilling from inside it as he forced the upper half of his torso through the gap, ready to grab any piece of burning wood that he could reach and set the match to this bonfire.

There was no fire. The heat was from dying embers, and sickness rose inside him as he smelt the horrid stench of burnt meat. Fridge's twisted, blackened remains lay curled in the corner of the fireplace, still smoking slightly. Fear and panic swelled inside him, feeling almost like a physical thing. He pulled backward but didn't move. He was stuck. The branches snaked and twisted around him, closing in tighter and tighter against his sides. Sam tried to yell, but the air was driven out of his lungs, and his words were swallowed.

✻ ✻ ✻

Gina heard the falls of the axe go silent and closed her eyes. It must be God's will, she decided. It was their time, and they would go out in happiness. She only wished she could spare James the agony that would no doubt signal their ascension. A creaking sound drew her eyes to the window, where the branches of the bedeviled Christmas tree covered the gap with sinister slowness. Splintering wood heralded the collapse of the door and Sam's hastily erected defense. She took a deep breath, trying to keep herself calm for James' sake. A movement on her shoulder brought her attention to another mass of branches that had wormed its way silently through the floor behind the bed, and was even now wrapping around them both.

Her eyes blurred as the truth of her situation hit home and the lies she told to herself and the world fell away. She had lost her faith years ago and had no idea what was to come after the tree was finished with them. Gina was terrified and brought James' face up to hers in a selfish move to try to find some measure of comfort in her son. Her last move was to scream as she saw the tiny tendrils of wood and vines that had snaked through his airways and around his eyeballs. He was dead, but his eyes watched accusingly as the tree invaded her open mouth, sealing her airway and choking her from the world.

O Christmas tree, O Christmas tree!
Growing so willfully!
O Christmas tree, O Christmas tree!

Come from where, did thee?

Wrapped around this family house
Your branches breaking brick and tile
O Christmas tree, O Christmas tree
Your influence spreading wild!

Five minutes after Gina lost her life, five armored vehicles tore down the quiet street, drawing a crowd from the neighboring houses as they surrounded the enmeshed dwelling. Squads of grim-faced men in army fatigues spilled out, evacuating the buildings to either side and setting up a quarantine zone thirty meters back from the writhing mass of branches.

Ten minutes after Gina lost her life, a helicopter hove into view above the road and settled down into a hastily cleared landing area. A starchly upright man stepped from the chopper, his oversized aviators projecting a veneer of disdain on the whole scene. He walked past the barricades and stood within three meters of the furthest-reaching branches, which were even now beginning to attempt to claw outwards for more sustenance to consume. A thin branch with eight finger-like tendrils extended from its end whipped out, the commando ducking at the last second, a combat blade unsheathed seemingly from nowhere chopping the offending limb apart as it passed. Just as suddenly, it was sheathed again, secreted somewhere on his person.

He sighed and turned back to the edge of the quarantined area, climbing unhurriedly back into the helicopter.

"They're long gone. Burn it all," was all he said. As he was born into the air, the soldiers produced flame-throwers and fireman-like hoses from their vehicles, trailing large tanks of flammable liquid. His last view of that house was of the flames beginning to take hold of the living fuel. He turned his head to regard the city, taking in the many smoke-wreathed dwellings scattered across the region that he had already put to the torch, and wondered how many more he would have to burn before the day was out. Anger suddenly stole through him and a scarred fist punched the bulkhead beside him.

"Damn scientists," he muttered.

"Sir?" the pilot inquired.

He shook his head. He'd forgotten the microphone in the headset he wore. "Just take us to the next one, son."

The pilot nodded as the man settled back into his seat, sighing and fingering the stripes on his shoulder. It was going to be a long Christmas.

✱ALL ✱I ✱WANT FOR ✱CHRISTMAS ✱IS ✱YOU
Mandy DeGeit

nopened Christmas cards lay forgotten on the shelf
So different is this holiday, since I'm all by myself.
Santa and his sleigh, towed by nine horned deer
Garland, balls and tinsel, all choke me with cheer.

Remember when we were happy, times so long ago?
I think of how you kissed me, beneath the mistletoe.
Once upon a time, you said, I'd make the perfect wife.
Together—you promised—for the rest of my life.

I smile as I think back to the moments we had.
My one little motion brought good out of bad
Never again, will we argue or fight
'Tis the season to begin what's finally right.

Your dark red blood has stained my floor.
I slit your throat as you spat the word "whore".
Your dead, rigid body lies wrapped under the tree.
The perfect boyfriend, from now on, you'll be.

The Red Man

Patrick Freivald

The elf clambered off the sleigh, her black claws digging jagged furrows into the snow-covered asphalt shingles. She shuddered in anticipation, ran a tongue over rows of razor-sharp teeth. Slitted nostrils flared as she crept to the cold chimney. She wiped drool from her lips and dared one last glance backward. And quailed under her master's gaze.

The Red Man huddled in his seat, wrapped warm in reindeer furs, his ashen, withered skin pulled too tight against his skull. Shriveled eyes glowed with reflected starlight out of sunken, black sockets. Nine deer stood motionless, not the slightest hint of breath fogging the air, white ribs showing through patchy fur, their eyes as red as the front one's nose. The Red Man stretched out a cold, skeletal finger. The elf vaulted the red brick masonry into the hole.

Chitinous claws dug into soot-blackened brick. At this height, the acrid smell of creosote almost washed out the smell of the sleeping boy. She crept down the chimney toward the dappled light below, careful not to make the slightest noise. The child-smell assaulted her nostrils as she pushed past the flue and hazarded a look. Only the tree illuminated the living room, casting multicolored shadows around the hearth. She scowled at the presents that scattered the floor; the parents had put out their store-bought gifts before seeking the shelter of sleep.

She dropped to the floor, then raised to her tiptoes and grasped the end table next to the fireplace, pulling her nose just over the edge. The scowl turned to a sneer at the crumb-dusted saucer and empty glass filmed with white milk residue. It stank of doubt and trickery, poisonous adult smells of a world too cynical to believe. She shied back, and followed the boy's vibrant and wondrous smell up the stairs.

This was a special year. The Red Man's list had told him this was the last year before the boy's parents told him the Great Lie: Elves don't exist. The Red Man doesn't exist. There is nothing but atoms and forces and the cold clank of machinery. This untruth would infect his mind, poison his soul, turn him into one of them. Already starving, the Red Man couldn't let this happen, not to one more child. If they wouldn't believe in gifts and grandeur, then they would at least fear the dark.

She climbed the stairs on all fours, nails leaving pinprick holes in the wood. She froze. Voices murmured in the next room, adult voices. Light sprang from the crack under the door, and she scampered into the corner. The door opened, and the man emerged. His powder-blue bathrobe split open to reveal a hairy chest as pale as his bunny-slippered feet. He yawned on his way to the bathroom, passing inches from the elf. She couldn't help it, the warm flesh so close and raw and inviting. Her jaw unhinged to take the calf whole, and she bit. Her teeth clapped together, passing through the leg as though there was nothing there.

She growled in frustration as the man stepped into the bathroom and closed the door. Without belief, the elf had no power.

"Mommy?" The voice came from the next room. The elf huddled in place, ruing the growl. When no one replied, the boy tried again. "Santa?"

"Just me, champ," the man said. "Go back to bed." The toiled flushed. "Santa won't come if you're not asleep."

The elf's flesh shriveled, her skin cracked. He had invoked the Red Man not to reinforce belief, but for the convenience of a good night's sleep. And in a spark of doubt, the boy knew it, if only for a moment smothered by hope.

She crept past the bathroom door, and recoiled from the man's reek billowing from the crack underneath. He stank of stolen milk and chocolate chips and cheap, box-store wrapping paper. Gagging, she flattened herself and slid under the bedroom door even as the man stepped out of the bathroom.

Sweet and bright with wonder and awe, the boy's scent encompassed everything the man's didn't. It filled the dark room, entwined the elf, giving fire to her heartbeat and strength to her muscles. Fueled by the energy, the elf grew, an expanding shadow of teeth and claws. Her feet left the ground. She hovered over the mound of covers on the bed, feeding on the energy of the dozing brown-haired boy. Dreams of the Red Man flooded through him, but it wasn't the Red Man she knew. The boy's Red Man was a stranger of time past, fat and jolly and full of good cheer.

The elf snarled when the Red Man suckled at the dream through their ethereal bond. The chord pulled taut as he slaked his thirst, leaching the boundless energies from the boy before she could even taste them. He gorged deep, and through the chord she felt his undying rage, mad with the knowledge that the Great Lie would destroy this font for all future years.

She knew she shouldn't resent the Red Man. Her creator had woven her from dreams such as these, had made her for this purpose. And like her, all over the world on this magical night, countless other elves did their master's work. They surrendered their feast so that the Red Man might abide another year of frozen solitude in the Arctic wastes.

Yet she knew that this night she was special as a few elves each year were: she wouldn't be going home. She would stay and foster the dregs of nightmare as the boy left innocence behind in the rush to adulthood.

A quiver of doubt shuddered through her. To never return to the ice caves, the frozen workshop, cold and cruel in its sparkling majesty, to abandon all she'd ever known for the warm land, hunted without mercy by the unbelievers… It was too much to bear, but bear it she must. The Red Man needed her. The boy must believe in *something*. She shook off her fears and looked down.

The blanket rose and fell. The boy's contented smile turned to a frown, then a grimace. The elf ran her tongue across her teeth, felt the flesh slice and tear, and tasted her own blood. Drunk on belief, her hands grew, black claws stretching like knives, knuckles popping as bones extended and muscles bulged. She grabbed the sides of the bed, pinned the blanket in place, and pulled herself down to within inches of the boy's face. She grinned her bloody smile, and exhaled. Hot breath fell like smoke onto the cherubic face. It slithered into the boy's nostrils and half-open mouth, grabbed his heart, and squeezed.

The boy's eyes snapped open and he shrieked, a too-human cry of primal terror. He thrashed and tore at the covers, but couldn't budge the elf's massive arms.

A stream of bloody drool fell from her mouth, spattering his face. Her jaw unhinged and opened wider and wider. The dark taste of his fear flooded down her throat and filled her bloated belly.

From down the hall a door crashed open. Footsteps thundered. In a blink the elf shrank and fell, then dove into the closet. It stank of old shoes and underwear and the delicious gobbets of imagination that clung to toys. She burrowed into the pile, glared once at the boy, who cowered in terror but couldn't peel his eyes away, and pulled her head back to disappear under the mess.

The bedroom door crashed open. Light splashed through the pile of dirty clothes.

"Hey, buddy!" the man said. "What is it?"

"A monster!"

The elf listened as the man consoled the boy, and strength leached from her bones when the man said that monsters aren't real. The closet light clicked on, then off, and her heart stuttered. The man swept under the bed with a flashlight and her skin withered; he checked the locks on the windows and bones grew brittle.

"But he was right there!" the boy said. A flicker of power infused the elf, a cool balm in a sea of burns.

"I already showed you there's nothing in there. Now go to sleep. Santa won't come if you aren't asleep." The elf shuddered at the cynical bribe, even as she feasted on the hope it brought.

"Here," the woman said from the doorway. "I brought Mr. Jangles. He'll keep you safe."

The elf smelled something new, feral and cruel and lazy

and spoiled. She dared a peek, and despite the smell she suppressed a dark chuckle. The fat orange thing's rumbling purr spoke of its softness as the boy hugged it to his chest. This wasn't a hunter, just a pale shadow of the tiger it resembled, a domesticated mockery of its true spirit.

The light went out as the parents left, but they left the door open a crack. The elf waited, pulling energy from the toys until ready to move. She pulled an extra jolt of essence from a discarded sock in the corner, relishing the lingering memory of a stick-fight with a "dragon bush", and dashed under the bed. She gasped at the massive cavern of black unknowns and dark mystery.

Driven by curiosity, she crept deep into the cave and smelled a coldness, a primal horror older than time. Beyond the darkness—beyond the *smell*—lay something alien, an undulating mass of inhuman, writhing *other*. The elf scrambled back before the music of nasal flutes and deep, monotonous thrumming could shred her essence and scattered it to the void.

She bolted for the closet. Under the bed was no safe place for an elf. That darkness wasn't like the Red Man, born of human faith and thus human in its inhumanity. The things beyond were older, past time and above space. The elf huddled in the pile of clothes and toys.

Eyes flashed in the darkness, bright green with thin vertical slits for pupils. The elf watched the orange thing's tail lash back and forth as it crouched, ready to pounce. She smiled and unhinged her jaw, ready for it.

The lazy thing must have thought it was fast. It had no idea. When it pounced, the elf opened her mouth wide. The plaintive meow drowned to nothing as her jaws snapped shut, and she licked her lips in satisfaction. This sustenance tasted different from what she's known. Meat wasn't spirit, but it was delicious. The world outside must have more; she'd have to explore when time allowed. The elf settled down to wait for the morning. Dawn would bring a big day. She closed her eyes, and dozed.

The boy's eyes snapped open a half-hour after dawn. She felt his heartbeat quicken, and drank his anticipation. Her bones stretched and cracked. Orange hair sprouted from her skin. Her head shrank, her neck bent forward. Rows of teeth became three, then two, then one, and they dulled to feline points. Her tail swished back and forth, an unfamiliar sensation. She hopped on the bed and licked the boy's face.

The boy giggled and pushed her to the side. "Mr. Jangles, I'm up!" He sprang from his bed, revealing red and yellow Iron Man pajamas. A mischievous smile on his face, he crept through the door and tiptoed down the stairs. The elf followed, padding across the floor with a domesticated lack of grace.

The boy shrieked when he hit the landing, a cry of unbridled joy that strangled the elf with its energy. She rubbed against a chair, skin crackling with power. With the magic of Christmas Eve behind them for another year, the Red Man couldn't steal this energy, and it filled her to bursting. She tore through the house, latching onto a present and raking it with her back claws, only to dash through the kitchen, around the dining room, and back to the tree.

The boy laughed and clapped his hands, but the spell had passed. The elf's hackles rose. She ducked behind the couch as footsteps descended the stairs. The man and the woman puttered about making coffee and English muffins, and all the while the boy's energies grew. When the time came, he tore into his presents: a video game console, a junior chemistry kit, and countless other distractions from the doldrums of school and chores.

The elf cringed and shriveled with each presentation. "This is from your uncle Vernon." "Your aunt Mary got you the green one with the red bow." "This is from your dad and I." There were no presents from Santa, only from relatives, and even untold the Great Lie took root—and the elf struggled to maintain its form. When the last of the presents lay open, she gasped in relief, gagging on a hairball as the boy lost himself in his toys.

She sat on his lap as he played his new video game, a gory slaughter of guns and tanks and extra lives that neither required nor provoked a spark of imagination. She purred as the boy petted her with fingers still warm with lingering wonder. She closed her eyes against the cold, lifeless hands of the man and the woman.

At last exhausted, the boy dozed on the couch, hugging her to his chest, his contented dreams a trickle of energy just enough to stave off starvation. Doubt ravaged his dreams, a world without Santa, without wonder, and she despaired.

The Red Man was right; wonder was too fragile. Belief must come from a deeper, more enduring place.

When the man carried the sleeping boy upstairs, she followed. She purred on the bed until the man turned out the light, then hopped off and trotted into the closet. She waited until the man and woman succumbed to their dreamless adult slumber and at last the house lay quiet.

In that silence, four legs writhed and became eight, stretching to three times their length, bristling with black, rigid hairs. Two eyes became eight lifeless, black orbs atop a face not quite that of a doll. Canines folded and stretched into great mandibles, bigger around than the boy's arms.

The spider-thing crept out of the closet and clambered to the ceiling. She crept over the bed, a giant stinger protruding from her abdomen and glistening with wet poison. She

wove a web of tangled dreams, waited to be noticed.
And feared.

Happy Christmas

Flo Stanton

Verditt accosted Patmun in the hardware section of S-Mart. He eyeballed a fourteen-foot wide wreath.

"What do you think, Patmun?" Verditt chuckled. "Your roof or mine?"

Patmun winced. Every year his neighbor added more crap to the tacky Christmas decorations he slathered on every inch of his property.

Verditt started this madness with 25,000 multi-colored bulbs on his roof spelling out "Happy Christmas" in a synchronized display. WKRZ dispatched a news crew, and Verditt was off and running. The following year an animated Santa climbing in and out of a chimney appeared on the lawn, and the next Verditt added eight custom-made reindeer pulling an authentic Victorian sleigh. Last year he erected a nativity complete with life-sized Mary, Joseph, baby in manger, wise men, and talking animals.

Bose speakers blasted holiday tunes while motorized spotlights crisscrossed the centerpiece, a twenty-five-foot Douglas fir anointed by two hundred battery-powered candles.

Patmun and the other residents of Avalon Hills suffered a relentless stream of traffic, noise, and blinding lights every hour of darkness from Thanksgiving until after New Year's, strangers parking on their lawns and demanding bathroom privileges and refreshments for their thirsty little ragamuffins.

So that day in the S-Mart Verditt was surprised when Patmun said, "George, you've been doing all the work yourself all these years." He slung an arm around his neighbor's shoulder. "This year, sit back and relax. I'll do it all myself."

For six straight days Patmun strung lights and set up displays, with no assistance from Verditt. In fact, no one had seen Verditt for a week.

The day after Thanksgiving everyone in town jammed the streets of Avalon Hills and nearby interchanges. They had to see the new display! The WKRZ van pulled up right at sunset and the station helicopter circled overhead.

Patmun finally threw the switch. WKRZ viewers witnessed a 50,000-light display of "Happy FUCKING Christmas!" before the frantic station manager cut to a commercial. Thousands of gawkers on the ground saw a reprogrammed Santa flogging his candy cane and the Grinch tonguing Rudolph's bum. Over in the nativity scene a very naked Mary and Joseph proved that Mary was no longer a virgin while drooling, lecherous elves sodomized Gaspar, Melchior and Balthazar as well as sacred corporate icons Strawberry Shortcake and Kim Kardashian.

In the middle was the Douglas fir with this year's addition–Verditt. He was posed as Vitruvian man, limbs outstretched, with the trunk of the Douglas fir rammed up his ass. Patmun had stripped the tree of its upper branches and honed the tips to a fine point, then jammed each bough under Verditt's skin. He replaced all two hundred battery-powered candles with real ones; the wax sizzled as it dropped onto Verditt's freezing skin. Verditt, still alive, made little whimpering noises.

Through a haze of anesthetics, barbiturates, and "Jesus Juice" the star atop the tree slowly became aware of the slack-jawed gaping of the awe-struck crowd and wondered, "How the fuck am I gonna top this next year?"

CHRISTMAS SHOPPING

Dan Foley

*F*uck, Skip thought as Deedee kissed the last of his in-
laws goodbye at the door. God, how he hated them
right now. Most of the year he could put up with
them, but not now. Now they were giving him an ulcer.

Her brother, George, was the worst. The only beer he
would drink when he was here at Skip's house was Heineken.
He went through at least a six-pack or two every time he
came over. When Skip went to his house, though, he was
always "out" of Heinie; all he ever had was Bush.

"Well, you'd better get started on this mess, or it'll still be
here tomorrow," Deedee said as she looked over the pile of
dirty dishes in the sink and on the counters. It looked like an
invading army had ransacked the house, ate everything in it,
and trashed what was left.

Skip wanted to say, "Fuck it, they're your relatives, you clean it up," but he couldn't. One year he had made the mistake of offering to do the cleanup because she did all the cooking, and now it was cast in stone. *What the hell was I thinking?* he thought as he stared at the piles of dishes on the counter.

It's the same every year, every fucking year, he thought. He could never curse like that out loud—Deedee would have a fit—but his thoughts were often riddled with obscenities when he thought about his in-laws. And this time of year, Thanksgiving Day and the four weeks before Christmas, was the worst.

Fucking leeches, he thought, and started loading one empty plate after another into the dishwasher. Every Thanksgiving they descended on his house like a horde of hungry locusts, consuming a twenty-four pound turkey, a five-pound bag of potatoes, a dozen sweet potatoes, two loaves of bread, bowls of vegetables, stuffing, a vat of gravy, at least four pies, a case of beer, two bottles of wine, and countless glasses of soda and juice. And not one of them contributed anything to the feast except an appetite. Skip had tried putting out a lot of snacks before dinner, but they went through them like Sherman through Georgia and still ate everything Deedee put on the table. They'd been coming to his house for years, and in all that time Skip had yet to have enough turkey left over for a sandwich the next day.

"What do you say we make it a pot-luck affair? We can supply the turkey and drinks and everyone can bring their favorite dish," he had suggested one year.

Deedee had flat-out refused. "This is our house and they're our guests, it's up to us to provide the food. When we go to their house, they provide the food," she had told him.

Yeah, right, we hardly ever go to any of their places, and when we do, Deedee insists on bringing something, he thought as he closed the dishwasher's door on what would be the first of at least four loads.

He might have been able to live with that once a year if it wasn't for Christmas. Deedee insisted on buying Christmas presents for every last one of them. For her parents, her three brothers and four sisters, and all their kids, regardless of age. All twenty-three of them, and it was a number that grew each year; one or another of them was always popping out another rugrat. This year it had been Carol, and from the way Mary was piling on the pounds, she'd be the next to announce. And Deedee insisted on spending a fucking fortune on each of them. At least her grandfather, the piggy patriarch, had finally kicked the bucket in June. *Too bad the old boy couldn't have gone a month earlier. It would have saved me the hundred bucks Deedee insisted on giving him every year,* Skip thought.

Now she wanted to spend fifty bucks on each parent, fifty bucks on each brother and sister, fifty bucks on their husbands and wives, and twenty-five bucks for each niece and nephew, for a grand total of nine-hundred-and-seventy-five dollars. And that didn't even count Christmas cards (and postage) and the individual ornament she insisted on attaching to each present. Skip still might be able to live with it if Deedee didn't rub his nose in it by insisting he do the Christmas shopping with her to buy all the presents. He hated shopping on a good day, and any day between Thanksgiving and Christmas was not a good day.

"I want to get an early start tomorrow," Deedee said as she carried yet another stack of dishes in from the dining room. "The stores open at six and I want to be there before it gets too crowded."

Jesus, what difference does that make? Skip thought. *It's the busiest damn shopping day of the year. Christ, I'll be lucky to drag your ass out of there before the place closes no matter what time we get there. And then you'll want to stop at Barnes and Noble on the way home.*

And Skip knew that tomorrow was just the start of things. For the next four weeks, his life was going to be a living hell. Deedee was going to drag him to every mall and shopping plaza within twenty miles of their house.

✳ ✳ ✳

It was five-thirty in the morning, and Skip already had a headache. *Where the fuck do all these people come from?* he thought as he cruised the already crowded parking lot looking for an open space.

"Just park already," Deedee demanded impatiently as he started down another row.

"Where?" Skip asked.

"Anywhere. Go out to the end."

"Fine," Skip agreed. Anything to shut her up.

"Wait. Drop me off here, then meet me at Sears at six o'clock."

Skip stopped as directed and let her out.

"And don't be late," she admonished him as she shut the door.

Skip parked the car in Lot T (there was no Lot U, or anything past that) and, looking at his watch, knew he'd be lucky to get to Sears by six-thirty. *Christ, why couldn't she pick a store at this end of the mall?* he thought as he started the walk back. A walk he would make several times this day carrying packages to the car.

They were just rolling back the gates at Sears when Skip finally reached Deedee. She was fidgeting at the entrance like a junkie looking for a fix when he walked up.

"What took you so long? We were almost late," she complained. Before Skip could answer, she was dragging him into the store.

"Deedee, we're going to be here all day, there's no rush," he said peevishly.

"Well, I just wanted to get started," she answered, hurt by his response. She enjoyed shopping so much; she just couldn't understand that Skip found it stressful.

"Okay," Deedee said, pulling her list from her pocket. "My dad's first, what do you suggest?"

Skip knew it didn't matter what he suggested—Deedee was going to settle on whatever she wanted anyway—but he took a shot at it on the off chance that she would listen to him. "How about a gift certificate? Then he could get anything he wanted. And he could hit the sales," he added, hoping that might help.

"Don't be ridiculous," Deedee answered immediately. "We can't give him a gift certificate. They're too impersonal. What else?"

"How about a book? He loves to read?"

"No. I'd be afraid of getting him something he's already read.'

"Clothes?"

"He doesn't need clothes."

An hour and a half later Deedee finally settled on a Black and Decker Leaf Blower. Actually, it was more than just a blower. It was a blower, vacuum, and mulcher—and it cost $64.99, excluding tax.

"Deedee, with tax this is seventy bucks. That's twenty more than we have budgeted. If we get this for him, we're going to have to cut back on somebody else. You know that, right?"

"But it's the perfect gift. He'd never buy it for himself, and he always complains about raking leaves," Deedee said in return.

He complains about everything, Skip thought but didn't say it. Instead, he said, "Okay, Deedee, but you know we're going to have to cut back somewhere else, right?"

"We'll cross that bridge when we come to it," Deedee answered, and he knew it was a lost cause. He just hoped she wasn't going to overspend on everyone.

"Okay, Mom's next," Deedee said, checking her list.

"No, coffee's next," Skip, insisted." I need a break." *Not to mention a couple of Aleves for this fucking headache*, he thought.

Twenty-five unrelaxing minutes later, Deedee dragged him out of the Food Court and back into the shopping wars. Two hours and no presents later, Skip was ready to kill something. He actually found himself peering into a pet shop window at a litter of puppies with malice in his heart when a flyer caught his eye.

"How about a massage?" he said, pointing to the flyer in the pet store window. "I think your mother would really enjoy one," he added, hoping he sounded sincere.

"You know, she might at that," Deedee agreed. "It would do her good. It might make her relax."

Great, another one down, and right on budget, Skip thought. The massage was exactly fifty dollars.

"But I'll have to get her something small to go with it," Deedee announced.

"What?" Skip asked, dismayed.

"She has to have something more than an envelope to open on Christmas. Half the fun is opening presents."

"Fine," Skip agreed. "Get her a romance novel. She reads enough of those."

"Good idea," Deedee agreed again.

By the end of the shopping day, they had only scratched four people off Deedee's list. Skip had taken more Aleves than that, and he still had a headache. Well, at least her mom and dad, her sister, Eve, and Eve's husband, Chuck, were taken care of. That only left their four kids and that whole family would be done. But they were already forty-five dollars over budget. *At this rate*, Skip thought, *it's going to cost me an extra two or three hundred bucks. Christ, that's another whole family. At least we don't have to buy for her grandfather.*

The next day was another disaster as far as Skip was concerned. He followed along behind Deedee, hauled the presents she selected to the car, and cringed every time she overspent on a gift. By the time they finally left for home, they were another fifty dollars in the hole.

Sunday was a day of rest for Skip because he worshiped at the altar of the NFL. He was a Giant's fan, but it didn't matter which teams were playing, Skip would be glued to his TV set. Not even Deedee could drag him away from the house on a Sunday, or on a Monday night for that matter. It was during half time of the Giants-Redskins game that Skip thought of Deedee's grandfather and a solution to his problem … his old .22 caliber target pistol. His dad had given it to him for his birthday when he had turned fifteen. He had told Deedee he had gotten rid of it when they got married, but he hadn't. It was hidden in the garage.

Skip was in a surprisingly good mood the following week. He even went shopping without getting a headache. On Tuesday night, two hours of shopping yielded a Dremel (a multi-purpose rotary tool Skip had coveted for years) for her brother, Charlie. It went for $69.95 plus tax. Then, on Thursday, Deedee found a gravy boat and pitcher to match Charlie's wife, Annette's, good dishes. To Deedee's surprise, Skip didn't complain about either of these gifts even though she overspent on both of them.

Saturday was another marathon, and once again Skip, though not a pleasure to shop with, was at least amenable. Deedee was thrilled that he was finally getting into the Christmas spirit. He even took the time to select his sister's gift. And for the first time in years, it was something other than a last-minute gift certificate to Penney's.

When Saturday's shopping was done, Deedee had worked her way through half of her Christmas list and an extra two hundred and fifty dollars of Skip's money. And still Skip didn't complain.

On Sunday, Deedee left for shopping at eight. Skip waited until she was gone, then went to the garage for the solution to his problem before going out for his usual Sunday breakfast. When he finished that, he drove the thirty miles to his brother-in-law's house.

Skip could never understand how Charlie and Annette could live so far out in the boondocks. Hell, nestled in the woods like it was, their house wasn't even visible from the road. It had always given Skip, a city boy at heart, the willies — but now he was thankful for it.

He parked his battered pickup at a picnic area frequented by hikers and hunters. It was two miles up the road from Charlie's house, but it was only a half-mile as the crow flies. Skip hiked it in less than twenty minutes.

When Charlie answered the knock on the door, Skip could see he was surprised to see his brother-in-law.

"Hey Skip," he said, looking past him for his sister. "Where's Deedee?" he asked, puzzled when he didn't see her.

"Shopping, where else?" Skip answered.

"Then what are you doing here?" Charlie asked.

"I got Deedee that treadmill she's been talking about for

Christmas. It's in my truck. I was wondering if you could keep it here for me until Christmas?"

"I guess," Charlie answered, but not very enthusiastically.

"Great," Skip said. Then added, "How about offering me a cup of coffee and then we can unload it?"

"Sure, but I'll have to get Annette to make some," Charlie agreed, and left to find his wife. Before following Charlie inside, Skip slipped on a pair of thin plastic gloves and retrieved the .22 from under his jacket.

"Hi, Skip," Annette said when they entered the kitchen.

"Hello, Annette," Skip answered. As he was sitting down, Annette gave her husband a "what the hell" look and started to make the coffee.

While Annette was busy with the coffee, Skip shot Charlie in the temple. He put the gun right to his head so there was no chance of missing.

When Annette turned around to see what had happened, Skip shot her in the face. He was actually aiming at her chest, but luckily he hit her in the forehead instead.

The .22 was so quiet it didn't even wake the boys. But that wasn't surprising; teenagers could sleep through an earthquake. Seventeen-year-old Matt was the first to receive an early Christmas present, although it certainly wasn't what he had been expecting. Nineteen-year-old Ben got his a minute later.

Before he left, Skip took the time to make the suicide look right. He placed the gun in Charlie's hand and squeezed off one more shot into a phone book (which he discarded in a dumpster on the way home) to leave gunshot residue on his brother-in-law's hand (thank you, CSI). Then he removed one empty shell from the revolver and replaced it with a full one. That done, he left the way he had come.

What he had done really didn't hit him until he reached

his pickup. Up until then, he had only been thinking about this Christmas. Now he realized that not only had been able to cut into some of Deedee's extra spending this year, but for every year to come. God, he wished he could get rid of a few more of them, but if they started dropping like flies, somebody would get suspicious. *Well, maybe one or two more, if I can think of a way to do it. If not, I've got a whole year to pare down the tribe.*

For now, there was one less family he had to shop for, and next Saturday he could return the presents Deedee had already bought for Charlie, Annette, and the kids. That was going to be the most fun he'd had shopping in years.

Checking It Twice

Stephen Roy

Santa's eyes were green and red. Timmy saw that clearly as he waited in front of Macy's toy department. Green and red. It was creepy. That poem said they twinkled, but he couldn't recall anything there about color. Emerald, flecked with bright, bloodshot bursts of red.

It was two days before Christmas. There were little kids everywhere. He was bored and tired and he'd been standing in line for over thirty minutes. What he wanted most was to go home and watch TV, but each year his mom insisted on a new picture with Santa. So here he stood, elbow to elbow with a bunch of hopeful little kids. Timmy had lived a world-wise nine years already and seldom indulged in hope. It seemed heavy baggage and unnecessary.

"Stop biting your lip, Timmy, it'll leave a mark," his aunt

called from where they'd roped off the harried and hard-pressed parents. "And push your hair back from your forehead. You want your mom to have a nice picture, don't you?"

Aunt Elaine had volunteered to take him again this year because his mom was "under the weather". That was how she described it. If being under the weather meant being sad, then yeah, she was under the weather all right, but other than unhappy, Timmy couldn't see a thing wrong with her. She did sleep a lot now, way more than when his real dad was alive, and she didn't smile much anymore, but that was all.

Timmy kept trying to hold onto the memories of those times, when his mom still smiled and when his father still came home each night and how sometimes they all went out to Brusters for ice cream. But the images had begun to fade, like they were drifting away down a slow, murky river. If he was honest, after three years he missed the thought of his dad more than the man himself.

"Timmy," his aunt called again from behind the rope. "Quit daydreaming. You're holding up the line. And stop chewing your lip." She smiled when she said it and he returned the favor. She had a nice smile.

"Yes, ma'am," he said. Aunt Elaine wasn't so bad, but she did nag a lot.

Timmy stood straight, puffed out his chest, and struggled to maintain his dignity. Still, he felt like a complete tool standing around with all these five and six year olds, and besides, he hadn't believed in Santa for two years, not since Hank, his stepfather, had set him straight.

"Get real kid," Hank had told him one night after work as he'd finished another can of Tecate and tossed the empty at the trashcan in the corner—and missed. "How can anyone know who's been good and who's been bad and all over the world? It don't make sense."

"Hank," his mom had scolded from across the kitchen. "Don't spoil Christmas for Timmy. He's only seven."

She'd still been willing to speak her mind back then.

"Hey, seven is plenty old enough to know where the bear shits, so shut your pie hole. Oh, and we're out of beer again."

Memories, memories.

"You're next, young squire," Santa's helper said as he guided Timmy forward with a bony grip. "Santa's ready for you now."

The fake elf was taller than the boy, but not by a lot, and his smile gleamed. To Timmy, that smile looked as sharp as a piece of glass and seemed wet around the edges.

Santa turned his head and peered down at Timmy. He looked awfully big, not fat, but tall and broad across the shoulders, and hard somehow. He wore a pretty good costume, though, better than most of the toy shop Santas Timmy had seen over the years. It was deep red, almost maroon, trimmed in white fur with a genuine leather belt and a brass buckle. His beard was real, too. It billowed across his chest in a crinkly white cloud, though the hairs poking out at the corners of his mouth had yellowed to a faded ivory.

Fighting back an ill-defined tightness in his chest, Timmy climbed onto Santa's lap and noticed a few dark smudges on his coat. They were a faded rust color against the red, as if someone had tried to wash away a pesky spill, then given up. He also noticed that Santa smelled a little like Hank did when his step-father stumbled home late at night. It was a spicier mix, though, not beer, something else. And, of course, there were his eyes. Up close, the green was remarkably clear and the tiny veins almost exploded in showers of red sparks. If he had to describe those eyes, he wouldn't have said they were mean really, but they were spooky.

Timmy shook his head and tried to find the comfort of his aunt's face in the crowd, but he couldn't catch her eye. She'd turned her attention apparently to a vibrating chair in the specialty furniture section next to the toy department.

"What do you want for Christmas, Tim?" the store Santa whispered, emphasizing the last word. That startled the boy. As far as he could remember, he hadn't told anyone his name and no one ever called him Tim. It was always Timmy.

"I don't know. Uberstix, maybe," he said. "It's this cool construction kit. You can build bridges and towers and stuff. Mom said she might get 'em for me this year."

"I know what Uberstix are, Tim," Santa said as he rolled those damn green eyes in disgust. "I'm Santa, for crying out loud."

A small smile tugged at the corner of Santa's mouth as he stole a glance at the electronic screen he held in his left hand. Timmy knew what an iPad was, but it surprised him to see Santa with one.

"According to my list, that's not what you really want, is it?" Santa said, looking up again. "But we both know moms don't always give us what we want, do they, Tim?"

"I'm not sure what you mean, sir."

"That's okay," Santa said with a wink and a nod. "We can talk about that later."

Santa's eyes did twinkle for a moment, just like the story promised, but then again it could have been the glare of the florescent lights. Still, they were hungry eyes, eyes that looked like they wanted to discuss every secret Timmy had ever known. They seemed ancient as well, and they sat in a face that had never been young, and as Timmy and Santa exchanged gazes, time slowed and the sounds of the store—and of the other children—died away.

"What are you t-t-t-talking about?" Timmy stuttered like he sometimes did when he got nervous. It was funny, but despite the thousands of parents and kids and shoppers around him, he felt alone and maybe a little more than scared now. Maybe damn near terrified. His aunt chatted up some old lady with blue hair and a cane, oblivious to her nephew's growing discomfort. The only eyes he saw belonged to that damn elf with his wet and nasty smile.

"Never mind, for now."

Santa winked again, then eased the boy off his lap. The elf had signaled it was time for the next child.

"The good news is that you're on the Nice List, Tim," he whispered as Timmy began to walk away. "That's important. You wouldn't like it on the Naughty List."

"Okay. Sure," he said. Of course, he'd have agreed to anything at that point.

Timmy snuck a last peak while his aunt paid for the pictures with her American Express, but Santa never looked back. That should have made him feel better. It didn't.

Aunt Elaine dropped him at his door soon after and Timmy let himself in through the kitchen. His mom was asleep again, big surprise there, so Timmy left the envelope with the picture in it on the counter and headed to his room.

In time, sharp voices drifted through the shallow waters of his sleep and brought him back to the surface of the world. He didn't remember much since getting home, but the shadows lay heavier on the wall now and the show he'd been watching was long over.

"I work my ass off every day, don't I, Evelyn?" he heard Hank say. "And all I ask is for dinner to be on the damn table when I get home and that there's some beer in the fridge. Is that too much for you to handle?"

No one was yelling yet, but soon.

"I'm sorry, Hank. I must have fallen asleep. I've been so tired lately, but I'll make something right now, okay?"

"You'll make something now, huh. Well, isn't that big of you? You'll make something now."

"I said I'm sorry, Hank."

Just a spark of challenge in her voice, but more than enough to push things forward.

"You said that alright, just like always. You're sorry. You tell me you'll do better, but then you backslide. And you do it every time, Ev. It's a flaw, that's what I think. It's a flaw in your character. My daddy always taught me that character was only built with hard lessons. It was the only useful thing that hateful son of a bitch ever said to me so maybe it's time for a little more instruction. What do you think, Ev?"

"No, Hank. Not again." She sounded frightened, but worse, she sounded resigned.

"Yeah, that might be just what we need here," Hank whispered. "Some good old time lessons."

Timmy knew how the rest of this story went, so he ran to his mom's room but Hank had already locked it up tight. He banged on the door and called her name but got nothing in return, save the sound of hard skin against soft, that and the muffled sobs. An hour passed in those few minutes and when at last Hank stepped into the hallway, he was sweating from the workout and smiling.

"What did you do to my mom?" Timmy said as he rushed in. She'd pulled on a long-sleeved blouse, but even in the growing shadows Timmy could see welts rising in red defiance where her collar and sleeves ended.

"Mind your own business, sonny boy," Hank whispered, "or you might get a little instruction yourself." It was an idle threat, of course. Hank had never raised a hand to the boy. Hitting kids apparently wasn't his thing.

"Mom, Mom! Are you all right?"

She turned and embraced her son, desperate as a non-swimmer in deep waters. They both cried as the front door slammed shut.

"Shhhh, Timmy. It's okay. You can stop crying now," she said, using her sleeve to wipe away his tears and then her own. "It was my fault. I should have had dinner ready."

Timmy loved his mom with the overwhelming focus only known to a child, but at times like this, he thought he might hate her a little as well. She was the adult. She was supposed to be strong. She wasn't supposed to be a dishrag.

"He doesn't have the right to hit you, Mom."

"He doesn't mean it, honey, and he's always sorry after," she told him again. "You'll understand when you grow up. It's just the beer that makes him impatient, and maybe I'm just not a very good wife anymore."

"No, mom," Timmy said. He tightened his hug, then let it loose as she stiffened with the pain.

"Maybe I haven't been a very good mom, either," she said, then lowered her face to his. "But I'll do better. I promise."

She was a good mom, that was the hell of it, and he was pretty sure she was a good wife, whatever that meant to a nine-year-old brain. What she wasn't was strong. She needed someone in her life and maybe it didn't matter who. His dad, at least what he remembered of his dad, had been there for her then and he was a good man. Hank was there for her now and he wasn't. Maybe the good part wasn't as important to her as the being there part.

Hank didn't make it home that night, nor most of the next day, and in his absence his mom rebounded some from the world of shadows and pity. The two of them baked cookies together and they wrapped a few last minute presents. She made meatloaf for dinner, which was Timmy's favorite, and an apple pie for the next day. They played Christmas carols and laughed like fools when Alvin and the Chipmunks sang "Please Christmas Don't Be Late."

It was the best day Timmy could remember in a long time, and for a moment the world held promise again, that is until the front door rattled at seven-thirty. He just focused on the TV as his mom rushed to the door.

"Hi, Evelyn," Timmy heard him say with practiced contrition. "I figured I'd give us a little space after last night. Sorry things got a little out of hand."

Hank walked into the living room and she followed behind.

"I know, Hank. I'm sorry, too," she said, handing him a Dos Equis. "You were right, I should have had dinner ready." She paused, then finished. She shouldn't have. "It's just that I'm always so tired lately."

"Tired," Hank said softly. He turned to face her as he rolled that pesky word over in his mind. "You're still tired?"

His mom saw her error and started to say something to change the dialogue, but Hank held his index finger to his lips, halting any explanation.

"I work all day. You know that. I work all day at a shit job taking all the crap they dump on me, but you're the tired one. How does that work, Ev? Are you sick? Do you need a doctor or something? 'Cause you look fine to me."

Timmy felt it coming hard this time, escalating quickly. It was a word he'd heard on TV, and even though he didn't know the exact definition, he knew that when things escalated, they got worse.

"I can't help it, Hank. It's not my fault," she explained, but Hank didn't want explanations and Timmy realized all at once that he wasn't drunk either, not tonight. Yeah, it was escalating alright; he was sober and Timmy didn't know where those two things would lead.

Hank held his voice low and he continued to shake his head back and forth, back and forth. Timmy could see a turning point coming, one where Hank would either swallow whatever was making him so angry or just let it out.

"So it's my fault, huh, Ev? You're such a mess because of me? 'Cause I'm what, a failure? I'm not what your husband was? Is that it? 'Cause I'm just not seeing it. What I see is an ungrateful bitch who doesn't know when to shut up." Though still low, Hank's voice coarsened all at once, crisp and brittle as overcooked bacon.

"We got a new year coming up, Ev, and you know what they say. New year, new rules. There's gonna be some changes around here, some big changes."

The race began to quicken, spinning away before Timmy's eyes. So he flipped off the TV and stood close, but not close enough to be noticed.

"Hank, please, let's talk about this later, okay?"

"Now you're telling me what to do. Is that it, Ev? I didn't come home to be lectured to."

Too late now, the anger wouldn't be swallowed. His eyes flashed and his face grew red but still his voice remained calm, and that scared Timmy even more.

"I'm sorry, Hank. I didn't mean…"

It sounded like a tree limb snapping when Hank backhanded her, fresh and clean and clear. Timmy had never seen Hank hit her before and the image was terrible and haunted his thoughts for a long time, but the sound was what he'd remember forever.

The blow lifted her off her feet and knocked her against a side table. The lamp fell, breaking the bulb and tearing the shade and the boy almost made it to her side before she hit the floor herself.

"Shit, now look what you made me do," his step-father said clearly and with not a trace of regret. He picked up the broken lamp and tossed it aside. "Why do you make me hurt you, Ev? It's just not right." He shook his head one last time, turned, and ambled out the door without a worry.

The spot beneath his Mom's eye ballooned at once and colored to the purple blush of a fresh eggplant. Timmy filled a washcloth with ice for her eye, then wiped a trickle of blood oozing from a ridge grooved in her cheek by Hank's ring. It was the championship football ring he always wore, even though high school was fifteen years in the past.

"Mom, this has to stop," Timmy pleaded.

"It will, Timmy. I'll do better. I know I can do better."

"That's not what I'm talking about," he said.

"I know, dear. I know. But it's all right now." She rubbed the back of his neck and kissed his forehead. "Why don't you get ready for bed?"

It wasn't even eight yet. What she meant was she was going to bed. He was on his own. Happy fuckin' Christmas Eve.

Timmy watched his mom shrivel before his eyes as she retreated to the comfort of her bedroom. Sleep offered oblivion after all. Timmy found what he needed on his own, the companionship of a television. But despite the cheerful Christmas specials, the evening wound down like a derelict wrist watch and that worm of hatred he'd felt toward his Mom earlier popped up again and began working itself into his heart.

Later, much later, Timmy lay in bed, the despair of a lonely Christmas Eve bitter on his tongue. He struggled to find even the rags of sleep, but it eluded him for what seemed hours. Then, just as his eyelids began to droop, a tired sigh floated from the next room, followed by the echo of ice cubes clinking in a glass.

It sounded like a church bell. It sounded like a mirror breaking. It sounded like Hank might have returned home, but brown liquor never sat well with his step-father; beer was his choice and never with ice.

Timmy slipped out of bed, walked to the door, and peered into the shrouded living room, seeing through the muted glow of the Christmas tree that he wasn't alone. A man, tall and broad, filled Hank's easy chair. A circle of red glimmered at the end of the man's cigarette and a large empty sack, red with a gold cord, lay haphazardly at his feet.

As he adjusted to the gloom, Timmy's eyes grew large. He knew this man. It was the Santa from Macy's.

"Hi, Tim," Santa said, his voice hoarse from cold winds and soot-filled chimneys. "I've been waiting for you."

Santa bogarted the last of his cigarette, flicked it into the fireplace, then emptied his glass. After a couple of seconds, he grimaced and spit back an ice cube.

"Kid, tell your mom to buy some decent scotch, will ya? I haven't had to drink Cutty Sark in twenty years."

He held up the glass, watched the lights from the tree sparkle in its cut edges. "At least it's not cookies and milk again. I've been a diabetic since FDR was president and that shit is going to kill me someday."

Timmy found it hard to take his eyes off Santa. Time drifted and he wondered if perhaps he was just floating through a dream, but then Santa sneezed twice, wiped a sleeve across his runny nose, and peeked at the results. No dream there.

"What are you doing here?"

"Where should I be?" Santa said. "It's Christmas Eve."

"But you're not ..."

"Real? Of course I'm real. You see me here, don't you? Just because you don't believe in it doesn't make something not real, no matter what your old man says. I'm real, you can take my word for it."

"He's not my father," Timmy screamed in a whisper. Of the thousand thoughts running through his mind, that one seemed the most important.

"Easy, kid. I know that mutt's not your father. He isn't capable of being anyone's father."

"Then what's this all about?" Timmy said. "I don't understand."

"Yeah, I guess it's a little confusing, but I really don't have time to explain. It's a busy night for me, you know."

"Look," Timmy said, "you better tell me what's going on or I'm gonna wake up my mom."

Santa raised his hand and relented, sporting the ghost of a smile as he settled back in the chair.

"Sure, but just the Cliff Notes version, okay?"

He stretched his legs and gestured to the floor by his feet. Timmy took his cue and sat.

"You see, kid, I've been around a long time, longer than you might imagine. There are all kinds of stories about me, what I do and why, and after a while, well stories begin to take on lives of their own. Some of what you hear is true, but some of it isn't, ya dig? Now, take those flying reindeer. I've never seen a reindeer get two of its feet off the ground at the same time, let alone fly. They're stinking, lazy, disgusting animals and mostly what they do is eat and fart and make little reindeer."

Santa shrugged, as if to say, "What are you gonna do?"

"And as for elves happily working twenty hours a day to make wonderful toys for little kids, well, that's a load of crap, too. You're lucky if you get one decent eight-hour shift out of 'em in a week, and even then they bitch all night about how hard the work is. They smell almost as bad as the reindeer and they drink all my scotch and the little bastards keep threatening to unionize."

Santa tapped another cigarette from his crumpled pack of Chesterfields and fired up a lighter engraved with two red Ks in overlapping scroll. He pulled a shred of tobacco from his lip, released an enormous cloud of blue smoke, and sighed as the nicotine rush hit. He started again, his voice milder now, either from the scotch or his interest in his own story.

"You see what I'm saying about those stories?"

It was Timmy's turn to shrug.

"Never mind, it's not important. But the lists, that part's true," he said, nodding three or four times. "We got lists on everyone and everything, you know, who's been naughty and who's been nice. We used to keep it all in these leather-bound notebooks. Those bastards weighed a ton and it was a real pain in the ass keeping that stuff up to date. I almost slipped a disc one year hauling those damned things around. Anyway, we converted to Apple PCs in '93 and that made things a lot easier, and once we went online, well, it's been a piece of cake ever since."

Santa held up the iPad Timmy had seen in the store.

"Hit one button and I get instant access to all my lists, no matter where I am, plus I get GPS thrown in for nothing. Hell, I know more about most people than they know about themselves."

Timmy struggled to take in what he was hearing and the fact that someone he'd given up as fantasy years before was sitting here in his living room. Still, the fact that Santa chain smoked Chesterfields and complained about the quality of his mom's scotch brought an edge of reality that was hard to ignore.

"So, why are you here?" Timmy said at last.

"Well, it's like this, Tim. You see, sometimes it takes a while, but eventually we get around to everyone, nice or naughty. Like I said in the store, you're on the Nice List so you get what you really want. It's your lucky day."

"It doesn't feel so lucky to me." The boy slumped back against the chair and folded his arms across his chest. He was a pretty sharp kid, but he was still a kid. The image of his mom scuttling into her bedroom was still raw in his mind and it released a short flow of tears.

The big man in the red suit placed his hand on Timmy's shoulder and said, "Give it time, kid. Anyway, before I go I needed to share a couple things with you."

Santa paused to make sure Timmy was listening.

He was.

"First, you need to give your mom a break. Lord knows she's no tower of strength. Anyone can see that. But she's a good person. Being good and being weak don't have a thing to do with each other. She needs someone, that's all. A lot of people do. It may not be fair, but for the time being, that someone is gonna have to be you, ya dig, little man?"

"Yeah, I guess so."

"Good. Now stop sulking and quit biting your lip, that self-indulgent shit really pisses me off."

Timmy took a deep breath and wiped his eyes as Santa continued.

"That's better. Now the second thing is important. It's the real reason I came by, so listen up. As you get older, you may decide to forget what happened tonight. It may not feel like something you want to hold onto or you may choose to remember it as a dream. Who knows, maybe you'll wipe it away altogether. That's okay. You don't need to remember exactly how things went down here. That's not the important part. But this is important."

Santa leaned forward, so close that the hairs of his beard tickled Timmy's nose while stale tobacco and a lifetime of scotch filled his nostrils.

"Stay on the Nice List, kid. That's all I'm telling you. You don't want to be on the Naughty List. Not ever, ya dig?"

The boy nodded. He was, after all, a pretty sharp kid.

"Then we're all ivey divey, my man," Santa said, ruffling Timmy's blond hair with nicotine-stained fingers. "Now off to bed. I still got a lot to do tonight and remember, no peeking. It's against the rules to see your present before Christmas morning."

Timmy watched Santa from the corner of his eye as he wandered back to his room. He expected the guy to lay a finger aside his nose and pop up the chimney at any moment, but as he closed his door, the last thing Timmy saw was Santa, back in the chair with that tiny circle of red glowing at the end of his Chesterfield.

Time passed, and though he may have dozed, he never actually fell asleep. His mind was too full of the possibilities and his thoughts raced in a hundred directions.

Just before three, Timmy heard the front door rattle under a balky key. Hank was home at last and his footsteps landed with the uneven grace of someone who might need extra effort to stay afoot.

"Who the hell are you?" he said, his words coming in one long, mushy phrase.

The springs on the easy chair groaned in gratitude as the large man stood. Timmy heard someone, almost certainly Hank, say, "What the...," followed by a sharply drawn breath. Its muffled release was almost imperceptible in the screaming silence, but it went on for a long time and it ended with a sound like a stretched piece of taffy snapping.

It took the boy nearly five minutes to gather his nerve, but when at last he padded to the door, he found the room empty. Santa was gone, Hank as well, but in the faint glow of Christmas tree lights, Timmy saw the sack, the red one with the gold cord, lodged in the mouth of the fireplace. It bulged and sagged, as if someone above struggled to wedge its now full girth up the narrow flue.

The bag dropped down for a moment and nearly hit the hearth's floor. Then, with a last great effort, the cord tightened and the bag inched its way back up the chimney with care, and just before it disappeared, it caught for a moment and something that looked like a hand popped free and banged against the brickwork. Then that, too, disappeared.

Timmy couldn't be one hundred percent sure it actually was a hand he'd seen; after all, it was dark and it was late and he was just a kid. But he was sure that something shiny fell from the bag as it was hauled up through the narrow opening. He walked to the fireplace, picked up what he'd seen, and marveled at the way Hank's football ring glimmered in the faint light.

He was so amazed at what had occurred that he might have stood there all night, but a voice wandered down the chimney and sent him scurrying back to bed.

"I told you, Tim. No peeking. Don't make me change that list."

The boy found his bed more inviting now. He slept like the blessed that night and his mom had waffles waiting for him when he woke. They exchanged gifts in a blizzard of wrapping paper and bows, and as he played with his Uberstix, his mom smiled briefly, like she used to.

Aunt Elaine came for dinner on Christmas night. They

laughed and they found peace somehow and they wished each other a better life in the silent recesses of their thoughts. And maybe they found that life and maybe they didn't, but they never saw Hank again.

As he grew older, the boy did forget quite a few of the fine details of that strange good night, but he never hated his mom again, and he never forgot to be there when she needed him, which wasn't nearly as often as he'd once feared. He was Tim from that night forward, no more Timmy. But mostly, he never forgot which list he wanted to be on, and for the rest of his life, on those rare occasions when he'd be tempted to forget, Tim would pull a thin gold chain from beneath his shirt and stare at the old football ring he carried on that chain, and he'd remember. Oh yes, he'd remember.

I'll Have a Blue, Blue Christmas

David Niall Wilson

Brandt filled his glass nearly to the brim with eggnog, the thick, sticky-sweet liquid coating the glass and running down the insides in opaque rivulets of milky white, glowing blue from the Christmas lights in the window. He turned to glance into the next room.

The tree glittered brilliantly, tin-foil-and-coat-hanger monument to his parent's long dead world, somehow found and resurrected by Sinthia and the Church of New Light Thrift Store. Brandt tipped the glass, letting the smooth, cold rum and milk slide down his throat. All of the bulbs on the tree were silver, a matched set, and whirring in the corner like an alien scanning device, the color wheel painted the tinsel, and the walls, the egg-nog, and Brandt himself, shades of red, and gold, green, and blue.

Brandt topped off his glass again, put the pitcher back in the refrigerator, and stepped into the living room, enjoying the silence. The holidays had changed subtly. The dates were the same, the eggnog just as strong—even the fucking tree was a ghost from his far-removed and well-forgotten past, but there was light in the small home. Though the eggnog was strong, there was no huge press of memories to wash away.

Against the wall in the corner, his guitar case rested like a forgotten soldier. Brandt sipped and smiled. For the first time in what seemed like a lifetime, he didn't feel like he had to have his fingers wrapped around the instrument's neck in a death grip. The music flickered through the back of his mind, but for once, Brandt listened. Another surprise—another difference. It had been a long time since Brandt had enjoyed music from the other side of the notes.

It was nearly dark. He moved to the window and stared out over the street. Synthia wouldn't be back for a couple of hours. She'd gone to the mall for a last-minute shopping spree—precursor to their first happy holiday in Brandt's memory. Shaver and Susan were due at 9:00, and Dexter would roll in eventually. The band was more a family than most of them had ever known.

As he stared out over the streets, Brandt's mind wandered. He thought of old Wally, wondered where the man had gone. In and out among the notes of the song that was never really silent in the back of his mind, Brandt could hear the notes of Wally's harmonica, cutting through the seams and re-arranging the notes. As he thought about that song, the streets grew darker, more shadowed.

The temperature in the room was dropping. Brandt glanced at the thermostat, then realized it was pointless. The temperature in the room hadn't changed, it was his own. He took a quick sip of eggnog, then shrugged and downed the entire glass in a warm, silky flood. Two hours until Synthia would be back, and already his buzz was fuzzing the light into a rainbowesque halo glow that lined everything.

Brandt felt the dull thud of his heartbeat blending with a darker pulse, thundering deep in his chest. Images flickered in and out of his thoughts, like a television obscured by storms. He saw firelight, flickering from the mouth of an alley. He heard the music rise and fall, sharing his breath. His fingers itched.

"Damn," he said softly.

Moving to the wall, he leaned in and grabbed his guitar case, wrapping his fingers tightly in the handle and gripping so that his knuckles went white. The color wheel slid through yellow to red, hesitating to pain the room a bright orange before slipping down. The tinsel glittered like rivulets of blood, and Brandt shook his head slowly, closing his eyes. The images hovered, just below the surface, sending tendrils of pain up to snag in his temples and dragging him down. When he opened his eyes, the room was a deep, glittering blue.

Without a word, Brandt turned to the door, grabbed his coat, and headed out into the night. As he stepped through the door, he turned, glancing at the warm, inviting room a final time.

"I'll be home soon," he whispered, willing the words to hang in the air and slip into Syn's ear as she entered.

Brandt turned, closing the door behind him, and headed out onto the street.

❋ ❋ ❋

The alley was just as Brandt remembered it. He'd half

expected to see the old woman leaning against the wall at the entrance, her faded Tarot deck spread before her like a gypsy's skirt. There was no one in sight, but there was a soft glow of light from the alley's mouth. The fires, always burning—always surrounded by those with such a darkness in their eyes the light could never touch it. Brandt stood, his toes and his fingers numbing slowly, stinging as the ice on the sidewalk ate slowly through the flimsy warmth of his boots and socks.

It was crazy. He should be home. Synthia would be getting back any moment, arms loaded with bags he wasn't allowed to peek into and eyes alight with the spirit of the holidays. The spirit Brandt hadn't experienced in so long he felt like a bit player in the billionth showing of *It's a Wonderful Life*.

"Where the hell is Charlie?" he whispered, images from that movie strobing with the firelight. The bridge. The café. Brandt glanced down at his guitar case, gripped in fingers that barely felt alive, and he shook his head.

Turning slowly, he entered the alley, and the world slipped behind a curtain of shadow. Two worlds, inside and outside. Real, surreal, and blending. Brandt stopped, blinking. He hadn't really studied the alley before. He'd seen it from the street, and that one night, so far in the past that it had blurred and reformed, he had the one drunken memory. Very suddenly the time dispersed, and he wondered if he'd ever really left. The only dead giveaway was that there was no Cuervo bottle, and his head was clear.

What had stopped him in his tracks was the center of the alley. One thing he should have seen, or sensed. The alleys stretched to his right, and to his left, and directly ahead, beyond the orange-tongued flames, a third disappeared into the shadows.

A voice floated from the shadows, chillingly familiar, making Brandt jump nervously. At the same time, it warmed his heart.

"Welcome back to the crossroads, boy. Tol' you more'n once. Crossroads don't get you, the cross hairs will. Good to see you still makin' the right choice."

"No choice involved," Brandt replied, stepping forward and holding out one numb hand. "Didn't know you'd be here."

"Just came to hang out with your friends, boy?" Old Wally smiled, and the world shifted. Brandt turned toward the trash can a few yards away.

"Got to warm my fingers if I'm going to play," he said softly.

"Guess you do at that," Wally said, grinning.

The two walked across the dirty alley to where flames danced brightly in an old trash barrel. Brandt would have sworn the barrel had been surrounded by thin figures draped in shadow, but now there wasn't a soul in sight. The wind had picked up, whipping down the alley and ignoring Brandt's coat on the way to his skin. He set the guitar case down and brought his hands up closer to the fire.

"Why did *you* come back here, Wally?" Brandt asked.

"Come, go, stay, all the same to ol' Wally, Brandt boy. The music takes me where it wants me. Always been that way, longer'n I can remember. Hoped you'd come tonight."

"Because it's almost Christmas?" Brandt asked.

"Nope," Wally answered, shaking his head and letting his gaze wander along the cracks on the dirty floor of the alley. "Hoped you'd come cuz fer once, I didn't have to be here, or anywhere. Got some time on my hands, and thought maybe I could tell you a story—if you're of a mind?"

Brandt rubbed the palms of his hands together—feeling

the pain-prickle of sensation returning. "A Christmas story?" he asked softly.

"Might say so," Wally nodded. "Might say it's the whole damn story, far as I'm concerned. Started on Christmas, though, so it's as much a Christmas story as anything."

The old man turned away for a moment, and the firelight glistened off his deep, chocolate brown skin.

"Got the first harp for Christmas, boy, so long ago you weren't even a dream in your grandad's childhood. Things was different then. Everything was clearer, the edges were harder, my Pa used to say. Men fought and drank, took care of their families. Kids went to school and studied and either went on, or came home to work. Not so many others sticking their fingers in the batter.

"Christmas wasn't the same then as now. Folks was deeper into it. Trees took days to cut and drag home and trim. My family gathered fifty deep for Gram's turkey and pie, every year. Every year I knew what I'd get for Christmas if I knew what my brother was getting, because I'd get his old one. Not a lot of money then. No K-Mart or Internet. Didn't matter. I'd been watchin' that harp two years straight. I guess what makes this story special is the surprise. That Christmas I was s'posed to get my first bike.

"It sat on my brother Daniel's dresser, right next to a short stack of faded, crimp-cover comic magazines and a picture of Pa from the war. It had been there since about two days after he got it, packed careful in a box and wrapped up in tissue. The harp, and the picture, they were about the only thing of Pa's Daniel had. I had a silver pocket watch that didn't work. Ma said we'd get it fixed one day, but I knew better. That cost money, and to spend food money on telling the time was a waste we weren't likely to condone. Didn't matter. Had Pa's fingerprints on it, still. I kept that wrapped in tissue, too, tucked in under my mattress, near to where my heart would rest on the bed.

"Pa went to defend the country from people so distant and different the whole thing might as well have been an invasion of aliens from space, far as Daniel and I could tell. Ma and her friends, my aunts and uncles, even the mail man when he stopped for cold lemonade each day, they talked about it as if they knew it. They traded words and stories, opinions garnered from close reading of the news and long hours with their ears cocked beside the radio.

"That war filled their lives, and it was as real to them as the road between my home and the general store. To me it was another story, like the ones Daniel had read to me over and over again from those comic magazines. Captain America. He fought in that same war—most kids wouldn't know that now. Lot to be learned by the words in those pages, but mostly we thought about Pa, waited for his letters and news about his unit. Ma had a scrapbook so thick with clippings and notes and letters that if you weren't careful it would all pour out on the table, or the couch, and she'd sit for hours, smiling and trying not to cry, putting it back the way she'd had it. Sometimes I think she poured them out on purpose, just so she could touch the words he'd written, knowing Pa had touched the paper as well.

"Anyway, that isn't the story. Your hands warm yet, Brandt boy?"

Brandt was surprised to find that they were.

"'Bout time you started playin'," Wally said softly. "Ain't meant to be told like this, you know? Meant to be lived. Lived it so many times already, one more shouldn't hurt."

"But it will," Brandt whispered. He bent to his guitar case, unfastened the snaps, and lifted the lid.

Moments later, he leaned against the nearest wall, tuning

the guitar slowly. Though he'd moved further from the fire, the cold still kept its distance. Wally stood his ground, gaze focused on some point far in the distance.

The guitar rested easily against Brandt's hip. He tuned quickly, no more than a couple of quick tweaks, and the notes rang pure and clear. Without waiting for more from Wally, Brandt reached deep inside, tugged at the block that stemmed the flow of inner pain. He felt it easing free, heard the soft whispered voices rising through his senses. Images coalesced and dispersed, only to reform each time. Brandt ignored them. He focused his gaze on Wally, and, after a few moments, the old man began to speak again.

"Ma had a *friend* to Christmas dinner that year. First time ever there'd been anyone but family. Daniel, he didn't like it. I can still see his face as Mama told him, explained he wouldn't be sitting in Pa's seat. That Phil Dresden would be joining us—that it was rude to ask a man to take second seat to a boy—even if that boy belonged."

Brandt's fingers strummed quietly, letting the words ripple through him and slip through his fingertips.   Wally's voice drew the notes from him slowly, first a trickle, then a slow, smooth flow of notes and chords—minor chords dripping sticky and bittersweet from Brandt's fingers. Brandt could still hear Wally's voice, but the words had blurred to a dull roar, filtered by the rush of other voices, other stories.

Brandt played through it. His mind drifted, and the world shifted. The alley faded slowly to black, then back to gray—and then white. Wally and the trash can disappeared, replaced by morning sunlight, bright, white snow, and a soft breeze. The wall at Brandt's back, now the trunk of a tree, coated in a frosted sprinkle of ice and blown snow.

Down a crooked lane, lined with trees, a low-slung house stood, new snow drifted against the walls. Nothing moved, at first, but whirling gusts of snow. Dangling above the railing on the porch, a wind-chime danced in slow circles, its chiming voice mournful in the early morning silence.

There was a single wreath hanging on the front door, just visible from where Brandt stood. A red bow adorned the wreath's center, and that red glittered too brightly across that long, brilliant-white expanse of snow. It looked as if the house were bleeding.

Brandt's fingers moved easily. He felt none of the cold, though icicles dangled behind his head and the rising sun shone through them to dance prismatically on the snow at his feet. The notes were slow—so slow it took a while for the melody to seep through Brandt's concentration. Nothing he could put his finger on—melodies joined and drawing tendrils of memory up from the sea of voices chanting in his mind. There was a sense of Christmas in it all, but not the happy, commercialized Christmas Brandt was familiar with— more a drop back to days he barely remembered—very young children gathered in front of a television and watching *The Nutcracker* on a fuzzy old color television with more red than green in the picture and strange music—stranger characters—playing out a fantasy holiday that never was.

A motion near the rear of the house caught Brandt's eye. A flash of bright blue, and a young man appeared, moving quickly, hunched low to the ground. Brandt blinked, wanting to shield his eyes against the snow-blindness. His fingers remained caught in a surreal holiday dance of chords and notes. With an effort, Brandt pushed off from the tree, meaning to follow the boy away from the house.

He needn't have bothered. The blue-coated figure turned straight at him, making surprisingly good time through the snow. Brandt played, and watched, and within moments a young black man was puffing through the snow, ignoring

Brandt, intent on some point far in the distance. Behind him, the young man pulled a battered red sled. His breath puffed white, tiny clouds drifting from his lips and dispersing.

Brandt shifted the music subtly, matching the boy's progress with the notes. There was no melt to the snow, though the sun was rising swiftly. The air was clean and crisp with frost. Brandt felt none of it. His fingers danced, his gaze tracked the boy across the snow. Moments later, Brandt could make out features. Bright eyes, dark hair pulled back under a hat. The jacket looked worn, but warm.

Brandt could hear a muffled voice—singing. The boy was singing, pulling the sled off into the woods in the snow. Brandt smiled. He let the music twist to the moment, drawing the Christmas tones from his guitar easily—notes he'd not played in years, melodies trapped too long in tinny muzak prisons in shopping malls. Music with feeling, and heart.

As the sled drew abreast of him, he saw the boy's face. Familiar, and not. Very much of Wally in those features, but chiseled of different stone. Again, Brandt smiled. Easy to drop into the music, to let it flow and to forget why he was there, why he was *always* there. The morning was beautiful, a world where Brandt had never walked—no cities, no buildings lined up to block the sun, no horns or screeching tires. Trees. Trees and snow, as far as he could see.

Pressing off from the tree, Brandt followed. The boy was moving at a good clip, gliding between the trees easily. Brandt lost sight, just for a second, and as he stepped forward in pursuit, the world shifted. His fingers ground nearly to a halt, notes sustaining impossibly until that sound rose, reverberating from the mountains in the distance and echoing through the trees.

Brandt stood at the top of a sloping open field. The field

was littered with pine trees. They were scattered, not even as those in the forest had been, nor as healthy. Brandt could just make out the nose of the sled around one of the larger trees. It poked beyond the lower branches, and through the patchy limbs, he could just make out the boy.

The solid *THUNK* of steel biting wood rang up the slope. An axe, something Brandt hadn't noticed in the boy's passing, swung up and back, glittering as it dove at the base of the tree, again—and again. The branches rattled, dropping snow in a slow crystalline rain that somehow wove itself into the music. Slow motion holiday video to Brandt's background of Christmas blended to pain.

Something else caught Brandt's eye. He turned, shifting his gaze to the side and down. Shadowy figures. One—a second, then a third. Moving parallel, one to the other, all working their way toward that tree—and that sled. One red cap, two black. All moving stealthily forward.

Brandt stepped onto the snowy slope. The boy was a short walk down—too far to see clearly, but close enough to hear. Stumbling, slipping, fighting for purchase on the slippery surface of the hill, Brandt started down. He gripped the neck of the guitar grimly, his fingers snatching the notes from the imbalance of the moment, making the odd, staggering steps work for and with him.

The other boys on the slope were moving quickly. More quickly than Brandt, and with surer feet. They had split wide, a three-pronged approach. Brandt caught a glimpse of a crooked grin, bright—glittering eyes that were too blue to be real— ice chips glinting from a pale face. Brandt tripped again, spinning forward. He cried out, his voice blending and sustaining and shifting. He could see the ground coming up fast, knew he had to stop, to reach out and stop that fall, to protect the guitar, but he couldn't.

If he stopped, it ended, and he would never know. If he let the moment slip away, he would lose it. Crossed roads only meet once.

Brandt closed his eyes, and he played. He gritted his teeth, preparing for an impact that never came and soft/cold snow sifted over his face and back and he fell and fell and fell and played, slowly, spinning—then standing. He nearly fell again, the sensation of firm ground was so sudden and intense.

The world focused. The sun was much higher overhead. Brandt stood between two snow-coated pines. Ahead, back to the tree he'd toppled, stood the boy Brandt knew must be Wally's brother. The axe was held high, and the boys eyes were wide, so wide they shone like white glittering plates against the dark lines of his face.

"You g'wan and let me be," the boy said shakily. Brandt played, falling into a Jim Croce-esque backbeat. "You Don' Mess Around with Slim" dancing down darker notes.

"You know we ain't gonna do that, *boy*," a tow-headed youth spat back. "You done chopped one 'a Poppa's trees."

"You don't learn easy, do you, *boy*?" a larger youth chimed in. This one was fat, so fat he was stretching the seams of his handed-down jacket obscenely. "Done tol' you last year. This is our hill. These is our trees."

"Ain't your hill," Daniel huffed. He gripped the axe tightly, not brandishing it, but not lowering it from his shoulder either. "My pa came here every year for our tree. Just a'cause a man dies don' mean you own the hill."

Daniel's voice was slow and even. There was a strength behind it, but the boy's eyes lowered somewhat as he spoke. Wars were fought behind those eyes. Brandt felt a pulse driving up from the ground beneath him, blood pounding too quickly. The rhythm was ragged, but steady for all that, and powerful.

"Give me that tree, *boy*," the third stranger said. "You give me that tree," he hesitated. "And that sled. You go on back to your mama, and you tell her you lost the sled—and the axe. You don't come to this hill again. Ain't no coloreds allowed on our proppity. You go, or I'm gonna have to tell the sheriff you was stealin' our tree."

"I ain't stealing," Daniel answered quietly. "I never stole a thing in my life. I aim to take this tree home to my momma."

The fat boy laughed. It wasn't a pleasant sound. There was no mirth, no enjoyment in that sound. He took a step toward Daniel, then another.

"You ain't taking nothin' nowhere," he said matter-of-factly. "You're gonna carry your *black* ass home. Matter of fact, I'm gonna whup it for you 'fore you do."

Daniel was trembling. Brandt felt the shift—felt the whirl—the song continued, beyond and behind him, but what he felt was solid. The axe in his hand and the too-wide set of stout legs. The muscles rippling through arms too short to be his own, and the fear churning with the anger deep in his mind.

"No," he whispered.

Images fought for control. He saw his mother's face, heard her voice. He saw the table, set for dinner, all the fine china and family silver laid out shined and polished. He saw that chair—his chair—his father's chair. Empty.

Then he saw Phil Dresden's face. He saw that expression, so close to hunger, the man laid on his mama every time he came around. The corner of the dining room was bare. As empty as it had been since Pa left and never came home. Since the last time they'd had a tree, or a real Christmas beyond the shell of emotion and pain that walled them off each year. No man. They had no man, and Daniel needed to fill that void. He needed to provide things he could not provide, to protect those he wasn't old enough to protect. He needed to bring home the tree.

The fat boy was moving close—too close—leering, hate-washed face suddenly impossibly large, voice blending to the notes of the song and back. Incomprehensible, and unimportant. Washing over and through Daniel's mind. Brandt's mind.

"Stop," Daniel said softly. "I don't care for you, John Melville, but I'll give a man fair warning. Don't you touch that tree, or that sled. Don't you try to touch me. My pa was a good man, and your pa let him be. It's Christmas, and I aim to take this tree home."

"You ain't taking a thing home black boy," John replied. "You be lucky if you take your hide."

With a roar that filled Brandt's ears, joining with the rush of adrenaline and blood and the smooth whoosh of steel slicing air, the song grew chaotic and powerful. He felt the ripple of muscle across shoulders and back, felt fingers gripping so tightly the wood seemed to compress. There were cries, anger and pain, and the solid *THUNK* as the axe bit deep. The fat boy had been charging, but that swing dropped him to his knees. The head of the axe was buried, the lower half unseen in a mass of blood-soaked cloth and flesh, head canted to the side, half torn from a body that knelt and trembled and shook. Blood gouted from John's mouth, washing away his sins to the pure white snow.

Everything stopped in that single moment. Brandt saw it captured, heard it floating in a whole-note, freeze-frame clarity that shivered up and through him so swiftly he nearly passed to darkness, fighting for breath, and for strength, fingers drawn on by the notes, not vice-versa as the images assaulted him in a staccato panorama of horror.

John's body slumped, and that motion tore the axe from Daniel's numb, unfeeling hands. The boy staggered back, nearly falling over his sled, and into the tree. He grabbed the rope, wrapping it over his shoulder. Desperately, he turned away, leaving the axe, the dead boy, and his screaming, crazed brothers without a second glance. Head lowered, Daniel started up the hill. Brandt heard the wailing cries, young bad-assed bullies melting to frightened children. He heard the soft shuffle of Daniel's boots, and the scuff of the sled's rails, gliding away.

Brandt stood once more alone, beside the trail. He played in numb horror, watching the trail of Daniel's sled moving on up the hillside. He turned to where the two boys were trying to raise their fallen brother. The axe tilted at a crazy angle, and blood spattered the snow—Rorsach blotch on a White-Christmas backdrop.

Brandt closed his eyes. Too much. The notes had slipped from holiday to dirge, rough and deep. Voices joined in, deepening the sound, but Brandt ignored them. Now the playing was his, the pain washing up and through, out the tips of his fingers and down the strings. He could sense the play of light and shadow across his eyelids. Firelight, or candles. In the distance, the voice of a single harmonica sounded. Not clear, or clean, but deep, clawing its way into the music, parting the notes and insinuating itself with raw emotion and blinding pain.

Brandt shivered, back arching as he opened his eyes. He'd felt and lived the pain of a thousand souls, played their pain to a world that soaked it in and spit it out, but he'd never felt such a singular stab of agony as the notes of that harp drew forth.

Brandt stood in an alcove, beside a fireplace. The door

was open, cold wind and flurries of snowflakes wafting in through the dark opening. A woman stood, back to Brandt, and the fire, staring into the distance. Her shoulders shook, arms tight-gripping a shawl around her shoulders. Oblivious to the cold, or the darkness, she stared. Behind her, to one side of the fire, a young boy sat. He held the old silver harmonica in a death grip. Tears streamed down his cheeks, but he played. No song Brandt had ever heard, just notes, long drawn out wails of sound that ripped from the tiny reeds and struck like daggers, shredding Brandt's nerves.

He snapped his eyes shut, stilling his fingers with an effort. His frame shook, suddenly cold, so cold he could barely stand on numb feet. The frozen bricks at his back dug through his jacket with ice-talons that worked their way deeper with each passing second. A few feet away, the flames still licked over the rim of the barrel. Only a miracle saved his guitar as Brandt lurched away from the wall with a gasp and staggered closer to the fire.

Wally was nowhere to be seen. Cold wind whipped down the alleys from all directions, and a dusty, snowflake whirlwind danced in the very center of that dark crossroads. Brandt lowered his guitar into its case and flipped the lid closed with the toe of his boot. Ignoring the pain in his fingers, he flipped each of the clasps closed before standing and holding his hands out over the barrel.

"Fuck," he muttered, shaking his head and instantly regretting that. Even his scalp was numb.

Brandt waited only long enough for the pain-prickle of sensation to invade his hands before leaning, gripping the guitar case tightly, and turning from the fire. He ignored the tiny whirlwind, but its soft, whistling voice followed him, sifting through his numbed mind.

"Found my own crossroads, boy. Made my choice. Long

way from here to there. You go back, you find that girl and hol' on tight. Come back and play some time."

Brandt stumbled out of the alley and down the street, the image of old rheumy eyes and gnarled hands fading to the too-young grip on a too-blue harmonica. Blood on a bright-white canvas. In the distance, a group of carolers filled the night with song.

Sudden images of the tree, the color wheel and its red to yellow to blue comfort, Syn's soft voice and softer skin, flooded Brandt's mind, and he hurried his steps. He wondered if, in all the world, there was enough eggnog to dissolve the chill in his heart. "Merry Christmas, Wally," he whispered.

The harp rose in answer, joining the carolers and dancing into the shadows, rimming them with silvery sound and the light of hope, draining away the pain. With tears wetting his cheeks and freezing to his skin, Brandt smiled.

Last-Minute Shopper

Mark Parker

"*Fuckin' wheel!*" David Sturgis grumbled, pulling the last of the shopping carts from the toy store's now-empty coral. Invariably, in any store he went to, he always managed to get the *one* malfunctioning cart that had a wildly swiveling wheel, which caused it to clunk along lazily with every labored push.

Turning away from the cart area, David reluctantly began to thread his way into the frenetic swarm of last-minute holiday shoppers. Overhead, the rows upon rows of fluorescent lights were near-blinding as he slowly edged his cart forward. Their brightness raining down on him made him feel conspicuous, like he had no business being here this late in the game. And, of course, he didn't. Once again, he was displeased with himself for having left his bit of the shopping to last possible moment. Thank God Beth had taken care of the rest. With every passing year, he vowed that *this* holiday season would be different, that he would get all his shopping done the week following Thanksgiving to ensure he had the best selection to choose from, as well as the highest seasonal discounts possible.

But, yet again, he'd failed by a full month. At this late hour, he worried he'd be forced to fight over whatever ravaged castoffs were left. But hopefully he would find the two most important things he needed to find. Troy, his twelve-year-old son, had asked for the latest *Quadcopter HD + drone*, and Emily, his nine-year-old daughter, wanted the *MiP Robot Miposaur*. Em wasn't your typical girlie-girl; she was always trying to keep up with her older brother, so she tended to go for the more-advanced motorized toys, and the *Miposaur* robot dinosaur was at the top of her list this year.

As a night shift cop, this was going to be David's first Christmas home with his family since being hired by the Bethlehem Police Department five years earlier. Although he considered himself more seasoned a cop than not, having transferred in from Pittsburg so Beth could take the Head Nurse position at Lehigh Valley Hospital-Muhlenberg in their Cancer Center, he was still considered a newbie by the more senior cops he worked with. But that didn't matter. All he cared about was that he would finally be able to enjoy the holiday with his wife and children, and not have to sleep all Christmas day to be well rested for his usual eleven-to-seven shift.

Looking over the shifting sea of heads spread out in front of him, David caught sight of a sign reading *ELECTRONICS*, which is where he needed to go. He kept telling himself that all he needed were the *two* gifts he'd come for, and then he could be on his way. He still needed to get something for

Beth and his sister, who was always the easiest person on his list to buy for. Mo loved to read, so every year he and Beth gave her a hundred-and-fifty-dollar gift card to Barnes & Noble, where she could load up on another year's worth of reading. But surveying the slow-moving mass of huddled bodies as they slugged along, he could see it wasn't going to be an easy task. A toy store was the last place he wanted to be on Christmas Eve. Again, he cursed himself for waiting until the last minute.

"Excuse me!" David said, louder than he actually meant to.

A large woman in a festive, bright red sweat suit—Bedazzled to the point where she looked like a walking Fabergé Christmas ornament—spun around and wagged a glittering, dangerously long, acrylic nail up at him and said, "You're gonna have to calm down and wait your turn, mister. We all *need* what we need, know what I'm sayin'!"

Indeed, he did. He smiled down at her, suppressing a chuckle at how she was dressed. She looked like a real-life version of *Elf on a Shelf.* After several minutes of stuttering along behind her, forcing himself to keep his growing frustration at bay, David was grateful when he saw that he was nearing the end of the aisle directly *next* to the one he needed.

As he slowly turned the corner, managing to avoid a near collision with a priest dressed in full clerics, who was not so successfully balancing a tall stack of board games in his full arms, David was astonished to see that the ELECTRONICS aisle was devoid of any shoppers. *Any at all.* Although the shelves had clearly been rummaged through, within a few minutes he was able to locate *both* items he'd come for. Though he was grateful, he had to laugh at his dumb luck.

He loaded the toys into his cart and pushed on. As he headed in the direction of the checkout lines, he could see over the heads of the customers in front of him that there were overfilled shopping carts lined up ten deep at each register. The scene reminded him of rush hour traffic on a busy Friday night. He was overjoyed when three 5 ITEMS OR LESS signs came into view. He was relieved to know he could use one of them once the shifting crowd dissipated.

Inching along, David stopped abruptly when something caught in the filter of his always alert cop's mind. It was an unavoidable aspect of his job that he often found nerve-wracking; never being able to turn off his hypersensitive mind when he was off-duty. It was an occupational hazard, to be sure, much like that of any other person acting in the role of first responder.

Glancing to his left, David felt a coil of apprehension tighten in the pit of his stomach. Something definitely didn't feel right. Maybe there was a scuffle brewing between two customers. Given the near-claustrophobic sea of people milling about, it would certainly be no wonder if one, in fact, did. Whatever it was that had his honed instincts heightened, this was yet another time David hoped he was wrong. Perhaps it was just a matter of his overactive imagination firing on all cylinders because of the swelling crowd. Cops were trained to always consider the worst-case scenario in all situations, so they were always on-guard and, therefore, prepared for anything.

And so he was.

Stealing another sideward glance, David caught sight of two college-age white males who appeared to be in some sort of disagreement with one another—a seemingly heated, though *quiet*, exchange. Acting as if nothing was out of sorts, he slowly began pushing his cart forward again, in the direction of the checkout lanes, clunking as he went. All the while, he kept his eyes trained on the, no doubt, strategically placed dome-shaped security mirrors hanging overhead. He glanced up periodically, taking in his surroundings in their gleaming convex surfaces. He was hoping to pick up on any sort of detail that might help explain what had set off his cop's radar, and now had it edging toward *red alert*.

Again, David noticed the two college-age guys, who were still immersed in their obvious, though guarded, discourse. And then something else caught and pulled at his attention. Something that, at least to him, presented as being far more worrisome, if not all-out *distressing.*

Behind the two college-age kids, David watched as a tall uniformed guy entered the store and sauntered right past the Rent-a-Cop, who was stationed by the electronic security arch in front of the exit, distractedly hunched over the glowing screen of his cell phone.

The uniformed guy—the *unpaid* one, that is—was dressed head-to-toe in all black and was carrying a large tactical-type black duffle bag low at his side. He nonchalantly threaded his way through the ebbing crowd with the ease of a shark's dorsal fin slicing through water. As he made his way deeper into the store, there was something surprisingly matter-of-fact about the way he was carrying himself. Either denoting his comfort with the situation—whatever the situation was—or entirely too familiar with the store layout for David's comfort.

Again, something caught in his cop's filter.

Even though the man appeared to be dressed in a uniform, there was nothing about his attire that suggested where he came from, what company he might work for, or what purpose he might have for being at the store on such a busy day, especially at this late hour on Christmas Eve. That's what had David concerned—that and, of course, the duffle bag.

As he looked at the shortening lines ahead of him, he was both grateful and now annoyed that he was almost at the *Express Lane* checkout.

Stealing another glance at the overhead security mirror, David could see that the exchange between the two college guys was quickly escalating. One of them was holding his hands close in front of his chest, guardedly motioning toward the front doors, where the security guard was still hunched over his phone. The other kid was shaking his head. Even though their voices were still muffled by the din of the crowd, their exchange was clearly more direct than it had been before, which made it possible for David to make out at least broken bits of their hushed conversation.

No…

Fuck…

Crazy…

As he tried to consider what the words might mean in their larger context, David found his eyes drifting back toward where the uniformed man had been standing. When he caught sight of him, he was alarmed to notice the man didn't have the duffle bag with him anymore. He was standing in front of a near-empty display of PlayStation 4s, conversing with a woman dressed in a blue t-shirt with the toy store's logo on it, pointing toward the back of the store, in the direction of the restrooms.

Oh, shit! David thought.

His mind began reeling wildly, kicking into overdrive while the wheel of his cart still stuttered along. Everything around him wound down to an almost uncomfortable, echoed silence, until all David could hear was the rabbit-like beating of his own heart in the dark hollow of his chest. Movement seemed to dissolve into a thick mire of staccato motion. Bright as the surrounding store was, looming seasonal displays rising up all around him, the whole scene abruptly drained of color, bleeding into an unsettling grayscale version of what he had been viewing only seconds earlier.

Blinking to clear his eyes, David saw the Bedazzled woman standing in front of him once again. She was wagging a *scythe* of an acrylic nail into the bewildered face of an elderly woman, from whom she was doing her best to jostle a toy away. Even in slow motion, David was grateful for the moment of comic reprieve. Anything to get him out of his own head.

But just as he thought how potentially dangerous that could be at the moment, he quickly steadied himself against the bright blue frame of his shopping cart and fought to return his focus where it needed to be. On the uniformed man who was now *without* his tactical-style duffle bag, heading toward the back of the store. Presumably to either take a leak—or blow the fucking place to smithereens.

In either case, a dozen terrifying scenarios began to play across the panorama of David's humming mind.

Elementary school children and teachers slaughtered in the Sandy Hook massacre.

The Boston Marathon bombings, enacted by two brothers using nothing more than kitchen hardware as their homemade "tools of terror."

A concert in Paris turned deadly, bringing the City of Lights to its knees.

And, most recently, a radicalized husband and wife team of Jihadists, turning their ideology-driven hatred back on friends and coworkers in the San Bernardino shootings, quickly turning a holiday party into an unspeakable bloodbath.

It was all he could do to not scream at the top of his lungs for everyone to get down on the floor. The cop inside him made him instinctively want to jump into action, calling out commands to prepare himself and the sea of shoppers around him to face whatever situation they were being confronted with. Of course, *terrorism* was first and foremost at the front of David's mind. But he knew it could be dangerous—even deadly—to jump to any overwrought conclusions without knowing anything for certain. He had to find a way to get closer to the two young men who were looking around the store nervously, as if they had insight into something he didn't. But first, he wanted to check out the guy with the duffle bag. Or, in this case, *without* it.

David knew any legitimate company-issued uniform would have the business's logo embroidered somewhere on it, announcing the man's company of origin and reason for being in the store in the first place. A nondescript, all-black jumpsuit was far too benign for David's liking. It could be viewed as something dangerous—or simply nothing at all. Either way, he didn't want to take any chances.

He was thankful he was wearing his ankle holster with his service weapon safely secured in it. At least he could defend himself if need be, or use it if something went horribly wrong. He had the police station programmed as #2 on his cell phone's speed-dial feature, HOME being #1. In case things went south quickly, he could have backup to the store in a matter of minutes.

Momentarily reluctant to relinquish his spot in line—or the two toys he'd come to buy—David turned his cart around and headed back the way he'd come. As he pushed the hobbled cart along, he loaded armfuls of other toys on top of his two, hoping to hide them from other customers who might want them for their own children. He knew it was a futile thing to do, especially given his current situation, but he did it anyway. If the college kids and Duffle Bag Man turned out to be false alarms, at least he'd have something to show for his efforts.

Abandoning his overflowing cart behind an enormous, picked-over display of *Star Wars* action figures, David rushed toward the back of the store with the hope of getting to the uniformed man before he had a chance to do anything to threaten the lives of everyone present. Knowing that the man was now separated from his large duffle bag had David the most concerned. Was he there alone, or working in tandem with someone else—or a *group* of others? David had no way of knowing at this point. Picking up the pace, he was now sprinting down the least-populated aisle, trying to get to the back of the store as quickly as he could.

Once there, he caught sight of the guy in the black jumpsuit following behind the same woman he had been talking to earlier. The woman was hunched over, keying a digital code into the security lock on a set of double doors. A loud beep sounded and she pushed the door open, and then closed it behind them.

David didn't know whether to be relieved or worried that the man was once again carrying the large duffle bag at his side. Running to catch the door just before it closed, David managed to slip inside behind them without being noticed. He hid behind a tall, gray filing cabinet and watched as the woman keyed in another code, followed by another beep. She then stepped aside and allowed the man to enter the room before following him in.

When the door whooshed shut behind them, creating an echoing vacuum sound as it did, David stealthily inched forward until he was standing directly next to the security door's keypad. Chancing a glimpse inside, David peeked through a small square of alarmed glass at the door's center and could see that the woman was kneeling in front of a large safe, spinning the dial of a combination lock left, then right, then left again, ending with a muffled *clicking* sound that could be heard through the door.

David watched as the woman handed a series of large

plastic bags filled with cash to the uniformed man, who then placed them inside the black duffle bag. Each bag was sealed at the top with a thick fluorescent orange stripe of tape, which David knew from experience was all but impossible to reopen unless you cut through it. Either the guy was from a security firm hired to collect the store's daily earnings and transport them to the company's bank of choice, or these two were collaborating to pull off a seasonal heist that would at least get them as far as Mexico or the Cayman Islands.

David tensed when he heard a muffled zipping sound followed by a loud *CLUNK* as the woman shut the safe door and spun the tumbler again to relock it.

When the door whooshed open once again, David was waiting there with his service weapon drawn and department-issued badge held out in front of him.

"I need to ask you a few questions," David said, motioning toward a closed door with a sign reading OFFICE on the front of it.

After he questioned the uniformed man, who actually *was* an employee of Brinks Security, and the woman who introduced herself as the store's second assistant manager, David followed them both back out into the front of the store, trying to appear as casual as possible so as not to draw attention to himself, or the bag of cash the guard was carrying.

When they reached the security arch in front of the store's exit, the Rent-a-Cop pocketed his cell phone and accompanied the Brinks guard out into the frigid early evening air. After the cash pickup was securely loaded into the truck and the vehicle pulled away from the curb, David thanked the young woman for her help and once again searched the store's waning crowd for the two shifty-looking college kids.

From where he was standing, he could see their reflections in one of the security mirrors off to his left. Both were now standing closer to the bank of cash registers at the front of the store, where the lanes were now each only several customers deep. David looked down at his watch. It was 5:55 pm. The store was scheduled to close in just five minutes, but it was clear that even if the doors got locked at that time, it would take at least another half-hour or so to process the remaining purchases and get everyone out.

The two kids appeared to be scanning the faces of the remaining customers, as if they were looking for someone in particular. David tried his best to isolate and focus on just their reflections in the curved mirror, but from this distance and angle it was impossible to see anything in any great detail. He began to inch forward, trying to appear as if he was checking out some bins of wrapping paper as he did. From this vantage point, he caught something he hadn't noticed before due to the throngs of people milling about. Though both men were easily over six feet tall and slender, their midsections—covered by coats of medium thickness—appeared oddly *bloated,* as if they were both attempting to shoplift something from the store and carry whatever it was outside undetected.

When David caught sight of the kid closest to him, their eyes met—and *locked.* The kid's eyes shifted wildly, as if hit by a beam of blinding light. When the kid looked up again, David could see that his eyes were as black as night. Despite his age, the kid's eyes looked as if they hid a host of dark secrets.

The young man elbowed his companion and they both glared in David's direction. In a movement that simultaneously appeared to be both quick and drawn out, the kids ripped open their coats, exposing something far worse than stolen toys. The all-too-identifiable black and white flag of Islam had been sewn to the lining of their coats, which concealed twin vests outfitted with rows of wired explosives.

In a sobering moment of realization, David found it impossible to believe what he was seeing. *"NOOOO!!"* he shouted, as he ran toward where they were standing. He opened his arms wide to take as many nearby customers to the floor with him as possible. He fell to the floor *hard,* looking up just in time to see a blinding explosion flower above him.

Both kids had detonated their suicide vests to eradicate as many Westerners in the name of Islam as possible. In this season of excessive consumerism, a retail-driven holiday such as Christmas was no doubt an offense to their Eastern sensibilities—if anything could be considered sensible about what they'd just done.

David's eyes stung with tears as acrid, fire-riddled smoke billowed out in every direction.

"What the *fuck* was that?" someone shouted from the back of the store.

"Kamikaze bombers!" yelled a man dressed in a jacket covered with Vietnam era patches. "In case you haven't been watching the nightly news, the miserable fuckers are all around us! Hell, it might as well be Pearl Harbor all over again. Fuckin' cowards!"

David searched for his cell phone and pressed the #2 key, which would call the police station. When a dispatcher's voice came over the line, David requested emergency service.

As he listened to the deafening sounds all around him— the frantic screams of customers rushing for the exits; wails of those set on fire from the explosions; the gluttonous crackling of flames as they ignited with a number of large toy displays and quickly climbed the store's cavernous walls—David was relieved when he heard the howl of sirens growing closer.

He lifted his pounding head from off the floor and tried to see through the wall of black smoke encircling him. His eyes burned as he attempted to look through a sharp sting of tears. As he did, his frantically beating heart sank in his chest.

It was like looking at human pieces of a puzzle. Dismembered body parts were smoking in piles all around him. The only thing he could make out with any certainty was the Bedazzled torso of the lady with the acrylic nails.

Ghastly images began to appear through the swirling smoke as it gradually dissipated. David could see displays of toys melting like too-warm ice cream. Racks of scorched greeting cards and bins of flaming gift wrap stood to his right. And, much to his dismay, he could now see the soot-streaked faces of customers who'd been set aflame, their hair singed to the scalp, the skin beneath bubbling like molten lava.

When the EMTs arrived and eventually made their way over to where he was laying, carefully rolling him onto a body board and lifting him onto a gurney, he caught sight of the severed arm of the Rent-a-Cop as they drew closer to the front doors. The damned thing was still holding its ever-present cell phone in its clenched fist.

As they reached the exit, the electronic doors whirred open and David was hit by a sudden in-rush of frigid air. Rolling through, he opened his eyes in time to see fat crystalline snowflakes beginning to fall from an overcast sky. Through the watery refraction of his smoke-induced tears, he thought they looked a lot like falling diamonds. Even if the night was a spinning kaleidoscope of red and blue cruiser lights, David was beyond grateful to be breathing in the fresh air for the first time in an hour.

As the gurney reached the rear doors of an idling ambulance, David heard a familiar voice filter through the wailing crowd.

"DAVID!"

It was Beth's voice. But that wasn't possible. She was home with the kids.

"DAVID—"

Bewildered, David looked to his left and saw his wife running across the car-filled parking lot, toward the building.

"Beth," he called out weakly, and by some miracle she heard him above the buzz of the crowd. She rushed to his side. "Honey … what are you doing here?" he rasped as she approached.

For a second he thought perhaps he hadn't made it through the blast, that he'd died and this was simply a matter of his waning memory conjuring the image of her. But opening his eyes again, he saw her pale, drawn face looking down at him.

"Oh, my God …" Beth cried. I heard about the explosion on TV. The kids are at home with your sister. I had to come and see if you were okay!"

David reached for his wife's hand and his body began trembling as he began to sob.

"I love you so—" he started to say. But his words were abruptly silenced by the roar of another explosion.

David searched his reeling mind for a way to make sense of the sound. How could it be that there'd been another explosion if the two college kids were already dead? It made no sense.

And then it came to him. Just before he'd locked eyes with the bomber closest to him, after clearing the guy in the backroom with the black duffle bag, David had noticed the kids looking over the heads of the crowd. *As if they were looking for someone else.*

Numbing realization hit. There must've been a *third* suicide bomber!

When David attempted to open his eyes again, expecting to see Beth's face smiling down at him, there was nothing but absolute blackness. In a millisecond, his world had been undone around him.

And, this time, him along with it.

Finally Christmas
Ellen Shaw

Evening was beginning to fall in the small town of Bakers, Maine. It had snowed heavily earlier in the day and the temperatures were hovering very close to freezing. The weather service promised it would only get colder as the holiday approached. Last-minute Christmas shoppers were out in full force, buying anything they could wrap and give as a gift to some unsuspecting friend or relative.

Winslow McTosh stood with his hands in his back pockets looking out from his bookstore window. He watched the people running around, smiling to each other, their breath rising in the cold evening air like individual chimney stacks. The sight of grown men wearing Santa hats made him cringe. He shook his head slowly. He did not like the holidays, especially Christmas, but he didn't mind all the money people spent on it in his bookstore. He smiled every time he put another deposit into his growing bank account. His store was located beside a small coffee shop, which worked out very well for him. People like to read when they drink coffee and he could certainly help them with that.

He opened his front door and looked to his left. The same dumb-ass kid was still there, outside the coffee shop, ringing that damn bell. It had been four hours today and Winslow had reached his limit. He waved the young man over, and thinking he was going to get a generous donation, he came, smiling.

Winslow leaned in close to the young man's ear and spoke clearly. "If you don't find another place to ring that freaking bell, I am going to shove it up your butt, and the only time it will ring is when you run like hell in the opposite direction."

He smiled and reminded the kid not to forget his bright red kettle. The young man was gone within two minutes. Winslow chuckled to himself as he returned to the warmth of his store. Ah, the Christmas holidays.

He closed at five, turning away a few last-minute shoppers who were knocking on the locked door by pointing to the sign listing the store hours. One of the younger ones flipped him off and Winslow simply smiled back. They hurried on, looking for other things on which to spend their hard-earned money.

He was headed home for a quiet night. He would settle in, and after a quick supper, he would spend the night sitting at his computer, working on his latest horror novel. He had some success in selling his short stories, but he longed for some sort of recognition for the long hours spent spinning tales of gloom and doom.

He worked on a new novel for close to four hours and finished with only five salvageable pages. Some stories write hard, and this was one of them. He stopped around two in the morning, saving what was on the computer and went to bed. He turned the heat up and noticed the severe drop in the temperature in the house.

He dreamt of fame, of the recognition he so badly wanted and felt he deserved. In his dream, a short fat man claiming to be a publisher had made an offer on his latest story. It was more than he had ever imagined getting paid for his writing, and this guy was talking a book deal. Winslow woke out of breath and covered in a cold sweat but with the sad realization that it had all been a dream. He swore in frustration. He showered and dressed for the day. He checked the heat again and then left without turning off his computer.

He opened on time, as he did every day, and the mad Christmas shopping rush greeted him. Everyone wanted the latest book written by that other author from Maine. He had to admit, it was a great story. He had read everything the guy had ever written. He wondered when he would get the break he had been waiting for. His stuff was good, he just had to get it into the right hands. He had mailed out a new story over a week ago and hadn't heard a thing back from any of the publishers he had sent it to. His own agent hadn't even returned his calls.

He worked on through the day, his only consolation was the money he was taking in from the sale of King's book. Christmas was only two days away and though he hated the holidays, he would enjoy the time the store was closed because of them. He could write uninterrupted.

The next two days went past in a blur, the register ringing up sales like never before. Taking a break, he looked out the front window and noticed a fully dressed Santa staring into the store. Feeling charitable, Winslow waved. The Santa didn't wave back. He just stood close to the window and stared. It appeared no one else on the street was bothering with the man in red because crowds were passing and no one seemed to notice him. Winslow turned away to take care of a customer, and when he looked back, the Santa was gone.

Time to close came fast and Winslow breathed a sigh of relief when he locked the front door and flipped over the closed sign. He rushed to the bank, and using the night deposit, he dropped in the last holiday cash bundle.

Despite his hatred for all things Christmas, Winslow had to admit that it twas the season for making money.

Walking home that night, he saw footsteps ahead of him in the fresh snow. They were larger than his feet, and from the depth of them, the person was of good size, both in height and weight. He had assumed all the town's residents were tucked in by a warm fire and drinking eggnog. He glanced around and saw no one in the square.

He didn't drive to work this morning, cleaning the car off was too much of a waste of time, but tonight he wished he had driven. He continued trudging through the deep snow, cursing winter and its white offerings. He thought he heard jingle bells, almost sounding like they were attached to someone's feet; with each step the bell would sound. He stopped and the bells stopped. He walked and the jingle bells rang. He was getting nervous. He had no cash on him, or valuables for that matter. He started walking faster, and though he saw no one, he had the feeling he was being followed.

He made it home in record time and quickly locked the door behind him. He peeked back out the window and noticed two sets of footprints on the walkway; his eyes followed them right up the porch to the door he had just locked.

"Ho, Ho, Ho!"

Winslow jumped and turned to face Santa. He was shaking his head in disbelief, moving his mouth but nothing was coming out but his own cold breaths.

I said, "Ho, Ho, Ho!"

The deep voice came from behind the beard. Santa took a step closer to the frozen figure of a man, now pressed up against the door.

"Who are you?"

Winslow's question was stuttered.

"I'm the Easter Bunny. What's the matter? Aren't you the guy that likes to scare people with your stories of demons and ghosts?"

"Yes."

"Well. Turn-about is fair play, isn't it?"

Santa slapped Winslow's shoulder hard, then walked into the kitchen to retrieve a cold beer from the refrigerator. He raised it up and nodded his head toward Winslow. Winslow slowly shook his head no. Santa made his way past Winslow and took a seat on the couch. He pulled off his big black boots and rubbed his stocking feet with his hands. He undid the belt around his waist and unbuttoned the collar from his neck. He took off his red stocking hat. When he felt comfortable, he turned and smiled at Winslow.

"Did I scare you?"

"Yeah, you did."

Winslow moved closer into the room where the big man was sitting, making sure to keep to the far side of it. He sat down on the chair beside his desk. He kept looking at Santa, watching him as he sipped the beer. Five long minutes passed until Santa stood up quickly and started walking around the room. Winslow sat still in the chair, frozen, and watched. He wondered what he was looking for.

"No tree, no lights, no freaking Christmas music, and no presents. No holly, no cards, no nothing." Santa was raising his voice with each missing item, and by the time he reached the last of his discoveries, he was screaming.

"You really do hate Christmas, don't you, Winslow?"

"Yes, I do."

"What's the matter? You didn't get the fire engine you wanted when you were ten?"

Santa was standing right in front of him now, and for the first time Winslow noticed the width and height of the man. It made him very nervous. He refused to answer but kept his eyes trained on the obese man, who looked like he was going to stroke out in his living room. Santa slowly returned to the couch and flopped back down, sinking into it. Winslow wondered if the couch would hold him plopping down on it like that too many times.

Santa sat staring at him, the same way he did through the store window.

"What do you want for Christmas, Winslow?"

"Would you leave, if I asked you nicely?"

Santa started laughing, and it was amazing. His big belly shook, his eyes twinkled, and his red nose turned up. A split second went by and Winslow actually thought this guy was the real deal.

Santa kept on shaking and laughing and Winslow felt a strong desire to join the rotund fellow in a good laugh.

But the longer Santa laughed, the stranger his laugh became. It sounded downright evil after a few minutes, and any thoughts of joining him quickly vanished.

"I am going to give you what you want for Christmas, Winslow. I am going to let your latest piece of horror crap become a best seller. Would you like that? Do you believe in Santa now?"

"I think this is all a bad dream. I will wake up and you'll be gone and my life will be just as it was before."

"So, you think I am the spirit of Christmas future and you'll be visited by ghosts that will change your little mind about the holiday? I suppose you believe that tomorrow morning you'll go out and buy the biggest turkey in the butcher's shop for some little crippled kid? Get a grip, Winslow. This is your one and only shot."

Winslow stood and walked to the window. He could see the neighborhood lit up with all the colored lights and fake ornaments, trees shining out through living rooms reflecting on the snowy blanket covering each yard.

There were snowmen on the lawns where children lived, and reindeer, elves, large candy canes serving as mailboxes, wreaths on every door, and neon lights attached to roofs that made them look like cheap hotel signs advertising the season. Winslow shook his head, thinking of the money wasted on it all. He turned back to Santa, who was still sitting on the couch, smiling. He sauntered toward him, never taking his eyes off of him until he was within a few inches of him. He looked down into the fat smiling face staring back up at him and spit into it.

"Get the hell out of my house."

Santa moved quickly. He was on his feet and had Winslow by the neck before he could even back away. Santa wasn't laughing anymore. He was downright pissed. Winslow felt his body leaving the ground and struggled to pull Santa's large hands from his neck. He could feel the room start to spin as the oxygen wasn't permitted entrance into his lungs. Just when he thought he was going to pass out, Santa let go and he fell to the floor in front of the big man's feet. He sat there rubbing his neck and coughing, trying to regain some sense of a normal breathing pattern.

"Sorry about that, Winslow. I do detest violence of any kind, but I won't be spit upon by the likes of a pathetic non-believer."

"You're crazy."

Winslow tried to stand and was lifted to his feet by the strength of Santa's right arm. Santa placed him back into his chair by the computer. When he was once again able to talk, Winslow started to pour out his story to the fat man. He told him how hard he had worked on his stories and they were good, "Honest, Santa," they were. He told him how he had given up the love of his life, a woman who loved him more than life itself and how he had broken her heart when he chose writing over her love. He told him of the lonely nights writing and rewriting until his stories sang with the words he created. He finally told him he wondered now if he had made a bad choice, and while his passion was for the written word, his life was incomplete.

"We all make choices, Winslow. Go get some sleep and in the morning things will be better for you, I promise."

Winslow slowly turned and shut down the computer, careful to save what he had written earlier that day. He turned at the foot of the stairs.

"Merry Christmas, Santa."

Before he finished the sentence, he knew the fat man was gone.

In somewhat of a haze, Winslow slowly walked up the stairs to his bedroom and undressed methodically, not feeling the bitter cold hit his naked skin. The windows were wide open and yet he simply threw himself onto the bed and fell into a deep sleep.

Ten O'clock on Wednesday morning, the day after Christmas, there was a constant knocking on Winslow McTosh's front door. A fat man with white hair and a rosy completion holding a brown envelope was banging and yelling for Winslow to open the door. It was his agent, Christopher Crinkle. Winslow's book had sold. It was the break he had been waiting for. His best seller was ready for printing. He continued to bang on the front door while Winslow McTosh lay frozen to death in his upstairs bed.

We all make choices in life.

Twas the Night Before Krampus

Rob Smales

The pillow struck Will right in the face. Unharmed and unsurprised, he peeled the soft weight away with a giggle and dropped it over the side of the bed.

"Stop it, Kev," he said, though his continued laughter robbed the command of any real force. "We *have* to get to sleep so Santa will come."

His brother's second pillow arced through the air to land, unerringly, on Will's face. Will grabbed at it and wrestled with it like it was attacking, all the while using it to muffle snorts of laughter. Across the room, Kevin stifled his own laughter: Santa may be able to see them while they were sleeping, but they didn't want Dad to hear they were still awake.

With that sobering thought, Will lobbed the pillow

gently across the room, aiming for Kevin's feet.

"We really *do* have to go to sleep. I don't want to miss out on Santa because I'm still awake when he comes by."

He rolled onto his side to emphasize his point, turning away from his older brother. He curled his legs underneath him and jammed a knuckle into his mouth, biting it to make sure he stopped giggling. For almost a minute, the only sounds were made by Kevin, stealthily retrieving that first pillow from the floor. Then Kevin spoke so low that Will barely heard him.

"You know ... Santa isn't really coming tonight."

A chill that had nothing to do with the cold wind blowing past their bedroom window touched Will's heart.

"What do you mean?" he whispered, the words sounding harsh as he flipped about to face his brother. "I been good! Me and Mom went over my list and she said I didn't ask for anything too big. I asked the Helper Santa we saw at the store, and he said I been good, and I even sent a letter to the North Pole and got a letter back saying I been good! What're you talking about?"

Kev sat up in bed, the dim glow of the SpongeBob night light enough to show his serious expression.

"It's not you, dude. You didn't do anything wrong."

The tightness in Will's chest started to relax, but that chill turned into a belly full of ice at his brother's next words.

"It's just that Santa isn't real, is all."

Now, Will was just six, but Kevin was ten, and he knew things no six-year-old ever knew. Will learned a lot just from watching and listening to his older brother. Mom told people he "looked up to Kevin" quite a bit, and that may have even been true, but Kevin was still a ten-year-old, and an older brother; he was not above playing a trick or three on Little Brother from time to time. In fact, had anyone ever asked

Will (not that they ever *did*, but, you know, *if* they did) he would have told them his older brother's main source of entertainment was playing jokes and tricks on Will.

That's what it has to be, he thought. *A joke. He'll laugh in a minute and tell me I'm a doofus.*

But Kevin didn't say anything. He didn't poke Will, didn't throw the pillow again, didn't even smile as far as Will could tell. He just lay there looking at Will.

Finally, Will could take no more of the silent stare.

"What are you talking about?" He tried to keep his voice from doing that scared little quivery thing, but he heard it in there anyway. "Of course, he's real."

But Kevin shook his head before Will had even finished speaking—not fast, or excited, or angry or anything, but slow, like their dad did when something was really serious.

"No. He's not. It's Dad."

For just a moment, Will pictured their father at the North Pole wearing the famous red suit, the front of it stuffed with a big, soft pillow, giving last-minute orders to the elves loading his sleigh.

"Mom, too," Kev went on. "But it's mostly Dad, I think. They get the presents and stuff and he sneaks them out there after we go to bed. Then in the morning they just *tell* us it was Santa."

"That's not true!" It was a loud, angry whisper, only a half-step away from shouting, really. "Mom told me there's a Santa Claus, and *she* wouldn't lie! Not like *you*."

Kevin was unfazed.

"You remember last month when Mom took you to see Doctor Oshea? When the doctor said you had to have a shot, what did Mom tell you?"

Will's face felt warm, and his eyes felt *hot*, and that flippery thing hanging down at the back of his throat felt huge and chokey. He swallowed twice, moving that big chokey-thing around a bit, then took the biggest chance he could recall taking in his whole young life.

"I don't remember."

He'd forced a lie out past the chokey-thing. A lie, on Christmas Eve, when Santa (*he's real, I **know** he's real*) was *sure* to be watching.

Kevin wasn't fooled for a second.

"I was there, remember? She said it wouldn't hurt, didn't she?"

Will nodded, slow and miserable.

"Did it?"

It *had* hurt, it had hurt like a hot coal on his arm, like a hundred *billion* mosquito bites all at once, and he had yelled and cried and hadn't stopped until they left Doctor Oshea's office and went up the street for ice cream. But he'd already lied outright, right there on Christmas Eve; Will didn't think a small fib would hurt him at the moment.

"A little."

Kevin was nodding along with him now.

"So she lied about that."

Will said nothing. The stupid chokey thing in his throat probably wouldn't have let him, even if he tried.

"And if she lied about *that*, then she could be lying about *this*, right?"

Will wasn't nodding his head anymore. He felt tired, exhausted, the way he always felt after a great big cry, the kind with snot-bubbles and the *hic-hic* breathing, the kind of cry that usually went on until Mom hugged it away, even though this time he'd swear only a couple of tears had rolled down his face in the dark. He flopped away from Kevin, lay flat on his back. His eyes felt like a thumb in a cartoon when someone's hit it with a hammer, all swelled up and throbbing.

He could *hear* them throbbing, just like in the cartoons. He forced the lids down over his cartoon-thumb eyes, even though that squeezed out new tears that ran back across his cheeks and made cold spots on his ears.

"Mom didn't lie. He's coming."

The voice didn't sound like his own at all, and seemed to quit before the words were out, making "coming" sound like "copik". He still heard his cartoon-thumb eyes throbbing, and that might have been why he didn't hear Kevin moving, but the next thing he knew there was a hand on his shoulder. It was a hand that had pinched and poked him, even punched him once, a hand that occasionally gave out the wickedest Indian burns, but this time Kevin's hand gave nothing more than a gentle shake.

"Hey, Will, I'm not trying to be mean. It's just the truth."

Will pulled away from the hand, turning toward the wall and pulling the covers up over his head.

"It's not. Mom didn't lie."

He sniffled prodigiously.

"You're just trying to trick me, and that's dumb, 'cuz it's Christmas Eve and Santa's watching. You're gonna wind up on the naughty list for sure."

The hand found his shoulder again.

"You're gonna have to learn this sometime, and I'm getting kind of tired of pretending. You think I'm lying? That I still believe in Santa? Come on—I can prove it to you."

❄ ❄ ❄

They crept down the hall on silent feet, right past their parent's bedroom door, Will's occasional sniffle the only sound. Kevin didn't even *shush* him; he simply pointed to Will, put a finger to his lips, and made a wringing-out motion with both hands. Will understood: if he kept making noise, Kev would give him an Indian burn. Maybe not right now, but Kev *never* forgot about giving Indian burns. Will muffled his sniffles and thought, *Yup, he's on the naughty list for sure!*

They tip-toed into the kitchen. Light spilling in from the hall nightlight augmented the trio of electric candles glowing on the windowsill

—to help Santa find us if there's fog, Mom says, and why would she say that if—

filling the kitchen with dim light. Will had no problem seeing Kevin turn and indicate the table with a grand gesture, a flourish, like The Amazing Prest-O, the magician they'd gone to see over the summer. He also had no trouble seeing what lay on the table.

A plate of cookies and a glass of milk.

"What are you—" Will began, but Kevin cut him off.

"Santa's milk and cookies, right?"

Will nodded. He'd picked out those cookies with Mom, special for Santa. Sugar cookies with pictures on them: Christmas trees, reindeer, and one with an image of Santa himself, sack on his shoulder. They'd put them there so the big, jolly man could have a little snack during his long night's work. They did it every year.

Kevin picked up a cookie, still with that showy magician's flourish.

"Would I do *this*, if I really believed in Santa?"

With that, The Amazing Kev-O began to make the cookies disappear.

He munched them down one by one, eating silently until the last cookie. For the last one, one with a picture of Santa on it, he made quiet Cookie Monster sounds, *num-num-num*-ing until there was nothing left but crumbs on the plate. Then he reached for the milk, a big tumbler Will had to hold with both hands, and *glug-glug*ged it all away, pawing at his cheek when a little rivulet of moo juice jumped the side of the glass and tried to escape across his face.

He placed the empty glass next to the empty plate with a quiet *Ahhh!*, then wiped a pajama sleeve across his mouth and looked at Will.

"There. You think I'd do that if I thought Santa was real? *Seriously?*"

No. There was no way Kevin would do something like that if he thought Santa was real. No way he'd do something so, so … so *in your face* like that to Santa, with no way to say it was an accident or a mistake. He was a little mean sometimes, but he wasn't dumb. He wouldn't give up on his chance to get toys and stuff just for a joke or a trick, even one on Will. But that would mean …

That means Kevin really *doesn't believe in Santa, and Kevin's ten, and he's smart, and he* knows *stuff, and Mom did lie about the shot … but* that *means* …

"So, can we go back to bed before Dad wakes up to sneak our presents out here and finds us?" said Kevin. He leaned a little closer.

"Or do you *still* believe in Santa Claus?"

Will stood there sniffling for a while—to heck with the Indian burn—and his answer, when it finally came, was in a whisper so low he barely heard it himself.

"I guess not."

As he said the words, he felt something. Something deep inside him, way, way down where he kept things like his memories of Mom, back when she was Mommy, and Dad when he was Daddy; where he kept how he really felt about Kevin, because he'd get teased if he told his older brother he really loved him. Buried deep within his Will-ness, where he kept all the important things, he felt one small, fragile thing, as brittle as a crystal snowflake, break with a silent *snap*.

There was a sudden, loud *thud*.

Kevin whirled to face the bedrooms, probably afraid it was Dad, though it hadn't come from that direction at all. Will thought it had—

The *thud* came again. Louder. From the roof. The boys looked at each other.

"What the heck was tha—" Kevin began, but Will cut him off with a short, breathy scream, finger pointing toward the window. Pressed to the glass, just past the trio of bulbs in the electric candles, was a hideous face. The brows were thick, dark in contrast to the white, *white* skin, and rising high above the wide eyes that stared in through the pane with a wild, brilliant blue gaze. The nose was wide and flat, made flatter as the face pressed to the glass, spreading across one cheek like a weird stain above a wide grin filled with sharp, triangular teeth.

Kevin had apparently given up on sneaking around because the yell that came out of him was so loud it snapped Will's attention away from the thing at the window.

"*Dad!*"

Without warning, the door leading out to the back hall exploded inward, split down the middle, one half spinning away across the room as the other smashed against the edge of the counter and fell to the floor. The brothers screamed as, from the darkness that seemed to pool out in the hall, a huge, hairy leg ending in a cloven hoof stepped across the threshold, landing so hard Will felt it in his feet.

In the stunned silence that followed, Will, too terrified to make a sound, clearly heard a clank, then a jingle, like Christmas bells. He had time to think *Santa's sleigh?* before the huge figure followed its hoof into the kitchen.

It seemed to unfold into the room, opening like some

dark and terrible flower, until it was taller and wider than the doorway itself. It stood on two legs like a man, but it was *not* a man. The legs it stood upon were *animal* legs, covered with thick black fur and bending backward at the knees, like that Mr. Tumnus, the faun in the movie about the magical wardrobe, but these were *huge*. The shaggy hair covered the whole beast. Long gorilla arms hung from shoulders humped and thick with so much muscle the head thrust forward and down, in front of those shoulders rather than sitting atop them. Even though the head rode low on the creature, its horns still swept up, over the head, over the bull-like mountain that was its back and shoulders to score deep furrows in the ceiling above.

Below the horns, the face was the only bit of the thing not covered in hair. It was a big face, a long face, as if someone had taken the faces of a man, horse, and goat, and only kept the worst bits of each. Round, red eyes glared from beneath a heavy brow, shining in the dim kitchen with a light all their own. Huge, square nostrils flexed as the thing scented the air, and the narrow, elongated mouth hung open, the lower jaw dangling as a tongue, longer and redder than it had *any* right to be, lolled from between thick, sharp teeth.

One hand came up, pointing at the brothers with what looked to Will like a whip, the long lash hanging down to coil on the floor at the thing's cloven feet.

"Destroyer!"

The voice sounded like Grandpa Willis's cough, the one he always did right before Mom told him the smokes would kill him someday: deep and wet, like something down in his chest had come loose on one side and was flapping about in there. Rattling. Just hearing it made Will's stomach lurch, and he might have thrown up right on the spot, if not for the blast of cold air that hit him as the kitchen window slid wide open.

The thing from the window landed lightly in front of the counter with a deep, menacing chuckle, bent legs absorbing all the shock. Will registered wide shoulders, arms and legs so burly and powerful the thing was bandy-legged, and the shocking fact that it was no taller than he—then the big one was moving, taking one lengthy stride to the other side of the kitchen table, a strangely fluid movement for a thing so huge. One long arm moved across the table, then the thing backed up half a step.

There, on the plate that had once held snacks intended for Jolly Saint Nick, was a candle, flickering in the breeze from the open window. The candle was thick and black, and it stood in the center of a small severed human hand.

"Destroyer," the thing repeated, that terrible rumble bringing Will's gorge up again. The whip was leveled once more, like a teacher using a pointer in school, but now the thing stood close enough that they could see exactly what it was pointing at.

Kevin.

"I come for you."

Even with the chill night air coming in through the open window, Will could smell the sharp, acrid stink as his older brother, king of the flinching game and master of the Indian burn, emptied his bladder.

"What?" Kevin's voice was a high, terrified shriek, but it was more than Will could have managed right then. "Who are you? Dad!"

That last was a scream, cast over his shoulder toward the bedrooms, his gaze never leaving that pointing whip.

"No aid will come, scream though you might. Answer to Krampus, you will on this night."

"K-k-Krampus? Who's Krampus?"

Wide nostrils flared as the thing leaned down, huge face looming over the boys, and Will detected the scent of smoke coming from the thick fur—not wood smoke, like from a fireplace, or when they went camping, but a bitter, nose-stinging smell, like burning plastic. With the thing this close, he saw the source of the jingling: wrapped about the thing's huge torso, crisscrossing the powerful chest like the bandoliers on the Frito Bandito, were chains, the links of which were hung with bells, tarnished nearly as black as the thick fur almost burying them.

The smaller creature began its evil chuckle once more.

"I am Krampus, punisher of children. For the crime of Destroying Belief, I, Krampus, the Stalker of Night, find you guilty."

The hand, now empty of the candle, reached to the chain wound about its waist and pulled loose a large canvas sack. Krampus, ignoring Will, leaned still closer to Kevin, the breath from that great horsey mouth actually ruffling Kevin's eyelashes.

"You're coming with me."

Will couldn't see into the sack, held out as it was toward his brother, but Kev could. And did. And what he saw within the depths of the big bag caused his mouth to drop open nearly as wide as that of Krampus himself. Out of that wide open mouth came a note of purest terror, and he wheeled about and fled toward the hall leading to the bedrooms.

With a casual, almost negligent movement, the hand not holding the sack went back, then came forward in a side-throwing motion. Rather than a ball, the business end of Krampus' long whip went snaking through the air toward Kevin's back. It was a narrowing space, however, and the lash struck the edge of the doorframe just as Kev turned into the hall, screaming for their father the whole way.

328

Roaring like a steam train with chest congestion, Krampus went after him, bells jingling as he slowed at the door, forcing his great bulk through the opening and into the close confines of the narrow hallway.

Will took a step or two after him, not knowing what he was going to do, but that thing was after his brother, and his mom and dad were down there, too. That was when the small one, the one with the white face, stepped in front of him, blocking his path.

"Now, now, that's nothing for good you to see.
You need to stay here in the kitchen, with me."

Will backed away from the creature, and it watched him go, rubbing its oversized hands and grinning with delight, those shark-like teeth protruding out farther than its lips. A gust of wind blew through the kitchen, and the tear tracks down Will's cheeks felt like ice.

"Who are you? What's going on?"

Those blue eyes, so pale they were almost white, lit up, and the wide smile widened, that jagged grin letting out a high, sing-songy voice.

"Santa you know, for he brings about toys,
but Krampus, he comes for the bad girls and boys.
And just as Santa has a helper, an elf,
I come along to help Krampus myself."

"But why?"

To his surprise, the ugly little man did a happy little dance (Will noticed then that though the creature was dressed all in grey leather, his too-big feet were clad in white Nikes) and answered him.

"The Krampus has come to cause pain, to cause grief,
and all of it based on one small thing: Belief.
And before you start cursing the thing that we do,
you should know the Believer who called us was ... you."

Will gaped at the sneaker-clad horror.

"Me? I didn't call anybody! I don't understand!"

"There is one thing left that a child can't do,
the thing that brought Krampus here, now, to you.
Believing in Santa must fade on its own:
for helping it die, helpers must atone.
Deep within you there once was a spark,
but your brother did smother it, leaving you dark.
From the South Pole we came, to take Kevin back
to the Krampus' lair, in his kid-taking-sack."

The white Nikes did another little happy dance as the thing clapped its hands in delight. In the background, Will heard Kev yelling for help while Krampus bellowed, wordless sounds of rage.

"My favorite part's when the kids try to run!
They scream and they kick when I fetch—it's great fun!"

Will listened to the capering little monster in growing horror, thinking he understood, but …

"You mean you're going to take Kevin away?"

The white face nodded, black hair jouncing.

"Forever?"

The hair continued its up-and-down dance, the odd eyes creasing almost shut with the width of the grin. Will tried to dart around the thing, to get to the hall, maybe wake his parents, though how they were sleeping through all *this* noise he had no idea. The nightmare in Nikes darted sideways, cat-quick, still blocking his path with those muscular arms. He tried a different tack.

"Dad! Mom! Help!"

"Shout all you wish, for no one will hear.
Not as long as the Krampuskandle stays near."

One of the big hands gestured toward the table, and the candle in its horrible five-fingered holder. Will had all but forgotten it in his fright.

"What? What is that thing?"

"Children taken by Krampus, they all cry a lot,
and their tears we do catch and then keep in a pot.
When they wear out and can no longer work,
we take all their hair, pull it off in one jerk.
The hair is all woven into one wick-like string,
and then into the tearpot to steep goes the thing.
While the wick soaks up all of the tears they surrendered,
their flesh into a nice little tallow is rendered.
Tallow and wick make a candle quite black,
and then it comes hunting along with the sack.
So long as the Krampuskandle burns in that hand,
no one in this house may leave Sleepyland."

The whole time he'd been talking, the little creature had shuffled forward with a slow, rolling gait, and Will had backed away, trying to keep his distance. The thing was looking Will up and down in a way he did *not* like, and after it had finished that little speech, it inhaled through its nose, leaning forward as if taking a big sniff.

"I don't understand," Will shouted as his back met the wall beside the splintered doorway.

"The best part I think, of the Krampuskandle so black," said the thing, pausing to lick those triangular teeth with a tongue as black as the candle itself. *"Is that when it's all done, I get the bones for my snack."*

It leaned forward again, nostrils flaring, and its bright eyes closed as it took the biggest sniff of all, then exhaled in a long sigh. The eyes opened, staring at Will with that expression again, and this time the boy recognized it.

The bandy-legged little nightmare with the mouth filled with shark's teeth was *hungry.*

"Wintzell!"

The eyes popped wide, mouth snapping shut so fast the teeth nearly cut off that flopping black tongue as the menacing little figure stood straight and spun about. Will looked past him to the dark, hulking form of Krampus, red eyes wide with rage, squeezing his way back into the kitchen.

"The brat has gone under his parents' bed where I cannot reach."

The long shaggy legs carried Krampus into the kitchen proper, hooves grinding into the linoleum. The whip pointed back toward the hall.

"Wintzell! Fetch!"

The hungry terror, the Wintzell, launched itself forward with a low growl, dropping down to run on all fours like some scuttling monkey. Will caught a flash of white as the Nikes rounded the corner, then the Wintzell was gone. His view of the hall disappeared behind a wall of black fur as Krampus stepped up to the table, tucking the coiled whip under one of his chains. Kevin's cries for help became wordless shrieks of terror as the Wintzell joined him under the bed.

Krampus turned from the table, one hand holding the sack, the other the Krampuskandle in its terrible holder. His blazing eyes fell on Will, and they narrowed.

"I came for one child, but here I find two. Oh, whatever shall Krampus do?"

The voice still sounded like it came from a throat filled with maggots, but had become lilting. Teasing. Krampus leaned forward, much as the Wintzell had, staring into Will's eyes.

"My counterpart's power wanes faster than mine, and faster every day. Would it be right to take one little boy but leave one behind? A witness? No ... that cannot be right."

The candle came down, hovering next to Will's face as the huge figure crouched low to look close.

"What say you, young Will? Will you leave your brother, your only brother to fend for himself in my care? Or shall I take two?"

Behind the Krampus, in the doorway to the hall, a grinning Wintzell appeared, bearing the struggling Kevin in its powerful arms. The sight was blotted out once more as the long, terrible face leaned still closer, and Will choked on Krampus' foul breath as the flame came so close it nearly scorched his cheek.

"What say you, Will? Have you been ... naughty?"

"No," said Will, and he blew out the candle.

He hadn't been sure what would happen, hadn't understood all of what the Wintzell had told him, but he'd understood the candle was important.

He hadn't known *how* important.

The great red eyes went round as a grunt of surprise, rancid and hot, washed over Will's skin.

"No!"

From down the hall, a new commotion began, barely audible over Kevin's screams for help. The sounds of a father and mother (*parents*, flashed through Will's mind) waking up to a disaster.

"Kevin? Will? What's going on?"

The Krampus stared at the smoking wick for an instant, then whirled, its hip striking Will, pinning him to the wall and smashing the breath out of him.

"You!" The deep, clotted voice was accusing and angry, and past the hairy bulk in front of him, Will saw the Wintzell's blue eyes widen in fear. *"I'll cut out your waggling tongue for this. How many times do I have to tell you—"*

"Boys? Where are you?"

Their mother's voice, coming from their bedroom.

"No time," said the Krampus, holding out the sack. The Wintzell all but hurled Kevin into the mouth of the bag and the Krampus drew the drawstrings tight, leaving Kevin's bare feet sticking out, kicking frantically. His muffled voice came through the burlap, words mixing in between terrified sobs.

"Help! Oh, God, help me, Will! Dad! Please, somebody!"

The Wintzell leapt to the open window, perching nimbly upon the sill, as the Krampus spun back to Will, teeth bared in a razor-sharp snarl.

"You defied me. Me! I'll not forget you, Believer!"

Krampus turned to the door as the Wintzell shot Will a reproachful look from its spot on the sill, a look that said *that goes for me, too, I'll remember you,* before ducking down and out, into the night.

A cyclone suddenly hit the kitchen, a hurricane, all the wind blasting out through the door and window. Outside the window, the Wintzell disappeared, while in the kitchen, the Krampus ducked his head and was blown right through the door by the great exiting wind. The smashed flinders of door were caught up by the blast, flying through the air, the larger pieces bouncing along like big wooden tumbleweeds. As the last of the cyclone left the room, the door re-assembled itself right in front of Will's eyes, all the pieces sucked into place by the wind and then slamming shut like a plug in a drain.

Will heard a faint cry and looked to the window. The exiting air had tried to suck the open window closed, but at the last instant those three tall, electric candles (*to help Santa find us if there's fog,* Will remembered) had tilted back, started to fall, and had gotten stuck in the closing window, propping it halfway open.

"Will ... please ... help!" came the voice, faint and far away,

carried through the stuck window on the cold night breeze. He shouted back through the window, his voice hoarse with tears.

"Kevin!"

"Will?"

It was his father, finally coming into the kitchen, unbelted robe swirling like a cape in the draft, hair and eyes wild.

"Will? What's going on? Where's Kevin?"

"They took him, Dad! They took him!"

That was all he could say before the world dissolved into uncontrollable tears.

✳ ✳ ✳

The rest of the night went by fast and slow at the same time. Dad yelling and crying. Mom hysterical. Neighbors in the back hall (the same hall the Krampus had used) wearing concerned faces. A man in blue doctor-gloves listening to his heart and putting that super-tight-cuff thing on his arm. Shining a penlight in his eyes. Police in the kitchen, dusting this and collecting that. A man in a suit who showed Will a badge and asked him questions. Will tried to answer the questions, but the man didn't want to hear his answers. Another man, another suit, another badge. The same questions. Will gave the same answers.

"I can't get anything out of this kid that makes sense," said the second suit.

"Paramedics say he's in shock," said the first suit. "Let's just let him rest. We can try to question him tomorrow if this thing hasn't resolved itself by then."

Then he was in bed, listening to police and parents, all talking and talking. It felt like forever. Mom had hugged him. Kissed him. Dad, too. It had all been good, felt good, and he had been comforted, but he still lay awake. Deep down inside him, buried inside his essential Will-ness, he stored the hugs and kisses from tonight next to the memories of Mom when she was Mommy and Dad when he was Daddy. And down there, as deep inside himself as he could go, he put the memory of Kevin, in a sack and screaming Will's name as he disappeared into the night.

And right next to that memory he found a small, fragile thing, like a crystal snowflake. It had a mark down the middle, where it had been broken and mended. The mended place looked thick and strong, much stronger than the rest of the thing. As Will lay there in his room (*His now,* he thought bitterly. *No brother to share with.*), he turned the crystal snowflake over and over in his mind, imagining it being wrapped in steel, encased; made unbreakable.

Much, much later, when the rest of the house was silent, police gone and parents in bed, Will quietly got to his feet. Out on the kitchen table, he saw the empty plate and glass and remembered the last thing he'd seen lying on that plate: a severed child's hand holding a magic candle made of suffering. The glass went into the dishwasher, but he threw the plate away, wearing Mom's big oven mitts to handle it.

He threw the mitts away, too.

He got out a fresh plate and glass, filled the one with milk and the other with cookies. Special cookies he'd picked out with Mom. He put the plate and glass on the table, stared at them for a moment, then went quietly to bed.

As he got into bed, he reached under his pillow, pulling out something he'd hidden there. Hidden from the police. Hidden from his parents.

When Krampus had whirled to face the Wintzell, it had bumped into Will, crushing him to the wall. Will had grabbed at Krampus, not to grapple with it, but as one does when flailing for balance, reflexively grabbing at anything within reach. He had managed not to fall, and had come away from that brief exchange with a little extra something clutched in his hand. He held it up now, looking at it in SpongeBob's dim glow.

A jingle bell. Battered and tarnished, nearly the size of a golf ball, and smelling faintly like burning plastic. The surface was slick despite the visible corrosion, and it just felt … wrong. Will gave the disgusting thing a little shake. A mournful note rang out, somehow warped and distorted, like a recording being played back too slow, or a finger slowing down a record.

In his mind, Krampus looked at him again, Kevin's feet sticking out of the sack on his shoulder. The Wintzell gave him a reproachful look.

"I'll not forget you, Believer!"

Will flicked the bell with a fingernail, summoning that tuneless little note. It sounded almost like a sob.

"I won't forget you either."

He tucked the bell beneath his pillow once more, then closed his eyes.

I'm coming, Kevin.

* * *

And so it begins…

ABOUT THE AUTHORS

Hal Bodner is a Bram Stoker Award-nominated author, best known for his best-selling gay vampire novel, *Bite Club,* and the lupine sequel, *The Trouble With Hairy.* He tells people he was born in East Philadelphia because so few people know where Cherry Hill, New Jersey is located. The first person he saw ever saw was the doctor who delivered him, C. Everett Koop, the future US Surgeon General. Thus, from birth Hal was ironically destined to become a heavy smoker -- a habit he greatly misses.

He moved to West Hollywood in the 1980s and has rarely left the city limits during the past several decades. In fact, he is so WeHo-centric that he cannot find his way around Beverly Hills, which is the next town over. In a burst of over optimism, he bought a six bedroom mansion in Highland Park, a supposedly up-and-coming area of East Los Angeles. After three years of watching the street gangs doing drug deals in his back yard, he fled back to WeHo.

During his sojourn in East L.A., he was protected from the harm because of his habit of chasing his escaped pet peacock down Figueroa Boulevard at night, dressed in his fluffy bathrobe and fuzzy Cthulu slippers while yelling "Apollo! Apollo! Come back!" None of the gang members would shoot him; they were laughing too hard.

His various professions have included stints as an entertainment lawyer, a scheduler for a 976 sex telephone line, a theater reviewer and the personal assistant to a television star. For several years, he owned Heavy Petting, a pet boutique where movie stars bought gold-plated water dishes and designer wardrobes for their Chihuahuas and Pomeranians.

In the erotic paranormal romance genre—which he refers to as "supernatural smut"—he is best known for having written *In Flesh and Stone* and *For Love of the Dead.* His comic gay super hero trilogy will hopefully debut shortly with *Fabulous in Tights,* to be followed by *A Study in Spandex.* He has recently agreed to write a series of mystery novellas featuring a gay detective and his Watsonian sidekick, who is the madam of a bordello.
Hal married a man roughly half his age who had no idea that Liza Minnelli and Judy Garland were related. In consequence, he has discovered that the use of hair dye is rarely an adequate substitute for Viagra.

Chantal Boudreau is an accountant by day and an author/illustrator during evenings and weekends, who lives by the ocean in beautiful Nova Scotia, Canada with her husband and two children. In addition to being a CMA-MBA, she has a BA with a major in English from Dalhousie University. An affiliate member of the Horror Writers Association, she writes and illustrates horror, dark fantasy and fantasy and has had several of her stories

339

published in a variety of horror anthologies, online journals and magazines. Her novels have included *Fervor*, a dystopian series, and *Masters & Renegades*, a fantasy series. Find out more at: http://chantellyb.wordpress.com

Tracy L. Carbone is the author of five novels, a short story collection, and dozens of dark fiction stories published in magazines and anthologies in the U.S. and Canada. The anthology she edited, *Epitaphs: A Journal of the New England Horror Writers*, was nominated for the Bram Stoker Award. She recently located from New England to Southern California and is hard at work on her newest novel, *The Rainbox*. She is an active member of the Horror Writers Association and its HWA LA Chapter.

Matt Cowan's love for the horror genre stretches back beyond his earliest childhood memories. At a young age he stopped having nightmares when he began enjoying them too much. His primary literary influences are Ramsey Campbell, M.R. James, and Algernon Blackwood. In addition to writing fiction, Matt also writes about some of the legendary names in the field at his Horror Delve blog (horrordelve.com). He lives with his wife Lynne in Indianapolis, Indiana where he's currently working on more stories. "The Collective of Blaque Reach" was originally published in 2008 by Dead Letter Press as the bonus story chap book for the *Bound for Evil: Curious Tales of Books Gone Bad* anthology. It was also featured on The Tales To Terrify Podcast in 2013 (read on episode #90). He's had stories in *Indiana Horror Anthology* (2011 and 2012), *Indiana Science Fiction 2011*, and *Indiana Crime Review 2013* from James Ward Kirk Fiction. "Numen" won an Editor's Choice Award for the *Cellar Doors: Words of Beauty, Tales of Terror* anthology in 2013 from James Ward Kirk Fiction. "Christmas Wine" appeared in *O Little Town of Deathlehem* in 2013. A shorter version of "Here He Comes A Wandering" was originally read on The Pod Of Horror Podcast (Episode #58) as the winning entry in their Christmas Horror Story Contest that year (2009).

Mandy DeGeit, author, chef, and farmer, hails from Nova Scotia, Canada, where she runs the Dandy Little Farm with her husband. When not writing, she's working on the business development plan for the farm or cooking something tasty in the kitchen. You can follow what Mandy's up to next on her blog www://mandydegeit.com. Her publication credits include: *Inviolable, Home Renovation, Does This Look Infected?, Le Petit Mort, Looking for Love Under All the Wrong Laces, She Makes Me Smile, Summer Break, This Only Happens In The Movies, The Only Way, Humanification, Dead Things Don't Rise, Morning Sickness, The Flight, F*cking The Dog, Hooray For Boners*, and *I Am But A Balloon, Fatty*.

JG Faherty is the Bram Stoker Award- and Thriller Award-nominated author of five novels, including his most recent, *The Cure*, along with nine novellas and more than 50 short stories. A life-long resident of New York's haunted Hudson Valley, he writes adult and YA horror, science fiction, paranormal romance, and urban fantasy. Follow him at www.twitter.com/jgfaherty, www.facebook.com/jgfaherty, www.jgfaherty.com, and http://jgfaherty-blog.blogspot.com/

Dan Foley currently lives in Connecticut. He grew up in New Jersey and then spent over seven years in the U.S. Navy. Much of that time was spent on nuclear submarines. He credits both of these factors for his slightly disturbed sense of humor and writing style. He is the author of the novel *Death's Companion, The Whispers of Crows*, a collection of short stories, and the novella *Intruder.* He has also published in various anthologies and magazines in the U.S. Canada, England and Australia. His next novel, *Abandoned,* is scheduled for release in June, 2016. Find him at ww.deathscompanion.com.

Patrick Freivald is an author, high school teacher (physics, robotics, American Sign Language), and beekeeper. He lives in Western New York with his beautiful wife, two birds, three dogs, too many cats, and several million stinging insects. A member of the HWA and ITW, he's always had a soft spot for slavering monsters of all kinds.

He is the author of *Twice Shy*, Bram Stoker Award-nominated *Special Dead, Blood List* (with his twin brother Phil), Bram Stoker Award-nominated *Jade Sky*, and the sequel *Black Tide*, as well as the novella *Love Bites*, a growing legion of short stories, and the *Jade Sky* graphic novella (with Joe McKinney) for Dark Discoveries magazine. There will be more.

Mark Allan Gunnells loves to tell stories. He has since he was a kid, penning one-page tales that were Twilight Zone knockoffs. He likes to think he has gotten a little better since then. He loves reader feedback, and above all he loves telling stories. He lives in Greer, SC, with his fiance Craig A. Metcalf.

D.H. Lewis lives in Winston-Salem, NC. When not writing about the weird and macabre, he spends his time working as a humble paralegal. He is married to a wonderful wife and has three vexing cats. You can visit him at http://barchiel1.livejournal.com.

Mark Parker is the founder, publisher, and managing editor of Scarlet Galleon Publications. His editorial credits include *Dead Harvest: A Collection of Dark Tales (2014); Dark Hallows: 10 Halloween Haunts (2015);* and the much anticipated *Fearful Fathoms: Collected Tales of Aquatic Terror (2016)*. Parker is the author of *The Scarlet Galleon, Biology of Blood, Way of the Witch, Banshee's Cry, Lucky You, The Troll Diner, Killing Christmas*, and *Born Bad* to be featured in the forthcoming anthology *KIDS: Vol. I* coming soon from Dark Chapter Press. Bestselling author of the *Witching Savannah* series writes of Parker's *Way of the Witch:* "Parker has a strong voice and is able to convey a sustained sense of time and place. Similar in feel to Richard Laymon's *Traveling Vampire Show*." You can learn more about the author/publisher by visiting his website www.scarletgalleonpublications.com

Evan Purcell is an American living and working in Stone Town, Zanzibar. His house is directly next door to a 200-year-old cemetery, which is probably why he's been writing so many horror stories lately. To find out more about his travels and writing, check out EvanPurcell.Blogspot.com.

Stephen Roy is an attorney by training and a business owner of necessity. However, he is a writer by choice because he believes that in the tales we tell, we find ourselves. He has numerous short story publications to his credit in both periodical and anthology formats and is actively seeking an outlet for his second novel, Wednesday's Little Girl.

A.P. Sessler A resident of North Carolina's Outer Banks, A.P searches for that unique element that twists the everyday commonplace into the weird. When he's not writing fiction, he composes music, dabbles in animation, and muses about theology and mind-hacking, all while watching way too many online movies. His short stories have appeared in audio podcasts such as Manor House and Human Echoes as well as print anthologies such as *Dandelions of Mars, Ain't Superstitious*, and *Hides the Dark Tower*. His short Beneath the Bell Bay Light was recently nominated for the Pushcart Prize.

Ellen Shaw grew up in Boston area and moved to New Hampshire. She has been writing for a long time but is only just now starting to share her stories. She has one fantastic son and works in long-term care.

G.G. Silverman is an award-winning author who lives just north of Seattle with her husband and dog. When not writing spooky stories, she trains on a compound bow in case of the zombie apocalypse.

Jeremy Simons lives with his wife and daughter in Grayson, Louisiana. He writes constantly in his spare time and aspires to one day become a full time novelist. His works have appeared with *Carnage Conservatory, Aphelion*-webzine, *The Horror Zine, Voices from a Coma, Hellfire Crossroads Volume 4, Short-Story.Me*, and *October's End* and the *X3* Anthology (both anthologies from Horrified Press). His debut novella *Buried Alive* is now available for purchase via Amazon and Smashwords in both paperback and eBook format. You can find Jeremy Facebook at Facebook.com/jeremysimonsauthor or follow him on Twitter, twitter.com/@jeremi1986. His website is jsimonsauthor.webnode.com.

Flo Stanton's most recent story appears in *Gothic Tales of Terror*. Others have appeared in *Traps, A Pint of Bloody Fiction, Indiana Horror Review, Ghosts Revenge, Tales of a Woman Scorned, Studies in Scarlet, Yellow Mama,* and others. Find out more about Flo at www.3amblue.com or follow her blog at http://flo-stanton.blogspot.com/

Rob Smales is the author of *Dead of Winter,* which won the Superior Achievement in Dark Fiction Award from Firbolg Publishing's Gothic Library in 2014, and the upcoming *Echoes of Darkness* (due out in 2016). His short stories have been published in two dozen anthologies and magazines. His story "Photo Finish" was nominated for a Pushcart Prize and won the Preditors & Editors' Readers' Choice Award for Best Horror Short Story of 2012. His piece "A Night at the Show" received an honorable mention on Ellen Datlow's list of the Best Horror of 2014, and earned a nomination for Best Short Story from the eFestival of Words. More about his work can be found at www.Robsmales.com. Visit him on Facebook at www.facebook.com/robert.t.smales.

Philip Thorogood is a Forensic Science graduate from Peterborough, UK, who started out writing fan fiction for Warhammer 40,000 and branched out into other topics. When he's not dreaming up too many ideas to put to page, Phil likes to immerse himself in the creative works of others in the shape of books, films and music. You can follow Phil on his Facebook page, www.facebook.com/thorogoodphil

DJ Tyrer is the person behind *Atlantean Publishing* and has been widely published in anthologies and magazines in the UK, USA and elsewhere, including *Chilling Horror Short Stories* (Flame Tree), *State of Horror: Illinois*(Charon Coin Press), *Steampunk Cthulhu* (Chaosium), *Tales of the Dark Arts* (Hazardous Press), *Ill-considered Expeditions* (April Moon Books), and *Sorcery & Sanctity: A Homage to Arthur Machen* (Hieroglyphics Press), and in addition, has a novella available in paperback and on the Kindle, *The Yellow House* (Dunhams Manor).

Max Vile is a prolific writer/actor working in Los Angeles & Las Vegas. He has been published in numerous anthologies & magazines both in the United States and abroad. On full moon nights & after intravenous tequila shots, he can be heard howling his insane nonsense, usually at full blast and accompanied by thrash metal electric guitar with a jazz flute kicker (lead vocals by Toto … no, not the band, not the dog—Toto's the schizophrenic gremlin who lives in Max's skull. At least, that's what he tells me …). If you're ever having a bad dream or a séance goes wrong and the Devil pops up, could you please tell him his son says hi? Max would really appreciate it.

David Niall Wilson has been writing and publishing horror, dark fantasy, and science fiction since the mid-eighties. A former president of the Horror Writer's Association and multiple recipient of the Bram Stoker Award, his novels include *Maelstrom, The Mote in Andrea's Eye, Deep Blue, the Grails Covenant Trilogy, Star Trek Voyager: Chrysalis, Except You Go Through Shadow, This is My Blood, Ancient Eyes, On the Third Day, The Orffyreus Wheel, Vintage Soul, My Soul to Keep & Others, Kali's Tale, Heart of a Dragon, The Second Veil, The Parting, Nevermore — A Novel of Love, Loss & Edgar Allan Poe , Killer Green & Crockatiel* — the newest novel in the new series O.C.L.T. David has also co-authored the Stargate Atlantis novel *Brimstone*, with Patricia Lee Macomber, and *Hallowed Ground* — written with International best-selling author Steven Savile. He has over 150 short stories published in anthologies, magazines, and five collections. His work has appeared in and is due out in various anthologies and magazines, including the upcoming anthology 2113 — stories based on the music of Rush, edited by Kevin J. Anderson. David lives and loves with Patricia Lee Macomber in Hertford, NC with their daughter Katie, and occasionally their genius college daughter Stephanie, three sons serving in the USN, Will, Zach, and Zane, their ridiculous Pekingese, Gizmo, their spaz of a Cocker Spaniel, Callie, their not-so-vicious cat, Sid, a never-to-become-a-coat chinchilla named Pook Daddy, Bellatrix LeStrange (the cutest cat in the world), and various other creatures. David is CEO and founder of Crossroad Press, a cutting edge digital publishing company specializing in electronic novels, collections, and non-fiction, as well as unabridged audiobooks. Visit Crossroad Press at http://store.crossroadpress.com. You can find David online at Facebook: http://www.facebook.com/david.niall.wilson; Twitter: @David_N_Wilson; and his website, http://www.davidniallwilson.com.

Grinning Skull Press Presents

The Place where it all started
O Little Town of Deathlehem

Twas the fright before Christmas,
And all through the town,
Not a soul stirred,
No one dared make a sound…

Welcome to Deathlehem,

where…
… Krampus, not Santa, brings the holiday cheer…
… the lights on the tree, so festive and bright, skitter and crawl and possess
a lethal bite…
… malicious little elves, not a jolly one, know if you've been naughty—or
nice…
and
… family gatherings often turn deadly.
So enter… if you dare.

A collection of 23 holiday horrors benefiting the Elizabeth Glaser Pediatric
AIDS Foundation.

Return to Deathlehem

Slay bells ring,
Kids are screaming,
In the lane, snow is blood stained.
There's nowhere to hide,
Krampus has arrived,
There'll be feasting in a winter slaughter land…

Welcome back to Deathlehem,

… where the office Secret Santa proves more dangerous than a game of
Russian roulette…
… where trips to Grandma's house are fraught with danger…
… where a traditional Nutcracker poses a threat to a pair of would-be
thieves…
… where ghosts of Christmases past haunt and take vengeance against the
living…
… and many more!

Twenty-three more tales of holiday horror benefiting the Elizabeth Glaser
Pediatric AIDS Foundation

www.ingramcontent.com/pod-product-compliance
Lightning Source LLC
Chambersburg PA
CBHW071516260626
47170CB00002B/388